Also by Emily McIntire

NEVER AFTER

Hooked

Scarred

Wretched

Twisted

Crossed

Hexed

SUGARLAKE

Beneath the Stars

Beneath the Stands

Beneath the Hood

Beneath the Surface

STAND-ALONES

Be Still My Heart (cowritten with Sav R. Miller)

Beneath the Stars

EMILY MCINTIRE

Bloom books

Published by Bloom Books, an imprint of Sourcebooks
P.O. Box 4410, Naperville, Illinois 60567-4410
(630) 961-3900
sourcebooks.com

Originally self-published in 2020 by Emily McIntire

Cataloging-in-Publication data is on file with the Library of Congress.

Printed and bound in the United States of America.
VP 10 9 8 7 6 5 4 3 2 1

For anyone who's been touched by addiction.

One second at a time.

READER DISCRETION IS ADVISED

Please note that while the main couple get their HEA at the end of this book, there are side stories and plot points that are not immediately resolved and will run through the series.

Suggested reading order:
Beneath the Stars
Beneath the Stands
Beneath the Hood
Beneath the Surface

Beneath the Stars is a full-length, interconnected stand-alone featuring strong language, explicit sexual scenes, and mature situations which may be considered triggers for some.

Full list of trigger warnings can be found by scanning the QR code below or on EmilyMcIntire.com.

Reader discretion is advised.

PLAYLIST

Rewrite the Stars—Zac Efron, Zendaya

Chasing Cars—Snow Patrol

Unsteady—X Ambassadors

Linger—The Cranberries

Who Knew (Acoustic)—James Bradshaw

see you later (ten years)—Jenna Raine

Bigger Than the Whole Sky—Taylor Swift

The Scientist—Coldplay

All Too Well (Taylor's Version)—Taylor Swift

Lover Of Mine—5 Seconds of Summer

You're Still the One (Acoustic)—Bailey Rushlow

Forever—Ben Harper

Listen on Spotify:

Prologue

ALINA

IT'S WHEN I'M WALKING TO THE BACK OFFICE THAT I feel it. The shift in the air. It's subtle—a ghost of a chill that flickers down my spine.

What the heck? I brush it off, straightening my shoulders and walking through the open door.

I don't see him at first, but when I do, that chill drops through my body like an iceberg free-falling, freezing me in place.

This isn't happening.

This cannot be happening.

"Alina! I was wondering if you'd even show up," my boss, Regina, says as she smiles thinly. She's annoyed, and rightly so. I should respond, but I don't. I'm not sure I physically can since my heart has stalled in my chest.

Chase Adams.

I'd love him if I didn't hate him so much.

There's a pencil behind his ear, a blueprint rolled up in his hand and another laid out on the desk.

But he isn't looking at that.

He's locked on me, mouth partially open, hand frozen halfway through his silky, dark brown hair. When he swallows, my traitorous eyes track the way his throat bobs. "Goldi."

The nickname travels across the room and pierces me in the chest, jolting me out of my shock. "Don't call me that," I snap.

He clamps his mouth shut and nods.

"You two know each other?" Regina points between the two of us.

"Yeah, actually we used—"

"Our folks are neighbors," I interrupt, tearing my gaze away from him to focus on her instead. "We grew up together, but no. I never really *knew* him."

I stand stoic, my gaze never straying from Regina, but I can feel him.

My body hums, reminding me of the first time I saw him at eleven years old, and just like then, I have to clench my fists to keep from reaching out.

Part One

Love is a single soul inhabiting two bodies.
—Aristotle

Chapter 1
ALINA

Eleven Years Old

I LOVE DANCING.

Always have and always will. Been in classes since I was four years old. Daddy likes to joke and say I'll dance my way into the worst kind of trouble, but I think that's a load of bull. Why would I want to get in trouble? I'm eleven now, way too big to be sitting in a time-out chair. It's just my favorite thing to do in the whole world and it's the only time I really feel *free*.

My older brother, Eli, will tell you I've got two left feet, but don't believe him. He just gets annoyed Mama lets me pick the music when she sends us outside to play.

I pick a new station on the radio and smile big, tapping my foot against the sidewalk.

"Lame," my brother huffs, shooting his basketball into the hoop. "Change it, Lee. You know I can't stand country."

My honey-blond hair tangles behind me as I spin to face Eli. I stick my tongue out at him and tell him to shove it where the sun don't shine before I turn to face our house. It's nothing fancy, but it's all I've ever known as home. A three-bed, two-bath, one-story right smack in the middle of Sugarlake, Tennessee, with white siding, blue shutters, and the prettiest tulips you'll ever see. I love picking them when they bloom in the spring, but Mama gets mad when I do because tulips are "a labor of love," so instead I just come out front and stare at them every chance I get.

Eli bounces the ball between his legs and groans, bringing my attention back to him. "Seriously. I can't practice my free throws to this shit."

I roll my eyes at his potty mouth. He thinks he's so big and bad because he's fourteen now, and he loves to curse every chance he gets.

"Don't let Mama hear you talk like that or she'll wash your mouth out with soap again." I stick my finger between my lips, making a loud gagging noise.

I've never had it done to me, but watching Eli go through it is enough to make me never want to speak a bad word *ever*.

He stops dribbling and runs his hand through his honey-blond hair, shaking his head. "Yeah, Miss Alina May, never doing a bad thing in her life. Why don't you leave me alone and go introduce yourself to the new neighbors?" He gestures to the house three doors down where there's a big moving truck in the driveway and a girl playing on the front lawn.

I put my hands on my hips and strain my eyes trying to see better. It's not the worst idea Eli's ever had.

The girl's smaller than me and hula-hooping away without a care in the world, her blackish hair swishing against her porcelain shoulders with every swing of her hips. She looks friendly enough, and since my best friend, Becca, is out of town for the summer at church camp, I really have nothing better to do than make a new friend.

"Okay, I will." I make my way across the lawn before spinning around and pointing my finger at him. "But *not* 'cause you told me to, Eli. I'm doin' it 'cause she looks nice."

He smirks and tosses the basket into the hoop again.

I'm almost to her house when a boy walks out of the front door and slams it behind him. I stop in my tracks and watch with wide eyes as he turns and flips off the closed door with both middle fingers, and then sits on the front steps and lights up a cigarette.

My brows shoot to my hairline.

He doesn't look that much older than me, definitely not old enough to buy cigarettes, but the way he's puffing on that smoke so well I imagine he has no trouble getting them whenever he wants. He leans his elbows on his knees when he inhales, and I'm mesmerized as it swirls into the air.

Is he the new girl's brother?

He has brown-black hair, although his is cut so short I can almost see his scalp, and he isn't as small, but he is kind of gangly looking.

It's only when he turns his head and stares straight at me that I realize I'm standing in the middle of our street gawking like a weirdo. My cheeks heat, so I quickly look down and start walking again.

No sense in turning back now, that would be even weirder.

The girl sees me as I get to the edge of their front yard, the Hula-Hoop falling down her body and a huge smile splitting across her face. She bounds over like a fairy flittering from tree to tree.

Dang, this girl is bouncy.

"Hi!" she squeals. "I'm Lily, what's your name?"

I open my mouth to answer but she keeps talking, so it's hard to get a word out.

"I've been so worried about not making any friends, but then here *you* are, and oh!" She pops up on her tiptoes, her nose almost brushing mine. "Your eyes must be the bluest things I've ever seen."

I stuff my hands in the pockets of my jean shorts and stare back at this girl who I think might be a little wacky.

I'm fixing to kill Eli for suggesting I come over here.

"Thanks," I reply.

I look behind her to where the boy is watching us, stone-faced.

Eli calls expressions like that "resting asshole face." I don't know if this kid is an asshole, but he sure doesn't seem happy to see me. I shift my focus back to Lily.

"How do you talk like that?" I ask. "Just goin' and goin' for so long without havin' to breathe?"

Immediately, I want to take my words back. Daddy says I have no filter, but I've always thought saying what's on my mind is the most honest thing I can do, and if I'm nothing else, I always want to be honest. I hate liars.

Guilt hits my chest when her smile drops, and I'm worried I hurt her feelings, but then she throws back her head and laughs, and I'm so relieved I join her.

She links her arm with mine and pulls me farther into the yard.

For such a small thing, she's awful strong.

"Just have a lot of energy, I guess." She pats my arm with her sparkly pink fingernails. "My mom used to tell me I had enough energy to light up all of Chicago."

"I think I believe her." My eyes are wide as I grin. "I'm Alina May Carson, by the way, but my friends call me Lee. I live three houses down that way."

Lily brings her hand up to cover her eyes from the sun while she looks toward where I point. "That your brother?"

"Yep, that's Eli." I glance at the boy on the steps again. "Does he like basketball? Eli never lets me play, he says basketball's not meant for girls, but he'd probably let another boy practice with him."

Lily scrunches her nose, twisting to look at the kid on the steps. "Oh, that's my brother, Chase. He doesn't like much of anything really unless it involves making our foster parents mad."

"Oh."

I'm not sure what a foster parent is, but I don't want to seem stupid, so I nod like I get it.

"Chase!" she yells. "Come here and meet Lee."

My stomach buzzes like a hive of bees as Chase crushes his cigarette beneath his worn black boot and stands, walking over to us. He doesn't stop until he's right in front of me, my eyes level with his chin.

When he's this close, I can see the scar running through his left eyebrow, and for some reason, there's an urge to reach up and trace it. My fingers curl into the palms of my hands to keep myself from actually doing it because *that* would be really weird.

There's something about this boy.

He hasn't said a word yet, and I'm already dying to know him.

"Smokin' kills, you know," I blurt.

His mouth twitches. "No shit?"

"Yep." I pop the *p*. "I'm a big believer in lettin' people know how I feel about things. You might as well get used to it since we're neighbors and all."

He runs his tongue over his teeth. "Yeah? And how are you feeling right now? You feeling good?"

"A little too hot, if I'm honest." I fan my face so he knows how serious I am. It *is* warm just standing here under the summer sun.

He chuckles and dimples mark his cheeks. "How old are you anyway, Goldilocks?"

I scrunch my nose. "I'm eleven and my name is Alina, not Goldilocks. Ah-lee-nuh. But if you start being a little nicer, you can call me Lee."

"Sure thing, Goldi." He tugs on a strand of my hair, then brushes past me.

My chest pulls tight because *doesn't he listen*? "Whatever, Boy Scout!" I yell at him. If he can make up a dumb nickname on the spot, so can I.

"You're the same age as me!" Lily pipes in, pulling on my arm again.

I had almost forgotten she was there.

"This is so cool," she continues. "We'll be in the same grade and everything. Have you lived here your whole life?"

"Born and raised."

"Lucky. I think it's the prettiest place I've ever seen." She sighs.

I smile, but my eyes move past her, hoping to catch another glimpse of her brother walking down the street.

Lily's gaze follows mine and she tugs on my arm again. "Don't worry about him. He's thirteen, and in middle school, so we won't have to worry about him being a jerk every day. You want to come inside?"

My stomach flutters because I don't know how to tell her I *wasn't* worried about him being a jerk, so I just nod instead and let her drag me into her house. But before we walk inside, I look back one more time in Chase's direction.

He has sad eyes and I feel like maybe he needs someone to make him smile.

I can be that someone.

Happy with my decision, I dance my way through the front door and into Lily's and Chase's lives.

Daddy *did* always tell me I would dance straight into trouble.

Summer turns into fall, bleeding into winter, and before I know it, the springtime flowers are blooming.

When Becca got back from church camp last summer—which she swears traumatized her for life—Lily and her got along instantly, bonding over their love of fashion and their heartbreak over the current "it" couple that broke up. I'll be honest, I was nervous about the two of them hitting it off, but Becca guzzles up attention like grass soaks up morning dew, so once Lily gushed over her curly red hair and emerald eyes, I knew everything would be just fine.

Right now, it's Wednesday after school—the only day Becca *can't* hang out because she has to go to church where her daddy preaches.

Lily and I are lying in the grass eating cherry Popsicles, the spring sun soaking into our skin. If I try hard enough, I can *almost* pretend it's summer.

A shadow comes over me and I shield my eyes to see who it is.

"Looking a little pink right…here, Goldi." Chase leans down and pushes his index finger into my cheek.

I prop myself up on my elbows and beam at him like a fool. "Hey, Boy Scout."

We joke around when we see each other, but that's about as far as it goes, and the fact he keeps me so far away bothers me something fierce. I don't know why he doesn't want to be my friend, but it is what it is, I guess. I've tried for months to get him to open up, but he's a brick wall and nothing but a wrecking ball will get through. Still, whenever he's near, my body hums and I crave his attention in the worst way.

"Want a Popsicle?" I hold out mine, the ice-cold goodness dripping down the stick and onto my hand.

"Nah, I came to get Lily." He looks to her and she sighs, pushing her bright-pink sunglasses on top of her head.

"Sam and Anna want us to come home, say they have something important to talk about."

"Something important?" Lily frowns. "You don't think they're going to make us leave, do you?"

"No, Lil, I don't think it's anything bad." Chase smiles, but to me, he looks a little nervous.

"Okay, let me go grab my things." She pops up and dashes inside, leaving Chase and me alone.

He drops onto the grass next to me, his knees bent and elbows perched on top. His happy face is all but gone now.

I don't know much about the homes they've been in before, but I don't like to bring it up. There aren't many times Lily shuts up, but you ask about her past and she clams up and looks about as lost as last year's Easter egg.

"You feeling good today, Goldi?"

"Eh." I shrug. "This Popsicle's makin' my mouth too cold."

He smiles at my answer and then gets quiet.

"You know," I whisper, "if you need someone to talk to, I'm always here."

He scoffs. "You're a kid. I'm not complaining to you about my issues."

Annoyance drops in my gut and I shove his arm. "Whatever, Boy Scout. You can act as grown as you want, but you're a kid, too. Plus, Daddy always tells me I'm an old soul." I puff my chest out in pride.

Chase snorts and drops back on his elbows, craning his neck to the sky. "Okay, *old soul*. I'll tell you what, you just keep being there for Lil, promise not to leave her, and I'll take care of you both. How's that?"

"Well, duh. I'll always be there for Lily. And 'sides…you two are the best thing to happen around here, other than Becca. Where would I go?" I raise my arms and look around. "But I'm your friend, too, not just Lily's, you hear me?"

"Yeah, I hear you, but I'm good. Promise."

I frown at him before leaning over, pressing my fingertip to his chest. "You can try to fool the world, sad boy, but you can't fool me. I see you."

A crease forms between his brows and he opens his mouth like he's about to say something, but before he can, Lily rushes out with her book bag hanging from one hand and a Coke in the other.

"Okay! I'm ready." She swipes the bangs out of her face, smiling as she looks between the two of us.

Chase reaches out and tugs on a lock of my hair before hopping up.

I watch them both disappear down the street, something sitting heavy in the center of my chest.

That feeling is still there while I'm lying in bed trying to fall asleep. My eyes have *just* gotten heavy and my brain's stopped buzzing when I hear my window slide open.

My heart slams against my chest and my breath catches in my throat. I had no idea it wasn't locked, and I'm so terrified someone's breaking into our house I can't move. I don't usually pray when Mama makes me go to church on Sundays, but right now I squeeze my eyes tight and pray to God Almighty that whoever is in my room decides to leave.

"Goldi."

Chase's voice calms me down, but now my heart's beating fast for another reason. The bed dips, and the comforter pulls back before a warm body slides down next to mine.

"Goldi, you awake?" It's a whisper but I hear it loud and clear.

I twist toward him, my eyes wide. I don't say anything. I'm still recovering from thinking we were being robbed, so I just blink at him instead. Besides, I'm super nervous he's here in the first place. Daddy would kill me for having a boy in my room, but there's no way in heck I'm telling him to leave.

"What are you doin' here?" I finally force out.

He blows out a breath, grabbing my hand in his, tangling our fingers. "Couldn't sleep and I needed someone to talk to. Your offer still good?"

Happiness pours through my body like sunshine on a summer day. "Yeah, of course."

We lie in silence for a long time, both of us staring at the glow-in-the-dark stars covering my ceiling.

"Do you ever look up at the stars and feel small?" he asks.

"What, the ones on my ceilin'?"

"No, the real ones, high in the sky."

I frown. "I've never really thought about it, I guess, but sometimes, I like to stare at the mountains and think about how little I am next to 'em. Is that what you mean?"

"Kinda. I just…sometimes I look at the stars and think about how none of this shit really matters, you know?"

I *don't* know, so I stay quiet.

"I think maybe that's why my mom could leave me so easily," he continues, his voice catching on the words.

My chest aches. "Because you're smaller than the stars?"

"Because to her, I didn't really matter."

I don't say anything right away. I just try to imagine what it would be like to not have a mama who loves you like it's the most important thing she'll ever do. I decide right then that I hate her, wherever she is, for making him feel anything less than what he deserves to be.

"You matter to me," I declare.

He swallows, the sound thick. "You matter to me, too. Promise you'll never leave?"

"Cross my heart and hope to die."

I squeeze his hand tight and my stomach flips when he squeezes back.

When I wake up in the morning, he's gone, but that night I make sure to leave my window unlocked, just in case.

Chapter 2
CHASE

Thirteen Years Old

I HATE SMALL TOWNS.

Over the past five years, I've been bounced from one small place to the next, and at the end of the day, they're all the same. Boring streets and boring people with pity in their eyes and force behind their fists.

Life with my mom wasn't sunshine and roses, but it definitely beats putting up with scumbags who pretend to care about kids in the system.

If I only had myself to worry about, I'd have made the jump to street kid before the first foster home. But it's not just me. I have a little sister to protect, and the thought of leaving her to the wolves makes me sick to my stomach. So I've taken the insults and the beatings for both of us with a smile on my face, knowing I'm protecting her the best way I know how.

At least one of us should make it out of this life without too much trauma.

The last piece of crap begged our caseworker to take us away after I caught him trying to sneak into Lily's room. I guess he didn't like a thirteen-year-old holding a knife to his dick. He liked it even less when I threatened to cut it off and shove it down his throat if he so much as looked at her again.

I asked Lily if he ever did anything, but she swears up and down nothing happened, and I have to believe her because the alternative means I have to murder someone, and I'm too pretty for jail.

They're not all bad, though. Our current foster parents, Sam and Anna, are a couple who just moved us from Nashville to Sugarlake, Tennessee: population three thousand.

Well, three thousand and four now, I guess.

They're different than others we've had. Nice even…but I still don't want them.

Like any kid, I just want my mom.

Considering she packed up our life in Chicago, trekked us seven hours to Nashville, and got high, forgetting us at a gas station, that seems pretty unlikely to happen anytime soon.

I'm angry at her. So, so angry.

But no matter how pissed off I am, it doesn't stop the dreams at night of her coming back. I hate those dreams because when I wake up, that hole she put inside me festers and rips open all over again, leaving behind nothing but a burning rage I can't seem to stomp out.

We've been here for a few months now, and still, every time we drive down the main road in Sugarlake, I'm reminded it's literally *called* Main Street. I scoff at the predictability.

Same cookie-cutter layout, new views.

"Tennessee is so pretty. I bet it's the prettiest state in the whole universe," Lily swoons, staring out of the car window.

I smirk at her. "That's just because you don't remember living anywhere else."

"That's besides the point, *jerk*. I'm sure it wasn't like this." She points toward the Smokies.

She's not wrong, it is a beautiful state. But how beautiful can something be if it's filled with the ugliness of your past?

"I've always loved Tennessee, too, Lily." Anna twists from the front seat and smiles. "You know, this is where I grew up as a little girl. I've always dreamed of comin' back one day and raisin' a family here."

She shares a heavy look with Sam. He places a hand on her knee and her voice cracks when she talks again. "I'm so happy you two are liking it."

I roll my eyes, that familiar burning simmering in my gut. Give it another month or two and Anna will be singing the same song as all the others. If it's not *them* being the fuckups, they quickly realize it's me.

He's too angry.

Curses too much.

He doesn't act his age.

I'm about to tell Anna exactly what I think of her empty words, but I glance at Lily who has the biggest smile on her face and decide to keep my mouth shut.

She deserves a little bit of happiness, even if it doesn't last.

It's only a few hours later I feel like I might have to eat my words. Lily's been at Goldi's for a couple hours, and I just grabbed her to come home so Sam and Anna could tell us their news.

They're adopting us.

Lily's sobbing next to me, her pink tipped fingers covering her face, the friendship bracelets on her arms clacking as she shakes.

I'm not sure how I feel. I guess I never really thought it was a possibility. I should be happy, ecstatic even. We're finally getting a family. A new last name.

Chase and Lily Adams.

Sam and Anna are good people, and they treat us well, even with the bullshit I put them through just by being *me*. I know I'm not an easy person to love, the memories of my mom telling me constantly play like a loop in my brain. Still, there's a part of me—a really small piece—that wants this time to work out differently.

"Chase, isn't this the best news?" Lily throws her arms around my neck. I shake myself out of my stupor and loosely hug her back.

"Yeah, Lil." I try to smile, but it feels more like a grimace.

Sam puts his hand on my shoulder, squeezing, but I don't think I'm fooling him. It makes me feel guilty because he's been nothing but the father figure I always wished for.

I'll try harder to be a better son for them.

That's what I am now, I guess.

A son.

Again.

Hopefully, it goes better the second time around.

It's late at night when my mind won't shut up, so I slip out of bed, unlocking the latch from my window and shoving it open so I can creep outside. It's surprisingly easy for me to sneak out of the house, so I do it a lot.

Usually, I just walk down the street to the open field, where I lie down and stare at the stars, wondering what I did to be the way that I am. I try to change, but it just never seems to stick, the anger coming back as soon as I think I get it snuffed out.

Tonight, though, there's something that makes me stop short in front of the little white house with blue shutters.

I war with myself over whether I should keep walking.

Goldi is everything good in the world. She's all innocence and sunshine, and I do my best to keep my distance. She doesn't need someone like me coming around and dirtying up her life. Someone like her deserves friends who are worth a damn, not me. But fuck, if staying away isn't the hardest thing I've ever tried to do. I've never had anyone look at me the way she does, like she sees straight into my soul.

I can tell she wants to be close, but I don't need another person in my life to disappoint, especially an eleven-year-old girl who's never had anything hurt her worse than a scraped knee.

Still, even as I repeat to myself that I can't be her friend, my feet move toward her bedroom window, where I slip inside.

Chapter 3
ALINA

Fourteen Years Old

A NEW BOY MOVED INTO THE HOUSE BEHIND US.

I haven't seen him much, but there's a small hole in the fence separating our backyards, and I'm not proud to admit sometimes I go sneak a peek.

He's got shaggy blond hair, and he's always hunkering beneath the hood of a car. Today, Mama caught me looking and told me to stop being a Peeping Tammy or she'd tan my hide. Then, she plopped her famous banana bread in my hands and shooed me on over to introduce myself, telling me it's the neighborly thing to do. I figure it's as good an idea as any, seeing as how I assume we'll be going to school together at Sugarlake High this year.

I'd rather not go to meet him alone, but Chase and Lily are on vacation in Florida, and Becca's once again forced to be at church helping her daddy, so here I am walking onto his porch all by myself.

The door swings open before I can knock, and out he walks.

I'm stunned a little stupid when I get a good look at him. I've never seen a guy with hair long enough to be pulled into a bun, but somehow it looks better on him than it ever has on me. His hair isn't what keeps my attention, though. It's that gaze of his. The strangest green, like God couldn't decide what shade to pick, so instead, he swirled around all the colors of the forest and placed them in his eyes.

"Hi." I force the banana bread into his hands, stepping back, plastering a smile on my face.

He quirks a brow, leaning against the wooden railing of his porch. "Hi yourself."

"I'm Alina May, but you can call me Lee. I'm your backyard neighbor and figured it's well past time for introductions, so here I am…you know, introducin' myself."

He tips his head down, lifting the banana bread to his nose. "What's this?"

"That right there is the best chocolate chip banana bread this side of the Mason–Dixon line." I say it proudly because it's true. No one can out-bake my mama; I dare them to try.

"Oh yeah?" He smiles and it draws my eyes to his perfectly straight, white as snow, teeth.

"Are those your real teeth?" I spout off before I can stop myself.

His smile widens. "You think I have fake teeth?"

"I mean…maybe?" I shrug.

He doesn't say anything, just stands there with banana bread in his hands and a goofy grin on his face.

"Gah, forget I asked that." I run my hands through my hair. "What's your name, anyway?"

He chuckles, straightening off the railing. "Man, are all the girls as cute as you around here?"

"Matter of perspective, I guess." My stomach flutters and I will away the heat surging through my cheeks. "You know, some say it's mighty rude to not return the favor when a person introduces themselves."

He places the banana bread on the ground, stepping over to me. I don't know how old he is, but I imagine he's a bit older than me because he looks like he hit puberty forever ago. His arms are all muscular and veiny, and he's so tall my head's level with the middle of his chest.

"My apologies, Alina May." He picks up my left hand. "My name's Jackson Rhoades, and believe me when I say it is my absolute *pleasure*."

I expect him to shake the hand he grabbed, but instead, he brings it to his mouth, lightly brushing his lips across my knuckles in a whisper of a kiss.

My heart skips and I laugh, jerking my hand back. "You know, I think you may be what the old biddies in this town call a shameless flirt, Jackson." I take a few steps away. "That may work on girls wherever you come from, but you really shouldn't waste your time on me. I don't fall for empty words and pretty smiles."

He nods, rocking back on his heels. "Noted."

"But if you're lookin' for a friend, I can be that all day long."

"In that case, how can I refuse?" He smirks.

I widen my eyes. "Well, I don't think you can. And since we're friends now, I suppose you can call me Lee."

"All right, Lee. Then I suppose you can call me Jax."

"Jax." I test the nickname out loud, happy with how it rolls so easily off my tongue.

"Do you always make friends like you're doing a business deal?"

I frown. "A what?"

He chuckles. "Never mind. What grade are you in?"

"I'll be a freshman when the semester starts. How about you?"

"Supposed to be a junior, but got held back last year when my dad got sick." He plays with a chain around his neck, his eyes flashing with grief.

"Is he better now?" I watch as the necklace rolls between his fingers.

"He's dead."

My gaze snaps to his from the sudden shift in his tone. "Oh," I whisper. "I'm so sorry."

I cringe as the words leave my mouth, and I don't think he appreciates the apology, but it's all I can think to give him.

"It is what it is." He shrugs. "Anyway, thanks for the bread, I'm sure my mom will love it."

"You bet." I slip my hands in my back pockets, rocking on my heels.

We both stand there, the air filling with awkward tension. I wish I could rewind time and bring back the Jackson from five minutes earlier.

"I'd introduce you to my brother, but he's always tied up with basketball." I change the subject. "But one of my best friends, Chase, lives around here. I'll send him over to say hi, although I don't think your charm will work on him."

He clears his throat. "Sure. Listen, as much as I'd like to stand around and chat about the who's who of Sugarlake, I've got shit to do, so if you're done with the twenty questions..." He turns his face to the side.

I inhale sharply, dizzy from the complete one-eighty of his personality.

"All right then." I purse my lips. "Look...Jax, I'm sorry if I upset you. I didn't mean nothin' by it."

He doesn't give me any indication he heard what I said, but he doesn't need to. I know when I've outstayed my welcome.

My shoulders hunch, embarrassment whirling through me like a tornado. "I guess I'll see you around."

I book it off his porch, each step allowing me to stew in my rising mortification. But honestly, *he's* the one who brought up his daddy, so how was I supposed to know? My breathing is choppy the whole time I'm walking home, and by the time I step inside our front door, I'm practically shaking from the anxiety. I take a deep breath to try to calm down, but it doesn't work, and Mama sees the nerves plain as day on my face.

She's in her favorite spot on the couch, a worn romance novel in her hand. "What in the world happened to make you so flustered?"

"I think I messed things up with the new boy. Everything was goin' fine till we started talkin' about his dead daddy." I chew on my bottom lip, walking over and plopping next to her. "Then he got plain mean, and now I think he hates me when he was the one who brought him up in the first place."

I'm getting upset even *thinking* about it. I can't stand when people think bad about me.

Mama sets down her novel and pats her lap until I rest my head on the top of her thighs. She smooths my hair, petting it in a rhythmic motion. "Oh, baby, we have no clue what that boy's goin' through."

"Yeah, well, now I don't wanna know."

"The best thing you can do is forgive his faults. Be there for him, it's what you're good at. He could probably use a friend like you."

"Fat chance. See if I'll be his friend now," I mutter, closing my eyes and sinking into my mama's embrace.

She kisses the top of my head. "Forgiveness is divine, Alina May. Remember that. You might need it too someday."

Becca convinced me to get this new cherry red polka-dot two piece, but I haven't worked up the courage to wear it out in public yet. In fact, I've been staring at myself in it for the past ten minutes, frowning at my reflection in the full-length mirror on the back of my bedroom door.

It looks fine, I guess, but no matter how I adjust the top, the dang thing is still like a big, bright sign advertising my newly acquired cleavage. I swear, I went to bed one night and woke up the next morning with two giant melons on my chest.

I cup them in my hands and marvel at the weight. Who knew they would be so heavy?

"What are you doing?"

Chase's voice rumbles through the air and I jump in shock, my hand dropping my breast and flattening against my chest instead.

"Good Lord, Chase. Knock much?" I complain, my heart racing underneath my palm. *I really hope he didn't see me groping myself.* "I didn't think you were back in town."

My eyes meet his in the mirror, and my mouth dries when his gaze darkens, trailing me from the top of my head to the tips of my red painted toes. Something takes flight in my stomach the longer he stares, and when he's done with his perusal, the air is heavy.

"What the hell are you wearing?" His tongue peeks out and

sweeps across his bottom lip, drawing my attention to the wetness left behind.

My breath hitches.

In moments like this, where the air is thick with uncharted emotion, I can almost convince myself he feels it, too. Whatever *this* is. Over the past three years, the vines of our friendship have grown and twisted, wrapping tightly around every single piece of me until I don't know how to get untangled. This new feeling is big and scary and I don't know how to handle it, so I pretend things are the same as they've always been.

But they're not.

I move my gaze from his lips, drinking him in. Gone is the gangly preteen with too-short hair. In his place is a full-grown teenager who sparks a fire low in my stomach. Sculpted muscles ripple under his shirt, fine-tuned from the summers spent at his dad's construction company, and his hair is longer now, mussed from those thick fingers that always find a home in the strands. Combine that with his angular jawline and boyish dimples, and I just know the girls at Sugarlake High go wild for him.

Something green and slimy sticks to my insides at the thought.

"Don't you worry about what I'm wearin', Boy Scout." I move to the small desk along my far wall and grab a pink robe that's thrown across the back of the chair, wrapping it around my body.

When I look back at him, he's grinning. "You feeling good today, Goldi?"

"Good as pie." I smile. "How was your vacay?"

He shrugs and sinks down on my bed, throwing his hands behind his head. "Sandy."

I place my hand on my hip and level him with a look. "*Sandy?* Sounds magical."

"I don't know, Goldi. It's the same as it always is when we go to Florida. Too many people and not enough beach." He glances at me, then flickers his gaze away.

"Well, there's been a whole bunch goin' on around here. Eli got offered a scholarship for basketball in Ohio, so naturally, Mama has lost her mind cryin' every day. She's dead set on tryin' to convince him to pick a local school instead, which is just ridiculous because you and I both know Daddy will have a conniption before he lets Eli go anywhere less than a D1 school."

I roll my eyes. Daddy and Eli have always talked about getting out of Sugarlake and being the next big thing, and now that Ohio's calling, there's no way they won't take advantage of it. Eli has dreams of making it all the way to the NBA, and I have half a mind to think he will.

The whole town lauds him as the hero anyway, so it won't surprise anyone when he does.

"No shit?" Chase says. "Good for him."

"Yeah, I guess. At least once he's gone, Daddy won't be tied up with his practices all the time. Mama gets lonely, I just know it."

I don't add that *I* get lonely, too. It's not fair how much time Eli gets with Daddy because he's good at throwing a stupid ball into a hoop when I can barely get him to show up to a dance recital.

Chase doesn't say anything, so I shake myself out of my stupor and think of what else to tell him. "Oh, and there's a new guy about your age that moved in, next door to Patty Lynne. I took him some of Mama's banana bread today."

This gets Chase's attention and he props himself up on his elbows, brows lifting. "You took *him* Mama Carson's banana bread? Is there any left?"

I scoff. "No, it was a welcoming gift. You can go ask her to make some yourself."

He huffs and drops back on the bed. "He probably won't even appreciate it."

"Who knows, he seemed nice enough." *Kind of.* "I'm sure Becca will be thrilled to have fresh meat to chew up and spit out, in any case."

"Why do you say that?"

"Well, you know how Becca is with boys, and this one's a looker." My cheeks flush when I think about how attractive Jax actually is, and how he was able to make my stomach flutter in a way no one except Chase ever has. "I'm also pretty sure he could charm the knickers off a nun."

Chase's demeanor shifts, his stare burning a hole in the side of my head. "Are you saying this new guy *charmed* you?"

I smile and settle down on the bed next to him, the back of my hand pressing to my cheek. "I definitely give him an A for effort, that's for sure."

He sits up fully now, his body hovering next to mine and creating a buzzing sensation that skitters over my arms. "Is he even your age? What kind of a guy flirts with a girl he just met?"

"He's *your* age, and I imagine most of them do." I frown at him. "What's your problem?"

"I don't have a problem, he just sounds like a douchebag."

I smack his arm and give him a saccharine smile. "Then you two should get along just fine."

He lies back again. "You don't have to make friends with *everyone* you meet, Goldi."

"And why wouldn't I?" I challenge. "Managed to turn your

grumpy butt into a friend, might as well extend my powers to the rest of Sugarlake."

Chase huffs again, and I give him a weird look because *what's his problem*?

"Anyway," I continue. "I told him you'd go introduce yourself."

He lets out a humorless laugh. "Fuck. That."

"Oh, come on, Boy Scout." I urge. "Just go say hi. I'll go with you if it'll make it easier. I know how much you dislike conversatin' like normal folk."

"No," he bites out. "In fact, I don't think you should go around him again, *ever*. I mean, he's my age, but he's flirting with *you*?"

My smile drops, anger swirling so hard and fast in my chest it feels like a tornado. I grab a pillow next to his head and whack him in the face with it, jolting farther up on the bed until I can straddle his hips and hit him again.

He chuckles, his hands snapping out and gripping my waist. "All right, all right, *fucking Christ*, I'll do it."

My breathing is heavy from exertion and I drop the pillow, sinking down on his lap and pressing my finger into his chest. "You know, I'm not eleven years old anymore, and I'm gettin' real tired of you treatin' me like I'm a little kid. I'm *not*, whether you want to admit it or not."

His fingers flex against my sides, and suddenly the air changes, my body becoming hyperaware of the position we're in. My stomach flips and free-falls and my palms grow clammy, but I don't move.

I'm frozen in place.

His gaze darkens and drops to my lips before he forces it back up. "Believe me, Goldi. I know."

Suddenly, I'm being tossed to the side roughly, Chase jumping from the bed and rushing to the window, slipping back out into the open air and leaving me alone, breathless and confused.

He doesn't return.

Which isn't unusual, to be honest. Whenever Chase gets into his moods, he disappears, but eventually, a day or two later, he's back again, acting like nothing happened.

Only this time, it's different, because it's been another week, and he still hasn't shown up, despite the fact I've lain in bed every night, listening for the slide of the window and the low rasp of his voice.

All I hear are the crickets chirping and the silence of his avoidance.

I've also decided avoidance must run in the family because it's been even longer since I've seen Lily. I keep expecting her to drop by and regale me with tales of Florida, but she hasn't given me so much as a phone call, which is why I'm so surprised to see her standing on my porch.

"Well, hi there, stranger." I lean my shoulder against the doorframe and smirk over at Becca standing next to me. "Look what the cat dragged in, Becca."

Becca's red brow arches and she looks Lily up and down, unimpressed. "Well, I do declare, Miss Lily Adams, gracing us with her presence. What *did* we do to deserve such an honor?"

Lily scowls at Becca before pushing her way inside, forcing me back a space so the door can open fully.

"I know, I'm the *worst*, but you two won't believe what I have to tell you." She walks straight into me, grabbing me around the waist and squeezing tight. "I feel like I haven't seen you in forever," she murmurs.

"Probably 'cause you *haven't*." I pull back, looking in her eyes, but she's got those giant sunglasses on that make her resemble a bug, and I can't see anything other than the bright-pink smile she has painted on her face.

"Ugh, I know, and I'm awful for it, but I have so much to tell you two." She continues making her way inside, and I shut the door, glancing at Becca.

She gives me a "what the hell" look and shrugs before following Lily then perching on the arm of the couch.

"I met this guy," Lily singsongs.

Becca smirks. "Oh, well *now* I'm interested."

"I knew you would be," Lily giggles.

I don't say anything, and honestly, I feel a little out of place here. They seem to be bonding over being boy crazy, and I…well, I've just never been that way. There's only ever been one boy on my mind.

"Well, go on. Tell us about him," Becca urges.

Lily beams. "He lives like an hour away."

Becca whistles. "Did you fuck him?"

I gasp and cut Becca a glare. *Is she serious?* Lily's fourteen. I'm about to say as much but the words die in my throat, anxiety curling through my middle when Lily sits up and blushes.

Becca squeals and slips from the arm of the chair onto the couch cushion, forcing Lily over. "You *slut*!"

The flush on Lily's cheeks darkens and she looks down at her lap, grinning. "I stayed at his place for the past few days."

"Whoa, whoa, whoa. Back up. You met a guy?" I repeat, my words slow.

"Yeah," she sighs.

"In the week since you've been back…"

"Yep."

"...and you had *sex* with him?"

"I know, right? It sounds crazy." She laughs, leaning back on Becca's shoulder and throwing an arm over her face.

"You can say that again," I mumble. "How on earth did you get your folks to okay this?"

Lily drops her arm by her side and gets a sheepish look on her face. "I may have told them I've been with you two."

I blink at her because...well...I'm not quite sure how I feel.

"That's fine with me," Becca interjects. "Just don't have them go askin' my folks because they'll know you're lyin'. I've been stuck doin' things for youth group the past few days."

My mouth pops open, but I can't form any words. It might be fine with Becca, but I'm not sure if it is with me. This is out of character for Lily. She's always been a fly-by-the-seat-of-your-pants kind of girl, but never reckless.

Becca looks at me and then nudges Lily, jerking her head in my direction.

Lily pops up, putting her hands together like she's praying. "Don't be mad, Lee. I know it wasn't right, but they never would have been okay with me going if they didn't think I was with you."

My gaze flicks back and forth between the two of them, and I try to relax, because maybe *I'm* the problem. Neither of them seems to think it's a big deal at all.

"Were his parents gone or somethin'?" I ask.

"No, he doesn't live with his parents." There's an edge of defensiveness to her tone.

"He doesn't live with his parents," I repeat Lily's words back to her again. "Who even is this guy? And how old is he if he lives on his own?"

"His name is Darryl and he's older..."

Becca sighs, twirling a piece of her hair. "I do love an older man."

Scoffing, I grab a couch pillow and toss it at her. "You don't even *know* any older men, be serious."

Becca grins, holding the pillow to her chest. "Don't have to know 'em to love 'em." She looks to Lily. "How old?"

Lily cringes. "Twenty."

Now Becca's face drops. "Lily..."

My stomach bottoms out and I feel sick.

I don't know much about people in their twenties, but I *do* know nothing good can come from one who wants to mess around with a fourteen-year-old girl. My body slaps against the couch cushion as I lean back, trying to process what she just told me. Part of me is angry because she's bringing me into her lies, but the bigger piece of me is sad that she felt she couldn't come to me sooner. The two weighted ends of my emotions toss me around like a seesaw, and I'm not sure which side I'm supposed to land on here.

Another thought hits me then, and it sends a shot of anxiety straight to my heart.

"Does your brother know?" I whisper, panicked eyes shooting to meet Becca's over Lily's head.

She stays quiet, but it doesn't matter.

Her silence is the answer.

Chapter 4

CHASE

Sixteen Years Old

I GET THE FEELING ANNA WISHES I WOULD CALL her "Mom." Lily had no problem taking up the moniker as soon as the ink was dry on the adoption papers, but I just can't bring myself to. Honest to God, I start every day with the intention of getting over my shit and just doing it. I can give this to her. She deserves the title after everything she's done for Lily and me. But then I think of my real mom, and guilt threatens to swallow me up whole. It's like no matter how hard I try to erase her, she's still the biggest part of the worst side of me.

Sam, however, is another story. I connect with him on a level that has me swallowing back the word "Dad" daily, and I'll be damned if I know why. Maybe it's because I don't have a real dad to compare him to? All I know is he doesn't push. He's just a constant, always steady and never changing, letting me just *be* without expectation or judgment. I've never experienced an adult like that before. Before the summer, I asked if he'd take me with him down to his business, Sugarlake Construction, and teach me the ropes. I shocked the hell out of myself when I realized how much I enjoyed it. There's something peaceful about the methodology in building something from nothing. There's no room for error, no guesswork. Everything is exact. Precise. Controlled.

Today, Sam sat me down and laid out his plans of eventually passing it on to me. I'll never tell him, but it's been one of the best days of my life.

I've never had someone believe in me, and while the feeling is intoxicating, mainly I'm just terrified of disappointing him. I've been dying to talk to somebody about it, but the only one who I'd want to listen is Goldi, and that won't work considering I'm doing my best to avoid her.

I don't know what the hell happened at her house the other day, but it freaked me out, and ever since, I haven't been able to get her out of my thoughts. She has this way of making everything around me disappear until all I see is her, and that's not good for either of us.

I thought with some space I'd be able to get my shit together, maybe gain some perspective, but the more I try *not* to think about her, the more she's there, front and center. And not in a "friendly" way.

It's not right.

Fuck, I know this.

She's my little sister's best friend. Hell, she's my best friend, and even worse, she's only fourteen. A fucking freshman. She's just learning about what it means to become a woman, and here I am thinking about how perfect her lips are and imagining what it would feel like to slide myself between her tits.

It doesn't matter, though. I'd rather torture myself into eternity than I give in. She means too much for me to ruin it by losing my self-restraint, and if I have to put some space between us and fill my days with all the other girls in town to get her out of my system, then that's what I'll do. I'd rather have her in my life from a distance than not have her at all.

I am, however, going to introduce myself to that prick who moved in behind her house. What's that saying? Keep your friends close and your enemies closer? Yeah. *Guess who's about to be your new best friend, buddy.*

I've just poured myself a bowl of cereal when the screen door slams. Looking up, I see Lily sludging her way into the kitchen, black smudged under her eyes and a sour look on her face.

"What the hell happened to you?"

There's only been a handful of times where Lily hasn't been one-hundred-percent put together, and it usually coincides with sickness or "Aunt Flow."

She plants herself in the chair across from me and groans, grabbing my bowl of cereal, the metal spoon clanking against the ceramic as she drags it over.

"Rough night."

"A rough night?" My brows furrow. "Didn't you spend it with Goldi?"

She's shoveling cereal into her mouth but pauses, looking up and pointing her spoon at me. "She hates it when you call her that, you know."

"She doesn't." My chest pulls tight. I don't want to talk about Goldi. "Answer the question."

"God, *Dad*, can you just relax a little?" she snaps.

I lean back and raise both my eyebrows, because what the *fuck*?

"Yes, okay?" she continues, rolling her eyes. "I was at Becca's with Lee last night. We stole some wine coolers from her mom's hidden stash, and my head's pounding, so just…lay off."

She's avoiding my stare, her eyes bouncing around the room like she can't decide where to focus.

I lean forward, resting my elbows on the table, uneasiness creeping up my neck like a spider. "Bullshit."

Her body stills. "What, so you're a lie detector now?"

"You're telling me if I walk over to Goldi's and ask her about last night, she'll have the same story?"

Lily shovels another spoonful of cereal into her mouth. "Mmhmm."

I rub my chin. "And they both were drinking?"

She nods, quirking a brow. "You gonna go over there and give them the third degree, too?"

No.

Mainly because going over there means I'd have to actually face Goldi, and that's a terrible idea. I am tempted though because I'm pretty sure Lily's full of shit. But I won't push her any more. If something serious was going on, she would confide in me. We've been one another's support our entire lives, no way that will change.

Sighing, I stand. "All right, whatever you say, Lil."

She drops the spoon in her bowl, her spine straightening. "You're not *actually* going over there, are you?"

I stare down at her. "Wasn't planning on it. Going to meet that new kid."

Her posture relaxes and she grins at me. "Oh. Well, have fun, don't do anything I wouldn't do!"

I leave Lily to wallow in her self-imposed misery and grab

my house keys before making my way to the street behind ours.

When I get there, Jackson's got his head buried beneath a royal blue Mustang parked in the grass, his white tank top smeared with grease.

There's music playing from a small speaker next to him, and he either doesn't hear me walk up or he doesn't care because his position doesn't change when I make it to the car.

I peer over the edge and whistle, even though I have no clue what I'm looking at.

"Looks good," I say.

Now he straightens, his eyes flashing as he reaches to a small makeshift table he has set up and grabs a blue towel, wiping his hands. "Yeah? You know how to fix a carburetor?"

I shrug. I don't, but fuck if I'm telling him that.

He laughs, tossing the towel down and crossing his arms. "You Chase?"

"Yeah. Jackson, right?"

He nods. "Jax. Lee said you might stop by."

My spine bristles because, what the hell does *that* mean? Has she been over here talking to him? Hanging out?

"Yeah, well...she says a lot of things," I reply like a jackass.

"I could see that." He watches me for a second, the corner of his mouth tilting up. "So, you don't fix cars...you drink beer?"

A slow smile spreads across my face because...yeah. A beer I can get into.

I might have been a bit preemptive in my assumption Jackson was a prick. We've been hanging out, mainly at his place while he works on restoring the '67 Mustang Fastback his dad left him. His mom isn't around much due to the fact she works twelve-hour days, three times a week as a nurse, and picks up shifts as a bartender at Mac's Dive here in town.

"How come your mom works so much?" I ask.

It's a hot August afternoon, and we're sitting on his back deck, sipping beer he schmoozed one of the housewives in town to buy us. I hate to admit it, but Goldi was right. He *is* a charming motherfucker.

"She won't be. Not for much longer, anyway. As soon as I convince them to hire me as a mechanic at the shop in town, I'll do enough to support us both." His fingers tighten around his bottle. "Our healthcare system is fucked, you know? When my dad got sick, it was...aggressive. We spent every dollar we had to our name doing whatever we could, just to give us one more day, but most of it was fighting with insurance about whether he really *needed* the meds or the PET scan his doctors ordered." He drains his beer, grabbing at the chain underneath his shirt.

"Sounds like bullshit."

He shakes his head. "Cancer's a business in this country just like everything else."

Laughter floats across the yard, muffled by the distance and the wooden fence.

My heart skips, but I don't look in that direction, because I just *know* it's Goldi. I can feel it. Condensation drips down my drink and onto my fingers, slipping over my knuckles, and I focus on the sensation to keep from doing something stupid, like jumping the fence, apologizing for ignoring her, and shoving my tongue down her throat.

I look back up and Jax is watching me, a knowing glint in his eyes.

"What?" I snap, setting my beer on the table.

"Nothing, man." He raises his hands up in surrender like he wasn't staring a hole through me. "It's just interesting, you know? I could have sworn Lee said you were her best friend when she pranced her cute little ass over here forcing her baked goods on me, but you haven't mentioned her once."

My body coils tighter with each word.

He leans back until his chair balances on the back two legs. "It's good, though. I thought maybe the two of you were a thing. What kind of guy can chill with a girl like *that* and not want to get it in, you know?"

"She's a little kid."

"Nah," he argues. "She's not."

Anger simmers beneath my skin, and I flatten my palms on my thighs, forcing them to not curl into fists.

I was right the first time. Jax is a fucking prick.

"I'm gonna snatch that up before some other guy has the chance," he continues, oblivious to the wrath building inside me.

I point a finger at him. "The fuck you will."

He throws his head back and laughs. "You should see the look on your face."

Grimacing, I run a hand through my hair. "I should fuck you up."

He's still laughing when he stands, pausing by my chair and clapping a hand on my shoulder. "You should figure your shit out and either lock that down or move the hell on because believe me when I say, a girl like that? She won't stay single for long once she's in high school. You want another beer?"

I nod stiffly, his words running through my mind on a loop. He's not wrong, it's unrealistic to think there won't be a guy eventually. I groan, throwing my head back. The thought of having to watch someone else touch her makes me sick to my stomach.

But I'm no good.

I'll hold on too tight and suffocate her with my need to stay close. To never let her leave.

She deserves more than that, more than me. She *deserves* soft and sweet, so even though it kills me, I'll stand back and let someone be that for her.

I drain the rest of my beer, the jealousy rising up my throat like acid.

Hours later, I'm still stuck on my conversation with Jax, and how it made me feel. My stomach is in knots knowing Goldi's starting school with us, and I'll have to stand back and watch those idiotic motherfuckers try to lay game on her.

She's too smart for that.

Even as I think it, I'm not convinced.

My mind volleys between slipping out of my window or staying in place. Up until now, I've been strong. For weeks, anytime I've seen her, I turn the other way.

But it doesn't stop my heart from reaching out for hers, trying to match its rhythm.

Tonight, though, I'm too weak to resist. It's been a long day with shitty feelings, and I'm suffocating without her.

As I open her window and climb inside, I tell myself that tomorrow I'll throw my feelings in a box and lock it up tight.

Tomorrow, I'll be strong.

It's dark other than the stars on her ceiling, and seeing them glow that neon color makes comfort blossom in my chest and wrap around me like a heated blanket. A few months ago, she talked about getting rid of them, but I made her promise to never take them down.

She hasn't asked why, but if she did, I'd tell her it's because they light the path straight to her.

Fucking pathetic.

Still, I like knowing that even without me here, she's kept them up.

When I reach her bed, she's sleeping, and I lean down, brushing the strands of her honey hair from her cheek. Little puffs of breath blow from her perfect mouth, dusting across my knuckles. My eyes drink her in, gliding over her like I'm parched for thirst.

She stirs as I trace my index finger along her jaw.

"Chase?" she murmurs sleepily.

"Yeah, Goldi. It's me."

She stretches her arms, her tank top lifting and revealing her midriff, and a shot of heat sparks low in my abdomen, so I swallow hard and look away.

I feel her stare, though.

She's the only person in my life that looks through all the bullshit and dives straight into my soul. The only person I'd ever want to.

"What's the matter, Boy Scout?"

I crawl over her, careful to make sure our bodies don't touch, and slip under the covers. "Just wanted to see you."

She turns to face me, frowning as she puts her hands beneath her cheek, sinking into her pillow. "I thought you'd gone and wrote me off. Then here you are crawlin' back in my window like you haven't ignored me for weeks."

I cringe. "I know. I'm an asshole."

"Is that your version of an apology?"

Reaching out, I pull her hand from beneath her face and tangle our fingers together in the space between us. "It's me saying I fucked up. You just make me feel…*so* much, Goldi. I don't know how to handle it sometimes."

Her gaze holds mine. "Apology accepted."

Guilt slithers up my spine knowing I'm not planning on changing my ways. "I'll probably fuck up again," I warn her.

She yawns and closes her eyes. "Yeah, probably."

My throat is tight, clogged from all the things I want to tell her. "You feeling good today, Goldi?"

She doesn't answer, already drifting back to sleep.

I lie in the silence, content to just be in her presence, my thumb stroking lazily over the back of her hand, and it's not until *my* eyes close that I hear her whisper, "You make me feel too, Chase."

I'm not even sure she's awake when she says it.

It's been a hard day, but like always, being around her lifts the heaviness from my chest, and for the first time in three weeks, I can breathe again.

Tomorrow, I'll be strong.

Chapter 5
ALINA

Fifteen Years Old

THERE'S A BONFIRE TONIGHT DOWN AT THE LAKE, an end of summer tradition. I'd rather stay home and curl up with a good book instead.

"I think I'll just skip out on this one," I tell Lily, spinning around in my desk chair while she ransacks my closet.

"Nope. I don't accept that. Here, try this." She doesn't skip a beat, thrusting a pink silk camisole in my face.

"Lil, I literally can't think of anything I'd rather do *less* than sit in front of a fire with a bunch of teenagers drunk and macking on each other."

Lily drops a shirt to the ground, cutting me a glare. "Yeah? Well, too bad, bitch. You didn't let me throw you a birthday party this year, this can be your apology."

I lift the pink tank from my lap. "I thought lettin' you dress me up like a Barbie *was* the apology."

"Nope, that's just you making good choices." She winks and hands me a jean skirt.

Laughing, I give in, both because arguing with her is useless—she'll always win—and also because it's nice to have her here.

She's been gone a lot lately. Hanging out with a new group of kids from a different town, and even when she is around, she's… different. Today is the first time I've seen a hint of *my* Lily. After I went mother hen on her over that creep she was dating, Darryl, she pulled away, but I won't apologize for my reaction. There's nothing okay about a grown man having sex with a fourteen-year-old girl, I don't care *what* Lily tries to spin it as.

She's lucky I didn't tell her brother. She swears up and down Darryl's out of the picture, but it's hard to keep the faith when she disappears for days at a time.

Sometimes I think I *should* tell Chase, or maybe my mama, but I know it will make Lily hate me, and the thought of losing her friendship entirely is worse than anything else.

Becca busts through my bedroom door, a bottle of cheap vodka in her hand I'm sure she stole from her mama's secret stash. "All right, bitches, they don't get me back till Sunday. Let's tear this town up. What're we getting' into?"

"Convincing Lee to come to the End of Summer Bonfire." Lily glares at me again, hands on her hips.

Becca laughs, placing the vodka on my desk and her bright red nails on my shoulder. "Lee, honey, it's adorable you think you have a choice."

I roll my eyes, shrugging her off me. "Who all's gonna be there?"

Lily moves to my full-length mirror, grabbing lip gloss and smearing it on her lips. "Everyone, obviously. There's only like twenty people in this town as it is, with nothing to do. Where else would they go?"

Becca snorts, walking to my bed and dropping onto it. "True. God, this town is lame as hell." Her brows draw down and she looks at her side where Lily's phone is tossed. She grabs it up and stares at the screen. "Speaking of lame, what kind of name is 'Big D,' Lily?"

Lily spins around. "What?"

"Someone named 'Big D' is tellin' you to be a good girl, and maybe he'll re-up your stash." Becca looks at her. "Kinky, what kind of stash?"

My stomach drops like a lead balloon.

Lily storms across the room and rips the phone from her hand. "Jesus, Becca, mind your fucking business."

Becca scoffs and sits up straight. "Excuse me, *bitch*? What crawled up your ass and died? Seems like I should make it my business."

My eyes volley between them.

Lily's body is coiled tight like a snake about to snap. "Just because your dad's the preacher of this Podunk town doesn't mean you have the right to invade people's lives whenever you please."

I'm too busy processing the fact Lily has a "stash" to be too offended by her words about the town I've lived in my whole life, but I can tell immediately that her words hit their mark with Becca.

She pops up from the bed and stalks toward Lily. "Let me tell you a secret, you rancid little witch, I don't need my daddy to—"

"Lil," I interrupt, shooting Becca a look. "What the heck is goin' on with you? You can talk to us, you know?"

Becca scoffs again, crossing her arms.

Lily, on the other hand, ignores me completely, her fingers flying over her phone screen, breathing heavy like she just ran a marathon.

"Hello?" Becca snaps her fingers in the air. "Anyone home?"

Lily's phone rings and she shoves it up to her ear, muttering something about needing a minute, and she'll meet us at the bonfire.

My mouth is hanging open as I watch her leave my bedroom, and then I twirl my chair, meeting Becca's eyes.

She raises her arms out to the side mouthing, "*What the fuck?*"

Lily doesn't come back, and so when it's time to head to the bonfire, it's just Becca and me.

It's a balmy night, and it feels like the whole of Sugarlake High is here. Even my brother made an appearance, which is unlike him. Usually, he steers clear, too busy with basketball to do normal things like get drunk on a lakeshore.

People cluster in groups along the bank, hollering and making general fools of themselves, and there are a few Adirondack chairs around the actual bonfire, which is where my booty is sitting comfortably for the duration. The smell of burning wood is strong, and I sink into the scent, loving the way it reminds me of when I was younger and we used to take our old RV up into the Smokies on the weekends.

Once Eli started becoming the next big thing in basketball, Daddy got too busy to keep doing silly things like family camping trips.

I'm nursing a warm, stale beer in a red Solo cup, pretending to listen to Ricky Walker tell me all about his daddy's brand-new fishing store.

But my eyes are on Chase.

That ratchet girl Suzy Abbott has her breasts pressed up so tight to his side, I'm surprised she can breathe.

She leans up to whisper in his ear, her hand trailing down

the front of his chest, and my stomach burns, scorching up my middle and into the back of my throat until I feel like I could spit fire.

He tips a beer bottle to his lips lackadaisically, his gaze skimming over the crowd before settling on me from across the flames.

I swear I try to tear my focus away, but I'm transfixed on the way Suzy tips her face closer to Chase's ear, her overly glossed lips whispering something that makes him smirk. Her hand keeps moving down, until she's palming his lap. Right in front of everyone, like it's hers to claim.

Like *he's* hers.

And through everything, his eyes never leave mine.

Suddenly, the warm beer in my stomach threatens to make a resurgence, nausea churning like a ship in a storm through my middle and coating the back of my tongue.

I'm not naive, I know Chase sleeps around. I've smelled the cheap perfume lingering on his clothes as he lies in *my* bed and tells me he's no good.

But to see it right in front of me? It makes me sick.

Is this what I'll have to deal with every day in school?

I turn sharply toward Ricky, looking him up and down. His blond spiky hair and dull brown eyes aren't really my thing, but he'll do.

Is he still talking? I cut him off. "Yeah, great. Listen. You want to get out of here?"

"Uh…yeah. Yes." He clears his throat. "Like, now?"

"Yeah." I spring up, letting my cup fall to the sand as I grab his hand, pulling him from his seat.

My vision swims slightly as I stand, and it's only right this second I realize maybe I drank a bit more than I thought. I'm not *wasted*, but I'm buzzing, my edges dulled and my limbs just a little warm and fuzzy.

Maybe that's why watching Chase be the biggest idiot on the face of the planet is affecting me so much. You'd think after all these years, I'd be used to his hot and cold act.

From my peripheral vision, I see him toss Suzy's hand from his lap, his eyes tracking my every move.

Good. Serves him right.

I thought losing my virginity would feel different.

But lying here in my bed, the breeze from my open window brushing my cheeks like a soft caress, I feel the same as I have every other night. I reach down and cup myself, thinking I should be…something. Sore or I don't know, maybe more like a woman.

Dang, that sounds stupid.

I thought it would make me more like Becca and Lily, I guess. Both of them have been with boys for a while now, and they act like having sex is the best thing that's ever happened to them, but honestly, for me? It was nothing to write home about.

Maybe I did it wrong.

Can't say I regret it, though. I've built up how my first time was going to go for months now, always trying to picture the perfect way Chase would take it from me.

What a joke.

The pressure of it living up to my expectations is gone now, at least.

"Goldi."

Great.

Out of all the nights for Chase to show back up in my life, it had to be tonight. I close my eyes because I'm afraid it will hurt to look at him.

"Goldi," he repeats.

His voice is closer now.

I crack my lids open and sneak a peek. He's peering down at me, his dimples on full display, and those deep hazel eyes searing through me.

Dang. I'm a sucker for the dimples.

Sighing, I give in and open my eyes fully. "Hey, Boy Scout."

"Where'd you disappear to tonight?" He sits back until he's perched against my nightstand, hands shoved deep in his pockets.

"Oh, you knew I was there?" My tone is sharp, but I can't help it. The scent of the bonfire is stuck on his clothes, and all it does is make me picture him with Suzy Abbott again.

He sucks on his bottom lip, dropping his head until a lock of his inky hair falls over his brow.

"Remember when we used to be best friends, Chase?" I murmur, my voice catching on his name.

His gaze snaps up to mine. "We still are, Goldi."

I laugh, rolling until I'm on my back. "Well, you must be the worst one I've ever had."

"Don't say that." His voice is rough, and he straightens, looming over me. "I warned you this would happen, fuck!"

"Quiet," I snap. "You want to wake Eli or, worse, my daddy?"

He grimaces, reaching up to grip his hair. "I just… I'm so fucking twisted. I see you and it's like all my shit gets thrown in the air, and I have no control over where it will land."

I sit up now, the comforter slipping down my body until it

pools in my lap. "You can't control everything, Boy Scout. That's not real life."

He scoffs. "What do you know about real life, Goldi? You're fifteen."

"Don't you patronize me!" My hands slap the mattress at my sides. "I know enough about life to know never takin' a risk is never really livin'. Mama says just to make sure the juice is worth the squeeze, that's all. I think *you're* worth the squeeze." My palm tries to rub away the ache in my chest. "I can't breathe sometimes with how much I wish you would think the same of me."

His knees hit the edge of my bed and he bends, calloused fingers, rough from construction, trailing down my jaw until he's cupping my chin.

I hate the way my heart flutters at the touch.

His Adam's apple bobs with his swallow and he gazes into my eyes, searching for…who knows what.

"Sometimes, I think I must love you, Goldi. That's the only explanation for why my chest feels like it's about to explode whenever you're around."

My lungs squeeze tight.

"But the last woman I loved more than the world? She decided I wasn't worth it, and left me with nothing but broken pieces and a baby sister to take care of." His thumb brushes over my bottom lip. "I ruin people's love. I don't want to ruin you, too."

I reach up, wrapping my hand around his wrist to keep him anchored to me, his pulse pounding beneath my thumb. "Why don't you let me worry about that?"

The muscle in his jaw tics, and he shakes his head, dropping my chin and stepping back. "You shouldn't *have* to."

Suddenly, I can hear the wood floor of the hallway creaking from someone padding down the hall.

Chase's eyes shoot to my closed bedroom door, and then he bolts to the window, not looking at me until he's got one leg out, his body straddling the ledge.

He stares at me for one second.

Two.

And then he slips away into the night, the same way he always has.

Chapter 6
ALINA

Sixteen Years Old

"REED STANTON ASKED ME ON A DATE," I SAY nonchalantly, my legs crisscrossed on my bedroom floor.

Becca's lying on the bed with a *Cosmo* magazine, but when I tell her about Reed, she drops it to the side, rolling over to give me her full attention. "And?"

"And…I said yes." I shrug like it isn't a big deal, but we both know it is.

"I'm sorry, what?" She cups her hand over an ear, a grin splitting her face.

"You heard me."

"I did, I just wanted to hear it again. I never thought I'd see the day."

"Is that really so hard to believe?"

"When it's someone other than the giant asshole with a chip on his shoulder, and a perpetual hard-on for everything on legs *but* you? Yeah, it really is."

I frown at her.

"It's about time, though," she continues. "Chase doesn't even see you."

My chest pinches. "He sees me."

"You mean when he sneaks into your room to use you as his emotional trash can?" She taps her chin. "Or maybe it's when he ignores you at school, too busy gropin' everything with tits."

"Chase is complicated. You wouldn't understand."

She huffs out a laugh, grabbing the magazine and flipping a page. "I understand he's a dick."

"Why are we talkin' about Chase, again? I thought I was tellin' you about my date with Reed."

Becca sits up, smacking her hands on her thighs. "Yes! Reed 'Lick Him Like a Lollipop' Stanton! Damn, that boy is finer than frog hair. Watchin' him throw the football in those tight pants is the only reason I fake school spirit."

I giggle at her theatrics. "Don't tell Eli you like football best."

She scoffs, falling backward on the bed. "Please, I'm not worried about your big-head brother. He can kiss my ass. How'd Reed get you to say yes, anyway?"

"He cornered me at my locker. Said the only thing better than winnin' the game on Friday will be when he gets to take me out on Saturday."

Her jaw drops. "He just said it to you like that? Didn't even ask?"

I shake my head, grinning at the memory.

Becca sighs dreamily. "Damn, I bet he fucks like a porn star."

"You are so crass, Rebecca Jean!"

"Best way to live, honey." She grins, tossing her wild red hair over her shoulder. "You know Lil's gonna want to dress you up for it. You tell her yet?"

My smile dims. "I haven't seen her goin' on three days now. She missed classes on Thursday and Friday." Worry bubbles in my gut over who she's spending her time with.

"I have half a mind to go over there and stick my foot up her ass." Becca makes a face. "In fact, there's no time like the present."

"You want to go over there? Like, right now?" I bite down on my lower lip at the thought of seeing Chase. "I've got dance in like...an hour."

"Then we won't take an hour," Becca replies, hopping up and grabbing her bag. "She can't hide from us forever, and I'm tired of her actin' like she can. Let's go."

My stomach knots tighter with every second as we make our way to Lily's house, and by the time we knock, I'm *sick* with nerves.

Chase opens the door, because of course he does.

He's got sleepy eyes and nothing on but low-hanging black basketball shorts. My eyes lock on those grooves in his hips, then slide up his chiseled abs and defined chest. My mouth runs dry.

Leaning against the doorframe, he glances at Becca before pinning his stare on me. I feel like an ant under a magnifying glass with the way he's burning me up. Lust and hurt mix together, seeping from my pores, and flooding the space between us.

Becca cuts the tension. "Hey, asshole, your sister home?"

He licks his lips, arm reaching up to rest on the doorframe. "Nope. Thought she was with you two."

Dang it, Lily. I can't believe she's still using Becca and me as her alibi. I stay silent, even though my mind is screaming.

"Well, you thought wrong," Becca says, side-eyeing me. "Mind if we hang around a while and see if she comes home? We need her fashion expertise. My girl has a date tonight with the quarterback, and I'm tryin' to guarantee some action, if you know what I mean." She nudges my arm, winking obnoxiously.

I watch closely for his reaction, searching for a sign that he feels something, *anything*.

But he's stoic. A statue of perfection that remains unchanged.

"Sure, come on in." He opens the door wider.

Becca rushes by, taking up residence on the living room couch, and I move to follow but get held back by a strong grip around my wrist.

My heart stutters as he closes the space between us, tugging my back to his front. Lips brush my ear, his breath prickling my skin with goose bumps. I squeeze my eyes shut, ignoring the way my body sings.

"If he touches you, I'll break his fucking hands," he whispers.

The thread holding my anger inside snaps and I whirl around, ripping my wrist from his grasp and shoving him in the chest.

He stumbles, his brows shooting to his hairline.

"Let me tell you somethin', *Boy Scout*. You're not my brother, and you're sure as hell not my daddy. You don't get to come and go from my life whenever you want, then think you get a say."

He rears back.

I don't let him go far, stepping into him and speaking low. "As a matter of fact, when you go out tonight and do whatever it is you do, with whatever girl you do it with…I want you to close your eyes and imagine Reed doin' the exact same thing to me."

His nostrils flare, but that's the only sign he's heard what I said. Probably because he doesn't care.

It doesn't matter.

I'm done playing this game with him.

Becca's staring, unashamed, as I walk to the couch and sit next to her. Her hand shoots up for a high five.

"Don't." I smack her fingers away before grabbing the remote and flipping through the channels. I try to ignore the feel of Chase's stare and relax. Hopefully, Lily comes back soon to serve as a distraction.

I miss dance because of how long we wait, but it doesn't matter.

She never shows up.

Reed Stanton is Sugarlake royalty, just like my brother. Maybe even more.

Not much has the power to unite small towns quite like football, and he's an all-American quarterback who's given our high school the best record in the past two decades. My daddy is an avid football fan, which is the only reason Mama got him to agree to this date.

Right now, Daddy's sipping beer in his recliner, his short dirty-blond hair mussed and his blue eyes alert. He's trying to pretend he's not waiting for the doorbell to ring, but I know he is. "What's this boy's name again?"

"Daddy, you know Reed. You were just singin' his praises last week about takin' us all the way to state."

He grunts. "That was before he went and got eyes for my baby girl."

"You started datin' Mama when she was younger than me," I point out.

"That was different, I was a gentleman who only wanted to hold her hand. Didn't even kiss till we were married. Kids these days act too grown."

"Don't you listen to that nonsense, Alina May. Your daddy was a hound," Mama teases, walking behind his chair and smacking him on the back of the head. "What time is Reed comin' to pick you up, baby?"

The doorbell rings.

"Right now," I say, lifting from the couch, my stomach flipping with nerves.

Daddy pops up and gives me a look before he speed walks to the door. I huff out a laugh. I knew he was waiting.

Wiping my clammy hands on the skirt of my yellow sundress, I follow behind. Other than the rash decision of letting Ricky Walker pop my cherry in the back of his pickup truck, I don't have much experience with guys so I'm a little nervous.

When I round the corner to the entryway, I can see Reed nodding to whatever Daddy's probably threatening, his silky brown hair just a little too long to be clean-cut, bobbing with the motion.

"Hi," I interrupt, walking up to them.

He shifts his focus over to me. "Wow. Hi, you look gorgeous."

"Thank you." My cheeks heat. "Ready to go?"

I side-eye Daddy as his gaze volleys between us, terrified he's about to embarrass me.

"Have a good time, baby girl." He kisses the top of my head and levels Reed with a stern look. "Have her back by ten, and no funny business. You hear me?"

"Yessir." Reed breaks into a smile so perfect, it's worthy of any parent's trust. My chest warms at the sight.

Grabbing a jean jacket on my way out, I close the door behind us and let Reed lead me to his car.

"I hope it's okay we're goin' to the lake. I brought some food and a blanket to lay out," he says.

"Like a picnic?"

"Yeah, just like that." He grins.

"Sounds perfect." I link my arm through his.

The lake is quiet for a Saturday night, just a few people splashing in the shallow water down the way.

Reed spreads out his checkered blanket and we settle in.

He opens a basket, pulling out various meats and cheeses, a baguette, and some grapes. My eyes widen as I realize how much effort he put into this.

"I was plannin' on an actual meal but was told this would be better to woo you with." He hands me a cup of sparkling cider.

"You were told, huh?"

"That's right." He grins. "By a very wise woman, so I thought it was best if I took her advice to heart."

I hide my smile behind the lip of my cup. "Reed Stanton, did you ask your mama for help with this date?"

He blushes, the pink peeking through the tan of his skin, and I worry I've embarrassed him. "I figured it was worth the risk."

"What's the risk of goin' to your mama?"

"Well, there's one of two possibilities. The first is that come Monday, you'll be tellin' the whole school how much of a mama's boy I am." He pops a grape in his mouth, chewing slowly.

"And the second?" I tilt my head.

"The second is you'll be tellin' them you're mine."

My stomach jolts with butterflies.

He leans in closer. "Now, I may be biased, but I'm hopin' for number two."

Heat rises to my cheeks as I open my mouth to respond, but he puts a finger over my lips. "Now I'll tell you a secret, Alina

May. I know you want to profess your love now, but I need you to keep me on my toes. I thrive under pressure."

I throw my head back and laugh. "Lord, you're cocky."

He chuckles, sitting back. "Always confident, never cocky. How do you think I win us all those games?"

"Same way you win everything, I imagine."

Before long the sun dips below the water, the moon rising to take its place. It's a clear night, the stars dotting the night sky like glitter, and lightning bugs hovering across the ground.

I drain the last of my cider and lie back on the blanket.

"Gorgeous out here, isn't it?" Reed settles in next to me, reaching for my hand. He laces our fingers together and it feels… nice. "I always love comin' out here when it gets dark. There's just somethin' about how bright the stars shine, you know?"

I hum my agreement, staring up at them.

It's been the perfect date.

Thoughts of being Reed Stanton's girl should be the only thing in my head.

But they're not.

Instead, my mind is filled with all the nights I held another boy's hand, under a glow-in-the-dark sky, telling him he was bigger than the stars.

Chapter 7
CHASE

Eighteen Years Old

FOR AS LONG AS I CAN REMEMBER, I'VE BEEN THE picture of self-control.

Since finding out about Goldi's date, I'm starting to understand people who let emotions rule their life.

I guess when it comes to her, I've always been weak.

It was a dick move to say what I did when I found out, and I knew it. I could see the confusion in her eyes as my words promised things my actions contradict.

Swear to God, I tried to stay away tonight. I attempted to drown out the thoughts with the sound of hammers and drills, but nothing worked, so here I am, waiting in her room, leg bouncing and gut burning.

There's a clock on her wall that ticks loudly, and it's the only sign the night is getting shorter, which means her date is getting longer. The otherwise silent air leaves me space to ruminate in thoughts of where they are…what they're doing.

I'm such a fucking idiot.

I've been torturing myself for years. Creating boundaries. Keeping her placed firmly as "little sister's best friend," refusing to let myself have her because it will hurt too bad when she leaves.

And everybody always leaves.

But I didn't realize it would be like this. Like my world is breaking apart at the thought of someone else getting to touch her, feel her, *love* her.

A car door slams.

My feet move before I can stop them, taking me to the window. Reed helps her out of the passenger side and they walk up to the door, the dim yellow porch light highlighting the way she's beaming at him.

My stomach twists.

Fuck.

He's tucking a strand of hair behind her ear.

I grip the windowpane, physically restraining myself from jumping through the glass and making sure the motherfucker can never throw a football again. My chest grows tight, exhaling choppy breaths.

Don't kiss him, Goldi.

She does.

And I'm in a special kind of hell.

Must be karmic retribution from when I sat across from her while Suzy Abbott had her hand on my dick, whispering how she wanted my cum on her tongue.

I ignored Goldi on purpose that night, pissed off she was cozied up to Ricky Walker, and clearly trying to prove a point, although I'm not sure to *whom*.

But I saw her watching. I saw her stand up and drag

Ricky away, disappointment and hurt marring her perfect fucking face.

I'm brought out of my regrets when she breaks the kiss. *Finally, goddamn.*

Reed says something that makes her smile, and I don't have to imagine the blush blooming on her cheeks for him. I can see it happening, live and in person.

My arms strain, fighting the urge to reach out and steal the color for myself.

They linger for another few minutes before she finally—*finally*—disappears inside and he drives away like the douchebag he is.

I watch until taillights disappear down the street.

Her bedroom door opens and then, "Chase, what the heck are you doin' here?"

I spin around, my chest squeezing at the sound of her voice.

She has no idea how much she affects me.

Running a hand through my hair, I force a cocky grin. "Thought I'd stop by…see how your date went. Get the gossip before everyone else."

She makes a sound of disbelief. "Really?"

A thousand words are on the tip of my tongue, dying to break free. *He fucking kissed you. Did you like it? Did you think of me at all?*

Instead, I lie on her bed and pat the space next to me, resting my hands behind my head like I couldn't give a fuck that she just had her tongue down another guy's throat.

She glances toward her door before walking to it and flicking the lock, then heading to the stereo and turning on music, most likely to drown out any noise so her parents don't try to walk in.

"Well, it went great, if you must know."

"Where'd he take you?"

"Down to the lake. We had a picnic."

"Original."

She smirks. "It was romantic."

The sting of teeth biting through my cheek is the only thing keeping me from losing my shit. "You going out with him again?"

A halo of hair whirls around her as she spins to face me.

Damn, she's pretty.

"What's it to you?" she questions. "You know, this overprotective big brother act is old, Boy Scout. You might want to spend more time worryin' about your real sister, instead of who's dippin' in my panties."

There's a brief moment where I focus on her bringing up Lily, but the visual of someone getting anywhere near her "panties" pumps rage through my blood until I can't think of anything else.

I jump up from the bed, stalking toward her. "Did you let that motherfucker *touch* you?"

She scoffs, propping her hands on her hips. "So what if I did?"

I chuckle, but I'm feeling anything but amused. "Answer the question, Goldi."

"That's none of your business."

"*Everything* about you is my business, don't you know that?" I argue. "Don't you get it yet?"

"What is there for me to 'get,' Chase?" She throws her hands up, her tone exasperated. "I can't do this anymore. You don't want me in the daytime, and I don't want to be your dirty little secret at night."

Fear of losing her chokes me and douses some of the jealousy stewing inside me. I soften my tone. "I'm not the right kind of person for you, Goldi. Believe me, I try every day to become something better. Something more." My fist smacks against my chest, and she flinches like I'm hitting *her*. "Whether I *want* to be around you has nothing to do with it."

"Oh, please." She rolls her eyes. "You only want to be around me when it's beneficial for you."

My brows raise, her words hitting my chest like a sucker punch. "You think it's easy for me to stay away from you?"

"Yes! I think it's easy!" she explodes, stepping forward and shoving me. "I think it's *easy* for you to climb in my window, as long as no one sees."

She pushes me again. "I think it's *easy* to drop my friendship and then pick it up when it suits you."

A third push. "I think it's *easy* for you to mess with any girl that has a pulse, and not care how it cuts me up inside."

This time, I grab her hands before they hit, jerking her body until she's flush against me.

She whooshes out a breath.

I can taste it on my lips.

The thread holding my restraint frays and snaps.

My hand grasps the nape of her neck at the same time she surges up, our teeth clacking together as we fumble to get closer, to taste deeper, and then she's climbing my body. It's clumsy, and new, but I don't care. I hoist her up, her ass fitting fucking perfectly in my hands, and her ankles locking around the back of my waist.

We move until I hit the edge of her bed and fall back, and then she's on my lap, and everything is…*fuck*… It just *is* everything.

My fingers thread through her hair and tug, pulling her mouth from mine because I want to look at her. I need to see every inch of her in this weak moment, but when I do, the pure adoration that's bleeding from her gaze makes my chest ache too bad, so I dive back in and press soft kisses to the nape of her neck, moving up across her jaw until I capture her lips again.

Goddamn.

My hand slides up her thigh and under her dress, teasing the edge of her cotton panties. She whimpers and shifts, and the tips of my fingers brush against her.

With my other hand, I tighten my grip on her hair, and she gasps, her perfect mouth popping open as I pull on the strands and expose her throat.

I cup her over the cotton between her legs. "Did he touch you here?"

"What?" she asks breathlessly.

"Did. He. Touch. You. Here?" I repeat.

She moans, and I trail a line of kisses up her throat, unable to keep my lips from her skin now that I've had a taste.

"Answer me."

"No," she admits.

The relief is sharp, even though deep down I know I have no goddamn right when it's *my* fault she wasn't with me instead of him in the first place.

I tilt forward, nipping her lips. "I want you so goddamn bad, but I want to take my time. I don't want to do anything you're not ready for."

She shimmies a little on my lap, like she's testing the waters, her movements unsure, and I bite the inside of my cheek to keep from thrusting up, or doing something even more embarrassing like ending all of this before it can really begin.

Her lashes flutter and I think my heart might explode from how stunning she is. Her hair is still fisted in my hand and I lean up, tugging on it until her head tilts to the side and I can suck on her neck, making sure to leave a mark.

Mine.

My abs contort under my shirt as her hand sneaks down my torso, like she's about to touch me there, and while I know it would feel good, I don't want her to think we have to go that far—do *anything* beyond what we're doing now.

Honestly, I could kiss her for the rest of my life and die happy. I release her hair and cover her hand with mine, stopping her descent.

"Please," she whispers. "I want to."

I shake my head. "I don't want your first time to be like this. We've got all the time in the world, baby."

She freezes, teeth indenting her lower lip, and suddenly her gaze is everywhere *but* on me. "You… I…" She runs her fingers through her tangled hair. "Chase, I'm not a virgin."

Her words hit my solar plexus so hard I can almost *feel* it physically breaking, and I shoot up from the bed, making Goldi fall to the side from the sudden movement. "I know you didn't just say what I think you did."

She rolls onto her back and looks up at me. "Well…what'd you expect?"

Running my fingers through my hair, I pull harshly, the pain doing nothing to ground me. "Who the fuck was it?"

Fire blazes in her eyes, her palms slamming on the mattress. "No! You don't get to ask me that. I'm not over here askin' for your list of a thousand hussies."

My teeth grind so hard, they'll turn to dust any moment, and I breathe deeply, my nostrils flaring as I attempt to calm that ever-present rage that simmers inside, but right now, it's a damn near impossible task. Even though I know everything she's saying is true; I have no right.

But I feel *sick*.

I was too much of a pussy to take what should have been mine, and she gave it away to someone else.

Exhaling, I crack my neck and admit, "You're right."

She props up on her elbows, surprise flickering in that big, blue-eyed gaze. "About time you realized that's usually the case, Boy Scout."

I smirk, moving toward her and leaning over the bed until she's forced back and my arms are caging her in. "You may have more...*experience*"—I grit the word out—"than I thought, but that doesn't mean anything needs to happen tonight. Okay?"

She nods, reaching up a hand and cupping my cheek.

My heart flutters like it's sprouted wings.

"You promise to never leave?" I ask.

"Cross my heart and hope to die," she replies, craning her neck and sweeping a kiss across my lips.

It's just a peck, but my chest cracks wide open, flooding with happiness I'll never deserve.

I can't offer her anything, can't give her the world, but I can't let her go, either, so I'll lay my bruised soul at her feet and hope she tends to the wounds.

It's always been hers anyway.

Chapter 8
ALINA

Sixteen Years Old

I'M CHASE ADAMS'S GIRL.

Those are four words I never thought I'd say.

I can't stop smiling.

Last night, after the high wore off, I was terrified of him running again. After all, it's what he's programmed me to expect. Instead, he admitted how tired he was of fighting what's between us, said I was his and he was mine, and that's all there is to it.

Maybe it makes me a sucker, but I believe him.

Chase is a lot of things, but he's never been a liar.

"So, let me get this straight, Alina May." Becca narrows her green gaze on me from across the worn brown leather couch in my living room. "You went out and had a great date with Reed. Gorgeous, charmin', totally fuckable, Reed. Am I right so far?"

"Yep." I nod.

"He wooed, you swooned. He was a perfect gentleman, not even sneakin' a titty grab all night and then… *Bam!*" She smacks her hands together. "The King of Assholes waltzes in, only *after* someone else shows interest, by the way, and you just jump in his arms and run off to live happily ever after?"

I sigh. "Well, when you put it that way, it sounds awful, but that's not what it's like."

"Then what's it like?" She crosses her arms.

"Listen, I like Reed. And maybe in a perfect world where my head rules my heart and not the other way around, he's the best choice for me, yeah. I can admit that."

"But..." Becca arches a brow.

"But Chase is my *person*."

Her nose scrunches up in disgust. "Yeah, well sometimes all your 'person' ends up bein' good for is disappointment. So I hope you're ready for that."

My stomach drops. "Can you at least *try* to be supportive? You're my best friend, and I need you in my corner. Lord knows how Lily's gonna react."

Becca's face softens and she reaches out, gripping my hand in hers. "Look, all I'm sayin' is this thing with Chase, it has heartbreak written all over it, sister. I've watched you pine for years while he tore you up, and I'm supposed to, what? Just forget all that, and suddenly be okay with this?" She shakes her head. "I don't think I can."

"I'm not askin' you to be okay with it, I'm just askin' for you to respect my decisions. Honestly, Becca, it's not your choice."

"He has issues, Lee."

"Who doesn't?" I shrug, defensiveness rising through me like hot steam.

She rolls her eyes and I snap, jerking my hand away.

"Rebecca Jean, you're my best friend, but I swear to all that's holy, if you don't get off your high horse and at least *pretend* to be supportive, I'll kick your butt straight out that door." I point toward the front entry, disappointment coloring my insides because she can't see how happy I am. "I won't sit here and justify my actions to you. Just 'cause you have issues with commitment, doesn't mean everyone else has to."

She scoffs. "I don't have issues with commitment, I just don't *do* commitment. There's a difference, honey. The church has me trapped enough." She wrinkles her nose, placing a hand on my arm. "All right, fine, *God.* If you're happy, I'm happy."

I blow out a breath. "Thank you."

"So…what was it like? And *don't* leave out the details." She wiggles her eyebrows. "I'll just pretend when you talk about Chase's dick that it's Brad Pitt's."

I grab a throw pillow from beside me and toss it at her, laughing, a little bit of lightness flowing back into the moment.

The doorbell rings and both of us snap our heads in its direction.

"Expectin' someone?" she asks.

"Never know around here, I guess," I say as I get up to answer.

She nods and stands, grabbing her book bag and following me. "That's fine, I've gotta go anyway or my folks will probably send out a damn search party."

I open the door and find Chase, one arm raised along the frame, his body towering over mine.

"Hey." His grin is wide, those dang dimples on full display.

"Hi yourself." My stomach flutters, lips curling up. "So you *do* know how to use a door."

He doesn't move to step inside, and I don't move to let him. We just stand in the doorway, smiling wide, locked in each other's gaze.

In my peripheral vision, I see Becca make a face like she's gagging. "Good God Almighty, y'all make me sick."

We ignore her.

"Lee, call me later, babe." She squeezes past Chase, waving her hand behind her as she walks down the drive.

I mumble a goodbye, my eyes never straying from Chase.

He finally moves, reaching out to press on my stomach, forcing me backward until I'm plastered against the wall.

My heart dances so wild in my chest I'm afraid I'll pass out.

He wraps his arms around my waist and pulls me into his body, my front grazing his chest. A pulse of heat shoots through me, and it catches me off guard because I'm not used to my body reacting this way. It's only *ever* been this way with him, and it was only in the past year it even started.

Chase leans down and takes my lips in a kiss, different from the ones last night, sweeter. Still, when his tongue teases my mouth, my body vibrates with *something*.

My eyes close and I lean into the moment, throwing my arms around his neck and trying to drag him further into me. He pulls back instead and then gives me a quick peck. Once…

Twice…

"I've been thinking of your lips all fucking day," he admits, kissing me again like he can't stay away.

I think I might burst from happiness.

My arms wrap around his neck, pulling him down so I can deepen the kiss. He groans, his arm tightening around my waist as he lifts me, pressing me harder into the wall. His hips push into mine, and I moan into his mouth, the ache sharpening between my legs, but he pulls back again, shaking his head and setting me back down.

"I don't want your parents coming home and seeing me mauling you in their doorway," he says.

My bottom lip sticks out in a pout, although I agree. Daddy would have a conniption, and Mama… I don't know *what* she'd do.

"So let's go somewhere else," I recommend.

He nods. "Anna's down at some job site with Sam today helping pick out interior designs, so they'll be gone awhile. We can chill at my place."

"What about Lily?" My stomach knots thinking of what her reaction will be to Chase and me. Like everyone else, she assumes we grew apart as we got older, not realizing her brother was busy tangling up my soul with his.

He shrugs like the thought hasn't even crossed his mind. "What about her?"

"I mean…is she home?"

"Probably. Who knows with her these days?" His jaw clenches, sadness sweeping over his features. "I'm trying not to be so overbearing because she gets pissed at me when I am, and it makes her disappear."

I cock a brow at him. "*You* aren't bein' overbearin'?"

He rubs his chin. "Yeah, I'm letting her live her life or whatever."

You shouldn't, I want to say.

Guilt stabs me for not voicing my worries. I promise myself that after we handle her finding out about us, I'll bring it up. I can't right now because if she finds out I narced on her *and* I'm dating her brother? She'll hate me forever.

"Do you, ya know, wanna tell her about us?" I break eye contact, peering down at my pink-sparkled toes. I guess the rips he caused on my insides are a little deeper than I thought because part of me is terrified he'll want to keep me a secret.

He tilts my chin up with his index finger. "I plan to tell *everyone* about us. I told you last night, I'm done fighting this. It's us now. Always."

My body releases the tension, relief flooding my veins.

He pecks my lips again, trailing his hands down my arms until our fingers lace together. "You feeling good today, Goldi?"

I smile up at him. "Just right."

He smirks, grabbing my hand and leading me out the door, making our way to his house.

Lily *is* home, and just as I feared, she does not take the news well.

She paces the living room, feet moving so fast I'm not sure how the rest of her body keeps up. She looks tired today, a raggedness to her features I'm not used to seeing on her dark brown hair hangs limp and stringy, no makeup on her face, the antithesis of what Lily Adams usually represents.

"Lil, come on," Chase pleads, standing in front of her.

She stops. "Don't you beg me, Chase. What am I supposed to do with this? I was having an okay day. Then in walks my brother, the one person I could always count on to put me first, and I find out my *whore* of a best friend has been stealing him out from under me all this time?"

My heart drops through my stomach. *Did she just call me a whore?*

"Hey." Chase's voice cuts through the air like an arrow. "Watch your mouth."

Lily scoffs, sneering over at me and crossing her arms.

He takes a step closer to her. "Put you first? Lil, you haven't *let* me put you first in a while. Every time I try, you call me overbearing, so don't play that card with me. You don't get to act like you're a victim here. This"—he gestures between us—"has nothing to do with you, Lil."

"This has *everything* to do with me." Her shriek grates my eardrums, making me flinch. "She's supposed to be my best friend! And you…you're supposed to be my brother. Didn't you care at all about how this would make me feel?"

She's sobbing now, her words coming out choppy and uncertain, and while I understand where she's coming from, this is an extreme reaction. I thought maybe, we'd at least get her to see it from our point of view.

Chase's entire demeanor shifts when she cries, his shoulders softening and grief splashing on his face like paint on a canvas.

He moves toward her and wipes the tearstains from her cheeks. "I'll always be your brother, Lil. It's us against the world, remember?"

She hiccups, turning her face away from him.

He sighs, and when he speaks again his voice is raspier, like he's trying to talk around a boulder lodged in his throat. "All I've ever wanted was to see you happy. Don't you want the same for me? She makes me *happy*, Lil."

Lily sniffs, staring hard at the ground like she wishes it would open up and swallow her whole. "I can't lose you, Chase. You're the only thing that keeps me safe."

I feel awkward, standing behind them, watching as Lily's scars from years I wasn't a part of rip open and bleed out on the floor.

Chase pulls her to him harshly, the muscles in his arms tensing as he hugs her tight, rocking them from side to side. "It's us against the world, little fighter. That's *never* going to change."

She nods against his chest.

My body relaxes, tension I didn't even realize I was holding melting away and being replaced with a warmth. Chase is a good brother. The best.

He lets her go after a few more moments and then turns to wink at me. "You want something to drink?"

I shake my head, still feeling off-kilter from Lily's reaction. He seems to think everything is solved but I can feel the weight of her glare.

When Chase goes toward the kitchen, I pivot.

"Lily, I—"

"Don't," she cuts me off, a look of disgust creeping over her face. "I thought I knew who you were. But looking at you now? I just see bumpkin trash."

Each word is a visceral pain making my stomach squeeze so tight I might throw up.

She moves forward until she's right in front of me, the energy of her anger whipping through the air and lashing at my skin.

I try to focus on what she's saying, but I'm distracted when she gets this close because her pupils are so big, it makes her eyes look black.

By the time I snap out of it, she's done talking, looking at me like she's waiting on a response. But I have no idea what she just said.

"God, you really are a selfish bitch," she hurls. Then she shoves by me, knocking my shoulder hard as she storms out the door.

Chapter 9
CHASE

Eighteen Years Old

I STARE AT THE LETTER IN SHOCK, PAPER CRINKLING as it sticks to my sweaty palms.

Dear Chase,

Congratulations! It is with great pleasure that I offer you admission to Eastern Tennessee University.

Accepted? I can't believe it. When Sam and Anna asked what my plans were for the future, I was adamant about staying local and working at Sugarlake Construction. There's no better way to learn a business than to be hands-on, and college was never even a whisper in my head. They convinced me to apply, saying the company would always be waiting and a degree in something like business management could be beneficial.

I listened. Partly because I can't stand the thought of

disappointing them, and partly because at the time there wasn't much—other than Lily—holding me here. But I never thought I would actually get in.

How the fuck am I supposed to leave now that I finally have Goldi?

"What's that?" Jax peers over my shoulder, being a nosy fucker like usual.

I ball it up quickly and push him back. "Jesus, get off my dick."

His eyes twinkle with mirth. "You're right. I think that's Lee's job now anyway." He puts his hand over his heart. "Let me be the first to tell you how happy I am to finally give up the title."

My mouth tilts up. "Isn't there some car that needs lubed or whatever the hell it is you do down at that shop?"

He smirks. "Know a lot about lube jobs, do you?"

"Why the fuck do I hang out with you?"

Jax shrugs in response, reclining on the couch and spreading his arms over the back.

I glance at the balled-up paper in my fist.

It's not a big deal.

The screen door on our house squeaks when it opens and I see Goldi standing in the entryway before she says hi.

Damn, she looks good.

"Hey, I thought you would be with Lil today." I shove the acceptance letter beneath a stack of magazines on the coffee table before giving her a kiss and pulling her to sit on my lap.

She gives Jax a small wave and turns her upper body to face me. Her hair brushes my neck, sending that vanilla shit she wears straight up my nose and I swear to God it makes my heart flutter.

"What?" Her eyebrows raise. "Why would I be with Lily?"

"Because she's your best friend? She told me she was going

to Chattanooga with Becca, I just assumed you would be with them."

"Uhh…nope."

Moving the strands of her hair to the side, I kiss the base of her neck lightly. "What's wrong?"

Her eyes flick from left to right like she can't decide where to look and then she sighs and meets my gaze. "Chase, Lily hasn't had anything to do with me since she found out about us, and if I'm honest, she was rarely around before that."

I laugh. "You fucking with me? She's always with you."

She shakes her head slowly. "No, Chase. She's not. You knew she was lyin' that day we showed up at your front door. You really thought that was a one-time thing?"

I was so lost in my head about Goldi's date, I guess I glossed over that fact. My eyebrows draw in. "Then who the hell *is* she with?"

Goldi's hands wring together, her teeth chewing on that puffy bottom lip of hers. She mumbles something, but I don't hear it.

"What's that?" My tone is sharp.

I'm not trying to be a dick, but I need her to get over whatever her issue is and spit it the fuck out.

"I said, I'm not sure, all right? A couple years back, she started seein' this guy." She's still shaking her head at me, her eyes glassy with unshed tears.

What? How could I not know this?

"I never met him, but he was older—too old for her. She swore she stopped seein' him, but all those weekends she said she was with us…" Her voice trails off, and my grip around her hips becomes tight.

She squeaks, smacking my hands off her.

"Fuck, I'm sorry, baby."

She hums and leans back, running her fingers through my hair. Her touch is normally calming, but right now I feel like a live wire ready to explode. "Why didn't you ever tell me about this?"

"You weren't exactly by my side much these past few years. What was I gonna do, yell it across the neighborhood? I figured you already knew."

Jax clears his throat and my eyes snap over. I forgot he was even here. "Not to intrude on what is obviously a personal moment between you two, but I did see Lily with some loser the other day down by the shop."

"What the fuck, man?" My eyebrows rise. *Does nobody tell me anything around here?*

He nods, leaning forward, elbows resting on his knees. "Yeah, bro. I was busy dealing with a customer, so I didn't pay much attention, but now that I think about it, shit looked kind of sketchy."

"I think she may be on drugs," Goldi blurts. Her eyes are wide, hands covering her mouth like she didn't mean to say it.

This conversation is the last thing from amusing, but I chuckle anyway. "And how long have you been thinking this?"

"A while, I guess."

Leaning back, I purse my lips.

"I was fixin' to tell you, I swear," she continues. "It just never seemed like the right time."

"Lil would never do drugs, Goldi."

She nods. "I'm sure you'd like to believe that. But, Chase, I'm tellin' you. Somethin's not right."

"Okay," I agree. "I'll talk to her."

The words roll easily off my tongue, but I'm not sure if they're the truth, because both of them are overreacting. They don't know Lily's past the way I do, and I *know* there's not a chance she's doing drugs. She knows what they do to people, what they did to us. I could, however, see her dating some dick bag and not wanting to tell me, afraid of how I'd react. Even I can admit that I'm not exactly known for my understanding and patience.

I push down the dread creeping up my throat and reassure myself. There's no fucking way she would get into shit like that. If she was having a hard time, she would come to me. It's us against the world. Always.

Jax hangs for a while longer before his mom calls him home, and when Goldi and I are finally alone, I bring up ETU.

"No way, Chase. Not on my watch." Goldi stares me down, hands on her hips, a serious expression on her face.

"Baby, it's not a big deal. I was never planning to go anyway. You're out of your mind if you think I'm leaving town now that I finally have you."

She rolls her eyes. "Good Lord, get over yourself, it's not across the country. It's ETU—a few hours away."

"A few hours isn't three houses down, and I don't want to be that far from you. What if you decide you can't handle long distance? What if something happens? I need to be *here*."

Her eyes soften as she puts her arms around my waist, kissing my chest through the fabric of my shirt. "That won't happen. You can come down on weekends, I can come up. I won't let you throw away college 'cause of me."

I blow out a breath, resting my chin on the top of her head. Anxiety is twitching in my stomach, but I ignore it because I want to be a better man for her, someone she can be proud to have by her side.

Maybe college *is* the right choice.

"I'll think about it."

A smile lights up her face as she raises up on her toes to kiss me chastely. "I'm really proud of you."

My heart pounds, a strange sensation filling me up.

Nobody has ever told me that before.

I like the way it feels.

Chapter 10
ALINA

Seventeen Years Old

IT'S BEEN SIX MONTHS SINCE CHASE LEFT FOR ETU. I'm crazy proud of him, but it would be a lie to say it isn't hard. When he was leaving, he swore he would be back every single weekend, but I don't think either of us realized how unrealistic that is. Between him working to pay for his apartment, and me teaching dance to toddlers at the local rec on the weekends, time—and gas money—has been difficult to come by.

I was planning to hop in my little Kia and drive up there at least once a month, but my folks said no way, no how could I go without a chaperone.

That's where Jax comes in, I guess. I don't know what he said to Mama, but she melted like butter and convinced Daddy that if Jax came along, it was okay to go. I about keeled over and died right there when they told me. *Jax? A chaperone?* I can't believe it, but I'm not about to look a gift horse in the mouth.

Jax and I don't know each other all that well. After our first disastrous meeting when I was a fresh-faced fourteen-year-old, we didn't really talk much. He became Chase's best friend, and since Chase was set on ignoring my existence, we ran in different circles.

We're friends now, but it's purely superficial so it's strange being in a car with him without a buffer.

Jax has one hand on the wood-rimmed steering wheel, and the other on the gearshift. He's relaxed, totally in his element, and I can see why he says cars are his calling.

"What are you thinking about so hard over there, Alina May?"

"What kind of car is this?" I look around the interior.

It sure is pretty.

When it comes to cars, I'm as dumb as a doornail, but I can feel the labor of love pouring out of these details.

He caresses the dash with his hand, the sun glinting off the blond hair on his knuckles. "Sixty-seven Mustang Fastback. She was my dad's."

"Oh." I get quiet, nervous to venture into this topic with him. Last time, it didn't go so well.

He peeks over at me, smirking. "It's okay to bring up my dad, I've had time to work through my anger."

"Oh, good. That's…good." I nod, still unsure what to say. Honestly, I'm not sure if I believe him.

The conversation subsides, falling into a comfortable silence. My head rests against the window, staring at the billboards cruising by, Tim McGraw serenading us through the speakers.

Jax turns the radio down, glancing over. "Let's play twenty questions."

I lift my head off the glass, angling my body toward his. "Okay, I'll bite. Who goes first?"

"Ladies first, of course." He tips his head.

I tap my finger on my chin, pursing my lips. "What's that necklace you're always messin' with?"

He grabs the chain around his neck and pulls, two pieces of metal clanking together as they fall on top of his shirt. "Dad's dog tags. He was a marine."

"Oh, wow. That's amazin'. Do you always wear 'em?" I lean over, getting a closer look.

"Never take them off. It makes me feel like a piece of him is still with me…guiding me, you know?" He shakes his head, his shaggy hair falling from where it was tucked behind his ears. "Shit, that probably sounds stupid."

I have the dog tags in my hand now, thumb brushing over the raised lettering of his daddy's name.

RHOADES,

JAMES A.

"No, not stupid. I think it sounds real, and real is beautiful, Jax."

Emotion swirls in his eyes as he glances down at me before focusing back on the road.

I drop the tags. "Okay, next question. What's your favorite food?"

His eyebrow quirks. "Isn't it my turn? This is your third question in a row. That's cheating."

"You took too long, which means you forfeit your turn."

He barks out a laugh. "You didn't even give me a chance, woman!"

I lift my shoulders. "That sounds like a personal problem."

He's grinning now, sneaking peeks at me from his peripheral vision. "Crab rangoon. All. Day. Long." His tongue peeks out to lick his lips, and he moans like he's in the throes of passion.

My nose scrunches. "What's that?"

"Don't tell me you've never had crab rangoon, Alina."

"Okay, I won't tell you that."

"That is entirely unacceptable." He tsks. "We were just becoming friends, too. It's really a shame."

I laugh. "Well, I don't know what you expect me to do about it right *now*."

"Next Chinese restaurant I see, we're stopping. No matter the time or place. I'll give your mouth the best experience of its life."

"Please, it can't be *that* good."

"Oh, Lee…sweetheart, you just wait and see."

His happiness is infectious, and I face forward in my seat, trying to suppress my smile. I think I quite like being around Jackson Rhoades.

It's another hour before we make it to Chase's apartment right on the edge of ETU campus, and there's a giddiness in my chest at the thought of seeing him. This is the first time I've been to where he lives. I reach in the back seat to grab my jacket.

It's too dang cold in February.

Jax walks around to open my car door, and he puts out his arm, winking when I take it. "You ready to go see your man, sweetheart?"

We don't get farther than the front sidewalk before Chase's door swings wide, and a blond girl steps out, pausing to speak with someone just inside.

I stop in my tracks, pulling on Jax's arm, confused. *Do we have the wrong place?*

My stomach flips and deep-dives when Chase follows her out, and she throws her arms around his neck, pulling him into a hug.

Okay, not the wrong place.

Flashes of our past play behind my eyes and that jealousy I haven't felt in so long comes roaring back to life. It's unwelcome, but I can't say it's not familiar.

Chase doesn't really hug her back, and his lack of response calms me, just a little.

He looks up and spots us, a smile that's only ever just for me lighting up his face. Stepping back from the blond, he briskly approaches. Excitement bounces around inside me, making it hard to stand still.

"Goldi," he breathes, wrapping me in a hug, lifting me up and spinning me around. The jealousy recedes, replaced by the familiar warmth of being in Chase's arms.

Jax waves his hand in front of our faces. "Oh hey, Chase. Nice to see you. Missed you, bro. Remember me? Jax. Chopped liver. Whatever name you prefer, really."

Chase laughs, setting me down, keeping me tucked into his side as he gives Jax a chin nod.

The blond girl appears beside us, her light brown eyes focused on me. "Chase, these your friends from back home?"

"Yeah. This is my girlfriend, Lee, and my best friend, Jax. Guys, this is Lindsay, she's in my Business and Professional Communications class. She was just dropping off some notes."

Lindsay plasters a smile on her face—a little too wide to be genuine—and puts out her long, manicured fingers to shake my hand. "Nice to meet you. I didn't know Chase had a girlfriend."

My spine stiffens, but I hear Mama's voice in my head telling me to be cordial, so somehow, I manage to keep the practiced grin on my face.

Jax must sense my irritation, because he chuckles, attempting to lighten the mood. "Typical Chase, keeping the best parts of his life all to himself. The greedy bastard."

Chase pulls me closer into his side. "The best and biggest part of my life." He drops a kiss on my forehead and gives Lindsay a look. "I've talked about Goldi. I mentioned last week she'd be coming up to stay the weekend."

Lindsay puts a hand up to her forehead. "Oh, that's right. It must've slipped my mind. We talk about so much, it's hard to remember all the details."

I know girls like this and can see her game from a mile away, but I'm not above marking my territory. I cup Chase's face, his stubble scratching my fingers as I pull him down to meet my lips, teasing the tip of his tongue with mine before moving back.

"You're the best and biggest part of me, too," I whisper against his mouth.

He buries his face in my neck, his cold nose sending shivers down my back. "Goddamn, I've missed you."

Jax glances over to Lindsay. "You coming with us on the ETU tour? Not really the best weather for it, but hey, 'when in Rome,' am I right?"

"No, no. I have things to do today. Like Chase said, I was just stopping by to give him a copy of my notes since he's missing tonight's study group."

"Your study group meets on Friday nights?" Jax is incredulous, his face a picture of disbelief. "What the hell kind of college experience are you living, Chase? To say I'm disappointed would be a gross understatement."

Chase lifts his head from my neck. "I'm not here to party, dumbass. I'm here to get a degree as fast as fucking possible so I can come home to what matters." His hands creep down low on my back, fingertips slipping under the waistband of my jeans.

The air of confidence from Lindsay's posture deflates, and satisfaction pours through me like wet concrete.

"All right, well, I'll see you later, Chase," she mutters.

Chase barely glances at her, mumbling a goodbye. His hand tangles with mine as he leads us up the sidewalk and to his apartment.

By the end of the weekend, I've already forgotten her.

I've been lost in the sights and sounds of the city, and the happiness that wraps my heart, making it beat out the rhythm of a love song.

"I don't want you to go back," Chase whispers into my hair.

I'm lying on top of him, our limbs entwined on his black leather couch, reveling in the peace that comes with his embrace. Jax is passed out in Chase's bedroom, and this is the first time all weekend we've been alone. We managed to sneak in a few make-out sessions, but even though I told Chase I was ready to take that last step, he didn't want to do it when Jax was in the other room. Said he wanted it to be special. Wanted to take his time.

"Bein' away from you is harder than I expected." I pout.

His arms tighten around me. "You aren't second-guessing things, are you?"

"No way. You're stuck with me for good, mister. I just miss you so much. We don't get to see each other as often as I imagined."

His fingers trail up and down my back, and he sighs. "It's hard for me, too. Not being able to see you whenever I want is fucking torture."

It *is* torture, but nothing compared to the torture of knowing he wasn't mine. This is child's play in comparison.

"Have you talked to Lily lately?" he asks.

My heart sinks. "Chase, she won't even look at me when she passes me in the halls at school, and she dropped out of dance to avoid me."

I've tried to talk to Lily a thousand different times. I thought after some space, she would have cooled off enough to hear my side of things, but there's only so much verbal abuse a girl can take. Eventually, I stopped trying.

"She's not answering my calls. Probably still pissed at me for leaving." He sits up, bringing me with him, and runs a hand through his messy locks. "Can you try to get through to her again, for me? I need to know she's okay, and I'll feel better knowing you're with her."

I love Chase with every part of me, and that's the only reason I agree.

For some reason, he's blind when it comes to Lily. Too scared to see what's right in front of him, maybe. He's not willing to admit she treats me like trash, let alone that she's off the rails and needs help. I just hope he doesn't look back one day and regret how he's handling things.

"Yeah, I'll see about her when I get back home. But don't get your hopes up, Chase, she really can't stand the sight of me."

He hums and smiles like I didn't just tell him my best friend hates me because of us. "Thank you, baby."

I kiss him, committing his touch to memory.

Who knows how long it will be until I get to feel it again.

Chapter 11
CHASE

Nineteen Years Old

GOLDI AND JAX MADE THE TRIP AGAIN AT THE END of March, Jax taking his "chaperone" role way too seriously and not giving us a moment of privacy. Not like I'd fuck her with him eavesdropping anyway. I want us to be alone for that, but who knows when we'll get the time.

Three weeks after they left, the ache in my chest from not being with her was too much to take, so I requested off work, filled up my gas tank, and took the trip home. Coincidentally, it's also Anna's birthday this weekend, and I'm happy I'm here to celebrate.

Goldi and I are at my house marathoning old horror flicks on TV, but I'm not paying attention. I'm too busy watching her.

Even though we've been together for a long time now, every day is still like I'm floating in a dream. I didn't know it was possible to feel this, like my world is spinning around her, surviving off her glow.

That makes me sound like a pussy, but I don't give a fuck. It's the truth.

Almost everything in my life is finally going right. I've got the parents. I've got the girl. I'm getting the education. The only thing I'd change is the deteriorating relationship with my sister.

Lily's the one thing I can't keep ahold of, and it fucking kills me.

I never imagined she would shut me out the way she has, and now it's too late for me to fix it. I spent too long not willing to see what was right in front of my face, and brushed it off like an idiot, reassuring myself everything was fine. But I can't ignore it anymore.

The movie ends, credits rolling across the screen. My fingers trail up and down Goldi's arm as she lies in front of me.

"I love havin' you home," she sighs.

"I love *being* home."

She pushes her ass into me, and I bite my lip at the feeling. With all the time apart, we haven't had too many opportunities to be with each other like this, and the nineteen-year-old hormonal boy is raging inside of me for some contact.

She reaches back and cups me through my basketball shorts, making the blood rush straight to my groin. She looks back and smiles deviously. "How long till your folks get home?"

"Who fucking cares?" I growl, lust overtaking rational thought. I grind into her hand, letting her feel how much she affects me.

It's been a year of foreplay, and I'm losing my fucking mind.

She moves suddenly, and before I can open my mouth to protest the loss of her touch, she settles to her knees in front of me, her hands sliding slowly up my thigh and over my lap.

My heart pounds in my ears, nerves racing through me like I'm a kid again.

I watch, transfixed, as she wraps her hand around me, looking at me with all the trust in the world even though I'm not sure I deserve it.

"Does that feel good?" she asks, her head tilting like she's trying hard to concentrate.

"Fuck. Yes."

Tentatively, she takes her other hand and moves it beneath the waistband of my shorts, tugging them down until I'm exposed.

"Can I?" she asks, her cheeks flushing pink.

The thought alone has me close, and I bite my cheek and think about math equations to try to stem the sensation. "Yes," I grunt out.

When I slide inside her mouth, she hums, and my hands grab fistfuls of her hair on instinct.

Shit.

I lose it almost immediately, and when I do, she *moans* like it's the best thing she's ever tasted, and fuck if that isn't the hottest thing she's ever done.

After, I collapse back on the couch, and she rocks back on her heels, grinning up at me with love shining through her bright blue gaze.

My chest squeezes tight from how hard my heart thumps against it.

She moseys back up onto the couch, curling herself in my arms, and gazing up at me. "Was that okay?"

I press my lips to hers, my body buzzing. "It was perfect… *You* are perfect."

And I mean it. She is.

Goldi goes home an hour later, and I help Sam cook for Anna's birthday. When Lily doesn't show up for the celebration dinner, I blurt out my concerns. They aren't surprised when I tell them—they've been having worries of their own. We should have had this talk a long time ago.

"Dinner's getting cold. We might as well just eat." I look at the spread on the table.

Anna sighs. "I guess you're right. Do you have any idea where she is?"

Guilt stabs my heart because I *should* have paid attention to where she's been for a lot longer than just tonight. But still, her question makes irritation simmer in my gut.

My head cocks to the side, eyebrows rising. "Do *I* know where she is? I'm not the one living under the same roof as her, Anna. Maybe you should pay closer attention to the girl you decided to play mother with."

"Watch your mouth," Sam intervenes. "We're all concerned, and I get emotions are running high, but disrespect won't be tolerated, regardless of you not living here anymore. Am I clear?"

I tug my hair, guilt slicing through my insides like a table saw. "I didn't mean that. I'm just worried."

Anna smiles softly, reaching across the table to cover my hand with hers. "It's okay, Chase. The truth is, we've been worried about her for some time. I've been treadin' lightly, scared to push her away even more. That might make me a bad mom, I don't know, but there's no guidebook on how to handle this."

Sam rubs Anna's back, his brows drawn down. "She could just be running late. Let's eat."

I swallow as much as I can stand, but the food tastes bland, overshadowed by the anxiety rolling in my gut.

Where is she?

I throw my utensils on my plate, feeling like I'm about to explode. Something's wrong. I can feel it. "I'm gonna go look for her around town, and drag her ass back home once I find her."

Sam nods.

Anna stays silent, a somber expression on her face as she stares at her dinner.

I drive around for the next few hours. I call Becca on the off chance she's with her, but unsurprisingly she hasn't heard from her in days. I'm stopped in a random parking lot, desperation creeping through my bones, when my phone rings.

"Hey, Sam. She home?"

"No, but I remembered something. We had her turn on the Find My Phone feature on her iPhone. I should be able to track her down that way."

Why the fuck is he just now telling me about this? I could have been to her hours ago. My leg bounces while I hold the phone to my ear. After what feels like a goddamn century, he gives me a location.

An hour later, a few towns away, I pull up to a single-story house. It's a small, run-down place, chain-link fence around the yard, and a square window on either side of the front door. The grass is overgrown, covering the sidewalk. If it wasn't for the streetlamp flickering outside letting me see cars in the driveway, I would think it was abandoned.

Anxiety tightens my stomach as I walk to the front door. I knock, but no one answers. I move over to the windows, peering inside, but the shades are drawn so I can't see much. I'm about to take out my phone and call Sam when I hear mumbling from behind the door. My stomach pitches into my chest as I rush back over, and a man stands in the doorway, eyes barely open, a cigarette dangling from his mouth.

My jaw tics as I take him in. He's skinny as fuck, has short brown hair tipped with blond, and pockmarks scattered across his face. He's wearing a white undershirt stained with something brown, and gold chains dangling from his neck. *Good.* Easier to strangle the life out of him if he's so much as touched my sister.

"Yeah?" he asks, scratching his stomach.

"I'm looking for Lily. Is she here?"

His eyes open a bit more, scanning me. "Who's askin'?"

"Her brother."

His posture straightens, a smirk covering his face as he moves to the side and waves his arm inviting me inside. "She's around here somewhere. Flyin' high in the sky."

My fists clench. *I will fuck this guy up.* I move past him, keeping the lid on my rage, and focus on what's important—finding Lily.

I walk into the house and scan my surroundings. The living room is trashed. A few random people lounge around in mismatched chairs and bean bags, and there are lines of white on the glass coffee table. My heart sinks.

Christmas lights are strung around the ceiling even though it's not the holidays, and I move down a hallway, checking rooms as I go. Finally, I get to the last one on the right, and before I even open the door the smell of burning plastic assaults my nostrils. Memories of a past I try to forget flash through my mind, the scent throwing me back in time, and making me spin with nausea. I close my eyes, breathing deep, fighting the urge to throw up my dinner.

When I've regained my control, I reach out to turn the handle, my fingers trembling and my heart blasting its beat in my ears.

I already know what I'll find.

And I'm not wrong, because when I walk into the room, my heart fucking stops, the silence making my vision blur and my ears hum.

Lily is laid out on a bare, stained mattress. Burned foil litters the floor around her, a lighter and straw next to her hand.

The lighting is low. Just a lamp in the corner of the room casting an eerie glow over this completely fucked-up situation.

"Lil," I gasp, rushing to her side, my stomach churning and rolling.

She doesn't stir.

I drop, foil crunching under my knees, and grab her shoulders. "Lily, fuck. Wake up." I shake her, but she doesn't fucking move.

This isn't happening.

Sliding my arms underneath her, I pick her up, her body limp in my arms, the same way my mother's used to be when I'd find her passed out on the living room floor of our apartment.

Back then, I used to rush to her side, my gangly arms trying my best to move her, and when that failed, I'd sit next to her all night long, memorizing the way her chest moved with her breathing.

That's the only thing keeping me together right now, watching Lily's chest move with her breaths. I focus on getting her the fuck out of this shithole and to a hospital.

The guy who opened the door is slumped on the couch when I get to the living room, Lily's head lolling to the side and knocking against my chest.

"Call an ambulance," I snap at him.

His cloudy gaze sweeps over Lily in my arms, but he shakes his head. "No can do, my man. If she dies, it ain't gonna be on my property."

Black rage surges through me, blinding my vision. If I wasn't terrified that every second wasted was a second closer to losing Lily, I would tear this motherfucker apart. Instead, I shake it off, rushing out the door.

I'm dialing 911 as soon as I get Lily in my back seat, my hands shaking so badly I can barely type the numbers. I'm panicking and have no clue where the fuck to go. The operator calms me down, letting me know I'm less than five minutes from a hospital. Somehow, I get us there in one piece.

There's a group of people in scrubs waiting for us outside the hospital doors, and I throw my car in park, jumping out as they move forward to take Lily from the back.

I try to pay attention to what they're saying, but the adrenaline pumping through me makes it hard to focus, and before I know what's happening, they whisk her away. I drop onto the asphalt, my knees screaming from the impact, and I use it to ground me.

Fear cripples my insides, the edges of my vision growing hazy as I try to regulate my breathing, or my thoughts, or fucking *anything* other than what's happening here.

But it isn't until I'm back in the waiting area with Sam and Anna, and the doctors tell me Lily's stable, that I find any type of relief.

How could I have let this happen?

The whisper of Sam soothing Anna while she cries makes me ache for Goldi, but I don't call her.

I don't deserve any solace.

Rehabilitation is mentioned, pamphlets are exchanged, and just like that the hospital wipes their hands of Lily, preparing to discharge her within a few hours.

Sam, Anna, and I go down to the cafeteria after Lily asks for a minute to rest. They're both talking to me, but I don't pay attention. I'm too busy sinking into the depths of my self-loathing.

This is my fault.

If I had just paid more attention. Not gotten so caught up in my own life…in Goldi.

Eventually, we make it back to Lily's room, preparing for the tough conversations ahead.

But when we walk in, the room's empty.

She's gone.

Everybody always leaves.

Chapter 12
CHASE

Twenty Years Old

"CHASE, ARE YOU EVEN LISTENING TO ME?" Lindsay asks as she tucks a strand of her bleached-blond hair behind her ear and sniffs like she has a cold.

Her pencil taps against her textbook and she quirks a brow at me from across the library table where we're studying.

"Yeah, I'm listening." I'm not.

She sniffs again, peering at me through her lashes, a small grin on her face. "What did I say, then?"

I don't answer because it's a little annoying she's being so pushy like this and thinking we're friends. We're not. Not really, anyway. She's just someone I study with whose company I don't *despise*.

Honestly, I'm not sure why I even bother with the charade of school anymore. Not sure why I came here in the first place after Lily disappeared, and whenever I think about it too long, guilt pounds against my chest, making it throb from the weight.

But Sam and Anna were convinced I should continue to "live my life," whatever the fuck that means.

We've been searching for a year now, and no luck. Sam and Anna hang on to hope, but I know better.

No love is greater than the toxic love affair with drugs.

If it weren't for me trying to avoid Goldi as much as possible, I'd be back in Sugarlake, doing *something* more than sitting useless in business economics courses and vacillating between hating Lily and missing her.

It's not that I don't love Goldi, I do. The problem is that I love her *too* much, and like usual, whenever we're together, everything else disappears until all I see is her.

And sometimes, looking at her hurts. If I hadn't given in to the pull between us, my sister might be healthy. Happy. Here.

I should have saved Lily from this. I *could* have saved her.

That ever-present anger swirls and tumbles through me like a tornado, picking up everything in its path and adding to its weight, and just like when I was a kid, I don't know how to control it. I see the pain I cause Goldi whenever she visits. Hear it in her voice every time we speak. I want to scream it's not her, it's me, but the words never come.

It's always me.

I should let her go; I know this because keeping her hurts. It's just that the thought of losing her hurts more, so I'm selfish. I keep her on my rope, knowing I'm slowly hanging us both.

Lindsay sniffs again.

I snap my eyes to her. "Are you getting sick?"

She rubs under her nose and looks up, her pen creating a steady *tap tap tap* from her twitching hand. "No, just allergies or whatever. Probably these dusty ass books."

I lean forward, looking at her closely. She's antsy. She keeps rubbing her nose, and her pupils are the size of quarters.

"Are you fucking *high*?" I hiss, my stomach churning.

Her gaze narrows and she crosses her arms, leaning back in her chair with a huff. "What are you, the DARE police?" she laughs.

My jaw clenches.

When she realizes I'm not laughing with her, her face drops. "Just a little pick-me-up. Everyone does it, it's nothing to freak out about."

"There's no such thing as a 'little pick-me-up,' Lindsay. What the fuck is wrong with you?" My voice rises.

She shifts in her chair. "Jesus, calm down."

"Don't tell me to calm down. I don't want you to be high when you're around me." I point my pencil at her, gripping it so tight I'm surprised it doesn't snap in half.

"Okay, fine. I didn't know you were such a Boy Scout." She raises her hands in surrender.

The words "Boy Scout" hit me in the center of my chest, gripping my heart in its tight claws and squeezing. I shake it off.

"I'm serious, Lindsay. I don't fuck around with that bullshit, and you shouldn't, either." I swallow around the sudden lump in my throat. "And don't call me that."

My phone vibrates on the table, Goldi's name flashing across the screen.

We haven't spoken in days, and I'm dying to hear her voice, but getting to the bottom of Lindsay's habit is more important right now. *What if she's an addict already?*

Visions of Lily, half-dead and sprawled out on a dirty mattress flash through my mind, panic spreading down my limbs and around my back, forcing the breath from my lungs.

Goldi will understand.

I silence the phone, slipping it in my pocket.

I invited Lindsay over and told her I want to help her…that I *need* to help. I didn't go into the details, but something I did got through to her because she broke down, admitted it was out of control and that she was scared.

Her quick acceptance just reinforces the fact that if I hadn't been so distracted with Goldi, maybe this could have been the outcome with Lily. From then on, whenever I'm not working or in class, I'm with Lindsay.

I don't particularly enjoy her company, but I don't want to give her the chance to shove more poison up her nose. Besides, it gives me something to do other than sit at my apartment and be alone with my thoughts.

Sometimes, I look at her and I swear it's my sister I'm seeing… not that they look anything alike.

Maybe it's my penance. Maybe if God exists, he's giving me a chance to right the wrongs of my past. Hell, I don't know. All I know is I couldn't save my mom or Lily.

I'll be damned if I can't save her.

But I'm still trying to figure out how to tell Jax and Goldi. It's been a few months, and both of them have been up my ass about why I've been so distant, so they decided to make a spur of the moment weekend trip.

They'll be here any minute, and Lindsay's here just to hang. My eyes keep skipping from the TV over to her, and every time she catches me looking, a small smile grows on her face, her cheeks flushing.

"What?" she asks finally.

I shake my head, glancing back to the show. "Nothing."

She snorts. "Yeah, okay. You just can't stop staring at me?"

"I'm not staring, I'm just… I want you and Goldi to get along."

Her face sobers. "Right."

Normally, I wouldn't worry about Goldi being insecure, but our relationship has been rocky, thanks to me and my revolving door of fucking issues, and now that I've taken on Lindsay as a sort of pet project, it's only made things worse. Mainly because Lindsay asked me not to tell anyone about her problem, especially Goldi and Jax. She doesn't want them judging her and I get it, I guess.

I *won't* say anything because it's not my story to tell. But because of that, I'm not sure what to say to Goldi about how I'm spending all of my free time with Lindsay, and I don't want to lie, so I've missed more than a few phone calls.

The doorbell rings and I'm swinging it open within seconds, the antsy energy whisking through my body and making me unable to stand still.

A swirl of vanilla and honey blond rushes into me, long legs wrapping around my waist.

I bury my head in Goldi's neck, gripping under the curve of her ass, holding her tightly to me. Immediately, the heaviness disappears from my shoulders, and the thoughts quiet in my brain.

She peppers my face with kisses and I chuckle, squeezing her ass in my palms. "Good to see you too, baby."

"Dang, I missed you somethin' fierce." She slides down my body and backs up a space, beaming up at me with those perfect blue eyes and gorgeous grin.

Jax is still in the doorway, but he isn't looking at me. His eyes are on Goldi. I clear my throat to get his attention, wondering why the fuck he's staring at her like that.

He moves his gaze to me, a lazy grin spreading across his face. "Sup?"

I raise my chin in acknowledgment, still watching him. He has his hands in the pockets of his jeans, and he's looking around the apartment like he's never seen it before. The moment he spots Lindsay, a saccharine smile spreads over his face. "Well, well, well. Who do we have here?"

Lindsay grins, walking over to stand beside me, her shoulder brushing against my arm. "Jax, right? Chase has told me a lot about you."

His eyebrows jump. "That's interesting. I don't think he's said a single thing about you, although I guess we'd have to be *talking* to hear anything." He looks her up and down, then glances over at Goldi, and I watch as what looks like concern fills his features.

Goldi's staring in Lindsay's direction.

I step away from Lindsay and closer to Goldi instead, reaching out to lace our fingers together. Guilt crawls up my throat and constricts the airways.

"I haven't heard anything about you, either, actually," Goldi says, her hand going limp in mine.

"Yeah, Lindsay and I have been chilling recently. I told her she could kick it this weekend, get to know you guys."

"You two have been *chillin'* recently?" Goldi twists and looks up at me, a crease between her brows.

Lindsay jumps in before I respond. "Goldi, right?"

Goldi's eyes narrow. "It's Alina."

Shit.

"Oh." Lindsay smiles nervously. "I'm sorry, I just assumed because that's what our guy always calls you. Thanks for sharing him, by the way. He's become a really important person in my life."

Unease prickles at my skin like needles.

Lindsay rests her hand on my arm at the same time Goldi rips hers away, stepping closer to Jax instead.

Why the hell would Lindsay say that?

Jax throws his arm around Goldi, which makes *my* brows rise to my hairline.

"Where's *my* thank you, Lindsay?" he asks. "Chase was mine first, you know."

My eyes don't leave Goldi, my heart beating so fast it pumps anxiety through my veins like blood. "Naw, man. I've always been Goldi's. She's had me since I was thirteen."

Goldi's features soften, her love pouring into the air between us as she looks at me like I'm the most important person in her life.

I revel in the warmth, knowing I don't deserve the comfort.

Chapter 13
ALINA

Eighteen Years Old

THINGS ARE DIFFERENT SINCE LILY RAN AWAY.

I can only imagine what losing her does to Chase's psyche, but just like when we were kids, he won't let me in. That brick wall I spent years smashing down resurrected seemingly overnight.

But I'm not a quitter.

So I'll stand at his back and sharpen his swords, hoping he slays his demons.

That doesn't mean I'm not hurting with every missed phone call or excuse as to why he can't make the trip home. I don't push him because I'm terrified he'll snap our connection in half, but in the back of my mind, there are red flags waving from the way he's using our distance as a shield. I know he's not treating me right, but I'm clinging on in any case, hoping it's just a phase. He'll come back to me.

Besides, it's not just *me* he's avoiding. Jax can't get a hold of him to save his life, either, so the two of us decided to take a weekend trip.

I didn't expect to find my boyfriend alone in his apartment with another girl, though, and I definitely didn't expect her to come with us to the restaurant.

Chase sits next to me, his head bobbing to the live band playing on the stage, an arm thrown lazily over the back of my chair. His fingers toy with the ends of my hair, and I wonder how it's so easy for him to go from not speaking with me to touching me like he'll love me forever.

Maybe I'm just bitter because Lindsay won't shut up about how close they've gotten over the past few months, the same months I feel like *we've* been drifting further away.

With every word out of her mouth, the urge to slap her silly grows, but Mama's voice in my head telling me to be a lady reigns supreme, and somehow, I hold myself back.

Jax keeps sending worried glances my way from across the table, and the attention feels nice, because at least *someone* around here seems to be on my side and realizes this isn't normal. Chase is acting like everything is copacetic and it most definitely is not.

Besides, Jax and I are friends now. Our car rides together are like therapy, letting me vent my fears and frustrations, and relieving me of carrying the burden alone.

It's a comfort to share the weight.

Chase leans over, running kisses down my hairline. I melt into him, the sting of jealousy ebbing away. He's mine, after all.

Lindsay's eyes glint, watching us over the rim of her water glass. "Chase, tell them about the spider fiasco at my place."

Chase's body tenses, his lips leaving my skin as he straightens in his chair. "They don't want to hear stupid shit like that."

I cock my head at him, jealousy growing like vines around my heart. "I'd like to hear it."

He sucks his teeth, glancing at me. "There was a spider at her place. She was scared of it, and it was hiding in her bathroom. I found the fucker and killed it."

Lindsay throws her head back and laughs and then pins her brown-eyed gaze on me. "It was a giant wolf spider. The thing was hanging out in my bathroom, and I was too terrified to even go in there, but luckily Chase was already at my place, so he went in to kill it."

"Wow, how fortunate," I deadpan.

She smiles. "You're telling me. Took him the whole weekend to find the damn thing and kill it."

My stomach drops. I slowly nod at her story. "All weekend, huh?"

Lindsay takes a sip of water and smirks before setting it down. "That's right. Chase and I have movie weekends all the time, don't we, Boy Scout?"

Chase's arm tightens on my shoulder, but I grow rigid beneath him, my chest throbbing like someone shot me in the heart, because *is he kidding with this?*

"What a riveting story," I say, looking up at him. "Can't believe you didn't tell me yourself, *Boy Scout*."

He physically winces at the term.

"When was this?" I ask.

"Oh, about three weeks ago, right, Chase?"

Chase shifts, clearly uncomfortable, and a forgotten gash reopens across my heart. Three weeks ago, the toddler dance class I teach had a recital. It was the first one I choreographed, and I was so excited for everyone to see all the hard work I'd put into their routine.

I *begged* Chase to come home for it.

But he didn't, saying he wasn't able to get off work.

Nausea swirls in my stomach at the knowledge he was with her.

Jax is staring slack-jawed from across the table.

Chase moves his arm, reaching down to my thigh and squeezing. I toss his hand off me, unable to stand the thought of his touch. Tears burn behind my eyes, and I push my chair back, the legs scratching on the tile floor, excusing myself to use the restroom.

Jax—not Chase—is the one who stands, trying to follow. I put my hand up to stop him, whispering that I just need a minute.

I lock myself in a stall, leaning my head against the cold metal.

Breathing deeply, I try to calm my racing heart. I'm sure there's a perfectly reasonable explanation for this. I don't think Chase would cheat on me, but him putting Lindsay before me hurts almost as bad. With a couple more breaths, I pull myself together and open the stall.

Lindsay is at the row of sinks, leaning against the counter, her arms crossed, and I make my way over there, turning on the sink and running my hands under the hot water.

She scans me up and down. "You know, I really don't get it."

"Mmm."

I don't ask her to clarify. I may be small town, but I'm not stupid. This girl is itching to start something.

"Yeah, I mean…when I found out Chase had a girlfriend, I was pretty torn up. I had my sights set on him from the jump." She laughs, tilting her head to the side. "And then I saw *you*, and realized maybe he's not so far out of reach, after all."

I meet her eyes in the mirror.

Usually, words don't affect me. Yet Chase's avoidance, coupled with the knowledge he's been with her all those times he could've been with me, grates my confidence until there's nothing left.

It's a few moments before I speak, after I've grabbed paper towels and wiped my hands.

"Lindsay, I don't know what game you're playin', but whatever it is, you're wastin' your time. Chase and I have belonged to each other since the moment we met."

"You stupid bitch." She steps closer, her tall frame casting a shadow over mine. "Let me paint the picture for your small-minded country ass. Every time you call and he doesn't pick up? I'm right there, watching as he declines the call." Another step closer. "When you beg like a pathetic dog, asking for him to 'please come home'? I'm listening to your whiny voice, because I'm cozied up next to him. All it takes is a single word from me, and he drops *everything*, including you." She taps her chin with her pink almond-shaped nail. "Now...I wonder why that is if you two are so meant to be. I'll let you think on that."

My fingernails dig into my palms so hard I'm sure I'm breaking skin.

I trust Chase.

I *love* Chase.

But I can't stand the way this feels.

Lindsay's leaving. *Finally.* Chase walks her to his apartment door, speaking low, his mouth so close to her ear it's almost brushing against it. I analyze every single moment between them, unable to tear my eyes away.

Anger buzzes so vibrantly beneath my skin, I'm surprised I can't see it as a tangible thing. Her earlier words have soaked into my skin. They've mixed into my bloodstream and reached my heart, causing fissures with every beat.

The couch dips beside me and Jax's arm settles around my shoulders, comforting me like a warm blanket on a cool night. "Sweetheart, you stare any harder, you'll burn a hole straight through her."

My eyes sting and I blink, trying to clear them.

"Just talk to him, Alina. Don't drive yourself crazy with the what-ifs." He pulls me closer, dropping a kiss on the side of my head. "And if you need me to beat his ass, just say the word."

I breathe out a small chuckle, but it's all I can muster because the hollow feeling in the center of my chest is making it hard to even breathe.

Chase walks back over, stopping short when he sees Jax and me on the couch. "You two look cozy."

Jax laughs. "Yeah, well…someone had to make sure your girl was taken care of while you were busy with the local trash."

I stifle a smile, my mood warming at Jax's show of loyalty.

Chase's jaw tics, like it always does when he's holding back what he wants to say. "What the fuck is that supposed to mean?"

Jax levels him with his stare. "Which part?"

The silence is deafening.

"Anyway, I'm beat. I'll see you two in the morning." Jax squeezes my shoulder before he stands and walks down the hallway, leaving Chase and me alone.

Chase sidles up to me on the couch, his arms winding around me, and I don't return the embrace, stiffening until my body feels like a wooden board.

"Baby," he whispers. "Come on, Goldi, don't be like this."

I bristle. "Were you ever gonna tell me, Chase?"

"Tell you what?"

"Oh, I don't know." I run my hand through my hair, my foot tapping. "How about we start with the fact you've been tellin' me one thing when you're really spendin' your nights in another girl's apartment."

He releases me, sitting back and running a hand through his hair, tugging on the roots. "I *did* work that weekend."

My stomach drops. "That's even worse! You left to go to work and then what, went back to her place after? Did she take your coat and cook your dinner, askin' how your day went before you both cuddled up in bed?"

He sighs, nostrils flaring. "It's not like that."

I scoff. "That's entirely besides the point."

"Listen to me, baby. Lindsay is just a friend." He scoots closer, reaching for my hand.

I jerk it out of the way. "She doesn't want to *just* be your friend."

"She's in a fucked-up place right now and needs someone to lean on. That's all."

"Oh, really? What's wrong with her?" I cross my arms.

He pops up, pacing the floor. "She asked me not to say."

I huff, rolling my eyes. "Predictable."

"Goldi, listen to me," he says, moving toward me and dropping to his knees, his hands gripping my thighs tightly.

Pressure builds behind my eyes, and I grit my teeth to keep from shoving him away.

"I don't fucking want her." His voice breaks. "I want you. I *love* you."

His words stab my insecurities, making them gape open and bleed, and that pressure explodes, tears bleeding from the corners of my eyes and staining my cheeks. "You have a real funny way of showin' it lately, Chase."

"Don't cry," he whispers, his hands gripping my face, calloused thumbs brushing the wetness from my skin.

I turn my head into his palm, hating how much I love his touch even now, even when I'm so hurt by his actions I want to scream. "I need you to choose me, Chase."

"I *do* choose you." His grip on my jaw tightens, forcing me to look in his eyes. "I've been fucked-up after Lily. I know that. I'll do better. Just…just don't give up on me. Please. You promised you'd never leave me."

The lovesick girl inside of me grasps his words, hanging on for dear life.

Chapter 14
ALINA

Eighteen Years Old

MY TODDLER GROUP'S SECOND RECITAL IS tonight, and everyone I love says they're showing up, despite me telling them it's nothing fancy, and "choreograph" is a loose term when it comes to two- and three-year-olds. Still, I never realized how much I would fall in love with teaching dance. When I was younger, I used to dream of *being* on the stage, and now I can't imagine doing anything else with my life besides watching others up there shining like a star from what I've taught them.

There's a studio about twenty minutes away that's offered me an internship. At first, I wasn't sure if I would accept because it would mean skipping college, but Jax encouraged me, saying college will always be waiting. He may be biased, though, considering he chose to stay in Sugarlake as a mechanic, instead of furthering his education. His late daddy always dreamed of having his car restorations in the movies, and Jax is set on seeing that dream through.

Daddy wants me to go to university, though, and so does Mama. They both see how well Eli's doing, but it's not the same with him. He's a basketball star, one for the ages, and I'm just…me. The only thing I've ever wanted to do is dance, and I don't know how a college degree would help further that along, and after a long talk, they both agreed to let me live life the way I choose.

I haven't told Chase about the internship yet, but I'm planning to this weekend. He was hoping I would apply to ETU, but I know if I don't take advantage of this opportunity, I'll regret it.

"Hey, sweetheart." Jax grins, shutting the sliding door to my backyard and waltzing into my living room like he owns it.

"Hiya, Teeth." I smile.

"Stop calling me that. These babies are one-hundred-percent au naturale." He runs his tongue over his pearly whites. "You ready for the big night?"

"Nervous," I admit. "But my girls will steal the show, you just wait and see."

He clicks his tongue. "I don't know. I heard the eight-year-olds have some killer moves this time. I'm not sure your toddlers can keep up."

I smack his chest, laughing. "You shut your mouth with that kind of talk, Jackson Rhoades. I'll have you know my kids can outdance those eight-year-olds all day long."

"Oh yeah? And why's that?"

"Because they have me, of course."

"Now *that* I believe."

My cheeks flush at the compliment, the air shifting as he loses his grin.

He clears his throat. "Anyway, I just stopped by to see if you needed help with anything."

I clap my hands together. "Yes! I'm in charge of refreshments for the recital, but I haven't had time to pick anything up. I'd love you forever if you'd do it for me."

"Is that a promise?"

"Would that make you say yes?"

His green eyes sparkle, and a lightness fills me. Things are so easy with him, and every day I'm grateful he's in my life. To be honest, without him and Becca, I'm not sure what I'd do these days.

He ties his hair into a bun and throws his hands up. "Okay, I'll do it. Cookies for the kids and veggie trays for the old people. I'll be back soon." He winks, spinning his key ring around his finger as he walks out the door.

My phone rings a while later, Chase's name flashing, and my stomach flutters, knowing in a few short hours I'll see him.

"Hey, Boy Scout."

"Hey, baby. You feeling good today?"

"Excited. Nervous. Mostly, I just can't wait to see you, though." I lean against the kitchen counter.

"Think I can steal you away after the show? I want to get us a hotel, spend some time together just the two of us." His voice quiets, whispering low and raspy in my ear. "I need to be *with* you, baby. I can't wait anymore."

Arousal shoots through me, mixing with nerves. I've been ready for what feels like years, but Chase has been adamant on taking things slow, and after this past year with him was especially rocky, I wasn't sure it would *ever* happen.

My grip on the phone tightens as I squeeze my thighs, trying to ease the ache. "Yes," I say on an exhale. I don't know how I'll explain it to Mama and Daddy, but I'll think of something later.

"Thank God. I know things have been…weird lately, but I—Hey, hang on a second."

Shuffling against the counter, I rest my cell between my shoulder and neck, lifting myself onto the ledge so I can sit. Anticipation lights up my middle because I'm pretty sure he's about to apologize for the way he's been acting, and quite frankly, it's about time.

He starts talking again, but the sound is muffled, almost like he's covered the phone with his hand. A girl's voice is in the background, and just like that, any hope withers and dies because I just *know* that's Lindsay.

It's like our fight about her didn't get through to him at all.

Or it did, and maybe he just doesn't care.

That nasty jealous feeling slithers around my chest and tightens like a snake, my lungs aching and my heart breaking.

"Chase," I snap. "I don't have time to just sit here and listen to you talk to someone else."

"What was that, baby?" he asks.

I hate that I'm not sure *who* he's talking to.

"Goldi?"

"Yeah," I reply.

"I'm gonna run a couple errands and take a quick nap and then I'll be there. I can't wait to see you."

My eyes flicker to the clock and back. "You sure you've got time for all that?"

He chuckles. "Come on now, don't worry so much. I'm setting an alarm. I promise I'll see you in a few hours, okay?"

"Is Lindsay there?" The words are out before I can stop them.

"Uhh…yeah." He clears his throat. "She just showed up."

"Mm." All the anticipation I was feeling disappears. I can't stand her and he knows it, but still, he keeps her in his life.

He chooses her when he should be choosing me.

Jax bursts through the door, hands filled with platters of cookies. "Just call me Sugar Daddy, sweetheart, because I've got all the sugar you need."

His eyebrows wag, and I snort out a giggle, a little bit of the heartache lifting when I see him.

"Is that Jax?" Chase's voice cuts through the line.

"Yeah, of course it is."

"What's he doing there?"

The question catches me so off guard I pull the phone from my ear and look at it with my brows drawn in. I put him on speakerphone and hop off the counter to go look in the grocery bags Jax brought. "The same thing he's always doin' here. Bein' my friend and helpin' out. He grabbed the refreshments for the recital tonight."

"How nice that you have him," he says dryly.

Jax scoffs and irritation slams into me, smashing my already thin patience into tiny bits that could scatter in the wind. "Yep. You have Lindsay, and I have Jax. Havin' *friends* is the best, ain't it?"

Chase is quiet for a few long, torturous moments. "That's not fair."

"What's not fair is you glued to a girl I've told you repeatedly makes me uncomfortable."

"And I've told *you* there's nothing for you to worry about."

"You haven't told me a *damn* thing, other than she's in a bad place and 'needs' you."

"She does."

"Well, so do I, Chase." I rub my forehead, the words catching on the lump in my throat. I'm so tired of having this same conversation. "Listen, I don't want to fight. I'll just see you when you get here, please don't forget you said you'd take me to the hall, so don't be late."

"I won't be, I'll be there at three thirty on the dot." He almost sounds offended. "And I don't want to fight, either, baby. I fucking love you."

Usually, whenever he says those words—the ones I've dreamed about since before I even knew what loving was—my whole body fills up like a balloon, giving me such a high I'm surprised I don't float away. Now, though, they barely touch me at all.

His words are just that.

Words.

I hang up without saying anything else because if I open my mouth, I'm liable to speak things I can't take back, and Mama always says if you have nothing nice to say, then you shouldn't say anything at all. And I *definitely* have nothing nice to say to Chase right now.

Still, I trust that he means what he says, because Chase is a lot of things, but the one thing he's always done is show up when I need him.

"What was that all about?" Jax says, leaning against the wall with his arms crossed.

Blowing out a breath, I run a hand through my hair and give him a small smile. "You know how it is. Just Chase being Chase."

His jaw clenches and he shakes his head. "You shouldn't put up with that shit, sweetheart. You deserve better and you know it. *He* knows it, he just also knows you'll let him get away with it."

Nausea curdles in my throat at the thought of Chase treating me this way on purpose, and not because he's going through something he just doesn't know how to control, but I push the feeling as deep down as I can and shake my head.

"He's just goin' through things, Teeth. You know how he gets, and what he's been through."

Jax breathes out a humorless chuckle, his fingers tugging on those dog tags around his neck. "Just because someone's got things they're going through doesn't mean they have the right to break someone else."

Pressure builds in my throat and behind my nose, spreading to my eyes. *Don't cry, Lee.*

Jax takes several steps forward, his finger and thumb gripping my chin and tilting my face to look up at him.

"You're far too special to be broken, Alina May."

I suck in a breath, gritting my teeth to keep the tears from escaping.

"Call me if he doesn't show."

And then he's out the door and I'm left with an emptiness in my chest, like someone took the light and snuffed it out.

At three twenty, I text Chase, asking where he is.

At three thirty, I call him.

At three fifty, I call my boss and apologize for running late, and then call Jax, asking him to come pick me up.

I'm backstage with the director and my girls, trying to pump them up.

It's fifteen minutes until showtime, and still no word from Chase. I peek around the curtains and see Jax and Becca in the front row, empty seats surrounding them. I give them a small wave, ignoring the black hole of disappointment trying to eat me alive. I don't see my folks either, which is strange.

I slip my phone out of my pocket one more time, checking for a call, a text, *something*.

It rings in my hand.

Unknown.

Confusion colors my features and I excuse myself from the group, moving into the audience and brushing by Jax and Becca when I do.

They're looking at me weird, but I shrug and make my way into the hallway just outside of the auditorium.

"Hello?" I answer, leaning against the white brick wall.

"Hi. Is this Alina Carson?" a woman asks.

"Sure is. Who's this?"

"Ms. Carson, my name is Judy Davis. I'm a nurse at CHI Memorial Hospital."

A foreboding tingle creeps up my spine, making me stand up straight. *Did Chase get hurt? Is that why he isn't here?* "Okay... How can I help you?"

"A Craig and Gail Carson were brought to us about an hour ago after being involved in a collision."

"What?" I suck in a breath. "Those are my folks. Are they okay?"

She hesitates on the line, and my stomach drops like a lead weight. "It's best if you just get here as soon as you can, miss."

I shake my head, my tongue sticking to the roof of my mouth. "Of course but...please, just... Are they all right?"

"Your father escaped with minor injuries."

"And my mama?"

She hesitates again. "The sooner you can get here, the better, Miss Carson."

My vision goes blurry, that black hole from earlier exploding like a dying star. The phone drops from my hand and clatters to the floor as I try to steady myself on the wall.

I can't breathe.

"Alina?" I hear my name, but it's distant, muddled.

Why can't I breathe?

Jax's face appears in front of me, his big hands on my cheeks. "Sweetheart? What's the matter?"

I look up at him, but darkness rims the edges of my eyesight and he's nothing but a blurry figure. I'm trying to find the words, but I can't talk because *I. Can't. Breathe.*

My hands claw at my blouse, the silky fabric suddenly choking me. If I can just get it off, maybe it will relieve the pressure pushing down on my chest.

"Whoa, Alina." I feel fingers grab mine, smaller ones than before, more feminine. "Lee, deep breaths, girlfriend."

My chest caves in and my back presses harder against the brick wall, my limbs feeling like they'll give out at any moment.

"Alina." Jax's voice is sharp and authoritative, his grip on my face firm. It cuts through the fog and helps me focus, my vision clearing, just a little.

Worried forest-green eyes stare into mine.

"Mama…hospital…please," I rasp out.

It's barely coherent, but it's the best I can do.

I collapse into Jax's arms, tears staining his shirt, my fingers gripping on to him like he's the only thing keeping me upright.

His torso pushes against my cheek with his abrupt intake of breath. "Your mom's in the hospital?"

I nod against him, my gaze flickering to Becca who's standing behind him with a worried look on her face.

"Which hospital, sweetheart?" he asks. "I need you to tell me where to take you."

I rack my brain, trying to remember what the lady on the phone said. "CHI Medical."

The next few minutes are a blur, but somehow, we make it to the car. Becca's in the back seat, murmuring soothing words in the way only she can, and Jax holds my hand in his while he shifts gears.

It helps, but what I really need, *who* I really need…is Chase. I try to call him. Over and over and over.

Please, Chase. Pick up. Can't you feel me breaking?

Eventually, it stops ringing at all and goes straight to voicemail.

I can't breathe.

The ride to the hospital is a blur, but we make it. Daddy's pacing in the waiting room with a white bandage on his arm and tears on his face when we get there, and I rush into his arms, the pressure in my chest easing.

"Daddy, what happened?" I cry. "Are you okay? Where's Mama? Have you talked to Eli?"

He brushes my hair with his hand, holding me so tightly it's like he's afraid I might disappear.

"Everything's all right, darlin'. God has a plan, and I won't lose your mama. He wouldn't take her from us…from me." His voice cracks and his body trembles like he's trying to hold back his tears.

"Is it that bad?" I force out, even though I'm dreading the answer.

He pulls back, his eyes dark and heavy as they gaze into mine, and he shakes his head. "God has a plan," he repeats. "All we've gotta do is pray."

So that's what we do.

We sit in small plastic chairs, and we pray.

A couple hours later and my panic has calmed. Jax is on one side of me and Becca's on the other, each of them holding one of my hands solid in their grasp. Daddy's been pacing nonstop, and other than him calling Eli and filling him in, he hasn't said a word.

I'm scared.

Mama is still in surgery, and nobody has told us anything.

Jax curses beside me.

"What's wrong?" I ask, looking over at him.

He's on his phone, but as soon as I ask, he puts it away and gives me a grin, his fingers squeezing mine. "Nothing for you to worry about, sweetheart."

His smile irritates me. "Don't you treat me with kid gloves right now, Teeth. *Please*..." My voice breaks. "Give me a distraction, tell me what you were lookin' at."

"I was just scrolling social media. Dumb stuff to pass the time." He won't meet my eyes, but he looks past me and gives Becca a look. The base of my spine tingles with awareness.

I pull my hand from Becca's and reach out, sighing. "Just let me see."

Jax purses his lips.

"Lee, maybe we should—" Becca starts.

I cut her a glare. "Don't you tell me what we should do, Rebecca Jean. Not right now."

She sucks on her lips, and nods, then gestures to Jax. "You heard her. She's a big girl, show her."

He blows out a heavy breath and hands his phone over, his screen lit up.

When I see the picture of a smiling Lindsay next to a sleeping Chase, wearing his shirt and in his bed, my heart shatters into pieces.

When Mama dies two hours later, those pieces turn to dust.

Chapter 15
CHASE

Twenty Years Old

AN ARM ON MY CHEST IS WHAT WAKES ME. I RUN my hands down my face, groaning, and reach over to pull Goldi further into me, but instead of soft curves, I grasp sharp angles.

The fuck?

My eyes open fully, and see bleached blond hair, not the honey-blond I was expecting.

Lindsay? What the hell?

Throwing her arm off me, I scoot back.

She stirs, blinking groggily. "Chase?"

"What the fuck are you doing here?" I ask, throwing the sheets off and jumping out of bed to find my phone. It's on my desk, and when I pick it up, I realize it's turned off. Unease trickles through me like a dripping faucet and I glance around to get my bearings.

The sun is streaming through the closed blinds, creating

thin slivers of bright spots in the darkened room. The clock on my nightstand says it's 7:30 a.m., which means I'm officially the world's biggest dick because I slept through Goldi's recital.

Fuck. Fuck. Fuck.

"Chase, what's wrong?" Lindsay pushes back the covers, sitting up in my bed, stretching her arms above her head.

Shock filters through me as I notice she's wearing nothing but my shirt.

Mistaking my wide eyes for something it isn't, she grins. "Looks good on me, doesn't it?" She sweeps her hands down her body.

"What the fuck, Lindsay?" I say, powering on my phone.

It vibrates immediately, over and over again.

25 Missed Calls. 10 New Voicemails. 7 Text Messages.

My stomach knots.

Lindsay stands, coming close to peer over my shoulder. "Your phone wouldn't stop ringing yesterday afternoon, so I turned it off. Thought you could use the rest instead. I know how tired you've been from school and work."

"What the hell are you even doing here?" I remember her leaving yesterday afternoon. Obviously, once I fell asleep, she decided to show back up.

She runs her fingers up my forearm, and I shrug her off, my teeth grinding. "Actually, never mind. Just leave so I can fix how hard you've just made things for me."

Lindsay scoffs. "Please, Alina will forgive you."

My gaze snaps to hers. "And how do you know that?"

"Because she always does." She shrugs.

Her words are a punch to the gut.

Self-loathing beats my insides with the fact that even *she* realizes how shitty I've been to Goldi. "Care to explain why you're even here? Or why you took it upon yourself to put on my clothes and sleep in my bed?"

"I was tired and didn't have anything to wear that was comfortable. I didn't think you'd mind."

"Of course I fucking mind," I snap, pinching the bridge of my nose. "Make yourself useful and go start some coffee."

I look down at my phone, pulling up Goldi's name and pressing call, turmoil thundering in my veins like a storm about to hit. I just need to explain. She'll understand.

She has to understand.

The phone rings, but her voicemail picks up. I try Jax next. No answer.

Shit.

I open up my text messages.

GOLDI:

I'm sorry about earlier, it's just hard with you being gone.

JAX:

Hey, bro. Excited for you to be back! Whoop! Let's chill tomorrow after you get your Alina time.

GOLDI:

Are you almost here? We need to leave soon for the rec hall.

GOLDI:

Chase. Answer your phone!

GOLDI:

I'm having Jax take me. If I wait any longer, I'll be late.

JAX:

Dude. Where the fuck are you?

GOLDI:

I'm done.

This is bad. This is really fucking bad.

I go to my call log next, realizing there's a string of calls from Goldi during the recital, which is weird because why would she be calling when her dancers are on stage? I keep scrolling.

Jax.

Jax.

Jax.

Becca.

I stop short, my thumb hovering over the screen. *Why the fuck did Becca call?* It's no secret we aren't each other's biggest fans, and her calling means one thing: I've seriously messed up.

Nerves skitter down my spine when I play her voicemail.

"You know, I've met a lot of assholes in my life, but you really take the cake. You and that no-good, flighty ass sister of yours have so much in common, it *disgusts* me. You better stay gone, Chase Adams. Do you hear me? I don't want to *ever* see your face around here again, and if I do? I promise I'll beat the shit out of you myself."

Becca's always been a bitch, but her reaction to a missed recital is alarming. I move on to the most recent message from Jax.

"I tried, Chase. I really tried to give you the benefit of the doubt, even after all the shit you've pulled. Losing your friendship myself was one thing, it fucking sucked but I could deal with it, because you know what? Despite you being a selfish dick, I love you, man. You've been like a brother to me, even though you've always been too lost in your own shit to see the forest for the goddamn trees."

My breath hitches.

"But this…I can't save you from this. And to be honest, I don't think you really deserve to be saved. For once in your life, think about someone besides yourself and call me back."

Panic suffuses my entire body, sharp pains spreading through my chest and down my arm, and I try Goldi again, throwing the phone on speaker so I can pull on the first pair of jeans I can find and a black shirt.

She doesn't answer, so I pull up social media, desperate to find some clue as to why everyone's freaking the fuck out.

Lindsay sashays back into my room, two mugs of coffee in her hands.

I give her a brief glance and then focus back on the screen, my heart stalling and free-falling to the floor when I see the new photo I'm tagged in.

My stomach bottoms out so fast it makes me dizzy, and I

practically fall onto the bed, sitting on the edge to keep myself from collapsing entirely.

"Here's your coffee, Chase." Lindsay sets the mug on the nightstand next to me, and I reach out fast, gripping her wrist so tightly I'm sure it will bruise, holding her in place.

"Ouch, what the hell?" She tries to wrench it from my grasp, but I tighten my hold.

"What the fuck have you done?"

She peeks at my phone screen, a soft smile taking over her features. "Honestly, Chase, I was tired of waiting for you to man up and make a move, so I figured a little push in the right direction was needed."

"And you thought this would make me, what...grateful?" My tone is incredulous.

She lifts a shoulder. "It'll get that pathetic lapdog of a girlfriend out of the way at least."

My mouth drops open and I finally let go of her wrist. "You posted this so Goldi would see?"

She smirks. "A girl can hope."

"Are you out of your goddamn mind?"

"Jesus *Christ*, I can't do this anymore," she complains, running a hand through her tangled hair. "Do you know how tiring it is to play the damsel in distress to your fucked-up issues every day? What happened to you, anyway? You have a serious hero complex."

Bile rises up my throat and my palms grow clammy. *Has she been manipulating me this entire time?*

My phone vibrates.

Jax.

I point my finger at Lindsay, anger swirling so strongly inside me that my hands tremble. "Get the fuck out of my sight before I do something I can't take back."

Her face turns down, lips puffing out like she thinks I give a single fuck about how *she* feels right now. "Come on, Boy Scout."

The thin threads holding together my sanity snap like broken rope, and I shoot to standing, marching past her to where her purse and clothes are stacked in a pile by the bedroom door. I pick them up and spin around, shoving them into her chest harshly.

She stumbles back, gripping them to her body.

"Don't you fucking call me that," I say quietly, my voice sharp as a knife. "Get the fuck out. Now."

"But I need to—"

"I don't give a shit," I interrupt her, reaching out and grabbing her arm, hauling her forward until I physically force her out of my door. "I swear to God, Lindsay, if I ever see you again, I will make you regret ever coming into my life."

She scoffs, her cheeks ruddy and her eyes wide with shock. "You're psychotic."

Leaning in, I lower my voice. "Then you should have known better than to fuck with me, bitch."

I slam the door in her face and turn the lock, before dialing Jax's number to call him back.

He answers on the second ring. "Chase."

"Jax. Listen, I can explain."

The line stays silent. I pull the phone away from my ear, looking down to make sure it's connected. "You there?"

"I'm here." His voice is flat.

"Look, I know this seems bad, man, but I can explain. Lindsay, she—"

A sharp laugh cuts me off. "We all know what Lindsay's been up to, you giant fucking douchebag."

His words cut through me, but I don't have time to focus on the feeling. Not when I need to get ahold of Goldi.

"You know where Goldi is? Are you with her?"

Usually, the resentment would rear its ugly head when I think of them together. But right now, if it helps me reach her, I welcome the thought.

"Yeah. I'm with her. No, you can't talk to her."

"Jax, come on, man," I chuckle, the sound hollow. "This is all just a big misunderstanding."

"A *misunderstanding*? Seems to be a lot of that with you lately."

My temper flares, burning like a fireball in my solar plexus. "Put Goldi on the fucking phone, Jax."

"You're one selfish son of a bitch. You know that? Not everything is about *you*."

My fingers rip at my hair in frustration and I pace a hole through my floor. "I never said it was."

"You didn't have to. Do you have any idea of what's been going on? Any clue as to what the fuck you've done?" he asks.

"I haven't *done* anything, if you'd just let—"

"Alina's mom was dying in the hospital last night, and instead of being here with the girl you claim to love, you were MIA. In bed with that snake Lindsay, so don't tell me what you have and haven't done, because I've seen the fallout. It's currently shattered into a thousand pieces on my living room couch."

I stop pacing, my footsteps halting so quickly I'm surprised I don't fall flat on my face. My heart bangs violently against my ribs, like it knows if it stays with me, it's bound to break. "What did you just say?"

He exhales heavily. “Look. Alina needed you last night, but she doesn’t need you now, so don’t waste your time and come back here when you’re not welcome. I won’t let you get near her again, and neither will anyone else. We’re done letting you ruin everything you touch.”

He hangs up.

The icy tendrils of dread creep up my back and wrap around my chest, squeezing the air from my lungs until I drop to my knees, nausea rising up my throat and making me vomit on the floor.

Jax is right. I’m a selfish son of a bitch.

Chapter 16

ALINA

Eighteen Years Old

I'VE DECIDED I HATE SOUND. SOUND REMINDS ME the world is somehow still spinning. People are still living. Time is still moving. Like nothing has changed. Like Heaven didn't just steal a piece of my soul.

I hate sound.

So today, I pick silence.

Lying in the middle of Mama's bed, the pillow that still smells of her catching my tears, I choose to be still.

At least here, I can freeze time. Just for a little bit.

I pretend I don't hear when the door creaks open, the *tap, tap, tap* of shoes scuffling across the wood floor. It's Jax, I just know it. He's the only one besides Becca who's been by my side through all this, and at this point, I can decipher who they are based on the weight of their walk.

The mattress dips when Jax's warm body sinks down behind me, cradling me in his arms, and I close my eyes, more tears slipping from the corners and onto the pillow. Jax is silent.

He knows what it's like to hate the noise.

It's impossible to explain this feeling. No words to express the pain of losing the one person who loved you most in the world. No way to describe the devastation in knowing no one will ever love you that way again.

If you've never lost a parent, you won't understand. But Jax does, because Jax *has*. I stay strong in the face of everyone else, but with him, I can break.

And I do.

Over and over, I break.

My tongue darts out to moisten my lips and catches on the rough, chapped edges. I swallow down the sadness, my throat so scratchy and dry it burns when I do.

A physical reminder that I can, in fact, still feel.

"Sweetheart," Jax whispers. "We have to go soon. Do you need help getting ready?"

I shake my head, but I don't move from my spot. I don't open my eyes, because once I do, time will start again. I'll have to wear my black dress and wave my white flag of surrender while pretending to give a damn that people are crying crocodile tears over Mama's casket. If I open my eyes, I'll have to watch them bury Mama six feet underground. I'll have to hear the strongest man I know break apart because half of him is gone forever. I'll have to taste the bitterness of knowing it took Mama's death to bring my brother back to town.

So I think I'll just keep them closed.

The service is beautiful. Yellow chrysanthemums and pink tulips line the pews, white stargazer lilies surrounding her casket. Bouquets and baskets sit on the floor in front of her picture.

Altogether, it's a moving image.

I'm numb.

While Becca's daddy preaches about the restoration of innocence for the departed and God's love, I sit in the front row with my head down, wringing my handkerchief so tightly my knuckles blanch and my palms sting. Jax is on one side, his hand on my knee, and Becca is on the other with her palm on my back, pillars of support holding me up while my family crumbles beneath my feet.

I feel their touch.

Still, I'm numb.

The service ends, and I stand between Daddy and Eli, lost in thoughts of who the masochist was that thought up the idea of a receiving line. My sweaty palms grasp a hundred different hands as they whisper their condolences, and I keep my head bowed and mumble my thanks. But then a different hand grasps mine, a flicker of static running through my fingertips.

I don't look up right away, but eventually, I do.

Chase's face is relieved. Like being in front of me is all he needed to feel whole again. Lucky for him, feeling whole is still a possibility. His hair is a knotted mess, the strands fighting over which direction to lie. Yet he's nearly perfect, of course. He always is.

But his beauty doesn't move me.

"Goldi."

I blink.

"Baby, I am so…" His voice cracks, lower lip trembling as he wipes his hand over his mouth. "Your mom. I can't even—"

"So don't." The words come across as flat as they feel rolling off my tongue.

He swallows harshly. His eyes bounce to Eli, then Daddy, until they land back on me, that hand of his tugging on his roots, the same way it always does when he's dealing with emotion he'd rather forget. "Maybe I shouldn't have come. But, fuck… I just want you to know I'm here. Take all the time you need, but, baby, I'll *be* here."

Laughter bubbles up inside of me, and as inappropriate as it is, I can't stop it from spilling out. It's brash. The sound echoes off the walls, reverberating, mocking me with its tone.

"I don't really give a *fuck* where you'll be, Chase."

His eyes grow wide.

"Are we done here?" I drop his hand.

Daddy doesn't even look at us, too busy taking sips from his flask of whiskey. Not that I blame him.

Chase is still as a statue when I walk away, his hand pressed against his chest and his eyes glossy with unshed tears. I should probably feel something after leaving him there that way, but I don't.

Usually, I depend on others to drive me around, what with me not having a car of my own, but today I've got the family car. Daddy's too drunk to get behind the wheel, and Eli's here so he can be the one to take care of getting him from place to place. I drive aimlessly around town for what feels like hours, until the blazing sun disappears, and the inky black sky takes its place, darkness blanketing the ground. With every street I turn down, there's a memory of Mama, and it hurts something fierce, almost as if every good thing in the world has been ripped out from under me, and all that's left is the pain of her absence.

Eventually, I find my way home, even though it's the last place I want to be. Earlier today was the first time I'd even been here in ten days. Ten days of avoidance, of not wanting to surround myself with memories and choosing to hide away in Jax's shadow and at his place instead.

I go straight to my room and lie in bed, staring up at the glowing stars on my ceiling.

They make me think of Chase.

Anger licks at my insides, and the blaze makes me gasp. Up until now, there's been nothing inside me but a hollow ache, and I've found comfort in feeling numb. The rush of fiery emotion is a jolt to my system.

How dare he come to Mama's funeral.

I grab on to the rage, marveling at how it unfurls inside me like an inferno. My heart pounds in my ears as I jump out of bed and rush to my desk in the corner, grabbing the chair and dragging it to the center of the room. My shin hits the wooden leg and makes me wince as I climb to stand on the seat, but the pain is muted compared to how I'm feeling on the inside. I reach up, the stretch radiating down my arm and side, my fingers grasping on to a star and ripping it off the ceiling.

My chest heaves as I watch it fall to the floor.

I repeat the action, fingernails tearing and knuckles bruising as I punch deep into the plaster, again and again.

Rip. Watch. Repeat.

Eventually, I collapse to the ground.

A graveyard of stars surrounds me.

I smile.

Heartbreak is easier to hide in the dark.

Chapter 17
CHASE

Twenty-Two Years Old

THERE'S THIS NASTY HABIT I'M TRYING TO BREAK.

I dissect every part of my past until the pieces are so skewed, I can't put them back together. Countless hours are spent trying to fit square pegs into round holes, deciding who I'm going to hold liable for my failings. I'm the fucking poster boy for the blame game.

When I lost my mom, I raged.

When I lost Lily, I grieved.

When I lost Goldi, I did both of those things.

I went to her mom's funeral with the stupid idea she would need me, not realizing I had taught her how to *not* need me long before then. I held her limp hand and stared into her vacant eyes, searching for the love she had always given freely and without constraint. The love I soaked up like a sponge, but didn't deserve.

How selfish of me.

Now, I realize the love I offered in return was twisted and

warped, bathed in my insecurities and modeled after the dysfunction I was born into.

But even back then, on some level, I knew. Maybe that's why I didn't go to her again after the funeral. I stayed that night at Sam and Anna's knowing I wouldn't return and drove back to ETU in the morning, desolate and defeated, hating myself for how heartbroken I felt when, deep down, I knew I had no right.

I'm a taker.

A controller.

These are flaws that exist within me and they always will.

The only difference between then and now is that now…I'm ready to heal.

So here I am, lying on a leather couch that creaks every time I move, and staring at a popcorn ceiling, wishing like hell I hadn't made the decision to see a shrink. He said I could sit any way I liked, but in the movies they're always lying down, and it's easier this way, I think—not having to look someone in the eyes while I divulge the weakest parts of myself.

"Chase. Why don't you tell me why you've decided to come here today."

Dr. Abernathy is an older man, late fifties with dark wavy hair graying at the temples, deep brown skin, and round glasses that sit on his crooked nose. His ankle is highlighted by orange and blue argyle socks and is crossed over the opposite knee.

I steeple my hands on top of my stomach. "Well, Doc. I'm fucked-up. I chase away all the good things in my life."

"Hmm…do you feel like you hold on to the bad?"

"I *am* the bad."

The room grows quiet when I don't continue. There's a small gold clock sitting on his desk, ticking away, and I wonder if that's on purpose. If maybe it's a way to remind me that even these minutes aren't given freely. That I have to *pay* to get someone to pretend they care.

Apparently, paying to sit in silence.

People actually need degrees for this shit?

I shift uncomfortably on the couch, the leather groaning again underneath my weight. I expected him to lead me with life lessons or, fuck, I don't know, maybe pass out a multiple-choice questionnaire? I'm low-key nervous, and I don't have any clue how this works. Turning my head to the side, I watch Dr. Abernathy as he taps the tip of his ballpoint pen on a legal pad that's sitting in his lap, ready to take notes on all the ways I'm fucked-up.

He'll need a lot more paper.

Finally, he speaks again. "What is it that makes you feel that way?"

I quirk an eyebrow and turn back to stare at the ceiling. "You want me to give like…examples?"

"That's up to you."

Groaning, I tug on the roots of my hair. "I don't think I have the money for the kind of time that will take."

He chuckles, but I wasn't joking.

"Why don't you start at the beginning, then," he suggests. "Your first memory of feeling like you were 'the bad.'"

Nodding, I blow out a breath. "All right, yeah." I close my eyes and search through memories I normally keep locked up tight, until I get to the earliest hurt.

And then there I am, clear as day in my mind's eye, four years old and desperate for my mom's attention.

I open my mouth to tell Doc, but nothing comes out, anxiety crawling up my throat instead of the words.

This therapy thing is harder than I thought.

It doesn't get any easier as I leave my session and stop at the store. I'm standing in an aisle filled with notepads and loose-leaf paper, feeling like a dumbass as I stare at the different options. Doc's "homework" was to start journaling.

Fucking journaling.

I scoffed at the idea. I told him I'm a twenty-two-year-old man, not a thirteen-year-old girl, but he assured me I would be surprised. Said it would help me work through things I couldn't voice. I'm not convinced, but here I am anyway, picking out a damn diary. I take my time perusing, finding one that really speaks to me.

If I'm going to slice open my insides and bleed out on the pages, I might as well do it in a book that I don't hate looking at.

After college, I moved to Nashville. Now, every few weeks, Sam and Anna make the long drive down. While it's mainly to see me, I know they enjoy the city, taking the opportunity to have romantic getaways and explore.

This time, though, it's only Sam here.

"How have things been at Benson & Co.?" He shakes the glass in his hand, ice clinking against the sides as the liquid sloshes.

Here we go.

I had a feeling he was here for a reason, and even though he doesn't admit it out loud, we both know he's dying for me to come back home and help him run Sugarlake Construction, the way we'd always planned.

But I can't.

"Things are great. Busy."

I've been with Benson & Co. Construction since freshman year. When I graduated with a degree in architectural engineering, specializing in construction management, Sam thought I'd resign from my position and run back home, but the map of my life changed course the second I lost Goldi.

He nods. "That's good, Chase. They're lucky to have you, you know?"

"Yeah," I mumble.

"Listen," he continues, leaning forward and resting his elbows on the table. "I know you're apprehensive about coming back home."

I chuckle, sipping from my IPA. *Apprehensive* isn't the word I'd use.

"But I'm planning to do a major overhaul, expand into neighboring towns, really grow the company into something bigger."

A pinch of longing tugs at me, because for years all I dreamed of was growing up and taking over Sugarlake Construction—making a life for Goldi and me. A good one.

"I'd really love it if you came home for that...if you were part of it," he says. "Let's build a legacy. Together."

Fuck. He really knows how to make it hard on a guy.

Guilt percolates through my system like slow-drip coffee and I take my time replying because, once again, I'm going to be nothing more than a disappointment with my response.

"Sam..." I start, shaking my head and leaning back in my chair. "The last thing I want to do is disappoint you, you *know* that, and if I thought coming back home was the right move for me—for anyone—" I pause at the pang of hurt that cramps my stomach. "I'd be there in a second. But it isn't. I've made a life here in Nashville. A good one, and I can't just walk away from it."

He sighs, bobbing his head like he knew my answer before I actually said it. "Are you happy, son?"

No. "I'm working on it."

A heaviness coasts across his eyes, and it makes the familiar ache of being a letdown bloom back to life, draping on my shoulders like a weighted blanket. I owe Sam for everything good in my life, and I wish I could be the son he wants me to be, but there's nothing left for me in Sugarlake.

Not anymore.

JOURNAL ENTRY #1

THIS IS FUCKING STUPID.

Chapter 18
ALINA

Twenty-One Years Old

IF YOU HAD ASKED ME WHEN I WAS ELEVEN WHERE I'd be at twenty-one, I'd tell you dancing on Broadway and still the apple of my daddy's eye. If you had asked me when I was sixteen, I'd say a college graduate, teaching dance in my spare time, with Chase at my side. At eighteen, I'd have been positive I'd be an instructor at the premiere dance studio in Chattanooga, planning the wedding of my dreams to the boy who's always owned my soul.

But life likes to throw curveballs, the changeup so extreme it spins you around and knocks you off home plate.

I reminisce on the notions of that young, naive, *stupid* girl, wondering what she'd think of the way her life turned out. I'm still living at home, taking care of the only parent I have left, one who can't stand the sight of me because I'm the spitting image of my mama.

My weeks are filled with teaching dance at the rec hall and

waitressing down at Patty's Diner on Main Street to make ends meet.

Someone has to make sure the lights stay on around here.

If it were up to Daddy, we'd be destitute by now.

There are moments, glimpses of the strong man who raised me. The man who told me I could do anything, *be* anything, but those moments are stretched few and far between, lost in a sea of amber liquid and glass bottles.

It has a name, this affliction of his, but I never speak it out loud.

If I do, I'll have to face the truth that another person in my life has failed to live up to my expectations. One more time I've been left on the outside looking in, no matter how hard I try to shatter the glass between us.

They're all too lost in their personal demons to care about mine.

Maybe I'm the problem.

All that to say, there's a new normal in the Carson family home.

The "normal" of starting the day with forced optimism.

Today will be the day things turn around.

Often, despite how hard I try to stay positive, it ends with a phone call from Johnny down at The Watering Hole, telling me Daddy is "causing a ruckus again."

This morning—like every morning—Daddy looks haggard and worn. His skin is sallow, whiskey and heartbreak oozing from his pores. I plate his breakfast of scrambled eggs and bacon, placing it in front of him at the kitchen table, before grabbing my mug of coffee, letting the heat of the ceramic warm my fingers as I slip into the chair across from him.

"Daddy, when are you gonna stop all this?"

He twirls his fork slowly, never looking up from his plate. Never responding.

At this point, I'm used to his silence. Between him and Eli, it's a miracle I have any family left at all.

"Eli tell you he's down in Florida now?" I try to change tactics.

Daddy grunts, reaching out to grab his coffee and chug it down.

"That's right," I continue like he responded. "Some big interview for a coachin' gig at FSU. You think he'll get it?"

Another grunt.

I tap my fingers on the table. "I reckon he will. Maybe him and Becca will run into each other, and she can smack some sense into him for never comin' back home. You know she just left the other day to finish up her senior year out there."

Daddy doesn't reply, but he does scoot back in his chair, stand, and leave the room like I was never talking to begin with.

The first year after losing Mama was a blur.

Eli was drafted to play basketball in New York shortly after her funeral. His new superstar life got too big for his small-town family, and I quickly gave up hope of him even acknowledging our existence. But then he tore his ACL, ending his pro career before it ever really began, and the selfish part of me was dreaming he'd come back home.

Three years later, I've given up that silly notion, because Sugarlake hasn't seen hide nor hair of Elliot Carson, and all Daddy and I get is an obligatory monthly phone call to "check in."

In fact, the only person who gives me the time of day anymore around town is Jax. He's steadily working on his daddy's dream, restoring classic cars, and he's gotten pretty well known for his work. But Jax doesn't ease the loneliness that slithers around the deepest parts of my soul.

Right now, we're sitting at Mac's Dive, like we do every week on my only night off.

"You know, I hear that's a sign of sexual frustration." Jax points his beer bottle at the shredded, soggy pieces of a Bud Light label I've torn apart on the table.

I give him a half smile, too worn out from wrangling Daddy back home last night to fake the energy for more. Jax doesn't know how bad it is with him, because it's embarrassing to talk about, and I know he'd rush in and try to help, take over to keep the burden from landing solely on my shoulders. He's just a good person like that, and he's the best friend I've ever had besides Becca, but I know he feels things for me that I can't reciprocate, and letting him in on the darkest parts of my life feels like taking advantage of those feelings.

"You okay, sweetheart? You've been quiet all night."

I squint my eyes. "You just think it's quiet 'cause we don't have Becca's loud mouth runnin' nonstop."

He laughs and takes another drink, and half the women in the bar turn toward the noise. "That's true, Sugarlake is quiet as hell when she's not around."

He catches the eye of a girl sitting next to me and tosses her a wink.

Jax is what you would call a player, and it's truly fascinating to watch. He only has to smile their way, and it's like open season, fresh meat they can't wait to dig their claws into.

Between him and Becca, I feel like a nun in a convent.

I've thought about it, of course, giving in to the chemistry between Jax and me. It would be so easy, because things always are with him, but the last thing I want to do is ruin our friendship. He's the only one on Earth who has seen the darkest, ugliest moments of my life and held them as if they were precious. So at the end of our night, when he has a girl on his arm and asks if I'm all right with him heading out, I encourage him to walk out the door, even though I can see it in his eyes that he's just waiting for the moment I say no and ask him to come home with me instead.

The next morning, I head to the graveyard behind the church to visit Mama. I've always been freaked out by walking on the grass at cemeteries, something about stepping over bones of the deceased just seems downright disrespectful. But since there's no other way to get to Mama's grave, I grit my teeth and bear it.

Crouching, I lay the bouquet of fresh tulips in front of the shiny marble slab. I visit her once a week, and I always bring her favorite flowers, because I like to think she appreciates her remains being surrounded by things she enjoyed. I trace her name with the tips of my fingers, that familiar ache in my chest becoming more acute with every letter.

Gail Elizabeth Carson
Your life was a blessing, Your memory a treasure.
You are loved beyond words, Missed without measure.

Sighing, I lie on the grass, staring up at the sky, and pretend she's next to me. If I strain my ears, I can almost hear her whispering secrets of how to navigate this thing called life.

She was always good at that.

"Hi, Mama," I breathe.

The breeze caresses my face and I smile.

"I miss you...*so* much. I'd give anything to have you here. You know, there's still this hole inside me from the pieces you took when you left, and I don't think anything on this Earth can fill it back up again."

A knot forms in my throat, and I close my eyes, tears seeping out of the corners. No matter how much time passes, the pain never fades, you just learn how to live with it inside you, careful not to pick the scab.

"I don't know if you've got any pull up there, but if you do... could you try to get Eli to come home every once in a while? We could really use him around here. I'm sure you know Daddy isn't doin' so well since you've been gone." I shake my head, laughing. "I bet you're sick of hearin' me say the same things week after week, but I wouldn't have to talk your ear off if you'd just give me a solution."

I pause, listening, waiting with bated breath for a miracle.

But just like every other time I visit, a miracle never comes.

Chapter 19
CHASE

Twenty-Five Years Old

"I HAVE A DATE TONIGHT."

Doc hums in his chair. It used to annoy me, but now the rumble is comforting. I don't need long responses, and he doesn't push me to verbalize things that are easier to write down.

Yeah, he was right about the journaling.

"Are you nervous?" he asks.

"I feel like I should be, right? I'm twenty-five and I've never gone on an actual date." The guilt knocks, trying to work its way inside as I realize I never even took Goldi on one.

"I don't really feel anything, to be honest. Her name's Marissa, by the way, not that you asked, which why would you care? It's not like you actually give a shit." I'm rambling, every second costing another twenty cents, but I can't stop. "I mean, do *you* think I should be nervous?"

"I think it's normal to feel nervous," he confirms. "Or excited. But remember all of your feelings are valid, Chase, no matter what they are."

I click my tongue, analyzing him. "Yeah, that's what you always tell me."

I've been coming to Doc for three years now, and some days, I feel like he's my best friend. *How fucking pathetic is that?*

There's a group of guys from work I grab beers with, but it's all surface level, especially once I was promoted to construction engineering project manager.

The pay is nice, but I found out quickly people treat you differently when you're above them in management.

That's how I met Marissa, though. She's a designer for one of our industrial complexes.

I've picked up a lot of girls in the past five years, always for a quick thrill and a release of tension, a nice, warm hole for my cock to disappear in for a while, but I've never given them anything more than that because I have nothing worthwhile to give.

At least, that's how I've always felt until Marissa.

I'm not sure what it was that made me ask her out. Maybe it was the conversation. She's the first woman to hold my interest long enough to look into her head instead of staring at her tits. Or maybe it's the fact that with her jet-black hair, tanned white skin, brown eyes, and legs for days, she's the exact opposite of the girl my heart still beats for, no matter how many times I try to change its cadence.

JOURNAL ENTRY # 156

I FUCKED A WOMAN TONIGHT. IT FELT GOOD. I MEAN, OBVIOUSLY. IT WAS SEX, SO IT ALWAYS FEELS GOOD. AND THIS ~~GIRL~~ FUCK, WOMAN, SHE SUCKED MY COCK LIKE A HOOVER.

I REALLY THOUGHT THIS ONE WOULD BE DIFFERENT, YOU KNOW? WE HAVE THINGS IN COMMON, LIKED THE SAME MOVIES AND SHIT. AND I SWEAR, I TRIED SO HARD TO BE INVESTED DURING DINNER, BUT EVERY TIME SHE LAUGHED, I COMPARED IT TO THE SOUND OF GOLDI'S. EVERY TIME SHE TOUCHED ME, I WAITED FOR IT TO BURN THROUGH MY VEINS, BUT WAS LEFT FEELING COLD. AND WHEN I CAME, I HAD TO CLOSE MY EYES AND IMAGINE IT WAS GOLDI, THE SAME WAY I HAVE WITH EVERY SINGLE WOMAN I'VE BEEN WITH SINCE LOSING HER.

JESUS, I HOPE NOBODY EVER FINDS THIS NOTEBOOK.

DOC THINKS MY PROBLEM IS THAT I WAS NEVER SHOWN HEALTHY LOVE DURING MY "FORMATIVE YEARS," AND HE'S PROBABLY RIGHT BECAUSE HE USUALLY IS.

THERE'S ONLY ONE TIME I CAN REMEMBER MY MOM EVEN SAYING I LOVE YOU. I WANTED TO TELL DOC ABOUT IT, SO HE'D KNOW MY MOM DID LOVE ME, AT LEAST A LITTLE. BUT LIKE USUAL, MY THROAT CLOSED UP AND MY CHEST CAVED IN, SO THE WORDS STAYED BURIED.

BUT HERE GOES, NOTEBOOK. I'M GONNA TELL YOU.

I CAN'T REMEMBER HOW OLD I WAS, I THINK MAYBE FOUR OR FIVE. LILY WAS STILL IN DIAPERS, I KNOW THAT MUCH.

IT WAS A GOOD DAY, THOUGH.

MY BIRTHDAY.

MOM WAS HAPPY, WHICH WAS FUCKING RARE. I DIDN'T KNOW ABOUT DRUGS BACK THEN, ONLY THAT SHE NEEDED MEDICINE AND GOT SICK A LOT WHEN SHE DIDN'T HAVE IT.

THAT DAY, THOUGH, SHE WAS GLOWING.

I REMEMBER HER LAUGH THE MOST. IT LIT ME UP INSIDE AND MADE ME WANT TO TELL THE WHOLE WORLD SHE WAS HAPPY BECAUSE OF ME.

SHE WOKE ME UP THAT MORNING AND SAID WE WERE GOING OUT FOR ICE CREAM.

"A BIRTHDAY TREAT FOR A BIRTHDAY BOY."

WE DIDN'T HAVE MONEY BECAUSE SHE USUALLY SPENT THE LITTLE WE HAD POISONING HER VEINS, SO LUXURIES LIKE BIRTHDAY PRESENTS WEREN'T REALLY A THING.

I WAS EXCITED, NATURALLY.

SHE HAD NEVER GIVEN ME A BIRTHDAY TREAT BEFORE.

WE WENT TO A LITTLE ICE CREAM SHOP DOWNTOWN, ONE I ALWAYS STARED AT LONGINGLY WHEN WE DROVE BY BUT HAD NEVER BEEN INSIDE. I'LL NEVER FORGET THAT MOMENT, I SOAKED IN ALL OF IT LIKE A SPONGE SUCKS UP WATER. THE BELL CHIMED WHEN WE WALKED IN, AND THE SMELL OF SUGAR FLOODED MY NOSE AND MADE MY STOMACH GROWL.

I PICKED VANILLA AND WAS VIBRATING IN PLACE WHEN I GOT TO LOAD IT UP WITH GUMMY WORMS, SPRINKLES, AND STRAWBERRY SAUCE.

IT WAS THE HAPPIEST DAY OF MY LIFE UP TO THAT POINT, AND EVEN NOW, THINKING BACK ON IT, MY STOMACH FEELS THE MEMORY OF THE FLUTTERS.

FUNNY HOW SOMETHING SO SMALL CAN HAVE SUCH A HUGE IMPACT.

WE SAT AT THE TINY METAL TABLE IN THE CORNER OF THE SHOP, THE STOOLS UNEVEN AND WOBBLY. IT WAS THERE SHE TOLD ME HOW MUCH SHE LOVED ME, BOUNCING LILY ON HER KNEE, AND MAKING ME PROMISE TO ALWAYS LOOK AFTER HER. "DO IT FOR ME, BABY BOY. THAT WAY I CAN REST EASY NO MATTER WHAT, KNOWING HER BIG BROTHER WILL ALWAYS BE THERE TO TAKE CARE OF HER. LIFE'S NOT THE SAME FOR A GIRL. IT'S HARDER."

I TRIED TO PAY ATTENTION TO EVERYTHING SHE SAID, BUT HER PROFESSION OF LOVING ME FILLED ME UP LIKE HELIUM, AND I WAS FLOATING ALL THE WAY HOME. MY WHOLE LIFE I TRIED TO GET HER LOVE, AND FINALLY, I HAD IT.

I REALLY THOUGHT SHE WAS BETTER. SHE HADN'T BEEN SICK ALL DAY, AND HOPE THAT THINGS WERE GOING TO BE DIFFERENT DANCED IN MY HEAD.

WE GOT HOME AND SHE PUT LILY DOWN FOR A NAP, TELLING ME TO TAKE ONE TOO WHILE SHE RAN TO THE CORNER STORE TO PICK UP SOME CANDLES FOR MY BIRTHDAY CAKE.

CHRIST. I'VE NEVER THOUGHT UNTIL THIS MOMENT HOW IRRESPONSIBLE SHE WAS LEAVING A CHILD AND A TODDLER ALONE IN THE APARTMENT. BUT BACK THEN, IT WAS A NORMAL WAY OF LIFE.

I FELL ASLEEP QUICKLY, PROBABLY FROM THE SUGARY ICE CREAM AND EXCITEMENT OF THE DAY, AND I REMEMBER LILY'S CRIES WOKE ME UP, WHICH WASN'T AN UNUSUAL ALARM CLOCK FOR ME. I GOT UP WITH HER A LOT, ESPECIALLY IN THE NIGHT WHEN MY MOM WAS LOCKED IN HER ROOM OR BUSY MAKING SURE EVERY SPECK OF DUST WAS GONE FROM OUR APARTMENT. SHE DIDN'T LIKE FOR US TO BOTHER HER WHEN SHE GOT IN ONE OF THOSE MOODS, SO I'D ALWAYS RUSH IN TO KEEP LILY QUIET WHENEVER SHE'D START WAILING.

THAT NIGHT, THOUGH, IT WAS STILL EARLY. BEFORE DINNER, FOR SURE. MY STOMACH WAS GROWLING, THE ICE CREAM AND REMNANTS OF MY MOM'S WORDS THE ONLY THINGS SLOSHING AROUND IN MY BELLY, SO I WENT INTO THE KITCHEN KNOWING LILY PROBABLY WANTED MILK AND A SNACK, ASSUMING MOM HAD PICKED SOME UP AT THE STORE EARLIER.

BUT WHEN I GOT TO THE FRIDGE, IT WAS EMPTY. ALL I

COULD FIND WAS A SLEEVE OF OPENED, STALE CRACKERS IN THE CABINET.

MOM WAS AWAKE. I COULD HEAR HER PACING THE LIVING ROOM, BACK AND FORTH, OCCASIONALLY GOING TO THE BLINDS AND CRACKING THEM OPEN TO PEEK OUT.

LILY'S CRIES WEREN'T EVEN ON HER RADAR. MY STOMACH SANK AS I PEERED AROUND THE CORNER FROM THE KITCHEN AND WATCHED HER.

I REMEMBER THINKING SHE MUST HAVE NEEDED THE GROCERY MONEY FOR HER MEDS, AND ALTHOUGH THE REALIZATION THAT SHE WAS STILL SICK...THAT SHE WASN'T ACTUALLY CURED THE WAY I HOPED, MADE ME SAD, I WAS MORE FOCUSED ON TAKING CARE OF LILY.

IF MOM NEEDED THE MONEY FOR HERSELF, I KNEW WE WOULDN'T BE GETTING ANYTHING TO EAT THAT NIGHT.

I CREPT BACK INTO THE KITCHEN, HOPING SHE WOULDN'T HEAR ME. SHE HAD A TEMPER WHEN SHE'D GET LIKE THIS, AND IT HAD BEEN SUCH A GOOD DAY. I DIDN'T WANT TO RUIN IT.

TURNING ON THE FAUCET, I GRABBED LILY'S PINK CUP AND FILLED IT WITH TAP WATER, HOPING IT WOULD HELP, AND THEN I GRABBED THE STALE CRACKERS AND TIPTOED DOWN THE HALLWAY TO OUR ROOM. I CRAWLED INTO LILY'S TODDLER BED AND LEANED AGAINST THE BACK WALL, HANDING HER THE WATER AND PUTTING THE CRACKERS IN BETWEEN US. EVENTUALLY, HER SOBS TURNED TO WHIMPERS, AND SHE MOVED NEXT TO ME, LAYING HER LITTLE HEAD ON MY SHOULDER, AND FALLING BACK ASLEEP.

ALL NIGHT LONG, I HELD ON TO THE WORDS MY MOM HAD TOLD ME EARLIER.

SHE LOVED ME AND I WAS A GOOD BROTHER. THE BEST.
I CONVINCED MYSELF IT WAS ENOUGH.

Chapter 20

ALINA

Twenty-Four Years Old

"HEY, I THINK YOU DROPPED THIS."

I ignore the stranger because I'm too busy digging through my bag while I rush out the front door of the rec center, trying to find my keys. I'm running late to my shift at the diner, and lord knows Patty will yell at me *again* and I can't afford to get fired.

"Hey, miss! Wait up."

Irritated, I spin around, coming face to face with Logan Baxter. I've turned so quickly, I stumble, my hands finding purchase on his chest.

My fingers dig in because his muscles are just *defined* as hell, and it takes me a few seconds for my brain to catch up, realizing I'm basically fondling him in public. My face flushes as I rip them away, and take a few steps back, but I can't help my gaze from drinking him in because he is a fine specimen of a man.

He's tall and handsome, and clearly coming from a fresh

workout if the sweat making his light brown skin glisten is any indication.

I know him, of course… Well, I know of him.

We went to school together, and by "together," I mean he was a senior when I was a freshman. Where Reed Stanton was the star quarterback, Logan Baxter was the shining wide receiver.

Logan grins his crooked smile, one that pulls up a notch more on the right, and his dark eyes sparkle with mirth. He reaches out, placing the missing keys in my hand.

"You dropped these." He trails his brown eyes from my plain ballet flats up to my flushed face. "Alina, right?"

"Uhh…yeah. Yep. And you're Logan." I stumble over my words.

"That's the rumor."

His laid-back personality reminds me of Jax, instantly putting me at ease.

"Well, thanks for my keys. I would have been up the creek without a paddle if it weren't for you." I smile, spinning my keys around my finger.

"Just happy I was behind you." He grins back, his gaze lighting a fire between my legs.

I shift on my feet. "You work out here a lot?"

He shakes his head. "I'm a personal trainer. This is where I meet my clients."

"Well, shoot, I can't believe I've never run into you before. I've been teachin' dance here for years."

"Maybe you've never seen me, but I've *always* seen you, Alina Carson."

"Oh, okay then." I look away, biting the inside of my cheek.

I really need to get my butt in gear, Patty will be fit to be tied and ready to rake me over the coals if I'm late. It's hard, though, when Logan keeps looking at me like I'm his next meal.

My heart doesn't react to his perusal, but my body sure does.

He reaches up, rubbing the back of his neck. "Listen…can I get your number?"

My brows draw in. "For what?"

Stupid, Lee. Obviously he's hitting on you.

His grin widens. "So I can take you out."

"Oh," I reply, butterflies flapping around in my stomach. "Yeah…yes, that'd be all right."

I rattle off my number and then my phone's ringing in my purse, and I cock my head, giving him a questioning look.

He winks. "Just makin' sure you gave me the real one."

A few days later, I'm with Becca for our Saturday brunch. After she graduated from FCU, she came home, accepting a social work position at Sugarlake High, and our brunches became a regular thing. She spent her whole life complaining about feeling trapped in Sugarlake, swore up and down she'd never wind up back here, but I guess time changed her mind.

I'll never say this to her, but I think facing the big, bad world scares her more. Better the devil you know.

She and Jax started forcing these "friend dates" on me when they were fed up with my self-imposed solitude, and normally he'd be here with us, but right now he's in California working with some fancy producer who hired him to be the car guy on their movie set. I'm so proud of him. It's what he's been working toward since forever, but I can't help feeling like everyone's life is moving forward while mine moves back.

I'm filling Becca in on my newfound "friendship" with Logan when my phone rings. Eli's name flashes. *Dang.* I forgot today was our monthly call. I chew on my bottom lip, deliberating whether to answer or to ignore him and just order another mimosa.

The mimosa wins.

"Who was that?" Becca asks with a mouthful of food.

"Eli."

She swallows, her fork scraping against her plate. "Oh. What's up with him lately?"

I shrug. "No clue, you know he doesn't tell me a damn thing. He's too busy thinkin' his money means he's showin' up."

Truthfully, every time Eli and I talk, it turns into an argument. He refuses to stop writing checks every month, and I refuse to let Daddy pour every dime of it down his throat.

"You should just take the money, Lee," Becca says. "He's clearly tryin' to help."

"He could help by comin' home," I snap.

"Have you even asked him why he won't?"

My eyes narrow, irritation tightening my throat. "Are you seriously defendin' him right now? Eli, the guy you've hated since you were a kid."

"I've never hated him."

I snort. "Yeah, okay."

She throws her hands up. "I'm just sayin'. Communication works both ways, girlfriend. You can bitch to me all day long and you know I'll listen, but at the end of the day, if you won't even ask him why he's not comin' home, then you don't stand a chance of ever gettin' him back here."

I huff out a breath, crossing my arms. "There's no chance, anyway. He's happy wherever he is with that girl he's datin'. What else is there to know?"

The sound of Becca's fork clattering onto her plate is jarring.

She recovers fast, clearing her throat and picking it back up, and I blink at her, trying to figure out why she's acting so strange.

Before I can ask what's wrong, she's onto the next subject like nothing ever happened.

I spend the rest of brunch listening to her telling stories of her college friends, and my heart squeezes at the thought I won't ever experience the kind of life she's lived. Even if I wanted to, I can't leave Daddy.

I'm all he's got.

Daddy's what I like to call a cycler. Some days he's quiet and ignoring me, but overall seems pretty normal. Well, as normal as someone can be with a gallon of whiskey in their belly. Other times he gets downright mean, taking his anger with God out on everyone around him. Once the dust settles—the lacerations barely healed from his cutting words—he's back to the sullen and distant man I've come to know. Those are the days I pray to hear he doesn't mean it when he says he wishes I'd disappear like Eli. Or that it's my fault Mama's dead.

I know it's the drink talking, not him. I have to hold on to the belief my real daddy is still in there somewhere. But, *dang*, it's exhausting.

He's got cement shoes dragging him under, and I'm the only one left to hold his hand, desperately trying to keep his head above water.

"Hey, Mama."

There's no breeze today, the Tennessee heat sweltering on my face as I lie in the summer sun.

"I met a guy. His name's Logan, I don't know if you remember him from back in the day, but he's nice, and I think you'd like him. We're not datin' or anything. I'm not interested in that, but he serves a purpose and makes me feel a little less lonely when we're together."

Sitting up, I throw my hair into a ponytail, the wispies sticking to the sweat on the back of my neck. "I'm sure you're turnin' over in your grave with that information. I'd like to think if it were a different world, I could open up and let him in, but..." I sigh, picking at a blade of grass and twisting it between my fingers. "The truth is, my heart's still taken by that broody boy who's bigger than the stars."

It's the first time I've admitted it out loud: Chase still has a hold on me after all these years. I hate him, but I'd be a liar if I said my heart didn't still beat for every piece of his damaged soul.

"Anyway. I'm not sure if you have any pull up there, but if you do..."

Part Two

Chapter 21
CHASE

Twenty-Eight Years Old

"GOD, GRANT ME THE SERENITY TO ACCEPT THE things I cannot change, the courage to change the things I can, and the wisdom to know the difference."

The voices repeat the phrase in unison, echoing off the walls in the basement of the church. The silence lingers for a few moments afterward, and I blink slowly, staring at everyone sitting in the fold-out chairs in front of where I stand.

"Thanks to everyone who showed up tonight. I know it's hard, but you're here, and we take it a day at a time. So whether you shared or just listened, thank you," I say. "See you next week, same time, same place."

I'm not a big proponent for God, but Nar-Anon's message is more about surrendering control to whatever higher power you choose to believe in. It's a crucial part of recovery, and while I'm not sure what that higher power is, I do believe there is one.

I have to believe there is one.

Two years ago, I finally opened up more to Doc, letting him read my journal entries. It's been a lot of inner work, but I've recognized how the drug addictions of my mom and sister were the biggest factors in shaping how I handle relationships. In shaping how I handle life.

I had never heard of Nar/Al-Anon groups, but Doc gave me pamphlets and explained how they were support groups similar to Alcoholics Anonymous, but for family members affected by addiction of their loved ones.

It took me two months to get the courage to go to a meeting. Six months to tell my story, but once I did, it was like a large boulder started getting chipped away, and the more I spoke, the less heavy it felt. For the first time in my life, I didn't feel so alone. And so began the biggest strides in my healing.

Four months ago, the woman who ran the local group here moved to Georgia, leaving a spot open for someone new to maintain it. I have no idea how it happened, but that someone became me.

I'm twenty-eight years old and it's the first time I can say I'm content with myself, but I guess that's what happens when you aren't harboring a lifetime's worth of self-hatred. That anger I spent years trying to douse is still there sometimes, but now I have the tools to keep it at a simmer instead of letting it erupt into an inferno every time something happens.

The hardest part has been facing my self-loathing from my culpability in Lily's downward spiral. I've struggled with it, but I've accepted she was battling her own demons, just like I was, and hers had nothing to do with *me*. Still, it's a regret I'll live with the rest of my life, knowing I chose to be ignorant to her pain.

Accept the things I cannot change.

I've tried to do the same work within myself over how I treated Goldi, but it's not quite as successful. Our "relationship" spanned seven years, and I can only remember *one* where she seemed genuinely happy. Guilt isn't a strong enough word for the emotion that drowns my body when I think of how badly I treated her. Of how much she must hate me.

So I write about her in my journals. Let Doc ask about her in my sessions. Open up about the pain of losing her in group.

People tell me first love is always susceptible to damage. It's fiery, intense, and usually burns out quickly. They say to forgive myself and move on. But they don't understand it's not my forgiveness that's needed.

I think about her all the fucking time, allowing myself to delve into soft honey-blond hair and the comforting scent of vanilla. It's self-inflicted torture remembering how every cell in my body reached out to fuse with hers. The feeling is still so intense, I'm convinced my memory exaggerates how strong our connection was, but I revel in it all the same.

I'm sure she's long gone from Sugarlake by now. On to bigger and better things.

Wherever she is, I hope she's happy.

Marissa zips her black pencil skirt and bends to slip on her high heels. My eyes track the movement, arousal spearing through me when she stands and turns, hands on her hips.

"See something you like?" she purrs, walking over to where I'm perched on the edge of the bed to give me a kiss.

"Just admiring the view." I smirk, palming her ass and pulling her into me.

Marissa surprised me last night, saying she had something "special" to give me. I was a little annoyed she showed up unannounced, but then she sucked me down her throat and rode me until I nearly passed out from exhaustion, and so I let her stay the night.

It's the least I could do after she put on such a show.

"You know, if you gave me a key, then I could have been waiting in your bed...*naked.*" She wraps her arms around my neck, peering at me from beneath her mascara-caked lashes.

I sigh, leaning my head back.

We've been together for three years, but I've been honest with her from the get-go about keeping things casual. I'm not interested in a serious relationship. I care about her, but it wouldn't be fair to promise something I'm not sure I can give, and while I keep waiting for that moment where a spark ignites, it still hasn't happened, and it doesn't feel right to force it.

But I suppose it's natural that after a certain amount of time, she'd start to want more.

Maybe if I hadn't met my soulmate when I was thirteen and lost her when I was twenty, I would be able to feel for Marissa the way I suspect she's starting to feel for me. But I *did* meet my soulmate when I was thirteen, and I *don't* feel that way about Marissa. I've tried to let her loose, urged her to meet someone who can give her everything she wants, but she sticks around, showing up and putting her pussy on a platter, insisting I'm enough.

So I'll give her the parts of me I can.

Marissa frowns. "Look, Chase, I'm not asking for a ring, hell, I'm not even asking for us to move in together, which if I was, after three years, could you really blame me? All I'm asking for is a level of trust. For you to show me that you want me in your life."

I run my fingers through my hair, blowing out a breath, the guilt pressing down on my chest.

Fuck it. "Okay, I'll get you a key made, but, Marissa, I've been honest with you from the beginning. I'm trying here, I am. Slow is what I need. Don't push me for more than I'm ready to give."

A smile lights up her face and she pecks my lips. "I think you're worth the wait. Your parents are in town tonight, right? What time are you meeting them?"

"Six. Do you want to come?" I ask.

Sometimes she tags along, but I'm hoping she says no. Spending quality time with the parents is literally the opposite of slow, and after me conceding to her on the whole key issue, I don't think I can take any more today.

"I'd love to, but I need to lay out these designs for the McKenzie project. I'll be locked in my cave for the rest of the night." She pouts, and I hide the relief flowing through me.

I shrug. "No loss. I'm sure Anna will be disappointed you're not there, but it'll be the same shit, different day, catching up on what's happening in our lives."

"You mean *your* life."

"What?" I look at her, my eyebrows drawing together.

"You had to have realized the conversation always centers around you and how you're doing *here*. I don't think I've ever heard them so much as mention anyone or anything from your hometown. Which, now that I think about it, is a little weird, don't you think? Their whole life is there, but they never say a word."

I let her words sink in, marinating in my brain. *Is that true?* Sam and Anna both know all things Sugarlake is a sore spot for me. I run through our past few dinners, realizing they've never once steered the conversation toward themselves. *Fuck my life.* All these years later, I'm still acting like a selfish prick.

Marissa unwraps herself from me and walks over to my dresser, picking up her earrings lying on the top and putting them in, one at a time. "You don't think they're hiding something from you, do you?"

I scoff. "No."

She lifts a brow like she's waiting for me to elaborate, but she'll be waiting a long time. No way in hell I'm bringing up my past with her.

Even though Marissa doesn't come with me to the restaurant, her words from earlier are stuck on a loop in my brain, making me feel like the biggest piece of shit to walk the planet.

I'll make an effort tonight, though. Ask about them for a change, even if the thought of hearing anything Sugarlake makes me sick to my stomach.

They're already seated when I arrive at the restaurant, and there's a tension in the air surrounding the three of us I haven't felt in years. It has me on edge.

I sip my beer, guilt billowing inside me. "So, what's been going on with you two?"

They share a look, and Anna places her hand on Sam's arm in a soothing gesture.

Sam rubs his forehead. "Well, there's actually been some things we need to talk to you about…with my health."

My beer goes down the wrong pipe, causing me to cough and sputter.

"Shit, that came out wrong. Don't worry," he rushes out. "It's nothing life-threatening, just a repetitive strain injury with my back. It's really not a big deal—"

Anna throws him a sharp look. "It *is* a big deal. He's been strongly advised by his doctor to go into retirement 'cause of this musculoskeletal disorder. If he continues to work, it'll only get worse."

Sam grimaces. "I'm fine. Just a twinge in the back that makes it hard for me to be in the trenches with the guys on-site."

Well, shit.

MSD is pretty common in construction. It's not unusual for workers to get strains on their ligaments and joints, causing restricted movement and severe pain, making it almost impossible for them to continue working. I've seen it before, but I never thought it would happen to Sam.

"Shit, Sam. That sucks."

He nods. "Yeah."

"So, what's the plan?" I ask.

"Well, you know what they say." He chuckles. "'Happy wife, happy life.' Anna wants me to go into early retirement, and bring on someone else to run the company."

His eyes meet mine, and my stomach fills with lead.

Anna nods, rubbing his forearm and gazing at him lovingly. "It's time to step back and enjoy the benefits of ownin' a company without the risks of workin'."

Sam's face softens, giving her a quick kiss before leveling me with a heavy stare. "Listen, I know we've already talked about this a million times, and I *know* more than likely, you'll turn me down again." He hangs his head, staring at the table, the muscles in his jaw clenching. "But before I go through the process of figuring out who I'll bring in—of figuring out who I *trust* enough to run everything I've spent years building—I have to try one more time." He raises his face until his gaze pins me in place. "Son, there's no one I'd want to run my company more than you."

I blink at him, anxiety scratching up my insides, making a sour tang hit the back of my mouth and the edges of my vision grow splotchy. I feel like I might pass out or throw up, I'm not sure which. I tamp it down and try to think logically. I've built a life here. I have a career I enjoy, respect from my peers, a girlfriend, a support system. In Sugarlake, there's nothing but painful memories and a group of people who made it very clear I wasn't welcome.

But it's Sam.

Everything I am, the man I've become is all thanks to him and Anna.

If they need me, then I owe it to them to get over my shit and show the fuck up.

God, grant me the serenity to accept the things I cannot change, the courage to change the things I can, and the wisdom to know the difference.

JOURNAL ENTRY #312

I'VE TALKED TO DOC ABOUT A LOT OVER THE PAST YEARS. BASICALLY VOMITED OUT THE WORDS SO THEY WOULDN'T KEEP ROTTING ME FROM THE INSIDE OUT.

BUT THIS ONE IS A MEMORY I'D PREFER TO FORGET.

SO HOPEFULLY, PURGING IT ONTO THE PAGES WILL MAKE IT FEEL A LITTLE LESS HEAVY IN MY HEART.

I WAS EIGHT WHEN MOM DECIDED SHE WANTED A NEW LIFE. I REMEMBER HOW SHE RAN INTO MY ROOM BRIGHT AND EARLY, PICKING ME UP OUT OF BED AND SWINGING ME AROUND WHILE

SHE SANG IN MY EAR. I ALWAYS CRAVED HER TOUCH, SO I LAID MY HEAD ON HER SHOULDER AND BREATHED IN DEEP, MEMORIZING THE SMELL AND FEEL OF HER. I NEVER KNEW WHEN THE NEXT TIME WE'D BE THIS CLOSE WAS.

SHE SAT ME AND LILY DOWN, DREAMING OUT LOUD ABOUT A MAGICAL CITY CALLED NASHVILLE. SHE HAD WATCHED THE MOVIE THE THING CALLED LOVE AND DECIDED IT WAS WHERE WE BELONGED.

MOM WAS ALWAYS GETTING FANCY IDEAS WHEN SHE WAS MANIC, BUT DECIDING TO UP AND MOVE US WAS EXTREME EVEN FOR HER.

BUT I WAS STILL A YOUNG BOY, EAGER TO BELIEVE IN FAIRY TALES. SO, I NODDED MY HEAD AS SHE SPOKE, MY BELLY FILLED WITH BUTTERFLIES OVER THE THOUGHT OF GOING SOMEWHERE THAT OUR LIVES COULD CHANGE. SOMEWHERE MOM WOULD BE HAPPIER.

SO, WE WENT. THAT FUCKING DAY. PACKED UP WHAT LITTLE BELONGINGS WE HAD, PILED INTO OUR BEAT-UP HONDA, AND STARTED DRIVING. I DON'T KNOW HOW LONG THE TRIP LASTED, BUT EVERY ONCE IN A WHILE, MOM WOULD PULL OVER AT A GAS STATION AND TAKE HER "MEDICINE" BEFORE WE GOT BACK ON THE ROAD. I WASN'T AN IDIOT—YOUNG, BUT NOT NAIVE TO THE UGLY TRUTHS. BUT WHAT THE FUCK WAS I SUPPOSED TO DO? MY MAIN PRIORITY WAS LOOKING OUT FOR LILY, NOT TRYING TO DIG MY MOM OUT OF A HOLE SHE FELL IN BEFORE I EVEN EXISTED.

I REMEMBER HER MOOD SHIFTING HOURS INTO THE DRIVE. SHE STARTED CURSING AND LOOKING AT THE MAP. SHE TOLD US SHE GOT LOST AND NEEDED TO STOP AND ASK DIRECTIONS, SO SHE PULLED OVER AT ANOTHER STATION IN THE MIDDLE OF

NOWHERE, TENNESSEE. SAID WE WOULD REST AWHILE AND HAD ME TAKE LILY TO A SMALL, PATCHY AREA OF GRASS AROUND THE SIDE OF THE BUILDING. THEN SHE LEFT, WALKING INSIDE THE STATION TO ASK FOR DIRECTIONS, AND SAID SHE'D BE RIGHT BACK. I WANTED TO GO IN WITH HER, BUT SHE TOLD ME TO WAIT INSTEAD.

SO I DID. AND WE WAITED. AND FUCKING WAITED. EVENTUALLY, I TOOK LILY AND WENT INSIDE TO FIND HER.

BUT LIKE A GHOST, SHE WAS GONE.

IT WASN'T THE FIRST TIME SHE FORGOT US, BUT SHE'D ALWAYS SHOW BACK UP EVENTUALLY. THE DRUGS HAD A WAY OF DOING THAT, OF MAKING HER NOT CARE ABOUT THE THINGS SHE WAS SUPPOSED TO CARE ABOUT THE MOST. WHEN THE HIGH WORE OFF, SHE'D REMEMBER.

I SAT WITH LILY ON THE SIDEWALK IN FRONT OF THE GAS STATION, WATCHING RANDOM PEOPLE FILTER IN AND OUT, THE SUN DIPPING BENEATH THE HORIZON AND THE CHILL OF THE NIGHT SEEPING INTO MY BONES. LITTLE BUGS WITH LIGHTS ON THEIR ASS STARTED LIGHTING UP IN THE BLADES OF GRASS, AND WITH EVERY MOMENT MOM STAYED GONE, THE FEAR AND ANGER BURNED A LITTLE BRIGHTER. I HID IT BECAUSE I DIDN'T WANT LILY TO REALIZE SOMETHING WAS WRONG.

IT WAS A DEFINING MOMENT OF MY LIFE, THE MOMENT I REALIZED SHE WASN'T ACTUALLY COMING BACK.

THAT'S WHEN I LEARNED YOU CAN NEVER TRUST ANYBODY, BUT YOU CAN ALWAYS TRUST THEM TO BE WHO THEY ARE.

AND MY MOM WAS THE WORST KIND OF JUNKIE.

Chapter 22
CHASE

"YOU'RE MOVING?"

Marissa sits across from me, her skin glowing in the candlelight. I brought her to her favorite restaurant, hoping it would soften the blow, and maybe give her less inclination to cause a scene.

"My family needs me, Mar. You know I wouldn't leave for anything less. I know what I'll be giving up here."

Honestly, the thought of going back to Sugarlake makes me want to throw up every time it crosses my mind.

"And what exactly is that?" She narrows her gaze.

"My career for starters."

Scoffing, she turns her eyes to the table, her lips pinching tight.

I'm an asshole for springing this on her, but *this* is exactly why I wanted to keep things casual. I don't want to cause her any pain, but I also don't want to feel like her emotions are my responsibility.

And so what if I'd have to give up everything I have here? It was my original plan to take over the company from Sam, anyway. Doc said we could do virtual calls, and I can make the drive down once a week for the Nar-Anon group.

Marissa, on the other hand…

"Listen, Sugarlake's not across the country. If you still want to see each other, I'm open to that, but my days will be filled with work there, same as it is here, so don't expect me to make a lot of extra time."

She reaches across the table and grips my fingers tight. "I just always assumed you hated where you came from, so I'm a little shocked. You never bring it up, never let *me* bring it up, and now all of a sudden you're picking up and leaving everything to go back?" She shakes her head. "I don't get it."

She's not wrong; talking about Sugarlake has always been a hard limit for me. It's none of her business, and I don't really enjoy bringing up the past when it still feels like a knife tearing me open from the inside out. "I don't *hate* it," I argue. "There're just memories I'd rather leave in the past, but Sam has done a lot for me, Mar. I can't leave him hanging on this, not when he needs me."

"What kind of memories?"

"The painful kind." I sip my drink, needing the burn of bourbon to chase away the bitter taste of Goldi.

And Jax.

And Lily.

She peers at me from over her wineglass, taking her hand away. Her ruby-red lips part, giving me a glimpse of her blinding-white smile. "Okay, so we'll do the long-distance thing." She pushes her glossy black hair behind her shoulder. "Besides, it could be fun. I'll visit on weekends."

I clear my throat, relieved that she's not making this a bigger deal than it needs to be. "Yeah, sure."

"Do you still have friends there?" she asks, cocking her head.

Regret burns my throat like acid. "Not really."

"Hmm..." She takes another sip of wine.

I follow suit, swallowing down more bourbon.

"Any high school sweethearts?"

My fingers tighten around the glass, jaw clenching so tightly, discomfort radiates up my cheek.

Even worse, the thought of Goldi makes my heart spasm, wondering if she'll still be there.

The idea of it has my stomach in knots. I'm not naive enough to assume I could get her back. I met her at the wrong time in my life and fucked it up before I could love her the way she deserved, but even though my brain realizes it, the rest of me doesn't, and my entire body aches with longing at the thought of being back in her orbit.

Not that it matters. I'm not the same kid I was back then. I doubt our connection would even exist with who I am now, who she may be.

"Who didn't?" I answer.

Marissa straightens, tension evident in her posture. "Well, I didn't."

"I doubt she's even still around. Haven't thought about it much, really," I lie.

"She?" Marissa prods. "So just one, then."

"Yep. Just the one," I say, shifting in my chair.

"How long were you two together?"

"What is this, twenty fucking questions?" I snap.

Marissa's eyes widen and she deflates, leaning back in her chair.

"Jesus, Chase, I'm just curious. Forgive me for trying to get to know the man I'm with a little better."

"Shit, I'm sorry." I tug on the roots of my hair. "I just…I don't like talking about things that don't matter."

She gives me a soft smile, but I see the questions in her eyes. "It's okay, I shouldn't have pushed. Just…can you do me a favor?"

I nod, even though I don't know what she's about to ask. I'd probably agree to anything right now as long as she stops talking about Goldi.

"Promise me once you move back, you won't shut me out."

I'm sick with the thoughts this conversation brings, so I agree.

Her grin widens and she changes the conversation, not bringing my past up for the rest of the night.

Two weeks later, and I'm already breaking that promise as I drive down Main Street in my hometown, silencing Marissa's call.

Sugarlake is thriving, and memories of the first time I drove this way in the back seat of Sam and Anna's Buick flash through my mind and make my chest ache. Back then, there were only five or six shops scattered along the street, but now there's an entire strip of local businesses, kids out on the sidewalks, and people at small round tables sipping on ceramic mugs and laughing on patios.

It's nice knowing the town flourished even when my world was falling apart.

I turn onto my old street and park in the driveway of what was once my home. I guess it technically still is, especially since I'll be staying here until I find my own place. I sit in my car, taking it in, surrendering to the storm whirling inside me. My knee hits the bottom of the steering wheel as I bounce my leg, and my fingers tangle in my hair, both nervous habits I've never quite been able to break.

God, grant me the serenity to accept the things I cannot change, the courage to change the things I can, and the wisdom to know the difference.

Exhaling a deep breath, I open my car door and step into the Sugarlake sun. The air feels different here, a soft breeze blowing over my face and keeping me cool despite the temperature. I've gotten so used to the hustle and bustle of the city, I had forgotten how nice it is to be surrounded by the calm of a small town.

I twirl my key ring around my finger and stare at the only childhood home I've ever really known. As I walk up to the front door, I can't help myself and glance at the house three doors down. I don't expect to see her, of course, but my heart races anyway.

Nostalgia hits me hard when I walk up to Sam and Anna's house and see the faded yellow paint on the front door, and before I can knock, it swings open.

"Chase." Sam has a wide smile and open arms, bringing me in for a hug. "I've been waiting for this day a long time."

The emotion in his voice reaches into the space between us and makes *me* feel choked up. "It's good to be back," I say.

"We'll give you the day to get settled, and then tomorrow we'll hit the ground running. Sound good to you?"

"Yeah, I'm ready to work. Let's dive right in."

His green eyes sparkle. "Good, good."

I follow him inside, taking note of the small changes to the décor since I was here last. The old blue couch in the living room is gone, replaced with a soft cream-colored one, and new pictures are sprinkled on the walls and along the fireplace mantle. Me graduating college. Them standing in front of the Grand Ole

Opry in Nashville. Jax and me grinning as we lean against his Mustang in the drive.

That one makes my chest pull tight.

Anna's in the living room, her face beaming as she reaches out to hug me and then pulls me onto the couch with her, talking a mile a minute like she's afraid if she doesn't, I might turn around and leave. I indulge her, because it's nice to be back here, and as long as she's gabbing in my ear, I don't have the space to think about anything else. Anything that *might* make me run from this place like the coward I still feel like on the inside.

When I finally make it into my childhood bedroom, everything is untouched from when I tucked tail and disappeared years ago. I'm not sure if it's being back in this place, or just par for the course, but when I fall asleep, I dream of honey-blond hair and vanilla.

It's the best sleep I've had in years.

I wake up bright and early, eager to jump into the nitty-gritty foundation of Sugarlake Construction.

Anna's pouring a cup of coffee when I walk into the kitchen, her navy blue robe wrapped tight around her, and her strawberry-blond hair wet from a shower.

She turns when she hears me and smiles.

"Mornin'," she singsongs, grabbing another mug from the cabinet. "Still take it black?"

"Like my soul," I reply.

She shakes her head. "So morbid."

I chuckle, enjoying the lightness that being around Anna always provides.

Sam wanders in a few minutes later, already dressed for the day, and he wraps an arm around Anna's waist from behind, tugging her into his front and kissing her temple as he grabs a mug for himself.

A pang hits my sternum and radiates outward, realizing I'll most likely never have what they do. It's painful watching how he cherishes her and she gives it back in spades even after all these years. Watching them makes me wish I had spent less time lost in my shit, and more time modeling myself after them. Maybe then I wouldn't have been so fucked-up.

"Are you two off to the office this mornin'?" Anna asks.

Sam nods, sipping from his coffee. "Yep, time to show Chase the lay of the land." His gaze moves to me. "A lot's changed since you've worked there. We've expanded, do a lot of work in the neighboring towns. In fact, we just landed a new contract, and it'll be the perfect project to get your feet wet. I know you're a big, bad boss in the city, but we do it a little differently out here, you know? Still gotta ease you in." He winks.

"You've got jokes," I chuckle. "What's the project?"

"A renovation to a dance studio a couple of towns over. They want the main area gutted and redone. Shouldn't be too much of a hassle, other than the owner being a bit controlling." He makes a face. "But you won't need to deal with her much. One of their office managers will be working with you on the details."

I grimace at the thought of someone who knows nothing about construction being involved in the details, but I can manage. Hopefully, they aren't a distraction.

JOURNAL ENTRY #315

IT'S EASIER BEING BACK THAN I EXPECTED. NOT GONNA LIE, PART OF ME THOUGHT I'D BE GREETED WITH PITCHFORKS AND

AN ANGRY MOB. BUT NOBODY EVEN KNOWS I'M HERE. THEY PROBABLY AREN'T EVEN HERE ANYMORE.

I WAS NERVOUS WHEN I STEPPED INTO SUGARLAKE CONSTRUCTION FOR THE FIRST TIME IN EIGHT YEARS, AND EVEN THOUGH I TOLD MYSELF I WOULDN'T, I KEPT LOOKING AROUND FOR GOLDI'S DAD, MR. CARSON, WHO WORKED HERE FOR YEARS. BUT I DIDN'T SEE HIM. I'M SURPRISED HE WOULD HAVE RETIRED BUT I CAN'T BRING MYSELF TO ASK SAM ABOUT HIM. THEY USED TO BE CLOSE AND HE HASN'T BROUGHT HIM UP, SO NEITHER DO I.

MARISSA CALLED, ALREADY WANTING TO COME DOWN, AND EVEN THOUGH I FEEL LIKE AN ABSOLUTELY ASSHOLE ABOUT IT, I MADE AN EXCUSE. IT'D BE NICE TO HAVE HER COMPANY, AND SOME RELIEF BY GETTING LAID, BUT NO MATTER HOW MUCH I TRY SHE JUST ISN'T GOLDI, AND I'M WORRIED THAT HAVING HER HERE IN SUGARLAKE WILL JUST MAKE THAT COMPARISON EVEN MORE STARK.

THE PAST WEEK HAS BEEN FILLED WITH GETTING ACCLIMATED AND I CAN'T LIE—I'M IMPRESSED AS HELL WITH WHAT SAM'S DONE. I SEE THE PASSION AND PRIDE IN EVERYTHING HE SHOWS ME. I HOPE I DON'T LET HIM DOWN.

I START AT THE NEW JOB SITE ON MONDAY. IT'S IN THE PRELIMINARY STAGES RIGHT NOW, JUST DESIGNS AND SHIT LIKE THAT. I'M MEETING THE PERSON WHO WILL BE MY MAIN POINT OF CONTACT AND I HOPE THEY AREN'T A NUISANCE. I HEARD THEY'RE NEW ON THE JOB AS THE OFFICE MANAGER, SO AS LONG AS THEY STAY OUT OF MY WAY AND LET ME DO <u>MY</u> JOB, THINGS WILL BE FINE.

Chapter 23
ALINA

Twenty-Six Years Old

"THAT'S BASICALLY IT."

I nod along with Regina, the owner of Tiny Dancers studio, and officially my new boss as of ten minutes ago. I'm not actually teaching dance, as much as I wish that weren't the case, but being the office manager is a foot in the door, and the pay is great. I'll be able to quit my job at the diner, and Tiny Dancers is one of the best children's studios in all of East Tennessee. So even if I'll be a glorified assistant, fetching coffee and Xeroxing copies till my fingers bleed, as long as I get to be part of something, I don't mind.

"…so enjoy your weekend, and be here bright and early on Monday morning, ready to go."

Blinking out of my daze, I smile wide, hoping she doesn't realize I ignored her. "Great!"

"Oh, before I forget," she continues, her short black bob swaying back and forth as she shakes her head. "You'll be the go-to for the incoming contractor. I've outsourced the renovation to a company about forty minutes away from town."

"You want *me* to be the go-to?" I look around the massive studio. "Don't you think it should be somebody, you know, who's worked here for more than a day?"

She laughs, her white teeth gleaming against her tawny skin. "Oh, honey, you'll do just fine. All I need you to do is be a glorified babysitter, make sure they don't make a mess of things." She waves her hand around the space. "You know how construction workers are, milking the clock and trying to make an extra dollar from their clients wherever they can."

I want to tell her my daddy was a construction worker, and so were my neighbors, but I grit my teeth to stop the sass that's dying to escape.

"Won't I be in their way?"

She gives me a pointed look. "Just keep an eye on them, keep them in line. Be professional and make sure they stay that way, too."

I nod. "Got it. Professional."

We wrap up our conversation and I walk outside to get a breath of fresh air. It's a beautiful day, and I finally feel like things are looking up. Sure, my boss is a teensy bit overbearing—but I already missed out on one opportunity to further my dreams, so I'm holding on to this one with everything in me.

About a year ago, I came across a quote by one of my favorite authors, C.S. Lewis, and it changed my life.

"You can't go back and change the beginning, but you can start where you are and change the ending."

Those words dug deep inside of me and pulled up the little bit of self-worth I had left. I was tired of waiting on a miracle, and

I wasn't taking any steps to change my own future. So I mustered up the courage to move out of Daddy's and into a place of my own, even though the guilt of leaving him eats me alive little by little every day.

It's been hard.

I feel like I've abandoned him. But he was sucking me down, and I realized in order to help him, I had to help myself first.

So here I am in my little 400-square-foot studio apartment, right above JuneBug's Bakery on Main Street. It's not much, but it's mine and I love it. I'm far away enough from Daddy where I get some peace, and close enough to be there when he needs me.

Now all I have to do is get him to admit he needs help.

Johnny from The Watering Hole has my cell number, and whenever Daddy drinks too much, Johnny calls.

There's never a time when Daddy *doesn't* drink too much.

I'm just getting cozy on my couch with a good book when my phone chimes with a text.

JAX:

> On a scale of 1–10, how much are you missing me?

I roll my eyes, grinning.

The truth is, I miss him a lot. He's away these days way more than he's home because he's in such high demand out in California. *Where dreams are made.* Movies need fancy cars, and fancy cars need someone who knows how to keep them pretty.

ME:

Like a hole in the head. Seriously, how long are you gonna be gone for?

JAX:

I'm not sure, but this producer is a pain in the ass.

Before I can respond, another text comes through.

JAX:

He's a ballbuster, and his daughter drives me nuts.

I smile, thinking about a little girl with a crush on Jax.

ME:

Oh, come on. It can't be that bad!

JAX:

It is. I miss you. You should come out here with me next time.

I laugh because he knows as well as I do that I won't be making the trip to California any time soon. I take my phone and move outside, sitting on the small Juliet balcony.

This is my favorite time of day, right before the sun meets the horizon fully, after the oranges and pinks disappear, and the sky is stuck in the in-between. Lightning bugs flicker to life and the world just seems…quieter. I close my eyes and relax, a genuine smile taking over my face for the first time in what feels like forever.

The grin is still on my face the next day when I show up at Logan's. It's been a week since we've met up, and I've gotten used to the type of relief he provides because our time together quiets the voices that beat down on my soul. He's a nice reprieve, one I have no shame about taking full advantage of. If men can do it, so can I.

"My ears are numb." I giggle, rolling over in Logan's bed, the silk sheets dropping slightly until they're only covering from my hips down.

He's standing by his dresser and smirks at my comment. "Your *ears* are numb?"

"Yeah, that never happens to you?"

"I can't say it does."

He moves toward me, crawling onto the bed until his body is covering mine, and he leans down to nibble on my neck. I laugh because it tickles, and he smiles against my skin.

It's nice what we have. No emotions, no strings.

No exclusivity.

It's the perfect arrangement, and I dread the day some girl sweeps him off his feet for real and he ends our tryst.

"I've gotta go." He stands, grabbing his jeans and pulling them on. "You can chill here if you want, just lock up on your way out."

This isn't unusual for us, him leaving and letting me take my time, so I head to his kitchen after he's gone and brew some coffee while I peruse the magazines on his counter.

"I Can't Help Myself (Sugar Pie Honey Bunch)" blares through the living room and I groan in frustration. Only Jax would set his ringtone to something so obnoxious. I stop snooping and head to my purse, opening it to grab my phone and answer.

"Hey, Teeth."

"Sweetheart. What are you doing right now?"

"Right now?" I look around Logan's living room and cringe. Jax doesn't approve of my situationship—which is rich considering he's the king of sex with no strings. "I'm havin' coffee at Logan's, thinkin' of all the ways to strangle you for messin' with my ringtone, *again*."

He groans. "When are you gonna cut that guy loose, Lee? He's only using you for one thing."

"I sure hope so."

"I just don't want you to get hurt," he sighs into the phone.

"Oh please, Jackson. I swear, I can't with you, actin' like a man can get his jollies anytime and a woman needs to wait for some big love."

He's silent. I know what this is really about, even if I don't want to admit it. Jax wants things to go further with the two of us, but I've never let it go further than what we already have. The truth is, I wouldn't be able to love him right, and if anyone deserves the "can't eat, can't sleep, can't breathe" kind of love, it's Jackson Rhoades.

I change the subject, not wanting to argue. "How are things on set?"

"Things are kind of bullshit, but I'm dealing with it."

"You're not enjoyin' it?"

"I've worked with some pricks, but this guy, Donahue, thinks he shits out gold." He exhales before murmuring, "He's a giant in this industry, though. My dad's dream is so close I can taste it, Lee."

"Then you've just gotta keep pushin' through it, Jax. Your work will speak for itself. Your daddy would be so proud of you."

"You think so?"

"I do."

He's quiet for a moment. "Did I tell you he has this daughter? She's annoying as hell and always in my ear asking a thousand questions about the cars I'm shaking down. I don't know why he lets her on set, it's not like she does anything except annoy the shit out of me."

"I thought you loved kids."

"I love *little* kids. Not nineteen-year-old brats who aren't used to hearing the word no."

My eyes widen. "Nineteen isn't exactly a kid, Jax."

"Tell me about it," he mutters.

I hear a faint knock through the line and know he's about to be stolen away.

"Shit, sweetheart. I've gotta go. I expect a phone call Monday night so you can regale me with stories of how you kicked ass at your new job."

"You got it, Teeth."

Melancholy seeps through every bone in my body when I hang up the phone. I'm so proud of him for all his accomplishments, but I'd be lying if I said I didn't miss my friend.

I spend the rest of the weekend wallowing in loneliness.

Jax is gone and Becca is busy doing her daddy's bidding at the church, but I could swear she's avoiding me.

Before I know it, it's Monday morning and time to start my new job.

Hope fills me up when I wake, because I'm determined to make today the start to the rest of my life.

No more settling. No more wallowing. No more misery.

Rolling over in my bed, I reach out to turn off my alarm since I never needed it and realize it never went off because it was set to p.m. not a.m.

Panic races through me, my heart flying against my chest with anxiety because, of *course* I'm about to be late on my first day at the new gig. My only saving grace is I laid out my outfit last night, and I rush, throwing on the black pencil skirt and cream silk blouse I borrowed from Becca. It's a little long on me because she's taller, and a bit tight around my curves, but until I get my first paycheck, this is as good as it's going to get.

I pull into Tiny Dancers five minutes late. There are two other vehicles in the lot and the lights are all turned on inside.

The contractor must be here already.

Even though I don't have the time, I take a deep breath to calm my nerves, wiping my sweaty hands on the seat's upholstery. I tell myself it doesn't matter if I'm a few minutes late. I'll kick butt today, wow this contractor so he'll sing my praises to Regina, and then I'll go home, open a bottle of wine, and call Jax and Becca to tell them how amazing I am.

With a nod of affirmation, I get out of my car, straighten my skirt, and walk inside.

Chapter 24

ALINA

IT'S WHEN I'M WALKING TO THE BACK OFFICE THAT I feel it. The shift in the air. It's subtle—a ghost of a chill that flickers down my spine.

What the heck? I brush it off, straightening my shoulders and walking through the open door.

I don't see him at first, but when I do, that chill drops through my body like an iceberg free-falling, freezing me in place.

This isn't happening.

This cannot be happening.

"Alina! I was starting to wonder if you would even show up," Regina says as she smiles thinly. She's annoyed, and rightly so. I should respond, but I don't. I'm not sure I physically can since my heart has stalled in my chest.

Chase Adams.

I'd love him if I didn't hate him so much.

There's a pencil behind his ear, a blueprint rolled up in his hand and another laid out on the desk.

But he isn't looking at that.

He's locked on me, mouth partially open, hand frozen halfway through his silky, dark brown hair. When he swallows, my traitorous eyes track the way his throat bobs. "Goldi."

The nickname travels across the room and pierces me in the chest, jolting me out of my shock. "Don't call me that."

He clamps his mouth shut and nods.

"You two know each other?" Regina points between the two of us.

"Yeah, actually we used—"

"Our folks are neighbors," I interrupt, tearing my gaze away from him to focus on her instead. "We grew up together, but no. I never really *knew* him."

I stand stoic, my gaze never straying from Regina, but I can feel him.

My body hums, reminding me of the first time I saw him at eleven years old, and just like then, I have to clench my fists to keep from reaching out.

Pathetic.

He clears his throat. "Right."

Regina stands and grabs her purse. My heart ratchets up in speed, because how am I supposed to be alone with him?

She *can't* leave.

But I can't tell her to stay.

"Well, that makes things easier then, considering the two of you will be spending lots of time together," she remarks.

Chase goes rigid. "She's my point of contact?"

I scoff and cross my arms. Who does he think he is having a problem with *me*? I'm the one who's allowed to be pissed off here, not him.

Regina arches a perfectly sculpted brow. "Is that a problem?"

He runs a hand through his hair and shakes his head. "No, I just—I was under the impression I'd be dealing with an office manager."

"She *is* the office manager."

He glances my way. "Not an instructor?"

I stay quiet, but the beat of my heart drowns the room with how hard it's slamming against my chest. All of my energy goes toward keeping it together.

Just a few hours and you can go home and fall apart in private.

Regina laughs, her eyes softening when she glances at Chase. *Oh, honey. Don't waste your time.* "Instructor? I don't need any instructors, I need someone who can file papers and show up on time. After this morning, I'm not even convinced she's capable of that."

Embarrassment rises to my cheeks, and I bite my tongue to stop the retort that wants to come out. Instead, I say, "It won't happen again."

I peek over at Chase, the blueprint in his fist gripped so tight it's crumpling.

Regina continues, "Anyway, since no introductions are needed, I'm off. You two have a lot to talk about, I'm sure. Chase, if you could just lay out for Alina what you did for me, that'd be great. I'll check in later." She turns toward me. "I left a list of things for you to complete before the end of the day. You've got my cell in case you have any questions?"

I nod.

"Great. Let's try to be on time tomorrow, hmm?"

And with that, she's out the door.

The room is jarring with its silence.

I keep my gaze locked on the desk, unwilling to be the first to break.

Because I was *always* the first to break, and I need him to see I'm not the same girl he once knew.

"Goldi, I—"

"I told you not to call me that," I spit out. "My name is Alina. Or, you know what's even better? Miss Carson." I bring my hand up to rub my pulsing forehead. "Can you just show me what you've got, so we can get this over with?"

"Yeah, yes. Sure." He shuffles his feet and attempts to smooth out the wrinkles on the blueprint he smashed.

I cross my arms as I watch him. I thought he was grown in college, but clearly, God wasn't done sculpting his masterpiece. His style hasn't changed, still casual in a black T-shirt and dark blue jeans. But the veins that line his forearms and the way the cotton stretches around his shoulders has my mouth running dry.

Crap.

My perusal continues, and I search for an imperfection, for *something* to show me he's had it just as rough as I have these past years. God wouldn't be so unfair to give him an easy time while I've been struggling so hard to stay afloat.

I suck in a sharp breath when I get to his face and find his gaze already locked on me. His stare burns, and my stomach clenches, the frayed edges of the threads that have connected us since childhood pulsing with the need to come back to life. They sizzle and pop, elated at our proximity.

"You look good, Alina." His voice is husky.

His words make me want to preen, but I catch myself—sickened by my reaction to him after all this time. After what he's done.

"And you look like my biggest regret." The words are out before I can stop them.

He winces, and I take pleasure in the fact my words have the ability to hurt him.

Serves him right.

He wasn't there when I needed him most. *Cheated* on me while my mom was dying in the hospital. He doesn't deserve my remorse or my kindness. He's lucky I'm even staying in this room.

Chase sighs and leans back against the lip of the desk. "Look, I had no clue you worked here, but I don't want to make things harder for you, so if this"—he waves his hand back and forth between us—"will be an issue, I'll tell Sam to put someone else on the project."

Sam?

"What?" I whoosh out. "Are…are you back home?"

His mouth lifts slightly. "Don't sound so excited."

"I'm not anything when it comes to you." I shrug.

My stomach churns, and my chest pulls taut because my body knows I'm a liar. I'm afraid when it comes to Chase Adams, I'll always be *something*, but I'll be damned if I ever let him see it.

I really want to tell him that yes, I do want someone else on the project. But the last thing I need is for Regina to think I threw a tantrum, especially when I'm on thin ice.

Sighing, I drop my arms by my sides and bite my lip. "You're already here so you might as well stay, but let's get one thing straight. We are not friends. We are not acquaintances. We are nothin'. In fact, we're less than nothin'. Let's just agree to make this process as quick and painless as possible."

He lowers his head and nods. The muscle in his jaw tics, and his fingers tighten around the edge of the desk. "Whatever you want, Go—Alina."

I let out the breath I was holding. "Good, now show me what you've got."

Somehow, I've made it through the day. I'm sitting at my kitchen table staring at the bottle of wine I've been saving for a special occasion. For *this* special occasion.

The celebration of my new job.

The start to the rest of my life.

Only, I don't feel much like celebrating now.

I never in a thousand years expected Chase to come barreling into my life again, and I'm left off-kilter and nauseous from the way he's spun me around. Even after all this time, the effect he has on me is heady, and it makes me hate myself.

It makes me hate *him* for coming back and tainting what was supposed to be the start of a new life with the feelings of my old one.

I tap my fingernails on the wood, eyes bouncing from the wine bottle to my phone. Jax and Becca are both expecting my call. I grab the bottle, ready to pour an ample glass, but before I get the chance to decide who to talk to first, my phone screen lights up.

The Watering Hole.

Of course. The perfect ending to a perfect day. I set the bottle back down, eyeing it longingly as I accept the call.

"Hello?"

"Hey, Lee."

I sigh. "Hi, Johnny. Daddy need a ride?"

"Yeah. He uhh...isn't takin' too kindly to being cut off. It's not a good night."

I bang my forehead on the table, praying I'll wake up and this day will have been a nightmare. "Okay, I'm on my way."

Daddy's sitting in his usual spot at the bar when I arrive. He's hunched around a glass of water, glaring at Johnny who's at the other end, pouring drinks.

"Daddy."

His head lolls over and he gazes at me through hazy eyes. "Gail?"

My heart clenches when he calls out Mama's name.

Bad night, indeed.

"No, Daddy, it's me. Alina." I reach out to put my hand on his back, but he shrugs me off.

He snarls. "They're always callin' you out here, like a…a goddamned babysitter. Go home, I'm just fine." His words are slurred, but years of practice have tuned my ears to understand the garble.

"You're not fine, and you're lucky Johnny's boss hasn't banned you from this place. Let's just get you home where you can get a good night's rest." I reach out again, looping my arm through his to support his weight as I pull him from the stool, sadness weighing me down more than his body ever could.

He complains but doesn't resist. I mouth "thank you" at Johnny while I walk Daddy out.

It isn't until we're in my car that I feel like I can breathe again.

After I get him settled at the house, I head straight to the cemetery to visit Mama. When Daddy's at his worst, being next to her, if only in spirit, is the only balm that soothes my soul.

"Hey, Mama."

My body's leaning against her headstone, and I finger the wilting flowers next to me. "Sorry I didn't bring any tulips, this wasn't exactly a planned visit. I just needed someone to talk to, I guess."

I lean my head back, staring at the stars. "You know what's funny, Mama? There hasn't been a single night in the past eight years where I've been able to see stars and not think of Chase. Not once. In eight freakin' years. But then last night, I sat on my patio and counted as many stars as I could find without him ever crossin' my mind." I huff out a laugh. "Joke's on me, huh?"

I don't say anything else, just close my eyes and try to find some peace, hoping she can calm the storm swirling inside me. I kiss my palm and press it against the engraving of her name. "I love you, Mama. I won't ask if you've got any pull up there…not tonight. I'll save that for our usual visit. Give you some time to come up with a different answer." I smile softly, even though I feel the pain of loss sneaking through the cracks of my heart.

Jax calls on the way home, complaining about that producer and his daughter again. I don't want to make his mood worse by bringing up Chase, so I don't.

There's always tomorrow.

Chapter 25

CHASE

"WHAT'S WRONG?" MARISSA ASKS, FROWNING through the screen of my phone.

"Nothing's wrong. Just tired, it was a long day."

"How was that new project?"

Shit. Why'd I have to answer when she FaceTimed? Honestly, I had been looking forward to talking with her, but after Goldi's presence slapped me in the face and turned my world upside down, the last thing I want to do is talk with Marissa about how my day went.

I lie on my bed and spew out random words, hoping they sound convincing. "It was good. I think it will be pretty easy. The owner's already got all the classes shut down. It's just an empty building, waiting for the reno."

"That's nice. Do they have a designer you're working with? Or should I offer my services?" She giggles.

I know she's joking, but the thought of her being in the same place as Goldi has me feeling sick.

"So listen," she continues, "I got an invitation in the mail today for Sam's retirement party. Were you ever gonna tell me about it?"

"What do you mean, tell you about it? I've only been back home for three days, Marissa. The party isn't until next month."

"I know. But… Well, do you want me to come?"

Not really. Not now. "If you want to." I sigh. "Listen, can we talk about this later? I'm beat."

"Okay. I'll start planning for that weekend so I can come down and stay. It will be fun! I'm excited to see where you grew up."

Nausea fights through the tightness in my throat.

I should feel good about my girlfriend coming to visit, and it makes me feel like an asshole knowing I'm dreading it instead. I've been trying to convince myself it's time to really make a go of things with Marissa for a while now.

She's been wanting more, and there's no reason why I shouldn't try to find happiness.

It will be a good thing, having her here.

Allow me to make new memories so I can focus on the future. Not fixate on feelings from the past.

"Yeah." I clear my throat, trying my best to not be a complete douchebag to my girlfriend. "Can't wait to see you."

She hums and says her goodbyes and then I'm tossing my phone to the side and staring up at the popcorn ceiling of my childhood bedroom.

Anna only told me about Sam's retirement party yesterday, and I had no idea she sent out invitations already.

Idly, I wonder if Goldi will be there, and the thought has my heart clenching tight, a pain searing down my middle and making my stomach drop like a lead weight.

If I ever had any doubt about the strength of our connection, it was put to bed after seeing her again. One look was all it took for my soul to light on fucking fire and my skin to prickle with the need to feel her against me.

I walk over to the en suite, ridding myself of my clothes, and starting the shower, sighing when the hot water runs in rivulets down my chest, and loosens the knots I feel in my back. When I'm soaping up my body, I try to wash away the desperation that clings to my skin from being around her, but all it does is make me think of her even more.

Fuck.

I picture how she looked today. Cheeks flushed, eyes wide, her tight as fuck clothes showcasing how well she's grown into her curves. Blood rushes straight to my cock, making it throb painfully. I groan, trying to ignore it.

I will not jerk myself off to thoughts of her.

My hand is already moving south as I think the words, wrapping around my shaft, sliding up and down once…twice…a third time. Slowly stroking. Teasing myself, as I close my eyes and let Goldi overtake my mind completely.

Fuck, that feels good.

I thrust into my fist, picturing myself ripping the buttons off that cream blouse she was wearing and having my hands on her, feeling the weight of her breasts. Having my tongue on her perfect little pussy. Her vanilla scent enveloping me as I feast on her, making her whimper and moan as I draw out her orgasm but tongue fucking her until she screams. That's all it takes for me to explode. Euphoria spreads through my body as cum shoots out of my tip, my head thrown back from the force, tingles shooting up and down my spine, my knees growing weak.

I lean my head against the wall, the cool tile calming my racing heart, panting from the exertion. *Holy fuck.* I haven't come that hard in years.

As the haze lifts, guilt weaves its way through my body. She would fucking hate me—more than she already does—if she knew I was getting off to her in the shower like that.

But that doesn't stop me from doing it all over again in the morning, because if I don't release the tension, I don't know how I'll make it through another day with her.

I stop at the coffee shop on my way into work and am standing in line when a voice interrupts my thoughts.

"I know my eyes are deceivin' me, 'cause there is no way on God's green Earth that Chase Adams is standin' here in Sugarlake."

Fucking perfect. I spin around, irritation lighting up my insides. "Hey, Becca. Long time."

"Not long enough," she responds, a smile as sweet as candy painting her face.

"Goldi didn't tell you I was back?" I smirk.

Becca's eyes widen before she schools her features.

"What Lee and I talk about is none of your concern. Actually, nothin' to do with Lee is your concern." She eyes me critically. "Are you back for good?"

I nod, moving up in the line. "Afraid so. Sorry to disappoint."

Her gaze ices over. "You think this is a *joke*?" Her finger pokes at my solar plexus, digging in just enough to hurt. "You better stay the hell away from Lee, Chase. I'm not fuckin' around. You have no business after what you did, and I swear to God I will kick your ass if you get near her."

"What can I get for you?" The barista interrupts, so I turn and order, moving to the side once I've paid.

The urge to walk away entirely and avoid Becca is strong, but I don't.

She orders and then walks over to where I am.

"Listen," I say immediately. "Not that I owe you any explanations, but I was a kid when I was with Goldi, and yeah, I screwed up. I wish I could take it back, but I can't. I would apologize, but the only person who deserves the words is her, and she isn't exactly open to hearing them. But I'm here, and I'm not leaving because my family needs me, and I'm tired of worrying about what everyone around here thinks. I don't want to cause any problems, I'm not *here* to cause any problems."

Becca squints, her head angling as she taps her high-heeled foot. "You're different."

My mouth quirks. "Yeah, well, growing up can do that to a person."

"Whatever," she scoffs. "Just stay away from her, Chase. Live your life and let her live hers. She's moved on and she doesn't need you messin' with her head."

The barista calls my name, handing over my coffee, but I've lost the taste for it after hearing that Goldi's moved on.

Ridiculous of me, but I can't help the way I feel. The way I think I'll *always* feel.

I think about Becca's words all the way to Tiny Dancers.

Cory, the head of my demolition crew, is waiting for me in the parking lot when I arrive. Today we're doing a standard walk-through of the property, laying out what needs to be done, and checking for hazardous conditions. If all goes smoothly, we'll start the demolition of the main area in the next couple of weeks.

"Chase, good to see you, man," Cory says when I walk up. "Is it just us today?"

"Yep. You and me, buddy."

I look around the lot, checking for Goldi's car, and find it almost immediately. My stomach sprouts wings of anxiety and I tap my foot to shake out the excess nerves. She's still driving that same shitty Kia she had eight years ago, and I wonder if she's holding on to it for sentimental value, or if she hasn't had the money to get a new one. I'm surprised as hell the thing even runs, but I guess if she's still friends with Jax, that probably explains it.

Becca's parting words filter through my mind.

Is she with Jax now?

My stomach curdles at the thought, and envy I have no right to feel spreads through my veins.

Cory pats me on the shoulder before heading inside, and I follow, stealing another glance at her car and trying to prepare myself for another day in her presence.

I don't see her at all while we conduct the walk-through, and I'm grateful for it, although even the thought of her has me on edge, side-eyeing the corners and empty rooms like she'll pop out and smack me across the face.

It's not until a few hours later that I finally have to suck it up and find her. She needs to know about the progress we've made, and some of the issues we've found so she can relay it to her boss.

I knock on the office door.

"Come in."

Her voice makes my stomach flip.

Get a fucking grip.

She's sitting behind the desk, her hands on the computer keyboard, looking beautiful as ever, but there's a heaviness to her shoulders that didn't used to be there, almost like the weight of the world finally broke through her sunshine wall and has started to press down, bit by bit.

"Hey, G—Alina." I grimace as I correct myself. It's hard not to slip up and call her Goldi. It's all I've ever known her as, and the name Alina feels like sandpaper on my tongue.

She continues typing on the computer, her jaw tightening.

I shift on my feet, uncomfortable with the way she's ignoring me. "So, we just finished the walk-through for the areas being renovated."

Still no response.

"Unfortunately, there are some issues."

Her fingers pause on the keys, the desk chair creaking as she leans back. "What do you mean, issues?"

"Well, there are some areas, especially in the front room, that are concerning. Possibly asbestos. My demo leader, Cory, is taking samples now to be sent to the lab for analysis."

She frowns. "How long will that take?"

"About a week. We'll have the results rushed, but there isn't much we can do in the meantime."

"What do you mean there's not much you can do? Can't you just work around the areas?"

I chuckle but stop when she glares at me. "No. Asbestos is harmless unless it becomes airborne. If there's a problem here and it gets disturbed, that's when it'll become an issue."

"I thought asbestos was regulated."

"Not when this was built, it wasn't. I was hopeful coming in this morning, but I knew it was a risk. We won't be able to start work until we get the results back from the lab."

She groans. "Have you told Regina this?"

"Nope. You're my point of contact, not her."

"So you expect *me* to deliver the bad news?" She covers her face with her hands. "You're just itchin' to get me fired, aren't you?"

"I don't mind calling her if you're that worried about it." I shrug.

Goldi peeks at me from between her fingers. "You don't?"

I shake my head. "Not if it makes your day easier."

She leans forward, her elbows coming down on the desk. "Okay, yeah. Okay. Well…wait a minute. If you call, she'll probably think I put you up to it. That I'm incapable of deliverin' a message. Maybe I should just call her?" She nods. "Yeah, I'll just call her and hope for the best."

I stifle my smile, my heart squeezing at how cute she is when she's nervous.

She continues to ramble as she reaches to grab the phone.

My hand shoots out to cover hers before I can stop it, and when we touch, electricity pulses through my fingers and up my arm, sparking to life like a long-lost reflex jumping into action.

She gasps and blinks up at me.

My heart spasms, slamming against my ribcage, and her tongue peeks out, swiping along her bottom lip before she bites down on the corner.

I track the movement, envious as fuck that her tongue gets to taste those perfect lips.

"Don't," I manage to rasp. "Let me do this. I'll tell her I wanted to be the one to deliver the news."

"Okay," she whispers.

My fingers tighten around hers and she breaks our gaze to stare at where we're connected.

Suddenly, her hand jerks out from under mine. "Is that all?"

I'm still rooted in place, my mind working to catch up. "What?"

"Is that all you have to tell me? If so, you can show yourself out." She angles her head toward the door, avoiding my eyes.

I step back, rubbing my chin and exhaling as I try to regain my equilibrium. "Yeah, that's it. We'll be here for a while longer finishing the samples and then we'll be out of your hair."

She nods, effectively dismissing me.

I walk back to where Cory is and try to calm the uneven beats of my heart.

JOURNAL ENTRY #316

I HAD A DREAM LAST NIGHT THAT LILY CAME HOME. I WOKE UP WITH TEARS ON MY FACE AND A HOLLOWNESS IN MY CHEST WHEN I REALIZED THAT'S ALL IT WAS...A FUCKING DREAM. IT'S BEEN ALMOST A DECADE SINCE I'VE SEEN HER. HELL, I DON'T EVEN KNOW IF SHE'S STILL ALIVE. BUT I BELIEVE SHE IS. I DON'T HAVE FAITH IN MUCH, BUT I HAVE TO TRUST IN THAT.

HERE'S ONE FOR YA, DOC. YOU KNOW WHAT I'VE BEEN FEELING RECENTLY WHEN IT COMES TO LILY? ANGER. FUCKING ANGER. AND I DON'T EVEN KNOW IF IT'S JUSTIFIED BUT IT'S THERE EITHER WAY.

MY WHOLE LIFE WAS SPENT PROTECTING HER. I FOUND COMFORT IN KNOWING SHE APPRECIATED ALL I DID FOR HER. BUT MAYBE SHE NEVER REALLY KNEW. OR MAYBE SELFISHNESS IS A FAMILY TRAIT AND SHE NEVER REALLY CARED.

THE FIRST FOSTER HOME WASN'T SUNSHINE AND ROSES. IT'S WHERE I LEARNED A LOT OF PEOPLE ARE IN IT FOR THE MONEY, NOT FOR THEIR LOVE OF CHILDREN. I WAS STILL NAIVE,

BELIEVING MOM WOULD COME BACK AND "SAVE" US FROM THE STATE SHE DUMPED US IN. LILY WAS JUST SCARED. TOO YOUNG TO UNDERSTAND WHAT WAS REALLY GOING ON. SHE ALWAYS HAD THIS ONE RAGGEDY STUFFED BUNNY RABBIT SHE HELD ON TO. NEVER LET IT OUT OF HER SIGHT SINCE SHE WAS OLD ENOUGH TO GRAB THINGS. IT HAD THREADS ALL OVER IT FROM WHERE I CLUMSILY STITCHED IT UP EVERY TIME IT RIPPED, AND IT WAS IN DESPERATE NEED OF A WASH. BUT IT COMFORTED HER, AND FOR THAT I WAS GRATEFUL.

OUR CASEWORKER TOOK US TO OUR FIRST HOME, SAID THERE WOULD BE OTHER KIDS TO PLAY WITH. IT WAS A NORMAL-LOOKING HOUSE IN A NORMAL-LOOKING SUBURB OUTSIDE OF NASHVILLE, A MARRIED COUPLE WITH TWO OTHER FOSTER KIDS AND A THIRTEEN-YEAR-OLD SON OF THEIR OWN. THEY WERE NICE ENOUGH, IF A LITTLE DISTANT. LEFT US TO OUR OWN DEVICES MOST OF THE TIME.

BUT THEIR SON WAS A FUCKING PRICK. HE LOVED TO PREY ON THE VULNERABLE, AND HE SAW IT IN LILY FROM THE JUMP. LINDA SAID WE NEEDED TO BE ON OUR BEST BEHAVIOR, AND I THOUGHT SHE MEANT IF WE WERE, MAYBE MOM WOULD COME BACK SOONER, SO I REALLY TRIED TO IGNORE THIS KID. BUT ONE AFTERNOON I HEARD LILY CRY AND WENT OUTSIDE TO SEE HE HAD RIPPED HER BUNNY OUT OF HER HANDS AND SHREDDED IT IN FRONT OF HER. MY FIST WAS IN HIS FACE BEFORE HE KNEW WHAT HIT HIM. PUNK ASS BITCH.

I GUESS HIS DAD DIDN'T THINK MUCH OF AN EIGHT-YEAR-OLD WHO COULD BEAT HIS TEENAGE SON'S ASS AND DECIDED TO TEACH ME A LESSON. BUSTED ME UP SO GOOD I STILL HAVE THE SCAR THROUGH MY EYEBROW. I REMEMBER THE POUNDING ACHE THAT THROBBED WHILE I TOOK THE REMAINING PIECES OF

THAT BUNNY AND RE-STITCHED IT TOGETHER FOR LILY THAT NIGHT.

WE WERE WITH THAT FAMILY FOR A LITTLE OVER A YEAR, AND HE TAUGHT ME A LOT OF "LESSONS" DURING THAT TIME. BUT THE ONLY THING I LEARNED WAS BULLIES HIT HARDER WHEN YOU CRY. THEY GET OFF ON THE PAIN. SO I TAUGHT MYSELF HOW TO LOCK IT UP TIGHT AND TOOK THE BEATINGS WITH A SMILE ON MY FACE, KNOWING THAT AS LONG AS HIS ATTENTION WAS ON ME, IT WASN'T ON LILY.

ON THE PLUS SIDE, HE NEVER BOTHERED HER AGAIN.

Chapter 26

ALINA

"YOUR BROTHER'S COMIN' HOME."

My fork is halfway to my mouth, but I place it back down without indulging. "I'm sorry?"

I blink across the table at Daddy. He says it so casually, like Eli visits all the time.

"Elliot's comin' home. Popped the question to that girlfriend of his, and she wants to meet the family, see where he grew up. Maybe look at our church to get hitched."

My mouth is gaping. Did I fall asleep and wake up in some alternate universe? I would swear Daddy's three sheets to the wind already, but he's not slurring yet, so I know that isn't the case. "Eli's gettin' *married*?"

Daddy nods, shoveling forkfuls of dinner into his mouth.

"Here?"

"Yes, here. Why wouldn't it be?"

"Oh, I don't know. Maybe 'cause he hasn't been home to see us since Mama died?" The words rush out, and I curse my lack of filter. *Dang it.*

Daddy's eyes darken. I flinch from the sound of his fork clattering to the plate. His chair scrapes back as he walks to the cupboard next to the sink, taking out his trusty friend Jim Beam and starts refilling his glass. His third since dinner started.

"Daddy, don't you think you've had enough?"

"Enough of what? Speak plain words, girl. I don't have time for your riddles."

"You know what." Nerves make my stomach churn, but I say what I need to say anyway, because one of these days maybe I'll get through to him. "Mama wouldn't want this for you."

He spins around, leaning his back against the counter as he brings the tumbler to his lips and takes a big gulp. "I try to share the good news that Elliot's comin' back around, and all you wanna talk about is your mama? Well, guess what, Alina, she's dead. She ain't comin' back. We were drivin' to *your* recital when we lost her forever, yet here you are sitting here with me. Family forgives each other, so you better find it in you to do the same with your brother. Although, you can't blame him for not wantin' to be around you when you're the reason his mama is gone."

I focus on my breathing. In and out, the same way I do every time he throws these accusations at me like serrated knives.

He doesn't mean it. It's not your fault.

Blinking back the tears, I murmur, "I just worry about you."

He grunts, his nose already back in his glass, taunting me with his disregard.

And so it goes.

I don't know how I'm supposed to feel about Eli coming home. I'm mad he told Daddy first and didn't think to include me, though, so I stomp outside, pulling up his name on my phone and pressing send before I can second-guess myself.

"Hey, Lee."

"Married, Eli? Really?"

I hear his heavy breath on the line. "Pops told you?"

"*Yes*, Daddy told me. What the heck, you can't call and tell me yourself? Gotta send the town drunk to do your dirty work?"

"Don't call him that," he snaps.

"Well, it's the truth, Eli. Not that you'd know about it."

"That's not fair."

"Don't get me started on what's fair." Pure, hot anger blazes at his careless words. Must be nice out in Florida, with his fancy girl and his fancy life. "Whatever, it doesn't matter. You gonna tell me about your girl? Sarah, right?"

"Yeah, Sarah. And there's not much to tell."

I snort. "Not much to tell? You sure do sound real wild for her."

He sighs. "Wild's the last thing I'd want to feel. You'll meet her soon, we'll be down there in three weeks."

"Three *weeks*?"

"Pops didn't tell you that part?"

"Daddy doesn't tell me much these days, Eli."

He hesitates. "Anyone else know I'm coming back yet?"

"Who cares? I'm sure the town will roll out the red carpet the same way they used to. They won't care you've been gone for years, they'll only care that you're back."

I lean against the wall and temper the rage, telling myself it will be nice to have him home, but it's hard to convince myself.

After the phone call with Eli, I'm irritated and in no condition to be around Daddy, so I go home instead and draw a bath, my muscles whining for relief. Dipping in the water is instant relaxation, and I lean back, submerging myself. My fingers accidentally brush against my breast, and I suck in a breath at how sensitive it feels. I repeat the motion and my nipples tighten, a spike of pleasure shooting straight to my core as I lightly tease my nipple.

It feels good.

I continue the soft touch, closing my eyes and imagining Logan here, his touch skimming up my sides and urging me to come for him, and my body heats, face flushing as my stomach tightens. Suddenly, Logan's voice shifts, growing deeper, huskier. My hand slips down between my legs and starts to circle my clit lightly, pinpricks of pleasure lighting me up as Logan's imaginary hands change into calloused fingers and rough touches, the same way Chase felt as he gripped my hand the other day. A moan slips out as another burst of pleasure runs through me.

My circular motions against myself pick up speed, and I give in to the visions of Chase being the one to urge me on, his palms gripping my body and his hot breath whispering against my neck, telling me how perfect I am and how much he's missed me, how good I look when I'm about to come. I move my fingers down, slipping them inside myself and starting a slow motion, in and out, while my palm continues to rub against my sensitive bud.

My core clenches, the muscles fluttering.

Water sloshes as my hips push forward for more friction, and warmth spreads from my chest, around my back and down my spine, pooling between my legs.

I bite my lip and my thighs tremble.

My breathing picks up as I picture Chase behind me, his hard chest against my back, his corded muscles wrapped around my waist while he holds me in place and plays me with *his* fingers. Whispers dirty words in my ear.

I want his hands all over me.

His arms surrounding me.

His tongue tasting me.

His thickness inside me.

"Come for me, baby, show me how good it feels."

My back arches at the memory of his voice, and I lose control, exploding into a thousand pieces. The wave of my climax washes over my body, my center pulsing as white-hot bliss surges through my veins.

Reason slowly filters back to me, and as the euphoria fades, disgust takes its place, sitting on the back of my tongue like sour grapes. I just masturbated to thoughts of Chase.

Nausea surges up my throat, and disappointment settles heavy in my center.

My bath is ruined from my complete lack of self-control, so I drain it and slip into my coziest pajamas, curling under the blankets.

I set my alarm so I don't miss brunch with Becca in the morning and send up a quick prayer that Chase won't be in my dreams.

God doesn't listen.

The next morning, I pull into the parking lot of the diner. I haven't talked to Becca since last week's Saturday brunch, even though she's been blowing up my phone. Avoidance—I've realized—is my go-to when it comes to telling my friends about Chase. But she'd kill me if I didn't show up today, and I don't think I can keep it in anymore. I'm no good with secrets.

She texts me as soon as I park.

BECCA:

Should I even bother waiting for you today? You've gone radio silent... wonder why that is?

ME:

Parking now! Just been busy.

I rush inside. Becca's glaring down at her phone, sitting at our usual spot in the back corner, and I slide in the booth across from her, a smile plastered on my face.

"Hey, girl."

She purses her lips as she gives me the once-over. "She lives."

I wave her off. "You know it's been crazy with the new job and all."

"Mmhmm." She sips from a mimosa and eyes me over the rim. "How *is* the new job?"

"It's all right. Nothin' I can't handle. I was lookin' forward to all the cute little kids in their leotards, but she's havin' renovations done, so there's nobody there except for me most days."

"Mmmm. Sounds thrillin'. An introvert's paradise."

I laugh. "I don't mind it."

She doesn't reply, and the silence makes me uncomfortable because it's not like her to not always have something to say.

The conversations from the tables around us fill up the quiet.

I fidget, taking a deep breath and vomiting out the words. "Chase is back."

She raises a brow. "I know."

I groan, throwing my head into my hands. "Dang it.

How'd you know about that already? Is that why you're bein' so weird?"

"Ran into him the other day."

Guilt crawls around in my chest. "I just didn't know how to bring it up."

She watches me for a few seconds, her eyes growing hazy before she snaps into focus. "I get it, I guess. We all have secrets. How'd you find out he was back anyway?"

"He's the contractor doin' the reno at the studio. Caught me totally off guard when I walked in on my first day, and he was just standin' there, lookin' perfect like the years have been good to him."

"What?" She laughs. "That's some twisted sort of luck. I bet Jax lost his shit when you told him."

My head drops and that guilt sprouts vines, wrapping around me like ivy and squeezing. The napkin I'm tearing apart becomes the most interesting thing in the world.

"Alina May...tell me you've told Jax."

"I swear, I'm gonna call him tonight."

She scoffs. "Girl, you better."

"Oh, and you'll never guess what else," I say, desperate to change the subject.

"Does it have to do with you, Logan, and a bottle of lube?" She grins.

I roll my eyes. "No, you deviant. Eli's comin' home."

She jerks, her body stiffening. "What?"

"I know, right? The audacity of him never ceases to amaze me. Daddy dropped the bomb on me last night at dinner."

"What?"

I nod and make a face. "I know. Get this, he's gettin' *married*."

"What?" Her voice is quieter now.

"Are you broken?" I joke. "Is that all you can say?"

Her arm wraps around her stomach, the color draining from her cheeks.

My brows furrow. "Hey, are you okay?"

She shakes her head, her fiery curls whipping around her face. "Yeah, I'm fine. Just those damn mimosas always fuckin' me up." She musters a hint of a smile. "I'll be okay, nothin' good food and some water won't fix."

I frown at her. "If you're sure."

Becca winks, taking a chunk of bread from the basket in the center of our table and starts rambling about how wild the high schoolers are these days compared to when we were kids.

I relax, knowing the Chase conversation is tabled, for now.

When I call Jax later that night, he doesn't answer.

Chapter 27
CHASE

IT'S MONDAY AND THE RESULTS FINALLY CAME back from the lab.

Luckily, asbestos is not a problem. *Thank fuck.*

I'm more than ready to get the ball rolling with this project, mainly because I'm anxious to prove to the guys on my team I'm more than just a nepo baby, that I actually know what I'm doing and deserve this position.

It's already past 4 p.m., but I tell Cory I'm planning to head over and work through the evening, anyway, because I want to catch up on lost time. He decides to join me and manages to grab a couple of other guys willing to put in some extra hours.

By the end of the night, we've made some nice progress, so I go tell everyone to stop at the local bar on the way back for a round, on me.

The bar's a little outdated, dark and dingy with sticky tables, but for a group of guys who are coming off a job site, a cold beer and a burger is all we need to be happy.

We're shooting the shit, winding down from the day when

one of the younger kids on the crew, Matt, leans back and groans. "Man, there are *no* girls in this place. I was hopin' I'd be able to find one and show her a good time before I head back home. Guess I'll have to call one of my weekend ladies, see if she's down for a Monday night special." He wiggles his brows.

Cory chuckles. "Son, who you tryin' to impress? No one at this table gives a damn about your made-up girlfriends. Save the imagination for later when you're entertainin' your hand."

I grin into my beer. Cory is the oldest one here, around Sam's age. There's a good dynamic he has going with his crew. It makes me confident in my decision to uproot my life and come back to run this company.

"Oh, shit. Look at this guy." Matt laughs, gesturing toward the bar.

My gaze follows where he's pointing. The bartender is leaned over the bar top, jaw set and hands tensed. The man he's talking to has his back to us, but it's clear to see he's smashed. He sways in place on his stool, stumbling as he moves to stand.

"I bet that dude's in here every night embarrassin' himself," Matt sneers. "Why the hell do people let themselves get sloppy like that? It's pathetic."

My head whips in his direction, an all too familiar ache springing to life in my chest. "Shut the fuck up."

Poking fun at a possible drinking problem is not the way to stay on my good side. I've seen what addictions can do—felt the judgment from people who don't understand. I won't sit back and let ignorant comments slide.

Raised voices bring my attention back to the altercation at the bar.

"I don't give a shit! I'm a goddamn…I'm a payin' customer

and I'm *payin'* for another… I want a damn drink, Johnny." The man flails as he reaches into his pocket and pulls out his wallet, slapping it on the bar top. His back is still toward us, but something about him pulls my stomach, jostling the contents and making me feel a little ill. He seems familiar.

The bartender throws his hands up and walks away, picking up the phone.

I scan the area, wondering if anyone else is paying attention. There are a few scattered people along the bar who spare him a glance, almost like they're used to his outbursts. At the tables surrounding the bar, though, people are gawking. Some have their hands over their mouths, stifling laughter, mocking the man who clearly can't handle his drink. Others watch with clear disgust and their phones out, recording every second. My temper flares.

Just like Matt, they judge him.

Profiling him as a disgrace.

An embarrassment.

Too busy on their pedestals to take a second and see the despair pouring out of him. Too good to walk a mile in his shoes.

My eyes swing back toward him as he quiets and tries to sit down. He loses his balance and falls, the smack of his body making me wince as it hits the concrete floor. *Shit.*

Laughter filters through the air as he lies still, sprawled out on the ground. I jump from my seat to help him because this is just sad, and it pisses me off everyone's watching him like a sideshow. He attempts to roll over and stand but struggles to regain his balance. I'm only a few feet away when he looks up. My stomach cannonballs and my steps falter.

Mr. Carson? What the fuck?

I hurry to him and squat, reaching out my hand.

He grabs it, hoisting himself into a sitting position. When he stands, I stay close. He's rocking in place, and I'm not sure if he's going to fall again. Finally, he manages to sit on his barstool.

I sit next to him, exhaling heavily as I take him in. He looks haggard. His skin is pallid. Dark circles mar his eyes, and blood vessels highlight the deep frown lines taking over his face. This is not the man I once knew. Clearing my throat, I try to find my equilibrium, because seeing him here like this has thrown me completely off-balance. Maybe I should offer to take him home? He's in no condition to be here.

"Mr. Carson?"

He grumbles, his head bobbing, nothing but an empty glass in front of him.

"Mr. Carson," I repeat.

His head snaps up, his eyes glassy and unfocused as they settle on me. "What's it to ya?"

"It's Chase, you remember me? Sam's kid."

"I know...who you are, boy." His words are so slurred it's hard to understand what he's saying.

The bartender walks over and places a glass of water down. "Craig, drink this, and for the love of God, stay calm, okay? I don't wanna throw you out, but there's only so much I can let slide."

The bartender seems familiar with him. *What's Mr. Carson doing all the way out here?*

"Do you need a ride, Mr. Carson? I came with a couple of guys from work, but I don't mind leaving early."

He ignores me, but the bartender's eyes glance my way. "He's got a ride. I've just called 'em. But if you two know each other, I'm sure he could use the company. Somethin' to keep him occupied." The bartender shoots me a pleading look, and I jerk my chin. I don't mind distracting him until whoever shows up, but there's a sinking feeling in my gut that it's going to be Goldi.

Mr. Carson fumbles toward the water glass, lifting it up to take a sip and scoffing when it's not the liquor he wants.

"How ya been, Mr. Carson? It's been a long time."

He looks at me, his frown lines deepening. "You back… You come here for my Alina?"

I force a chuckle through the sudden tightness of my throat. "No, sir. I'm pretty confident your daughter wants nothing to do with me."

He mumbles. I'm not sure, but it sounds like he says I can have her. As if she's his to give. *Like he doesn't want her.* But that's fucking crazy because if there's a man who cherishes his daughter more than Mr. Carson, I've yet to find him.

"Daddy."

My heart beats double time in my chest. I knew it. *Of course she's his ride.*

Goldi's voice comes closer as she repeats herself.

My gut pinches, knowing she'll hate that I'm here for this, but it's too late, she's already next to him, staring at me with wide eyes.

"Chase?" she gasps.

I attempt a smile, and reach out, gripping Mr. Carson's shoulder. "Hey, Alina. I was just keeping your old man company for a bit. Catching up."

"Oh. Okay." She looks back and forth between us as she chews on her lip, color flushing high on her cheeks. She puts her hand on his arm. "Daddy, come on. Let's go home."

He twists in his seat, smacking her away. She stumbles back.

I grasp the edge of the bar to keep myself from reacting.

"I'm not goin' till I'm good and…till I'm ready. And I sure as hell ain't goin' with you. Johnny!" He slurs across the bar. "How many times do I gotta tell you I don't need no…damn babysitter."

"Daddy, stop it." Her voice cracks as she reaches out again, and again he smacks her off him.

I blow out a breath and stand because they're both out of their minds if they think I'll stand here and watch him treat her this way. The only thing that stops me is when I peer at Goldi. Her shoulders are tight and her face is stone, mask firmly in place. I've seen that mask before. Hell, I've worn it. I know the suffocation of trying to breathe underneath.

Johnny walks up, slinging a towel over his shoulder. "Hey, Lee."

She sighs, throwing up a half-hearted wave. "Hi, Johnny. Thanks for callin'."

"No problem." He pauses like he doesn't want to say what he's about to. "Listen, Lee… I can't keep lettin' this happen. It's no good for business, and to be frank, it's irresponsible on my part to keep servin' someone who clearly doesn't need the drink."

"What am I supposed to do?" Her voice is a whisper and her eyes are glassy. I'm sure she's trying to keep me from hearing. She turns toward her father. "Did you hear that, Daddy? You've gone and lost your favorite place with the way you been actin'."

Mr. Carson doesn't react. He's gone from mildly coherent to passed out on the bar top. *Jesus.* Goldi shakes his shoulder and gets nothing more than a grunt. She peeks over, her body rigid, obviously uncomfortable with me witnessing her vulnerability.

Doesn't she know I'm the last person who would judge her for this?

"Daddy, come on." She shakes his shoulder again.

I make a split-second decision and lightly put my hands on her hips, ignoring the way the contact singes my fingertips as I move her to the side. I put her dad's arm around my shoulder and hoist him up by the waist. She looks like she's about to protest but I silence her with a look. "I've got him, Alina. Please, just let me help."

She sucks in a breath, analyzing the way her father's weight rests against my side, and then she squeezes her eyes shut and dips her head. "Yeah, okay. I'm parked right out front."

I half walk, half carry Mr. Carson outside, and get him settled in before I close the door and turn to face her. She stands behind me, keys in her hand, chin high, her beautiful blue eyes steely like she's preparing for a battle, and maybe she is. Whether it's against me or her father, I don't know.

"You good?" I ask.

"Yep." Her jaw stiffens.

"I'm staying at Sam and Anna's if you need anything, okay?"

She runs her fingers through her hair. "Look, we've been fine since you've been gone. Actually, since before you were gone. You can't just show back up years later and think I'll be waitin' around for you to come save me. I'm not."

"I know you're not, but I know how hard it can be." I gesture toward her passed-out dad in the car.

She straightens. "You don't know *anything*."

My heart turns to lead, sinking inside me at the strength of her resentment. "Fair enough."

I stuff my hands in my pockets and watch as she rounds the car. It's only when she's long gone that I finally move back inside.

A few hours later I'm back home, surfing channels. There's nothing on, but I settle on *Hoarding: Buried Alive*. I need something to take my mind off the ache my soul feels knowing Goldi would rather suffer in silence than accept my help. I'm about to grab a drink when there's a knock on the door. I glance up the stairs, hoping the noise doesn't wake Sam and Anna. *Who the fuck would be here this late?* I'm stunned into silence when I see who it is.

"Hey." Goldi looks up at me through her lashes, and I swear my fucking heart skips a beat. *She's so goddamn beautiful.*

"Can we talk?"

Chapter 28
ALINA

MY PALMS WON'T STOP SWEATING.

I don't know why I'm here, standing in the middle of Chase's living room, but when I was driving Daddy home, the night kept playing on a loop in my mind.

Getting the call from Johnny.

The way my chest caved in when I saw Chase.

Me, selfishly letting my emotions get in the way of him helping.

So, here I am, attempting to swallow down my pride long enough to apologize.

"I was unfair to you earlier tonight," I force out.

Chase's brows lift, but that's the only response I get. I grind my teeth as my anxiety rises, the shame over what he saw threatening to drown me. "I should have told you I'm grateful for your help. With Daddy, that is."

He's silent, still just staring at me from across the room.

"Say somethin'." I smack my thighs.

"What do you want me to say?"

"I don't know, call me a bitch or…or tell me it's okay. That you forgive me."

He sighs, wiping his hand across his mouth. "Out of the two of us, Alina, you're not the one who needs absolution."

His words surprise me. They roll around in my head, and I'd like to pretend I feel nothing, but the twinge in my chest lets me know that's not quite true. Regardless, I'm not here to talk about our past. "I don't wanna talk about any of that. I just—I got Daddy home and then I realized I never even thanked you. So, thank you, I guess. You didn't have to do what you did."

I shuffle my feet, my hands going to my back pockets.

His eyes are searing, leaving me raw and exposed. It's uncomfortable, and I wish he'd quit staring at me like that.

Finally, after a few torturous moments, he breaks his gaze, grabbing his keys off the rack on the wall. "Will you come with me somewhere?"

"What?" I breathe. I came over here to apologize, not to torment myself by spending hours in his presence. I don't know if I can be around him and pretend the scars I wear weren't made by him.

"Just…come with me somewhere. Please."

I should leave. I should turn around and march back out that door, but instead, I stand here like an idiot.

Say no. "Okay."

A grin overtakes his face and those dang dimples knock the breath from my lungs.

I follow him outside and down the driveway into his shiny, blacked-out Ford F-250, and the entire drive is uncomfortable and silent. At least for me, it is. He seems calm, like this whole situation isn't wild to be experiencing after all these years.

I side-eye him every few seconds, my legs tense and my body angled toward the passenger side window, trying to keep as much space as possible between us. The air likes to spark with tension whenever we're near each other, and it's the last thing I want to feel.

We turn into familiar territory and I realize he's taken us to the lake. He bypasses the lot, driving us right onto the sand, backing up so the bed of his truck faces the water. Lightning bugs flash in the grassy areas, and the moon shines high, reflecting off the water.

I've never been to the lake in the middle of the night. *Why did he bring me here?*

He turns off the engine and hops out. I suppose I should follow him, but I'm twisted around in my seat, looking back and admiring the lake instead, marveling at the stillness of its inky black surface and wishing I could take some of its serenity for myself. I jump when the passenger door opens.

Chase is standing there, a boyish grin on his face as he holds out his hand. "Not much point of being here if we don't get out and enjoy the view."

I peer down at his outstretched palm. The memory of what I imagined those hands doing to me earlier makes heat coil low in my gut and it's enough to make me not want to touch him at all. Instead, I maneuver around him and slide off the seat onto the ground, taking in my surroundings.

It's deserted. I guess midnight on a Monday isn't a peak time for lake goers.

Chase moves and I expect him to walk toward the water, but instead, he goes around to the back of his truck, dropping the tailgate and hoisting himself up before turning to look down at me with his hands on his hips. "Come on, Alina May. Let's stay awhile."

I walk to the side and peer into the bed, watching as he spreads out a large, thick green blanket. *Does he just keep that back here?* "Do this a lot, do you?"

"You know the motto. Always be prepared." He smirks.

I can't help the laugh that escapes. "Whatever you say, Boy Scout. Although, let's be real with each other and admit you've never really been one."

"Yeah, well there were a lot of things I should have been. Guess I was just a little late in learning the lessons." He comes to the edge of the truck bed, reaching down to help me up.

This time, I do take his hand.

We settle in, lying on the afghan as we stare at the sky. It's clear tonight. Peaceful. At least, it would be if I weren't right next to the man who broke my heart, pretending like everything's fine and dandy. The space between us is charged like it always is when we're around each other, and I clear my throat, shifting slightly as I stare up at the stars twinkling in the sky.

His voice pierces the silence. "Do you want to talk about it? Your dad, I mean."

Yes. "Not really."

He nods. "I figured as much. Sometimes talking fucking sucks."

"You can say that again." My chest tightens. "You know, I've never been out here this late before."

"Really?" He looks over at me. "After I got my license, I used to come out here all the time, usually after leaving you in the middle of the night. I'd lay down just like we are now and think about all the ways I wasn't good enough. All the ways I had failed the people in my life." His voice is heavy. "All the ways I was scared of failing *you*."

My stomach flips, old wounds gaping open, and I close my eyes, willing the burn away. "I thought you said talkin' sucks."

"I did. And it does. But I've learned it also helps."

"*You* talkin'?" The corner of my mouth lifts. "I don't believe it."

He chuckles. "People change, Alina. I'm not the same fucked-up kid I was back then. Not really, anyway."

My stomach drops, because do I believe people can change? Ask me that years ago and my answer would have been no, but I've seen my daddy go from one extreme to another like the man he was never even existed, so I guess it's not out of the realm of possibility. "He wasn't always this bad, you know?" I blurt.

Chase's head turns toward me, his hazel eyes piercing. "Your dad?"

I nod, sucking my teeth, willing away the embarrassment that's filling me up like helium. "Yeah. At first, it was just a way for him to cope because losin' Mama was hard on him, you know? He never really learned how to live without her, just turned to the drink instead, and by the time I realized it was out of control, he was already gone. Lost at the bottom of a bottle."

Chase doesn't say anything, and I'm grateful for it. I don't need someone telling me how to feel or trying to justify Daddy's actions. But it's cathartic, speaking my truths out loud.

"Stupid me, huh?" I huff out a hollow laugh. "I just thought…" I shake my head, not able to speak around the lump in my throat.

"You thought you'd be enough?" he whispers.

"Yeah." My voice cracks, a tear slipping down the side of my face. "I thought I'd be enough."

He reaches over, hesitating before he links our hands.

Warmth spreads through me, comforting all of my broken pieces.

And at least for tonight, *that's* enough.

Chapter 29

CHASE

TODAY, I WOKE UP FEELING HOPEFUL. IT'S NOT AN emotion I'm used to having, but it's there, so I'm holding on tight. If someone had told me a few months back I'd have Goldi in my life again, I would have laughed and tried to ignore the throb in my chest caused just by hearing her name.

But now I'm here, and so is she.

And while I don't have any grandiose ideas about where our relationship can go, I can't help but feel like maybe there's a reason beyond Sam's retirement that I'm back.

I'm a little surprised Sam hasn't told me about Mr. Carson's drinking. It makes me wonder if he knows, if anyone around here really knows, or if Goldi has been carrying the weight of her father's problems all on her own.

It's our first official day back on the Tiny Dancers project. Demo day. I *love* demo days, and I'm like a kid again knowing I'll see Goldi. Life is brighter with her in it. Colors more vibrant, birds fucking sing and all that shit. I had forgotten what it was like to live a Technicolor life.

In fact, I've been in such a good mood that I stopped by the coffee shop and picked up some caffeine for the crew on my way in. Impulsively, I got some for Goldi, too. Maybe it's a pipe dream thinking we can be civil, that maybe we can even be friends again, but if there's even a slight possibility, I'm not going to squander the opportunity.

When I get to Tiny Dancers and make my way down the hallway to the offices, my stomach flutters with anticipation. The door is propped open, so I nudge it wider and peer inside. Goldi's standing in the far corner, bent over what looks like a laptop bag, digging around for something in one of the pockets. My stare is greedy, taking in the flare of her hips and the curve of her ass in that spectacularly tight skirt she's wearing. I know I should look away, but I don't think I can. Heat flares in my abdomen and my cock twitches, longing mixing with the lust I always feel when I'm around her.

Goddamn.

I bite the inside of my cheek, my fingers tightening around the coffee cups to keep myself from doing something stupid like walking over to her, lying on my back between her legs and demanding she sit on my face. I shift on my feet, clearing my throat to get her attention.

She stiffens, her spine straightening as she looks over her shoulder.

"Oh! Chase, hi." She brushes a loose strand of hair behind her ear.

"I heard a rumor you were up late last night. Thought you might need some coffee." I wink, then mentally bitch-slap myself for doing it. *A wink, you fucking douchebag?*

She looks down for a second, running the palms of her

hands over her outfit, straightening the wrinkles. It's an innocent gesture but fuck if it doesn't make me think of how I'd like to glide *my* hands all over her body. I wonder if she'd feel the same as she did back when we were younger. If I'd remember exactly where to touch her to make her moan, like a muscle memory that's engrained forever.

"Oh...um, yeah. Thanks." She walks over and takes the coffee.

Our fingertips brush.

The contact lasts for less than a second, but a jolt shoots through me, catapulting my heart into my throat.

She backs away quickly, rounding the desk and sitting. I lean against the opposite wall, crossing my legs at the ankle and taking sips from my cup as I watch her.

She's nervous around me, and a small smile curves up my mouth as she stacks random piles of paper and moves around folders, her fingers fumbling.

Eventually, she realizes I'm still in the room, tracking her movements. Honestly, I could stay here all day and soak her in without complaint.

Her head tilts as she looks at me, and her voice comes across cold and cutting. "Do you need somethin' else?"

My gut tenses with the shift in her demeanor. I take another sip from my coffee before saying, "Is this how it's gonna be, Alina? Hot and cold all the time?"

She looks to the ceiling before heaving a sigh. "Listen. I don't—I don't know what you're expectin' from me. But I can't do this." She points back and forth between us.

My chest pinches, the lightness I felt this morning disappearing with the weight of her words. "What do you mean *this*?"

"This! Us! You can't just bring me coffee, and—and be all sweet and charmin', and think I'm just gonna forget about the past. About who you *really* are."

"People can change, Alina. Maybe you should get to know the new me."

"I don't wanna get to know you," she bites out, her eyes narrowed. "Last night was a mistake. I should never have gone with you."

That high I've been on all morning pops like a balloon pierced by a needle. My soul is raging against her words, beating against my insides and trying to tear out of my skin to get to her. To remind her. I grip my hair, the sting of the roots keeping me grounded, and I watch her for a few seconds before relenting. "Okay."

"Okay?"

My hand drops to my side, and I swallow down my want—my fucking *need*—to beg for her forgiveness. To let me atone for my mistakes. "Okay. Yeah, I get it. I thought maybe we could move forward and be friends, fuck, you have no clue how badly I want us to get back to that. But if you need me to stay away, if I've been too much of a fuckup in your life to ever make up for it, then okay. But can you do me a favor?"

I walk over, ripping a corner off a piece of paper, and grab a pen from the cup holder, writing down my number and sliding it to her across the desk.

She glances at it. "What's this?"

"That's my number. Put it in your purse, or better yet, program it in your phone. Just… I want you to have it. Just in case you need it."

Her chin juts out. "I won't."

"Okay." My fingers press down on the paper and slide it farther. "Keep it anyway, and know that I'm here."

A sharp laugh escapes her. "I've heard that before."

Fire sparks in my veins, frustration grinding my teeth together. The need for her to see me for who I am now rages like a hurricane, but I push it down as far as it will go, trying to keep my temper in check.

I lean forward, my knuckles pressing down on the desk, my voice low and sharp. "You heard that from a dumbass kid who took *everything* that mattered for granted. A kid who didn't know how to hold on to the best fucking thing in his life. Believe me when I tell you, that kid is gone."

She sucks in a breath, her baby-blue gaze searching.

I point to the piece of paper. "Keep it. Just in case."

My heart's beating so fast I can hear it pumping in my ears, and I spin, walking out the door.

It's not until the end of the day that I feel her eyes on me again.

I'm a sweaty mess. All the other guys have left, but I stuck around, taking my frustration from our earlier conversation out on the walls.

Who needs Doc when you've got a sledgehammer?

I drop the hammer to the ground, my torso twisting as I look at her.

She's in the middle of the room, gawking at the destruction.

I smile at her. "Not what you expected?"

"No. Not really. It's a mess in here." She narrows her eyes and takes a step closer. "This is what we're payin' y'all to do?"

Chuckling, I take off my eyewear, setting it on my head, and lift my shirt to wipe the sweat from my brow. Her eyes sear into me, mouth parting as she gazes at my stomach, watching as the fabric falls back down. "Do you wanna try?" I ask.

Her mouth snaps shut, her eyes widening as they flick up to mine. "What? No, I can't do that."

"Why not?"

"I've never even held one of those things before. Daddy never let me near 'em when I was a kid." She points to the sledgehammer on the ground. "I wouldn't know what to do."

"Not much to it." I shrug. "Come here, I'll show you."

She backs up. "I'm really okay."

"It will make you feel better."

Her hands go to her hips. "Who says I don't feel good?"

I smirk at her, waiting.

"Ugh, fine. Just hand me the stupid thing." She marches past me to pick it up, and I grab her around the waist without thinking.

Electricity sparks, a thousand fireworks detonating where we touch, and we both freeze. Her breathing is heavy, chest rising and falling, and I'm straight-up holding mine, afraid if I move even an inch, she'll force me to let her go.

She feels so good in my arms.

I lean in, my lips brushing her ear, my stomach flipping like I'm on a roller coaster. "Not so fast."

My fingers dig in tighter, and she doesn't resist when I spin her around until she's facing me. Our energy weaves together, buzzing between us, attracting like magnets. I try to ignore the way my heart thumps in my chest as I take the eyewear from my head and gingerly slip it over her face.

My hands slide along the curve of her ear and down until they rest on her neck, and I feel her pulse beneath my thumb.

Her lips part, that perfect, pink tongue peeking out to swipe along the bottom, and it would be *so* easy to lean in and taste her. I can feel how much she wants me to.

But I know she'd regret it after and push me away. So even though it's the last thing I want, I drop my hands and step back.

"Go ahead, pick it up." I gesture toward the sledgehammer.

She's still standing there, chest heaving as she blinks at me a few times and then snaps herself out of the daze by shaking her head. Brushing by me, she picks it up and then looks at me from over her shoulder.

"What do I do?"

I stick my hands in my pockets, trying to calm my racing heart. Trying to keep myself from grabbing her back into my arms. "Think of whatever's pissing you off and swing."

"That's it?"

"That's it."

She turns toward the wall, raises the hammer above her head, and brings it down. Not technically the proper way to do it, but she'll be all right.

By the third attempt, she's got it down.

I can tell the moment she really lets go, her anger breaking free with every swing. She's a goddess in her turmoil.

My heart fucking beats for her.

I was foolish to think it had ever stopped.

JOURNAL ENTRY #320

I WAS IN SECOND GRADE THE FIRST TIME A TEACHER NOTICED SOMETHING WASN'T RIGHT AT HOME. MRS. GRADY WAS HER

NAME. SHE'D ALWAYS PULL ME ASIDE AND ASK ME QUESTIONS ABOUT MY LIFE. I WAS SO STARVED FOR ATTENTION, I ATE IT UP LIKE CANDY, THINKING SHE JUST LIKED ME ENOUGH TO WANT TO KNOW.

THE DAY CPS KNOCKED ON OUR DOOR ALSO HAPPENED TO BE THE DAY I BROUGHT HOME MY FIRST OFFICIAL "REPORT CARD." ALL A'S. MRS. GRADY TOLD ME HOW PROUD SHE WAS AND I THOUGHT SURELY IF SHE WAS PROUD, HOW COULD MOM NOT BE? I RACED OFF THE BUS, EXCITED TO SHOW HER, BUT WHEN I WALKED INTO THE HOUSE THERE WERE STRANGE PEOPLE THERE. MOM HAD A BIG SMILE PLASTERED ON HER FACE AND SHE USHERED ME IN, HANDS ON MY SHOULDERS AS SHE INTRODUCED ME TO THEM. I DON'T REMEMBER THEIR NAMES, ONLY THEIR EYES AS THEY CATALOGED ME FROM MY WORN SHOES ALL THE WAY UP TO THE BUZZED HAIR ON MY HEAD. THEY MADE ME UNCOMFORTABLE AND I LEANED INTO MY MOM FOR SUPPORT. SHE SQUEEZED MY SHOULDERS, THE GRIP BRUISING.

ONCE THEY LEFT, THE SMILE DROPPED AND HER EYES LOST ALL THEIR WARMTH. TOLD ME HOW EMBARRASSED I MADE HER. THAT IT WAS MY FAULT SHE WAS LIKE THIS IN THE FIRST PLACE. HOW IF I WASN'T AROUND, SHE WOULDN'T NEED TO MEDICATE SO MUCH, AND HOW DARE I TRY TO PAINT HER AS THE PROBLEM. THAT MAYBE IF I WAS A BETTER SON, I'D WORK A LITTLE HARDER AT LIGHTENING HER LOAD.

FOR A FUCKING SEVEN-YEAR-OLD, THAT SHIT HITS YOU DEEP. FORMS SCARS YOU CARRY WITH YOU FOR THE REST OF YOUR LIFE. I CRIED IN MY ROOM THAT NIGHT, LYING IN BED WITH MY REPORT CARD ON MY PILLOW CATCHING MY TEARS.

IT TOOK...A LONG FUCKING TIME TO REALIZE THE WAY SHE WAS WASN'T MY FAULT. SO MANY RELATIONSHIPS RUINED AND

SO MUCH TIME LOST FROM BELIEVING HER LIES. FROM CARRYING RESPONSIBILITY THAT WAS NEVER MEANT TO BE MINE.

PARENTS' WORDS BECOME THEIR CHILDREN'S INNER VOICE.

IT'S A HELL OF A THING, LEARNING TO IGNORE IT.

Chapter 30

ALINA

"LUNCHTIME!" I SAY, WALKING INTO THE STUDIO. I raise my arms, showcasing the bags of burritos. It's Friday, and Cory asked if I'd be willing to pick up something for the crew. I was content hiding out in the office, but he said my lunch would be covered, and I couldn't say no to a burrito bowl.

Besides, I can't avoid Chase forever.

He has me so confused, I can't tell my head from my toes. Our invisible tether vibrates to life whenever I'm around him, and this time he isn't the one trying to snap it in half.

I'm not sure how to handle a Chase that isn't pushing me away.

It's mystifying. One minute I'll want to strangle him, hurt him as bad as he's hurt me. Then the next, I'm convincing myself maybe we *can* be friends.

I set up the food on a clean table along the wall, grabbing my burrito bowl and sitting down in a fold-out chair in the corner. It's been a long time since I've been on a construction site, and I had forgotten what the process looked like. Honestly, it reminds me of Daddy, but those memories hurt because that man doesn't exist anymore, so I've tried to steer clear.

Now, after literally smashing down walls, I find myself wanting to sit in the middle of it, breathe it all in.

My stomach jumps when Chase enters the room. I tell myself to stop watching him, but I can't look away. He takes in the room and all the food, and then our gazes lock. I'm mid-chew and I just sit there, staring at him. I can't help it. For the thousandth time since he's been back, my brain and heart war with each other.

It's hard being around him.

But lately, at least some of the time, when he's around I don't think about the past, and when that happens, being with him is as easy as breathing. He quiets the doubts—the voices. But I can't let myself go through this again. Not in general, and especially not with him.

Letting Chase Adams break my heart one time was foolish, but letting him in to do it again? Well…I think that might be catastrophic.

A couple of younger guys come in, and Chase's attention is off me as they say something to him. His eyes crinkle as he throws his head back, his deep laugh causing me to cross my legs against the sudden ache flaring between them.

I look down at my watch, checking the time. I'm leaving early today to pick up Jax from the airport. He's coming home for the next two weeks before he has to hightail it back to California, and I can't wait for him to be here. Jax has been hard to get ahold of lately, so I haven't had the chance to warn him about Chase. I won't lie and say that I haven't been avoiding him, too, because the thought of even broaching the subject makes anxiety cramp my insides.

Regina waltzes through the door right as I check the time again, giving me a passing glance on her way to the office.

Okay, I guess that's my cue.

When I throw my trash away, I catch Chase leaning against the wall, watching me, his arms crossed and his square jaw tensing.

Fire blooms on my cheeks.

I can't wait until this renovation is over and I can get some space. Right now, I can hardly breathe.

"Sweetheart."

"Teeth!" I yell, running around my car to jump in his arms. "You've been gone for way too long."

He sets me down, cupping my face in his palms and smiling wide. "Seems like you survived without me."

"Barely." I beam back at him.

Once we settle into the car, he chuckles and pats the dash of my Kia. "I can't believe this thing's still running."

"Hey, you watch your mouth. She's a labor of love, is all. You've done her proud and I ride her gently." I side-eye him. "So how's the big time, Mr. Hollywood?"

Jax sighs, tucking his shaggy blond hair behind his ears. "It's different than I expected."

"How so?" I keep my eyes on the road, merging into the line of cars trying to leave the airport.

"It's a bunch of bullshit and red tape. The guy pulling all the strings, James Donahue, is a dick."

I flip on my blinker. "Why are you workin' with him, then?"

He grins. "Because at least he's the biggest dick in all the land.

All I want is to see my cars on the big screen, and he's the way to make it happen."

I nod. "Makes sense. His daughter still followin' you around like a lost puppy?"

"She's not so bad."

I widen my eyes. "That's quite the attitude change after spendin' countless hours and texts complainin' about her."

"Yeah, well… It's not like I *want* her attention, but you get used to it after a while." He shrugs. "What's been going on around here? Mom told me Sam's having some retirement party?"

My grip tightens around the steering wheel, nerves making my stomach buzz. This is my moment to bring up Chase. "Yep. Life's full of surprises."

He raises his brows, his arm resting on his propped knee. "Is it now?"

"Mmhmm."

"What's up with you, Lee?"

"Why would you assume somethin' was up?" My fingers tap on the wheel.

"You're fidgety."

I make a face. "Fidgety?"

He gives my fingers a pointed glance. "Fidgety."

I keep my eyes on the road, my bottom lip raw from how hard I'm biting into it. "Chase is back."

"What'd you say, sweetheart?"

I glance at him. "I think you heard me."

"Oh, I did. But I swear you just told me Chase was back, so I need you to repeat it."

Blowing out a breath, I say again, "Chase is back."

I peek another look at him, gauging his reaction. Losing

Chase was hard on him, too, and I've always felt a massive amount of guilt over the way their friendship ended.

He frowns. "Has he been bothering you?"

I force out a laugh. "What? No."

"So, you haven't seen him?"

"I have," I say slowly.

"Sweetheart, I'm really trying to keep my patience here, but you're not making it very easy with your cryptic answers."

I swallow down the rest of my nerves, feeling them settle in the bottom of my belly. "You know how I told you Tiny Dancers is havin' a reno done? Well...she hired Sam's construction company and Chase is the lead on it."

Jax scoffs. "He's working with you?"

I cringe. "Not *with* me. Just...around me."

"Big damn difference, Lee."

"Look. I didn't ask for this, all right, so don't get a tone with me. But...it's fine. He's different than he used to be."

Our night at the lake drops in my mind, and I smother the grin wanting to break free when I think about it.

Jax narrows his eyes. "Alina. Tell me you're not falling for that."

"Fallin' for what?"

He waves his hand through the air. "For his shit."

"There's nothin' to fall for."

"Alina."

"Jax," I mock.

He blows out a breath, rubbing a hand over his face. "I want to talk to him."

I flip the blinker and focus on turning the wheel. "That's your prerogative."

"It is." He nods. "It's also my prerogative to kick his ass."

I snort. "Oh, please. What happened with him was a long time ago. It's fine. *I'm* fine."

"I didn't say you weren't. Some things aren't just about you." He watches me, his forest-green gaze noticing my every twitch. "Just promise me you'll stay away from him."

My heart stalls. I can't promise him that, and even worse, I don't know if I want to. "Hard to do that unless you're expectin' me to quit my job."

"You know what I mean, Lee. I don't want to see you get hurt again. And he *will*. All he knows how to do is hurt people."

The words strike a chord in me, ringing true. Staying away from Chase *should* be a no-brainer, but my feelings muddle and twist until they're so complicated I can't tell whether it's my head or my heart making the decisions.

So I don't promise, because I don't want to be a liar.

Jax comes back to my place and we spend the evening hanging out with Becca. He regales us with tales from California and the soreness in my belly from laughing is a nice respite from the hollowness that's usually there. There's a different energy around Jax than before. Or maybe it's just the way it feels between him and me. He isn't clinging so tight, and I'm not sure what to do with the shift. All night I obsess over what's changed, and while I can't pinpoint it, I realize maybe I depend on him a little more than what's healthy or normal. After Mama's death, he wrapped himself around me and I never really let him take his arms back.

Maybe it's about time I do.

Chapter 31

CHASE

THE SECOND I'M IN MY NEW PLACE, MARISSA surprises me with a weekend visit.

I should be thrilled the woman I'm in a relationship with is here, and I swear to God I try to be the type of boyfriend she deserves, the kind that wants her around and isn't spending all of his time thinking of another woman, but I'm failing miserably.

"I'm so excited to see where you grew up," she says, making herself comfortable on my couch.

"Mmm." I sit next to her, but I'm distracted.

"What's wrong? Are you upset that I came?"

Blowing out a breath, I lean back and run my hand through my hair.

Her eyes track the movement. "What is it?"

"Nothing," I reply, my tone defensive.

She points to my hand that's still tugging on the roots. "That's your tell. You *always* mess with your hair when you're nervous or stressed."

My palm drops to my side, and I stare at her silently for a few moments, surprised she knows that about me.

But why wouldn't she? I tilt my head and blink at her, trying to figure out if there's anything about *her* that I know. Small things like that, things that seem inconsequential but make us who we are at the core.

I come up blank.

"Not upset."

She frowns. "Are you mad that I'm here?"

Shaking my head, I reach out and grip her hand. "Not mad, just… I wish you would have called first."

"I thought it would be a nice surprise," she says, her face dropping. "You've been tense whenever we've talked on the phone, you know? Thought you might need some *relief*."

Grinning, she takes her hand from mine and slides it down my abdomen until she's palming my lap.

I've been half-hard all week from thoughts of Goldi, so it doesn't take long for my body to react, my cock stiffening under her touch, and I wish I was the kind of guy I was back in high school. The kind that could shove all my emotions into a small, square box and move on autopilot, not caring how shitty of a person it made me, but I'm not that person anymore, and Marissa touching me right now makes me physically sick to my stomach.

I push her hand off, and she scoffs, crossing her arms.

I haven't really been stressed like Marissa thinks, just distracted, mainly with thoughts of Goldi. How she's dealing with her father. How badly I want to take away the sadness from her soul, even though I know it's not my place anymore.

She has Becca.

Jax.

Envy slithers up my spine and squeezes like a constrictor when I think of them together.

He was always half in love with her, and I'm sure over the years, the feelings have only grown stronger.

It doesn't matter, I tell myself.

"Are we…okay?" Marissa's voice cuts through my thoughts.

She sniffles, and once again, I feel like a complete asshole.

Another flash of Goldi with Jax flows through my mind, and then the memory of her wanting absolutely nothing to do with me, both at her mom's funeral and at almost every encounter we've had since I've been back.

Regret and longing fill up my chest, but they're blanketed by a type of acceptance. One that might be coming years too late, but I guess better late than never.

I focus my attention back on my actual girlfriend, the woman who *does* want me. One who I haven't fucked up beyond repair yet.

She's here. She's trying. And with her there's an actual chance of a future, so maybe it's time I accept reality and really give it a shot.

Reaching out, I run my hand up Marissa's arm and over her collarbone until I'm cupping the nape of her neck, tangling my fingers in her hair. I drag her toward me, resting my forehead against hers, and press a kiss to her lips. A chaste one. Just to see.

It's nice. But my heart stays steady and my brain is calm.

Maybe that's for the best.

"Yeah, we're okay," I murmur, pressing my mouth to hers again.

She grins against me and moves quickly, sliding into my lap

and shoving her tongue down my throat, and I accept it all with a certain type of numbness.

Guess that high school kid isn't too far gone, after all.

All my pent-up energy goes into fucking Marissa. But afterward, I feel dirty. Like I cheated on *Goldi*, which is truly an extra level of some fucked-up shit.

Marissa's lazing in bed next to me, still naked, and when she sees me watching her, she rolls toward me, throwing her leg over my hip, her fingers playing with the dusting of hair on my chest. "Mmm… I could get used to this. Being here, I mean."

I absentmindedly rub her back as I ponder whether this is something *I* could get used to. Could I see myself with her here? It's not unpleasant, having her warm my bed. There are worse things to come home to.

My phone vibrates on the end table and Marissa jerks her head up from where it's resting on my chest to look at the screen. It's a random number she wouldn't recognize, but I sure as hell do.

I'm grabbing it to answer before I even recognize that my heart's picked up speed.

"Goldi," I say as I move Marissa off me and sit against the headboard.

I'm not sure what's going on, but I doubt she'd call me unless it was an emergency, as much as I hate to admit it.

She says she needs me and I'm out of bed in seconds, holding the phone between my ear and shoulder as I throw on my clothes.

"What are you doing?" Marissa asks, leaning on her elbows.

I hold up my finger so she knows I'll answer her in a second. I'm sure she's wondering who's on the phone, but my mind is only worried about Goldi. Complete tunnel vision. I repeatedly fucked up when she needed me before, no chance in hell I'm going to let that happen again.

She rattles off her address, which isn't far from me, and then I'm hanging up the phone and grabbing a jacket from my closet.

Hands creep around my waist after I get it on, and my stomach drops.

"Are you going somewhere?" she asks, her fingers rubbing small circles on my abs.

"Yeah." I clear my throat. "A friend needs some help. Car trouble."

She gives me an incredulous look. "At 10 p.m.?"

Sighing, I turn around and lift a brow. "You think cars normally fuck up during business hours?"

She steps back, giving me an odd look before picking her dress up from the floor. "Well, hold on a second. I'll come with you."

Panic chokes me, and I walk to her and rest my hand over hers, stopping her from getting ready. "No, no. You hang out here. I'm not sure how long this will take."

Her dress hangs limply in her hand and she frowns. "Are you sure?"

Fuck yes, I'm sure. Having the woman who wants my heart around the reason she'll never get it? Hard pass.

Marissa's eyes narrow. "Who's the friend, someone from work?"

"Oh. No, it's..." I debate how to handle this situation. Why is it even a question? I'm not doing anything wrong, and I have no reason to lie. "It's a friend from when I used to live here. Alina."

"Alina. That's a pretty name." She slinks over to me, running her hand down the front of her naked body. "Doesn't she have someone else she can call? Another friend, a boyfriend of her own?"

I shrug, but her words invade my brain. *Does she have a boyfriend?* God, I'm fucking pathetic. "I don't know, but I won't ignore her when she needs me."

Marissa's fingers ghost over her nipples and tweak them. "*I* need you."

I grit my teeth. "Marissa…I can't right now."

She huffs, dropping her hands to her sides. "Fine. I'll just be here, waiting for you to get back, I guess."

I feel like an asshole, but not enough to make me stay.

"How long will you be gone?" she prods.

"However long it takes, I guess. I'll leave some money on the coffee table so you can order some food. I don't have much here yet."

"Okay." She goes up on her toes and leaves a lingering kiss on my lips.

I let her because I don't know what else to do.

Chapter 32

ALINA

JAX AND BECCA FINALLY LEAVE, AND EVEN THOUGH I'm exhausted, I draw a bath.

I've just dipped my toes in when my phone vibrates. I look down at the display, already knowing in my gut who it is.

The Watering Hole.

Of course.

For the first time in a long time, I've had a good day. It's only natural something would come along and screw it all up.

Johnny begrudgingly informs me he'll be forced to call the police if Daddy doesn't leave. He made a scene again, and it's the final straw. Johnny says he's not allowed on their premises anymore, and he isn't listening when they ask him to stay gone. *How did this become my life?* I should just let him get arrested, but I know I won't. The part of me that believes all of this is my fault forces my hand.

Daddy wouldn't be the way he is if Mama were here. And she *would* be if they hadn't been coming to my toddlers' recital.

I grab my keys, lamenting the fact I'm dealing with this again.

What would I have done if Jax and Becca had still been at the house? *What you've always done. Make an excuse and get 'em to leave.*

Once I reach my car, I realize the interior light is on. "Come on, come on, come on. Work with me," I mutter, turning the key and watching the lights on my dash flicker. I hear clicks, but no engine. *Shoot.*

I should call Jax, but if I do, he'll ask where I'm going, and I'm not ready for him to know about Daddy. I'm not ready for anyone to know about him. I lean my head against the headrest, closing my eyes.

"Keep it. Just in case."

My eyes snap open as the words filter through my head, and I dig in my purse to grab the piece of paper with Chase's number. Every bone in my body is telling me this is a bad idea, but unless I want to air out my family's dirty laundry, I don't have any other option.

With shaky fingers, I call him.

"Goldi?"

My stomach clenches at hearing the nickname, but I don't correct him. "How'd you know it was me?"

"You've had the same number since high school. It's burned into my memory. Is everything okay?" he asks.

I lean my forehead against my steering wheel. "My car won't start."

"Do you need me to come look at it?"

"No. Daddy's causin' trouble down at The Watering Hole and I need to go pick him up. I just... I didn't have anyone else to call." I lift my head, raising my eyes and willing the tears to stay at bay.

It's silent on the line and I pull the phone away from my ear to make sure it's still connected. I hear rustling on the other end and a female voice in the background, mumbling. My stomach bottoms out. *Is he with someone right now?* "Oh, you're busy. I shouldn't have called."

"No," he barks. "No, I'm not busy. You can *always* call. Just tell me where you're at and I'll be there."

My chest warms with relief and something else I refuse to identify. I ramble off where I live and then I wait in my car until headlights are coming down the street.

It's probably stupid, but I don't want him in my apartment. It's the one place in town that doesn't remind me of him, and I'd like to keep it that way.

Chase pulls in behind where I'm parked, and I'm out the door and over to his truck before he can turn off his engine.

"Hi," I say, strapping my seatbelt on.

He smiles. "Hey."

His hair is mussed like he just got out of bed. Like fingers have been tugging on it. Something that feels a lot like jealousy crawls up my throat, squeezing as I remember the woman's voice on the phone. "Thanks for this. I'm sorry to interrupt whatever you were doin'."

He glances at me. "You didn't interrupt anything."

"Oh, I just heard a woman on the phone and assumed…"

His features tense, but he stays silent.

Guess that answers that.

I shouldn't want to know anyway. It's not my business.

He runs his hand through his hair. "You left work early today?"

"Yeah. I'm surprised you noticed with how busy y'all were."

"I always notice you."

My rebellious heart skips.

"So where'd you go?" he continues. "Or can I not ask that?"

"You can." I side-eye him. "I picked up Jax from the airport."

"Oh. You didn't want him to come look at your car?"

"No, I… He was tired from travelin'. I didn't want to bother him." I stare at my hands, heat rushing to my face.

"Hmm."

It's quiet for the rest of the drive and I'm thankful. When we get to The Watering Hole, I see Daddy slouched against the wall outside.

Chase sighs as he pulls up to the curb. "Let me go grab him. You just stay here, okay?"

I start to take off my seatbelt. "No, I—"

His hand covers mine, preventing me from unbuckling myself. "Alina. Trust me, stay here." I shouldn't trust him. I know this. But I lean back and listen to him anyway.

Surprisingly, he gets Daddy into the back with no fuss. It occurs to me that if I had gotten out, Daddy may have caused a scene. Maybe Chase knew that, too.

I wait until we're on the road again before twisting in my seat. Daddy doesn't seem too gone yet, and it makes a bit of the despair that's clinging to my insides loosen. "Daddy, you all right?"

He ignores me and looks to Chase. "I thought…you said you weren't back for her."

An invisible fist lodges in my gut. *He said that?* I sit forward, looking out the windshield. I can't pay attention to their conversation; I'm too busy wondering why it hurts so much to hear it.

Chase glances in the rearview mirror. "I'm not."

My chest pinches.

Daddy grunts and then finally acknowledges me. "I should have…have known Johnny would be callin' you out here."

"If it wasn't me, it would be the cops," I reply. "Then where would you be?"

Chase is silent. Maybe I should feel embarrassed for hashing it out with Daddy right in front of him, but I can't find it in me to care.

"You know you can't keep showin' up, right? They don't want you in there, Daddy."

He waves me off. "They always say that. It's fine. I'm their best…their best damn customer."

"Why don't you come hang with me instead of goin' to a bar? You can finally come see my place."

I turn around again, watching for his reaction.

His eyes are ice. "I already gotta look at you enough."

My eyes flutter closed as I will my heart back into my chest. No matter how often I take his jabs, they still leave a bruise.

Chase's fingers tighten around the steering wheel.

"I'm just sayin', maybe you should try not goin' to a bar for a while," I try again.

"Don't you lecture me, girl. I'm the parent here, not you."

I laugh. "Coulda fooled me."

Daddy leans forward, and his breath reeks so much of whiskey I can smell it from the back seat. "Yeah? Well…I'm the only one you got. You can thank yourself for that."

My already weathered and beaten soul is crippled further by his words.

"That's enough." Chase's voice is sharp, his eyes glacial as he looks at Daddy in the rearview mirror.

Like a reflex, and without much thought, I put my hand on Chase's forearm to keep him calm. I don't know how his temper is these days, but the Chase I knew had a short fuse, and the last thing I want is for him to fly off the handle when we've already got enough going on with my father.

His muscles tense under my fingertips, and something hits me in the center of my chest when I recognize that I'm willingly touching him, and even worse than that, it feels easy to do.

"It's okay, Chase. Daddy didn't mean it," I say.

His jaw tightens and he glances at me before staring back at the road. "I don't give a fuck if he meant it. I won't let that shit fly, Alina." The car rolls to a red light and it gives Chase the perfect opportunity to focus on Daddy. "You hear me, Mr. Carson? If you disrespect your daughter again, we're gonna have problems."

"I ain't sayin' nothin' she don't already know," Daddy slurs.

The shame burns my cheeks, his words slamming into me until they ring true like a reverb in my ears.

Chase's mouth opens but I squeeze his arm tighter.

"Please…leave it." My voice is a whisper.

Chase stares at me, his shoulders tensing before he nods sharply and puts his attention back on the road.

The rest of the car ride is silent, but we get Daddy home in one piece.

We pull up to the driveway, and my belt buckle is undone before Chase has a chance to turn off the truck.

I glance at him. "You can wait here."

He shakes his head. "Absolutely not. I'm making sure he gets inside and that you get back out here before he abuses you more."

My stomach cramps. "He doesn't *abuse* me."

Chase looks at me, his eyes sad and his lips slightly pursed.

Embarrassment fills up my chest with every second he stares, and I break our connection, looking back at Daddy who's passed out, his head against the window.

"Yeah, well, let me help anyway," Chase finally replies.

Pressure builds behind my eyes and I will away the burn, nodding and hopping out of the truck.

Watching Chase walk around and maneuver Daddy until he's practically carrying him is another hit to the shield I've built up over the years, and when he gets him inside and sets him up in his recliner with a glass of water and some ibuprofen on the end table, that shield crumbles even more.

"You don't think he should go into bed?" I ask, chewing on my lip.

Chase shakes his head. "Keep him upright in case he throws up."

Swallowing, I nod, giving one more glance to Daddy.

Chase walks toward me, and before I can stop him, his right hand is cupping my cheek, and the other is tilting me up by the chin, forcing me to meet his gaze.

"You okay?"

I can only nod, unable to force the words out.

His thumb brushes against my skin, and my eyes flutter closed, hating myself for taking solace in the comfort.

But I'm too weak and worn down to resist right now.

"Come on," he says. "Let's get you home."

I'm relieved once we're back in his truck.

The boulder of Daddy's problems and my shame for causing them sits heavy on my shoulders, and I prefer to wallow in my misery alone.

Chase sits with both hands on the steering wheel, the engine running but the car staying idle. His cheek muscle twitches and he says, "Go for a drive with me."

I grip the handle of the passenger door. Part of me is screaming to open it and run away from him.

But the bigger part of me wants to give in, so I nod and give in to the moment, not caring if it makes me selfish or stupid to do it, and before I know it, we're back at the lake, lying beneath the stars.

Chapter 33
CHASE

WHEN I ASKED IF GOLDI WANTED TO GO FOR A drive, I didn't plan to end up at the lake, but here we are. I have so many things I want to say, but I'm silent because I know it's not what she needs to hear, and I've spent enough time over the years being a selfish prick when it comes to her.

My phone vibrates in my pocket, and I ignore it, already knowing it's Marissa trying me again. I'm a shit boyfriend for not responding, but when I look at Goldi, it's hard to care, because for the first time tonight, she looks relaxed, leaned back on her elbows in the bed of my truck as she stares at the water.

I love seeing her like this. It reminds me of when we were kids.

"Do you remember that date you went on with that fuckface Reed? He brought you here to the lake."

A soft smile grows on her face. "Yep. It was a great date."

I scoff, decades-old jealousy creeping into my bones. "You mean it was great *after* the date."

She laughs. "You really need me to stroke your ego that badly?"

"I was so fucking jealous," I admit.

Goldi looks at me. "I know you were."

"The thought of him touching you made me lose my mind. It was all I could think about. And when I found out he brought you out here..." I shake my head, chuckling. "I thought I'd go insane with how much I wanted to take his place. He was doing things with you I wanted to do. Things I wouldn't let myself do."

She turns her head, resting against the blanket I've laid out and watching me with sad eyes.

"Even after we were together, I never really let myself. I didn't have the balls to be what you needed." I suck on my teeth. "I guess it doesn't matter now."

"Why do you bring me here?" she asks.

That's a good question, and it takes me a minute to answer. Not because I have to think of why, but because I'm not sure she really wants to hear it.

"Because life gets noisy, and when I was a kid...when I was in your room, under your makeshift sky with those tacky glow-in-the-dark stickers, the world would get quiet." I wave my arm at the Tennessee starlight. "I thought maybe this could do the same for you."

She stares at me, and I watch the delicate slope of her neck as she swallows. "Sometimes...sometimes I look at you and I wanna punch you in the face."

I laugh. "Don't sugarcoat it, damn."

She grins. "It's the truth." Her smile fades. "But then...then there are other times, like now, when I'm happy you're back, and that makes me feel stupid 'cause I should know better than to let you into my life."

I try to tamp down the emotions her words cause, but the

happiness infuses my chest anyway, swirling around and mixing with the sharp stab of knowing she thinks I'm just another bad decision. I turn until I'm on my side, propping my head up in my hands and locking my gaze on hers. "I messed up with you, I know that. I didn't put you first, and I wasn't there for you the way you've always, *always* been there for me. The truth is, I didn't know *how* to put you first when I had never done it for myself. I'll live the rest of my life with that regret."

She blinks at me and then nods. "Good."

"I'd love to have a conversation where I tell you all the ways I know I've fucked up, but I know that's not what you need from me. Not right now."

"I may never be ready for that, Chase."

My heart splinters, even though I've known that for a while. Since I've been back, if I'm being honest. "I respect that, but can I say one thing?"

"Chase, I—"

"Just...please." I reach over and put my finger on her lips. Her perfect fucking lips. My chest aches from what I'm about to say, and I know she can feel my finger trembling. "I'm sorry, Alina. I'm so sorry. I know they're just words and they don't make up for shit, and I know they're eight years too late. But there they are."

Her lips part, and I watch as my words sink into her. Desperation claws at me and I do my best to ignore it. There's nothing I want more than for her to forgive my sins, but I won't ask that.

Forgiveness isn't mine to demand; it's hers to give.

She pulls away from me and faces the sky. I follow suit, lying against the blanket, my apology lingering in the space between us.

"Thank you," she speaks into the silence. "For the apology... and for bringin' me here. It helps."

I was hoping it would. Her dad has a serious problem, and he talks to her like an asshole. Blames her for things he has no fucking business laying on her shoulders. I know what that can do to someone's psyche.

Chewing on the inside of my cheek, I peek at her from the corner of my eye. "Do you want to talk about it?"

"Not really."

I nod. There are a million things I want to say. *You're beautiful. I still love you. Your mom's death is not your fault and fuck your dad for making you think it is.* Instead, I reach into the space between us and grasp her hand, squeezing lightly, my blood pumping as I wait to see if she squeezes back.

She does.

Chapter 34

CHASE

IT'S SUNDAY MORNING AND I'M DRIVING BACK TO Nashville for both my appointment with Doc and then Nar-Anon group this evening. This weekend has been eye-opening, to say the least. Marissa stayed all weekend and now I'm following her back to her place. She was pissed when I came home on Friday night, but not pissed enough to leave, and even though I know that I need to end things, I was too much of a pussy to do it right then. Instead, I let her order furniture for my house.

I spent the whole time feeling awkward as fuck because she kept trying to get me into bed and I…couldn't. I've been trying to feel a sliver of the way I do for Goldi, but for Marissa instead, and it hasn't happened.

Marissa's a good woman. She's just not the woman for me.

Now, I just have to figure out the best way to tell her.

Courage to change the things I can. I repeat the serenity prayer before parking behind her and following her into her house.

I'm surprised she's been dropping hints about moving to Sugarlake when she has such a nice setup here. My stomach rolls when I think of how invested she must be in our relationship to feel that way.

"Do you want anything to drink?" Marissa walks to the fridge.

I lean against her kitchen island. "Can we talk for a sec?"

Her hand pauses midair and she spins to face me. "Talk about what?"

"About what we're doing here. With this. With us."

"With *us*?" She frowns. "I thought we were doing kind of good in that department, so I'm not sure what we need to talk about."

"Do you really feel that way? You can honestly stand there and tell me you're one-hundred-percent happy with how things are?"

"Yes. We're very compatible." Her voice deepens.

Damn. She's not gonna make this easy. Blowing out a breath, I run a hand over my face and pin her with a heavy stare. "The past few years have been good. You've been a great friend, and yeah, the sex is…"

"Awesome," she finishes. She closes the fridge and then moves around the island until she's directly in front of me. "So why do I get the feeling you're trying to ruin it?"

My chest pulls, because I don't want to hurt her. "You deserve better than me."

She scoffs. "I don't want better."

"I want better *for* you," I argue.

"I'm a big girl, Chase. I can decide for myself what and who I want."

My throat's tight, anxiety threatening to choke me. I don't want another woman's hurt on my conscience, but she's not getting the picture. "Marissa, be serious. You're pushing me for things I've told you time and time again I'm not ready to give."

"You *are* giving me what I need." She rests her hand on my chest. "I know you feel what's between us, Chase."

My jaw clenches to keep the harsh truth from spilling out. I *don't* feel it. Maybe in another life—if Goldi didn't exist—then the comfortable warmth Marissa provides would be enough.

But it's hard to appreciate warmth when you've been consumed by fire.

I grab her hand and move it off my chest. "I care about you, but you deserve someone who's able to give you everything. That man's not me."

"That man's not you." She repeats my words, her eyes shuttering. "Is this about that girl?"

My heart pounds. *Fuck.* "What girl?"

"That Leah girl you ditched me for this weekend."

"Alina." My response is automatic. I cringe, knowing I just made things worse.

She laughs, backing up a step. "Unbelievable. I tried to look past it when you left for hours and then didn't want to touch me. I forgave you when you came home at one in the morning, after spending time with someone who gave you a look on your face that you've never given me."

It's a struggle not to show the guilt on my features. She really knows how to paint the picture of an asshole.

Marissa's head tilts. "Did you fuck her?"

"No." *But I wanted to.*

She crosses her arms. "I don't believe you."

"I may be an asshole, but I'm not a cheat…and this isn't about her. It's about me not being able to give you what you want."

"All I want is you!" Her hands smack the marble of the island.

I blow out a breath. "I'm trying not to hurt you."

"Well, you're doing a shit job."

Groaning, I tug on the roots of my hair and then stare at her. "What do you want me to do, Marissa? Continue to play house with you? Let you uproot your life and move in with me when I know damn well I won't ever love you?"

She freezes in place. *Shit.* I didn't mean to say that last part out loud. Her eyes become glossy and she stiffens her shoulders. "Get out."

I sigh. "I'm sorry, I shouldn't have said it like that. But you'll see this is what's best in the long run."

"Get. Out!" she screams. She takes off her shoe and throws it, narrowly missing me as it crashes against the door.

Jesus.

It's clear she doesn't want to hear any more, so I leave. I hope in time she realizes this is what needed to happen, and even though it was difficult, I'm not sad over the end of our relationship.

All I can feel is relief.

I head straight to my therapy appointment with Doc, pulling him in for a hug he doesn't return. *Stingy fucker.* "Damn, Doc. It's good to see you." I move back, grinning at him before making myself comfortable on his sleek, black couch.

"Chase. How are you?" He sits in the brown leather chair across from me.

"Good, real good." I lean forward and rest my elbows on my knees.

"You seem to be in good spirits."

I can't help the smile that overtakes my face. "You'll never guess who works at the job site I'm on."

He raises a heavy brow.

"Goldi."

"Hmm. And how is that?"

"It's…amazing. And frustrating. And torturous." I pause, looking up. "You're married, right, Doc?"

He nods.

"Do you love your wife?"

"Very much."

"Can you imagine being around her and knowing she hates you? What it would feel like to not be able to touch her…to kiss her?"

He's silent.

"I know you won't actually answer that. It's a rhetorical question, I guess. But I forgot what it felt like, you know? I can't fucking breathe with how bad I want to touch her. Make her smile." I shake my head.

"Is that something that's on the table? Something you think she'd allow?" he questions.

My heart sinks. "Nah. But we're kind of, sort of…friends now, I guess? I don't know if you can really call it that. There are some things she's going through and I just—I see the same haunted look in her eyes I've spent my life trying to hide. I want to be there for her."

"Does she allow you to be there the way you want?"

"Sometimes." I shrug.

He writes on his notepad.

"I broke up with Marissa," I blurt.

His pen pauses as he looks at me from over his tortoiseshell glasses. "Oh?"

"We should never have been anything more than friends. She

wanted so much from me, and I didn't want to give it to her. I never even told her I was adopted, or that I have a sister. How could I make a life with her?"

"You never spoke of your past with Marissa?" Doc sounds surprised.

I lift a shoulder. "Marissa isn't the type of person I'd want to share stories with. That's why she was great, though, you know? She never pushed to know about my past. It was purely physical, and that's how I liked it." I frown. "At least at first."

"Hmm…let's change course for a moment. Is being back in Sugarlake bringing up any feelings for your sister?"

Ice races through my veins and my mouth clamps shut. Talking about Lily is hard for me, even after so many years. The cuts from her abandonment run deep.

I miss her, and I'm extremely fucking pissed at her.

"I don't want to talk about that."

"Then I hope you'll consider writing about it."

JOURNAL ENTRY #327

BEING BACK HOME MAKES SLEEP HARDER TO COME BY. LILY SURGES FORWARD IN MY DREAMS, CHOKING ME WITH HER MEMORY. BUT I'VE ACCEPTED THE REALITY THERE'S NOTHING I COULD HAVE DONE TO SAVE HER FROM HERSELF. PEOPLE ARE IN CHARGE OF THEIR OWN HAPPINESS. IT'S UNFAIR TO PUT THAT RESPONSIBILITY ON OTHERS.

BUT IT DOESN'T STOP THE NIGHTMARES.

SOME DAYS I WAKE UP IN A COLD SWEAT NOT KNOWING WHERE I AM, THINKING I'M BACK IN THAT LAST FOSTER HOME BEFORE WE WERE ADOPTED. THAT PUDGY MOTHERFUCKER WHO

THOUGHT HE COULD SNEAK INTO HER ROOM AND NOBODY WOULD NOTICE. IT REPLAYS IN MY SUBCONSCIOUS WHENEVER I'M ASLEEP, EXCEPT THE DREAMS ARE DIFFERENT THAN HOW I REMEMBER REALITY. THEY TWIST AND GET MUDDLED UNTIL I'M NOT SURE WHAT WAS REAL AND WHAT WASN'T.

SHE WAS STILL YOUNG. WE WERE THERE FOR A LITTLE OVER A YEAR, AND SHE PROMISED ME NOTHING EVER HAPPENED. BUT IN MY DREAMS, SHE'S CRYING, ASKING WHY I DIDN'T SAVE HER SOONER.

SOMETIMES, ON THE REALLY FUCKED-UP NIGHTS, SHE'LL SHIFT INTO A VISION OF MY MOM, TELLING ME WHAT A SHIT BROTHER I AM.

I THINK I HATE THEM BOTH FOR MAKING ME LOVE THEM SO MUCH.

BUT THE HATRED DOESN'T TAKE AWAY THE URGE TO FIND LILY.

MAYBE I DIDN'T PAY CLOSE ENOUGH ATTENTION. I STILL HAVE NO FUCKING CLUE WHY LILY FELT LIKE SHE NEEDED TO RESORT TO DRUGS AND BAD PEOPLE TO ESCAPE HER REALITY. A REALITY SHE CONVINCED EVERYONE SHE WAS HAPPY WITH FOR SO MANY YEARS. I DON'T FUCKING KNOW, MAN. MAYBE I'LL NEVER FIND THE ANSWERS, AND THAT'S HARD FOR ME TO ACCEPT.

I HOPE THAT WHEREVER SHE IS, SHE'S SAFE.

Chapter 35

ALINA

IT'S ONLY WEDNESDAY AND I'M DRAGGING. Between Logan's, working, and rushing straight to Daddy's to make sure he stays home for the night, I'm drained. Not just physically but emotionally. Daddy knows just how to slice, his barbs cutting deep, and I wonder how I survived living under the same roof as him for so long.

Regina and Chase are having a meeting, so I've been relegated to the office couch. Chase keeps giving me glances, probably because I can't stop yawning.

Finally, they wrap up, Regina giving me some tasks to do before she's out the door. She never stays, just comes and goes when she's needed.

It must be nice to be an owner. One day, maybe I'll get there, too.

Chase hangs back, leaning against the desk while I stand and make my way over to Regina's computer.

He quirks a brow.

"What?" I ask.

"You okay?"

"Yeah, why wouldn't I be?"

He shrugs. "You seem tired."

My instinct is to get defensive and hide the truth—and the truth is that making sure Daddy doesn't end up in jail is a hard job. I'm about to keel over from either exhaustion or stress. I open my mouth to brush off his concern, but then I remember Chase already knows about Daddy. There's no reason to hide it from him.

Sighing, I admit it. "I am tired. I've been headin' straight to Daddy's every night to make sure he doesn't get himself in trouble. I can't stop the drinkin', but I can at least try to keep him home and safe. If he goes back to Johnny's bar, they'll throw him in jail."

Chase crosses his arms, his lips pursing. "He putting up a fight?"

I roll my eyes. "Daddy lives and breathes to fight with me. So yeah, it's not easy. But I can't just do *nothin'*." My neck pinches and I gasp, reaching back to try and rub out the kink. "I don't think I ever realized how uncomfortable the guest bed was, though."

His brows raise. "You've been sleeping there?"

"What am I supposed to do?" I throw my hands out to my sides. "Although sleepin' is a generous term. More like I lay in the guest room and spend all night worryin' he's gonna get alcohol poisonin' or wake up and try to leave." I laugh and stare up at the ceiling. "When did I become the parent?"

"Why don't you just stay in *your* room?"

"Daddy moved all his stuff in there and turned my room into a 'man cave' as soon as I moved out." I wave off my statement like it doesn't bother me. "Anyway, I can't wait till Eli gets in town. They're gonna stay at the house, so I just have to keep it together till then."

"Hmm." He hums, that dang stare of his penetrating through to my bones. I'm not hiding anything, but it unnerves me either way.

I don't mention that my extracurricular activities are also tiring me out. I've been going to the rec center and having quickies with Logan on my lunch break. Normally I wouldn't be so desperate for an orgasm, but Chase being back has me confused and I need some relief.

Besides, Logan turns off my brain for a while, and that particular brand of numb feels nice.

My phone dings with a text and it's the perfect excuse to break this weird stare-off with Chase. I look down, and like I thought him into existence, there's a text from Logan.

LOGAN:

Any surprise visits from you today? I'll be at the rec until 3.

I grin, unlocking the screen to respond.

ME:

I can stop by on my lunch break at 12:30?? It will have to be quick.

LOGAN:

> Must be my lucky day. I don't have a client until 1:30. Feel like sneaking into the men's locker room?

I can't deny the thrill that spikes through me. I never thought I'd be into public places, but I've found out this past week it turns me on somethin' fierce. Biting my lip, I type out a reply.

Chase clears his throat, and I glance up at him. He's staring at me, his body tense like he knows what I was texting about.

I give him a sheepish smile, my cheeks heating. "Sorry, just makin' lunch plans. What were we talkin' about?"

He taps his knuckles on the top of the desk and grins, although it doesn't reach his eyes. "Nothing important. I gotta get back to work. Try to get some rest, yeah?"

My chest pinches. "Yeah, sure."

He rushes out the door, but my gaze lingers for a few minutes longer, wondering why I feel sad that he's gone.

I don't see him again, and I don't look for him as I leave and head to the rec on my lunch break. The quickie with Logan is just what I need to take the edge off, and the high from our tryst lasts through the rest of my workday.

It isn't until I'm walking through the grocery store that it starts to wear off. I take my time picking up different items and reading labels, mainly because I dread having to stay up all night worrying about Daddy sneaking out, so I'm putting it off for as long as I can. Part of me is worried he'll be gone by the time I get home, but so far, he hasn't snuck out once. Just drinks himself silly at home, drowning himself at the kitchen table or in his recliner.

I cannot *wait* for Eli to get to town. I'm not sure how much longer I can keep this up. Daddy needs help and I'm not fit to be giving it to him. I'm trying to get my life together, but for some reason, I keep slamming myself against the walls of his animosity. I decide on burgers for dinner, hoping he isn't already three sheets to the wind. Maybe I can convince him to man the grill—remind him there's something he's capable of doing other than drinking himself into oblivion.

When I finally make it to Daddy's place, I'm exhausted. I turn off the car and then move the rearview mirror so I can see my face, pinching my cheeks to try and get some color back.

This is as good as it's gonna get.

There's nothing I can do to hide the dark circles that line my eyes or the exhaustion seeping from my pores.

I load the groceries into my arms before heading to the front door. I realize I'll have to ring the bell since I don't have a free hand to turn the handle, and I send up a prayer that Daddy is still coherent enough to answer.

Let it be a good night. Let it be a good night, I repeat mentally, shifting on my feet and ignoring the weight of the bags.

My heart stalls when the door swings open because it isn't Daddy who answers, it's Chase.

He grins, propping his arm on the frame and leaning forward. "Hi."

"What are you doin' here?"

I'm too stunned by his presence to argue when he opens the screen door and takes the groceries from my arms. He turns around and walks down the hallway. I follow, mouth gaping. *Is he just gonna ignore my question?*

"Chase, what are you doin' here?" I repeat once we make it to the kitchen.

He sets the bags down on the counter and spins to face me.

"Thought I'd drop by, keep your dad company." He says it so casually, like the words coming out of his mouth are completely normal.

I twist around, searching for Daddy. "Where is he?"

"We're hanging out on the back patio."

"You're just…hangin' out?"

"Yep."

Daddy walks in through the back door and I turn my attention to him. "Hi, Daddy."

He makes eye contact and I lose my breath at seeing how clear his gaze is.

"What's for dinner?" he asks.

I get no greeting, but that doesn't surprise me.

"I thought we could make burgers. You up for some grillin'?" I smile wide, hoping he's in an amicable mood.

He's already shaking his head, but Chase cuts in.

"Hell yeah. I hope there's enough for me, too." He smirks. "Think you can teach me a thing or two, old man?"

To my shock, a grin pulls at Daddy's lips. *What in the world?*

"There's an art to grillin', boy. Not sure you're cut out for it." He looks him up and down.

"Lucky I know you, then." Chase glances at me and winks. "Unless you're not up for the challenge."

My eyes spring back and forth between them. Daddy mutters something about checking the propane and disappears out the back again.

I'm standing in the middle of the kitchen, gobsmacked. What the *heck* is going on?

Chase moves toward me, angling his head down to look in my eyes. "I hope it's okay I'm here."

"Uhh…yeah. Yes, it's—it's fine. What—how…"

His eyes twinkle with amusement as I stumble over my words.

"I was at Sam and Anna's, figured I'd walk over and keep your dad company, give you a break."

My heart trills. "You're here for me?"

He puts his hands in his back pockets, briefly lifting his shoulders. "You need rest." He says it like it's no big deal—like he'd do this for anybody, and maybe he would. I'm realizing I truly don't know this Chase at all.

"That's…" So much gratefulness surges I have to choke it back down. "Thank you," I manage to whisper.

He walks toward me and cups my cheek, the way he's been doing almost every time he's seen me lately. And like usual, I lean into his touch instead of turning away.

"You're welcome," he says.

Chase stays for dinner. He mans the grill next to Daddy, who is laughing at something he says. Honest to God, he's *laughing*. My heart soars at the sound, but the lighthearted moment doesn't last, because like usual, Daddy drinks himself into a stupor and starts slurring during dinner.

But he's home. He's safe. And he had a good day.

I stare at Chase across the table, my body tingling as I look at him. He didn't have to spend his time like this, and I know he did it for me—and maybe a little bit for Daddy, too.

I'm the first to stand from the table, picking up the dirty plates and taking them to the sink. Daddy stumbles out to sit in his recliner and watch TV, and I can feel as Chase moves behind me, the static buzzing from how close we are. My hands clench.

He reaches out until his forearms surround me, uncurling my fingers slowly as he places my car keys in my palm.

My eyebrows furrow as I look down at them. "What's this for?"

"Go home, Alina. Get some sleep. I'll stay here and make sure your dad stays put. Try out that guest bed and see if you're lying about how comfortable it is," he teases.

"What?" I gasp, spinning around. The front of my body brushes against his chest from how close we are, and my hands rise to push against him. "You don't need to do that. Honestly, Chase, you've done more than enough."

A strand of my hair falls forward, tickling my cheek. He brushes it behind my ear, his fingers lingering, skimming down my face until he's cupping my jaw. Butterflies erupt in my stomach and my mouth parts, my breathing growing choppy.

"Let someone take care of *you* for once, Goldi." His eyes glaze over as his thumb swipes across my mouth.

I bite my tongue to keep from licking my lips so I can taste his touch, and I step away instead.

His hand stays in the air for just a moment before he comes back to himself and drops it down. "Go home. I've got it under control."

I shouldn't accept his offer. The beat of my stitched-up heart remembers how he shattered it and warns me not to trust him again.

But I'm *so* tired, so I swallow all my doubts and nod. "Okay. But call me if anything, *anything* goes wrong, and if you decide you wanna go home, you can call, too, just let me know. It doesn't matter if it's—"

"Goldi." He chuckles. "It's fine."

"Right." I blow out a breath and start backing up toward the hallway, my eyes never leaving Chase's. "Thanks, Boy Scout."

His face breaks into a huge smile at the nickname, and those *dang* dimples make me grin, too, my heart fluttering.

When I get home, I'm out as soon as my head hits the pillow.

I don't talk to Chase at work the next day, but I feel his eyes on me.

It shouldn't excite me the way it does.

And when I get to Daddy's house that night, Chase is there again, cooking dinner and then pushing me out the door, saying he'll stay instead.

By the end of the week, we're in a routine, and as I watch Chase slip Daddy a Dr Pepper instead of a whiskey, I let myself imagine what it would be like if he were mine.

I don't hate it as much as I should.

Chapter 36

ALINA

"WANT TO CATCH A MOVIE TONIGHT?" JAX ASKS at brunch.

I look at Becca, sipping on her second mimosa and shoveling pancakes in her mouth. She shakes her head. "Can't. Have a date."

"*You?* Have a date?" I point at her, narrowing my eyes. Becca loves men, but she isn't the dating type. Growing up, she was a firm believer that commitment of any kind was a waste of time. Now that she's an adult and still living under her daddy's—a.k.a. the church's—thumb, that lack of commitment has only grown. I don't know if I've ever seen her go on an actual date in my life.

"Yep." She looks up, realizing we're both staring at her. "What?" she mumbles around a mouthful of pancake.

Jax laughs. "You can't just say something like that and not expect us to need more information. Who's the date with?"

She swallows, looking down at her plate. "You don't know him, he's from out of town."

I squint my eyes. "What's his name? How'd you meet him?"

She runs her fingers over her curly hair. "His name's Braxton and I met him online."

Jax is still chuckling, but his face drops when he sees the glare Becca is sending his way. "Tell me you're joking."

"And what about it, asshole? I like him. He's nice."

"He's *nice*?" I exclaim, sharing another look with Jax. "Who are you and what have you done with my best friend?"

She throws her arms up. "I just—don't you think it's time I start takin' life more seriously? Try to settle down? We're gettin' old as shit. I've got crow's feet, for God's sake."

My face scrunches. "Are you feelin' okay? What happened to the 'I don't do commitment' Becca?"

She grabs her mimosa, downing it before looking around for the server. "She grew up, I guess."

Jax gives me a "what the hell" look and I shrug in return.

"So that's a no from Becca who's busy getting busy with *Braxton*. That leaves you and me, sweetheart. Wanna get crazy tonight?" He grins, leaning his elbows on the table. "Maybe dinner *and* a movie?"

I smile, but my stomach flops while I try to think of an excuse for why I'm saying no. One that doesn't involve babysitting my drunk daddy and letting Chase cook me meals. "I can't. Gotta help Daddy prepare the guest room for Eli and his girl."

Becca makes a face and Jax sticks out his bottom lip. "Fine, ladies. Leave me all by myself. A lone cowboy riding into the night."

Becca snorts. "I'm sure you won't have any trouble findin' a replacement for the night. One that will be all too willin' to give you a *ride*."

Jax grips his heart. "That hurts, truly, Becs. I'm more than my gigantic cock."

"Oh? You into kinky shit?" She raises an eyebrow.

"I don't speak of private activities." Jax smiles, winking. "You've never been curious?"

"Um…no."

"Never wanted a one-way ticket on the Jackson express?" He wiggles his brows.

Becca gags. "Darlin', I'd break the train down."

I giggle into my sweet tea and take another sip.

"Anyway." Jax shifts his attention to me. "When's Eli getting here, sweetheart?"

"A little less than a week. That reminds me, Becca, you think your daddy can sit down with them and talk about havin' their weddin' at the church?"

Becca chokes on her drink, coughing until her eyes water and her hand smacks against her chest.

"Lord, are you all right?" I ask.

She wipes under her eyes. "He wants *my* old man to marry them?"

"Why not?" I frown at her. "Eli asked me about it the other day. I'm just the messenger."

"*Eli* asked?" She blinks at me. "What the hell's he expect me to do about it?"

My forehead wrinkles. *What's the big deal?* "Haven't you been helpin' around the church since summer break started? I mentioned it and he asked to see if you could work somethin' out."

She slams her body against the back of the chair. "Well, he's an idiot."

"Okay, that's it. What happened between you and Eli? You never used to have a problem with him, but anytime I bring him up, you get weird."

She rolls her eyes, tangling her hair in her fingers. "I don't get weird. I just think your brother's a jerk with a head big enough to take up the entire state of Tennessee. I never thought he'd come back here, let alone bring a little hussy of a girl wantin' to parade their love through the town."

"That's a little harsh," I chide. "We don't even know her."

She throws her hands up. "Ugh. You know what? I have to go. I need to get ready for my date."

"With Braxton. The 'Becca tamer.'" Jax pipes in.

He is *so* not helping.

Becca sends him a glare and throws her napkin down on the table. "Just for that, you can pay for brunch. I'll see y'all later."

We both watch with big eyes as she leaves the restaurant.

"What the hell was that about?" Jax asks.

"Beats me. She's been weird lately. I think maybe her and Eli got into it or somethin' when they were both in Florida."

"She's never said anything?" He tilts his head, staring after her.

I shrug. "Nope. She doesn't talk about it."

"Weird." He takes a bite of his food before sticking out his bottom lip. "You sure you can't come tonight? You're really gonna leave me all alone?"

"You're a big boy, Jax. I'm sure you'll find somethin' to do."

"I suppose I'll have to," he says.

I try to pay attention to Jax for the rest of brunch, but my mind is busy replaying Becca's actions. She's always been as stubborn as the day is long, so when she doesn't want to talk about something, there's no changing her mind. But I wish she'd tell me about Florida. I make a mental note to ask Eli next time I talk to him.

Enchiladas are on the menu for Saturday night dinner, courtesy of Chase. I haven't cooked a single thing all week, and I've gotten a solid eight hours of sleep each night, so I'm feeling better than I have in a while. Still, this weird family dynamic with Chase and Daddy should have alarm bells sounding in my head. Maybe this fuzzy feeling of comfort is making my ears numb to the ringing.

I've just taken my first bite when the doorbell rings. I look over at Daddy, furrowing my eyebrows. "You expectin' someone?"

"Who would I be expectin', Alina?" he barks.

The bell rings again. Chase stands before I can, putting his hand on my shoulder to keep me in place. I sit back down, keeping my ears strained so I can hear who it is.

"What the fuck are you doing here?"

Shoot. My fork drops and I close my eyes, guilt churning in my stomach. I should have known this would happen.

Before I can even think about defusing the situation, footsteps stomp through the hallway and a raging Jax enters the kitchen.

"Can I speak to you for a moment?" he hisses through clenched teeth.

"Sure." I scoot my chair back, laying my napkin on the table.

Chase is standing behind him, his fists clenched and hazel eyes stormy as they bounce between the two of us.

Jax knocks into his shoulder as he walks by.

I cringe, expecting Chase to react, but he doesn't.

He stands stoic, only the twitching of his jaw letting me know he's holding himself back.

When we reach the front porch, Jax spins to face me with a glare, the screen door slamming behind him.

"*This* is why you couldn't hang out with me tonight?"

"I told you I was gonna be here with Daddy." My voice is weak. I've never seen Jax upset like this.

"And you didn't think to mention you were playing house with Chase?"

"I'm not *playin' house* with him. He's just been showin' up. Helpin' out. It's not like I invited him over."

"But you didn't tell him to leave."

I look down, the guilt chiseling away at my insides. "No."

He lets out a disbelieving laugh, his hands on the top of his head. "I can't believe this, Lee. I mean, what the *fuck*?"

A bit of anger spikes through my middle. I get that he's upset about Chase, but it isn't his decision. It isn't his life. "Listen, you don't get to be mad at me, Jax. I didn't tell you because it's none of your business and I knew you'd react this way."

He rears back. "None of my *business*? Was it my business when you used my shoulder to cry on every time we'd go visit him?"

"Jax—"

"No." He cuts his hand through the air. "Let me ask you something, Lee. When he fucked around on you the same night your mom died…who was it that held you? Because it sure as shit wasn't him. Was it my *business* then?"

Tears well in my eyes, the words dying on my tongue. "Jax…"

His cheeks are rosy with his anger, and he steps in close, lowering his voice. "Is it really that easy?"

"Is what that easy?"

"To forgive him? To take him back like nothing happened?"

"It's not like that, I swear. We've just been friends and—"

"I've waited years for you to give me a chance, Alina. Fucking *years*, hoping his memory would loosen its grip on your heart enough to just let you fucking *see* me. Chase treated you like shit, and somehow you still choose him over me, every single goddamn time. Less than a month he's been back, and you just open your arms to him." He raises his face to the sky and his voice cracks. "You've never even given me your hand."

I feel like I might throw up. I swallow around the knot in my throat, searching for words to make this okay. "Jax, I… You know I love you."

He blows out a breath, pinching the bridge of his nose. "Just not as much as you love him, right?"

My clammy hands wring together. "Don't do that. It's different."

His fingers tease the chain around his neck as he hangs his head, shaking it slightly. "I'm gonna go."

He stomps by me and I reach out, grabbing the back of his shirt, trying to anchor him to me, my throat swelling. "You're my best friend, Teeth."

"Yeah, well, that's the problem, isn't it? I don't *want* to just be your friend."

I close my eyes.

"Do you hate me?" I whisper.

He doesn't turn around, but he sighs and his stance softens. "I don't think it's possible to hate you, Alina."

And then he walks down the steps of the front porch, and I watch helplessly as he peels out of the driveway.

It's not until he's gone that I collapse on the ground, covering my mouth to keep the sobs at bay.

This hurts.

I'm not sure how much time passes with me sitting outside, staring at the empty spot where Jax was, but I'm snapped out of my stupor when I hear the screen door open.

Chase sits next to me, his elbows resting on his knees and his eyes straight ahead. "Do you want me to go?"

I shake my head, a tear slipping down my cheek.

"Are you okay?"

I shake my head again. Another tear, and then another, until I'm crying all over again.

Chase wraps his arm around me, pulling me into his side. I lean into him, knowing I shouldn't accept his embrace but basking in the solace, nonetheless.

"I'm sorry," he says.

I bite my lip, keeping the words "It's not your fault" from escaping. Because it is. At least a little bit.

Eventually, we go back inside and finish dinner.

Daddy's already incoherent, and as I watch him, I can't help but feel relieved Jax didn't stick around. Things would have been much worse if he realized I kept Daddy's issues from him. The fissure in my stomach gapes wider and threatens to swallow me whole.

I don't feel happiness when I leave tonight.

I don't sleep soundly in my own bed.

Instead, I try to keep from drowning in my failures.

Like every other Sunday, I visit Mama's grave. There's nothing I wish more than to have her hold me and tell me everything will be all right, but I'll settle for spewing my broken heart all over her memory to help ease the ache.

By the time I get to Daddy's for the night, I'm feeling a bit more put together. Chase isn't coming, he has some business over in Nashville on Sundays, and honestly, it's a good thing he isn't here. After the blowout with Jax, I need some breathing room.

I'm getting lost in my feelings and forgetting how hard it was to find my way back last time.

But I guess my self-control is weak because I only make it through dinner before I give in to the urge to text him.

ME:

I think Daddy misses you.

I press send and toss my cell to the side, lay my head on the table, groaning. *Why did I do that?* My phone vibrates and I scramble to pick it back up.

CHASE:

Just him?

My stomach flutters.

ME:

Yep, just him. He's pouting in his recliner as we speak. He's gotten used to having you here and it doesn't feel the same when you're not.

I see the three dots appear and disappear over and over. *Stupid, Lee. You're stupid.*

CHASE:

I miss you, too.

The butterflies jump into my throat. I wish he was here and that's a dangerous thing for me to want. My mind goes back to the woman's voice I heard at his place.

Is he in a relationship? Is that why he went back?

ME:

What's in Nashville? Visiting friends?

I chew on my lip and spend the next ten minutes burning a hole through my phone with my stare. He doesn't respond and I start to curse my nosiness. *Is he with her right now?* Jealousy bubbles through my veins at the thought of some other woman getting all of his attention. Feeling his touch.

ME:

Sorry, forget I asked. Not my business.
Hope you have a good weekend.

I force myself to put my phone away, and it's not until that night when I'm lying in the guest room, trying to find Chase's scent on the pillows, that I pull it back out to check.

CHASE:

> You can ask me whatever you want. Have an early morning meeting with my therapist and then a group thing tomorrow night. Lots of that bullshit talking stuff you don't like.

A therapist. Does he talk about me?

I shake my head. Why would he? We're ancient history, and he definitely had a woman in his place last week. Heck, he moved on before we were even apart.

The thought's a dagger to the heart.

Asshole.

Just like that, the anger I've been missing rears its head. The more I focus on our past, the more I realize how naive I've been. Jax is right. I've been so stupid, letting him play me like he hasn't already broken all my strings.

I exit out of our text message and pull up Jax's instead.

ME:

> Can we talk?

I wait all night, but there's no reply.

Chapter 37

CHASE

THIS PAST WEEK WAS A BIT SURREAL. I'VE FALLEN into a new normal with Goldi and her dad. I went over there the first time because I could see the strain on her face, could sense it in the slump of her shoulders and the circles under her eyes, and I just wanted to give her the night off, let her get some rest. I *keep* going because I can't fucking help myself. I look forward to our conversations, even the ones with Mr. Carson. When he's not sloshed beyond recognition, there are still hints of the man underneath.

When I answered the door on Friday and Jax was on the other side, it was a rainbow of emotion. I've missed my best friend, but my anger and jealousy knowing he has Goldi burns the sadness away, leaving an anger in its place that I don't know how to tamp out. I hate it because it reminds me of when I was a kid, with emotions so big and trauma so strong I spun out of control constantly.

I don't know what was said between Jax and Goldi when they went out front, but inside, it was easy to hear the raised voices, muffled through the walls. *Did she not tell him about me?* The thought makes me feel dirty. Like a damn secret.

It *hurts*, and for the first time, I think I understand what Goldi felt like all those years ago when I kept our relationship hidden in the dark.

Needless to say, I was more than ready to see Doc over the weekend. There were a thousand things to unload and even more for him to read from my journal. He's always good at giving me guidance.

Especially on the Marissa front.

I've been getting messages from her since last Thursday. They started out innocent, asking how I was doing, wondering if we could still be friends. I responded because I didn't want to hurt her more than I already have, and I figured if we *could* be friends, maybe it would lessen the sting of the breakup. I quickly realized my mistake when the messages started to escalate. I was in my hotel room getting ready to see Doc the first time she sent a picture of her pussy. What the fuck am I supposed to do with that? I erased the image and didn't reply. More came in through the day, like clockwork—every hour on the hour—until I finally told her to knock it the fuck off. There hasn't been another one since, but I'm not an idiot, and I know it's only a matter of time before she reaches back out.

Despite all of that, I've been eager to get back to Sugarlake. Back to Goldi. Now that it's Monday, I'm tempted to go straight to the work site to see her, but I need to stop at the home office and do a few things first.

I'm rushing around, fumbling through the papers on my desk, when Sam walks in. He makes himself comfortable in the chair across from me, crossing his ankle on his knee.

I give a wave. "Hey, what's up?"

"Hey, son. Just checking in. How are things going with Tiny Dancers?"

"Great. We're ahead of schedule."

"I saw that. I knew you'd knock it out of the park. The owner giving you any flak?"

"Nah, I don't really see her too often." I narrow my eyes at him. *Does he know about Goldi working there?* "You'll never guess who the office manager is."

"Who?"

"Alina."

He sits forward, uncrossing his legs. "Craig's daughter, Alina?"

I can feel the happiness on my face as I think about her. *Damn, I can't wait to see her.*

Sam watches me, his jaw pinching more with every moment. "Be careful, Chase."

"What do you mean 'be careful'?"

"I mean…last time things went south with Alina, you disappeared for eight years. We just got you back. It would break Anna's heart if you were to leave again."

My smile drops along with my stomach. I thought it was beyond obvious the downfall of our relationship was on me. The fact he's insinuating otherwise is fucking crazy. "Are you blaming *Alina*?"

He watches me carefully. "I blame the circumstances. Anna still has a hard time accepting that Alina ran you out of town."

I frown. "She didn't run me out of town, what the hell are you talking about?"

"Well, you ran off without telling us anything and we were left to make our own assumptions. The heartbreak was written all over your face, Chase. It wasn't difficult to put two and two together."

I'm sure it was. I remember what it felt like—can't imagine how it came across to others.

Sam's eyes soften. "I've always loved Alina, you know that. I'm just saying maybe the two of you are better apart than together. Don't put everything you've worked for in jeopardy because of some old feelings from back when you were a kid."

I'm shocked this is even a conversation, and to be honest, it's pissing me off.

"A lot of things happened, and I know I never opened up to you or Anna, but I'll say this, and I'll say it to her, too…and please, listen close because I really don't want to have this conversation again. Alina was not the problem. It was all me. *I* was the fuckup. So, if you're gonna place blame somewhere, make sure it's in the right direction."

Sam rubs the back of his neck as he nods.

"Speaking of Alina, how come you didn't tell me about Mr. Carson?"

His face drops. "What do you mean?"

My chin raises and I squint my eyes. "What do you think I mean?"

"I have no damn clue." Sam laughs. "The truth is, after you left, it was hard for us to stay close with Craig. He was grieving, and being around Alina was hard for us. Especially for Anna. Can't really look at the girl and not feel the loss of both you and Lily."

My heart weighs heavy with his words, stomach sinking at the realization of how much my actions affected the way they are with Mr. Carson. *With Goldi.* "But you still saw Mr. Carson here at work, didn't you?"

Sam's head shakes and he purses his lips. "He took personal time after Gail's funeral and never came back. I've thought about reaching out over the years, but I never know what to say. Other than a wave here and there when I see him in the neighborhood, we haven't really talked."

I'm surprised as hell they didn't try harder with Mr. Carson. Honestly, I'm a little disappointed. But this does answer my question.

Sam doesn't know about his drinking.

Goldi's avoiding me. Instead of the shy smiles and eye contact that heats my veins, we're back to cold shoulders and turned heads. I'm willing to bet it's because of Jax. Once again, I feel like her dirty little secret and the feeling fucking sucks. I don't want to come between her and Jax, even though the thought of them together makes me fucking crazy. *Okay, that's a lie.* I'd love to come between them, make her realize it's *us* who are meant to be, but I'm not going to do that. If he makes her happy, I'll suffer through her friendship for the rest of my life and find a way to be content.

Work is busy, so I don't push a conversation with Goldi. If she wants to pretend we're back to being strangers, I'll let her be. But if she thinks I'm not showing up to her dad's tonight, she's in for a shock. As long as I can help, I will.

There isn't much conversation during dinner. Mr. Carson's in one of his moods and has learned quickly if he has nothing nice to say to Alina, he needs to keep his fucking mouth shut—at least when I'm around. But that tension that had all but disappeared between Goldi and me is back, twisting the air and pulling it tight, letting me know things are *not* okay with us. I'm racking my brain to figure out what the hell it is I did to make this sudden one-eighty shift.

I set her dad up in his recliner after we eat and hang out with him until he starts to doze off and then I head back to the kitchen to check in on Goldi.

She's at the sink, soapsuds up to her arms as she slowly washes the dishes. It looks like she's in a trance, staring out the window, lost in her thoughts. I walk up beside her, wedging myself between the corner of the fridge and the counter, watching her rub the wet sponge over the surface of a red plate.

"You feeling good today, Goldi?" Every time I use her nickname, I hold my breath, waiting to see if she gets upset. I've slipped up a few times and she hasn't called me on it, so I use it now to test the waters.

Her arms pause and her jaw tightens, but she doesn't correct me. She just looks back down to the plate and resumes washing it.

I cross my arms, my forearms flexing. "Did I do something to upset you?"

She peeks over at me but bites her lip to keep from saying anything.

I chuckle in frustration. "Now I *know* something's up. It's not like you to hold back. You finally learn how to hone that filter?" I go for teasing, but it misses the mark as she drops the plate and sponge in the water, twisting her head to shoot me a sharp glare.

Even with the rage that swirls around her irises, she's fucking beautiful.

"Don't act cute," she hisses, pointing a soapy finger at me.

I raise my brows and gesture at myself. "Me? What am *I* doing?"

"You know exactly what you're doin'. Comin' in here, takin' care of me and Daddy like you have any right. Tryin' to weave your way back into my good graces, and make me forget about the past. Well, I'm done playin' your games, Chase Adams. I won't be made a fool of again."

"Whoa…that is *not* what I'm trying to do. There isn't some ulterior motive here, Goldi."

She slams her hands on the edge of the sink, the sharp slap making me wince. "Stop callin' me that! You don't *get* to call me that anymore. It's confusin'. Makes me feel like we're still…"

"Still what?" I ask, moving closer to her, my heart racing.

She exhales. "Still us."

My insides burn at her words, and I take another step. "We'll always be us, Goldi."

Her head jerks, eyes like ice. "I don't accept that."

"You don't have to." I shrug. "Doesn't change the fact."

"Here's a fact. You were sleepin' with someone else while my mama was *dyin'*, so…" She inhales a shaky breath, her voice breaking. "You can't just come back here and expect things to magically be okay."

My stomach drops to my feet. *What? Does she think…* I cover my mouth, the realization she's spent the last eight years thinking I cheated on her making bile burn my throat. *What the fuck.* I grip her hips, turning her to face me. Her soapy hands soak through my shirt as she tries to push me away, but I glide my palms up her sides until I'm firmly gripping her shoulders, anchoring her in place. I need to keep her here. Make sure she hears what I'm about to say. This is important.

"Alina…" She stops fighting. "I've done a lot of things I regret when it comes to you. To *us*. Got lost in my head and let you slip through my fingers, instead of treating you like the fucking queen you are. I know I'm guilty of that."

She looks to the side. I put my fingers under her chin and turn her face back. "I have *never* cheated on you. There isn't anything in this world that would make me pick a quick thrill over what we had. What we still have."

"I don't believe you," she whispers.

My gut tightens, but I'm not surprised by her words. "That picture on Facebook looked bad. Missing your recital was bad. Being blind to Lindsay manipulating me, allowing her to come between us, was beyond bad. But that's all it was, Alina. Lindsay's manipulations and my fucked-up brain thinking she was my penance. A way to right my wrongs with Lily and my mom."

Tears well in her eyes. I'm desperate to get it all out while I have her attention. "I passed out that day. Do you remember me saying I was about to take a nap?"

She nods.

"Lindsay was there, which I admit, was fucking stupid. I'm not justifying my actions. She turned off my phone and slipped into my bed. But, baby, I was *asleep*. You have to know—" My voice cracks, and I swallow around the lump in my throat. "Lindsay was a horrible mistake, but she wasn't that kind of mistake. You have to know I would never do that to you."

She gazes at me, searching for the truth. "I don't know anything about you. Not anymore."

The side of my mouth lifts, even though my chest feels like a bleeding puncture wound.

"You know that's not true. When it comes to us? We'll always know each other." I move my touch from under her chin, dipping down to her neck, her pulse jumping beneath my fingertips. "We could go our entire lives without speaking, and still, I'd know you in the next one."

She exhales a shaky breath, and I rest my forehead against hers. Her hands are still on my chest and I grab one, moving it until her palm is resting on my heart. "Do you feel that?" I whisper. "Feel how fast it's racing? Feel what you do to me?"

"Yes," she whispers.

"My heart fucking beats for you, Goldi. So please, let's not pretend we don't know each other. The sole reason for my *existence* is to know you. In this life, in the next…it doesn't matter."

Her fingers tighten, bunching the fabric of my shirt.

"I'm not asking you to forgive me. I'm not even asking for us to be together, although, if that's something you decide you want, I'll grab on and never let go. But it doesn't matter. Call it kismet, call it fate, call it whatever you want, it doesn't change the fact your soul is meant for mine." My heart slams against my chest, trying to break through my skin to lay itself in her hands. "*Knowing* you is the only thing I'm sure of."

She leans back, her searching gaze meeting mine. "You really didn't sleep with Lindsay?"

"That's what you got out of all that?" I move my hand that was on her neck up to her cheek and cup it. She turns into my touch, and fuck, I'd spend every night for the rest of my life with just this, and I swear it would be enough. "I never slept with her. The only person I've ever wanted is you."

The air thickens, weaving around us and tightening until I'm sure I'll burst if I don't get closer. My grip strengthens, pulling her against me. Her hands clench my shirt and she rises up on her toes.

"Chase—" she breathes.

My eyes are locked on her mouth, desperate for just a fucking taste of her. I lean my head down, lightly grazing my lips across hers. The touch shoots a tingle through my body, and my stomach somersaults with anticipation.

Slam.

The sound of a crash breaks us apart. Goldi's eyes widen as she stares at me, her hand touching her lips. She turns and runs into the living room, and I follow.

Her dad's fallen out of his recliner, passed out on the floor.

She sighs and walks over to him. "Daddy," she says, even though we both know once he's out, he's out.

I want to go back to a few seconds ago, but instead of pulling her into my arms, it's Mr. Carson I go for.

By the time I get him settled in bed, she's already gone.

Chapter 38

ALINA

KNOWING CHASE DIDN'T SLEEP WITH LINDSAY IS A balm to the wounds of my heart, although it doesn't change the fact that he put her before me time and time again. Maybe I shouldn't believe him. After all, it's easy for someone's words to be just that. Words. I should know, I've been a sucker for Chase's a million times. But it's exhausting trying to hold on to the anger after all these years, especially when all I'm really searching for is peace. Plus, he's not the same boy I once knew. He's changed, grown. Probably more than I have, to be honest. He's seeing a *therapist*. That's more than I've ever done, and Lord knows I could use one.

I called in sick to work on Tuesday, unable to face him after our almost-kiss. I *did* send him a text asking him not to come to Daddy's that night, and even though I wasn't sure he would listen, he did. The real kicker is that I missed him when he wasn't there. Somehow, he's wormed his way back into every single piece of me, and I don't want to fight it anymore.

I've decided I'm not going to.

Work isn't the best place to air all of our dirty laundry, so I'm hoping he'll come back over to Daddy's and we can talk after dinner. I haven't even thought about how I'm going to tell Jax or Becca. Seeing as how Jax still isn't speaking to me, I figure that's something I'll worry about later. I'm a little nervous about their reaction, but it doesn't really make a difference either way. Chase makes me happy. He did back when we were kids, before things went to crap, and I know deep in my bones he'd make me happy for the rest of my life if I would only let him. It's like he said… we're meant to know each other.

The butterflies flop around in my belly as I pull into Tiny Dancers and see Chase's truck. I search for him when I get inside, but I know he isn't in the front area. The pull in the air whenever he's near is missing.

Walking into the office, I stop short. Chase sits in the desk chair, leaned back with his feet up and ankles crossed, dark hair mussed and looking like he doesn't have a care in the world. My heart skips at the sight of him.

"Hi." My nervous energy shows itself on my cheeks.

"We missed you here yesterday." The chair creaks when he stands and walks around the desk, resting against the edge of it and crossing his arms, his muscles flexing and those veins running from his hands and disappearing beneath the sleeves of his shirt. "Missed you last night, too."

My heart speeds up, beating so hard it's bound to burst out of my chest. "I just needed some time to think."

I don't have to be looking at him to feel the way he's taking inventory of my body.

"You planning on keeping me away again tonight?"

His voice is low. Raspy, even.

I raise my face to his as I shake my head no. He steps in closer, the tips of his shoes brushing the closed toes of my pumps, his chest grazing against mine with every inhale.

"So, you've had enough time to *think*?" he murmurs.

My mouth dries as the energy crackles between us. My insides are on fire, the heat between my legs threatening to consume me, and I'm tempted to climb him like a tree right here in this office. Anything to alleviate this ache.

There's a knock on the door and we jump apart.

"It's open," I holler, trying to get a hold of myself.

Benny opens the door and peeks his head in. "Boss? You got a minute? We could use an extra set of hands. Matt just went home sick for the day."

Chase clears his throat. "Yep, I'll be right out. Just finishing up with Alina."

He nods and leaves the door open as he walks away.

Chase is undeterred, stepping back into me as soon as he's gone.

My hands fly to his chest, fingers caressing the defined muscles before I can stop myself. "Can we talk tonight?"

"We can do anything you want, baby."

Baby. My heart dances inside my chest, and I can't stop the way my lips curl up. "Good. I'll see you tonight, then."

His dimples come out to play as he gives me a blinding smile, and his calloused hand cups my cheek, causing a shiver to race along my spine. A kiss brushes against my skin, so close to my lips I can taste him. Heat flares from my cheeks down to my toes.

"I'll see you tonight," he whispers.

He doesn't wait for a response, just brushes by me and closes the door on his way out.

I'm nervous the rest of the day. Like, hands sweating, knees knocking, body buzzing nervous. I feel like I'm a teenager again, about to leap into something I know nobody will approve of. Chase and I still have some things to work through—I know that. Hurts like what he caused don't go away overnight, but I can't keep holding the sins of a boy against the soul of the man.

He beat me to Daddy's, like usual. I see his truck as I pull in behind it. Laughter filters through the front door and I smile, happiness spreading through my veins at the thought that Daddy has someone to talk to. It just further cements the fact that moving forward with Chase is the right choice. I want him here. With us. With *me*.

I walk into the kitchen and stumble over my feet, my stomach dropping to the floor when I realize the laugh didn't come from Chase.

It came from Eli.

I'm frozen in the doorway taking in the scene.

Chase is at the stove, sautéing something in a pan, while Eli and Daddy sit at the kitchen table. There's a beer in front of both of them and a pretty strawberry-blond thing sitting next to Eli. They haven't realized I'm here, and I soak in my long-lost brother. It's been a long time.

He's always been a fit guy—basketball keeps you in peak physical condition—but the last time I saw him in person was eight years ago. He's grown up. There's a twist in my heart knowing I didn't get to experience his transition into adulthood. He looks relaxed. His legs are stretched out in front of him, so long they touch the other side of the table, and his hair—the same sandy-blond shade as mine—is longer than he used to keep it. If it wasn't for his slicked-back city style, I imagine pieces would be flopping on his forehead. He's tan, probably from the Florida sun, and his smile is so easy, so laid-back, that a bit of anger flares to life in my chest.

Because, *of course*, he has it easy. He hasn't been here.

Eli's eyes are still crinkled from laughter when he sees me in the doorway. "Hey, Lee. About time you got here. Pops and I were about to start in on all of your embarrassing stories."

"Eli." I glance over at Chase. His back is to me since he's at the stove, but he twists around and winks. Clearly, he's the one cooking dinner. For *all* of us. This is…strange.

Eli kicks the leg of the chair across from him, making it screech against the tiled floor, and I walk toward it, falling into the seat and staring at him. "I thought y'all weren't gettin' here until Friday."

"We decided to come early. Not excited to see me?" Eli chuckles. Like it's *funny* he just showed up. Like it's no big deal he's able to sit down and laugh with Daddy as though nothing's changed.

My nails dig into the tops of my thighs as the resentment builds.

"Just surprised is all." I nod toward who I'm assuming is his fiancée. "Big city life make you forget your manners, Eli? You plannin' on makin' any introductions?"

Eli's smile drops. The blond reaches across him, sticking her hand out. "I've heard a lot about you, Alina. I'm Sarah, this big guy's woman." She jerks her elbow into his chest with her words.

I take her hand, smiling at her easygoing nature. *She seems nice.* "Pleasure's all mine, Sarah. Welcome to Sugarlake."

Her sky-blue eyes twinkle against her pale skin as she tucks her long, glossy, straight hair behind her ear. "It's totally my fault we're here two days early. I wanted to have time to sightsee before we start nailing down wedding details."

I stifle the smirk that's creeping onto my face and look over to see Chase's shoulders shaking. The fact she thinks she can "sightsee" Sugarlake only shows how little Eli has talked about his hometown.

"Well, I'm sure you'll have plenty of time to see everything we have to offer." I lock eyes with Eli. "Speakin' of weddin' details, I'm just gonna give y'all Becca's number so you can call her yourself."

His shoulders stiffen. "What? I don't want to do that. Why can't you just talk to her for me like I asked you to?"

His tone grates on my nerves. "For one thing, Eli, I'm not your dang servant. For another, I *did* ask her and she wasn't exactly responsive." I think back to how weird she got when I brought it up. "What happened with you two, anyway?"

Eli rests his hand on Sarah's thigh, his eyes hardening. "Nothing."

I laugh. His accent is barely noticeable after years of being away. "Well, she gets agitated whenever I bring you up. Acted like I was the Devil himself for askin' her to help. I'm not in the business of tickin' off my best friend, so like I said…I'll give you her number."

Sarah pats the hand on her thigh and smiles at me. "That'd be great, Alina. I have no problem giving her a call and setting something up."

Eli grimaces.

I let it go for now, not wanting to delve into that conversation with an audience. "How'd y'all get here, anyway?"

"Pops picked us up a couple hours ago," Eli says.

My head turns sharply toward Daddy. "You *drove* to the airport to get them?"

"Why wouldn't I? He's my boy. If he needs me, then I'll be there."

My teeth grind. Of course, he'd be there for Eli. Even though *I'm* the only one who's been here for him. "So you knew they were comin' in today and didn't tell me?"

He shrugs and necks his beer. I wonder how many he had before he left to pick them up. Too many to be on the road, that's for sure.

I glance at my lap, trying to stem the tears that want to bubble up. Eli's eyes bounce between us, the wrinkle between his brows deepening.

His stare continues to burn all through dinner, because Daddy doesn't put his best foot forward for company. Try as he might, the drink always wins the battle. By the time we're having coffee and dessert, he's switched to whiskey and is well on his way past coherent.

"You want to come with us tomorrow, Lee? Help me show Sarah the town?" Eli asks.

I choke on my coffee, surprised he's inviting me, and irritated he thinks we can just hang out like no time has passed.

"I have to work."

He smacks his forehead. "Right. It's so strange to see you grown. Sometimes I forget."

"Maybe it wouldn't be so strange if you'd been around for all the years in between." My face muscles burn from the effort of keeping my smile in place.

"Alina. Mind your manners. We got…we got company." Daddy's voice is loud but slurred. The whiskey makes his tongue thick and his mind sluggish.

Chase shifts in his seat and I scoff. "I'm just speakin' truth, Daddy."

Eli sighs. "You don't know what you're talking about, Alina."

My eyebrows raise. "Oh, no? Why don't you enlighten me then, big head?"

"*Don't* call me that," he snaps. "Don't you ever fucking call me that."

My brows shoot to my hairline.

He runs a hand over his face and continues, "I would have if you had ever taken the time to ask."

My mouth parts, surprise rendering me speechless at his words. *I ask... Don't I?*

"Your mama. She would be disappointed in you, girl." Daddy points his finger at me, the usual sneer on his face.

The table falls silent.

Chase's chair scratches against the floor and he comes around to stand behind me, squeezing my shoulders. "Craig, with all due respect, it's not Alina that Mrs. Carson would be disappointed in right now."

Daddy's eyes flare and he slams his coffee cup on the table. "You think you can speak to me that way just 'cause I been lettin' you... You've been...playin' house here with my girl?"

Chase doesn't back down. "I think I've made it clear that you disrespecting your daughter won't ever be something I'll tolerate, regardless of where we are."

Daddy raises out of his chair, pointing at Chase. He wobbles, unsteady on his feet, and has to catch himself on the edge of the table.

"Pops, you okay?" Eli is half standing, his eyes volleying between the three of us.

Sarah sits next to him, her mouth gaping open. *Welcome to the family.*

"Of course he's not okay. He's never okay," I spit, glaring at him. "You would know that if you had spent more than ten minutes here in the past eight years."

"Sis—"

"Don't you 'sis,' me, Eli."

"I'm fine, damnit!" Daddy's voice roars, cutting off the argument and blanketing the room. "And I'm a goddamn adult. *I'm* the parent, and this—this is *my* house." He points to Chase and me. "You two, go on…get. I don't want you here."

"Pops," Eli whooshes out.

Tears fill my eyes, but I straighten my shoulders and raise my chin. "I don't need this anyway." I look at Eli. "Have fun catchin' up on your missed years with Daddy. I'm sure he and this town will be thrilled to have you back. Sarah, it was nice to meet you. I'm so sorry you had to see this." I stand and face Chase. "Come on, let's go for a drive."

"Anywhere you want to go, baby." He slides his hand down my arm, tangling our fingers, leading me out the door. Away from my dysfunctional family.

I'll deal with them tomorrow.

Tonight, I think I'd like to hang out at the lake with the boy who's always been bigger than the stars.

Chapter 39

CHASE

BETWEEN SUNDAY NIGHT'S ALMOST-KISS AND Wednesday morning, I've had a lot of time to think. About Goldi. About me. Our past. Our future. About how perfect she is and how I'd spend the rest of my life loving the hell out of her if only she'd let me.

I used to think I didn't deserve her. That I couldn't be who she needed me to be. Hell, I still don't think I was wrong; that boy was in no shape to handle Goldi. But I'm a man now. I've weathered the storms and forged through the rubble of living a life without her. I don't want to know that type of emptiness anymore.

She may be with Jax, but she was mine first.

I'm not surprised when she doesn't show up for work, even though I know she isn't sick. I figured she'd be scared off by what almost happened between us. What *keeps* almost happening between us. She better buckle up, because if she thought I was hard to handle before I decided to fight for her, she has no clue how difficult I'll be now.

She lets me touch her in the office. Lets me call her Goldi. *Baby.* The sudden change in her demeanor makes me dizzy, but it's not unwelcome. I'm fucking giddy over it.

I show up to her dad's house eager for our "talk." When I see Eli and his girl sitting at the kitchen table, laughing with Mr. Carson and sharing beers over their memories, my stomach sinks with worry. I don't think Goldi knows what she's about to walk into, but fuck, I'm glad I'm here, so she doesn't have to face it alone.

All through dinner, I keep my eye on her, assessing her face, watching her body language. I know the bough is about to break before it happens. I should have guessed it would be her father that adds the pressure to make it snap.

I won't allow his disease to be an excuse for treating Goldi like a punching bag. It's beyond obvious he hasn't healed from his wife's death and she's taken the brunt of the fallout. She lost her mom, her dad, her brother, and me all in one go. My heart weeps for what she's had to endure.

I'm thankful when she decides to get us out of the situation, instead of feeding into the toxic environment of her family dynamic, and even though she asked for a drive, I know where she really wants to go—what she really needs.

Fuck her family for making her deal with shit like this. For the thousandth time, I wonder why Jax and Becca aren't around to help her carry the weight, but I'm pretty confident she hasn't told them. Shame is a hell of an emotion. I felt it every day with my mom.

We get to the lake and I pull into our usual spot. When I look over at Goldi, her face is drawn and she's lost in her thoughts. I reach out, tucking a strand of hair behind her ear.

Come back to me, baby.

She turns, smiling. "Thanks for bringin' me here. How'd you know this is exactly what I needed?"

"How many times do I have to tell you I know you before you start to believe me?"

She takes a deep breath, hopping out of the truck and running around the back. She jumps in the bed and starts laying out the blanket.

My heart skips as I watch her. She's so comfortable in my truck, by my side, with my things. *With me.* I'm so busy staring, I don't make a move to leave my seat. She pushes her hair out of her face and glances at me, her hands on her hips.

She speaks loud, making sure I hear every word through the back window. "Well, Chase Adams...you just gonna sit there like a dud, or you plannin' on comin' back here to woo me?"

My stomach somersaults as I open my door and walk around, leaning my arms over the side of the truck bed. I arch a brow. "Who said anything about wooing?"

She plops down, crossing her legs, her eyes twinkling. "I did. Just now. Your ears broke?"

"Maybe I don't woo. You know it's never been my strong suit."

She rises on her knees, scooting closer to the side of the truck. "Lucky you have me here to practice on then, huh."

My heart skips. "Is that what this is? Practice?"

"No," she whispers, pushing her body against the truck's metal frame. "This is the main event."

My eyes follow her fingers as they slide up my forearms and rest on my shoulders. Every nerve lights up at her touch. "Are you saying what I think you are?"

Her cheeks flush and suddenly pink is my favorite color. She leans her forehead against mine and her breath fans my face. "I'm tired of bein' angry with you."

My lungs squeeze tight. "You are?"

She nods.

"What would you rather be, instead?"

"Yours."

I'm on her in the next breath, stealing the remnants of her words. Drowning in her forgiveness. Her mouth opens immediately, warm honey and vanilla coating my senses and slinking through my veins, heating me up from the inside.

Goddamn.

My entire being groans from the taste of her. *Finally.*

I reach around the back of her head to pull her in closer, my fingers knotting in her hair. I tug on the strands, and she gives me the sweetest moan. *Fuck this truck for being in my way.*

She rises up on her knees, leaning over the edge until her breasts push into my chest, her mouth pressing harder against mine. Her tongue delves deeper, then retreats only to be replaced by her teeth nipping my bottom lip.

Arousal flares, blood rushing to my groin.

The sound of laughter down the bank interrupts the moment and has me slowing our kiss, trying to regain some sense. Her hands clutch the fabric of my shirt, pulling me back, like she's desperate for more. I've dreamed of this moment, so I give in, losing myself in the euphoria of her touch.

Finally, I break away, my chest heaving.

Goldi grins at me, her eyes glazed, her cherry lips swollen.

My soul fucking sings.

I peck her lips again because I can't help myself, trailing a line of kisses along her face until I reach her ear. "Promise you're mine?"

She smiles against my cheek. "Cross my heart and hope to die."

JOURNAL ENTRY #347

SHE'S MINE. I'LL NEVER LOSE HER AGAIN.

Chapter 40

ALINA

CHASE AND I KISSED OUR WAY BACK TOGETHER, and all I want is to drag him to my place and make up for all the lost years between us. Instead, he's walking me to my door and leaving me there, just a big ball of pent-up hormones.

He says he's trying to be a gentleman.

Regardless, I'm floating through my tiny apartment on a cloud, feeling lighter than I have in years. I had forgotten what it was like to become Chase Adams's girl, and I'm basking in the happiness. There are still a lot of things that we need to deal with. Things I know we'll have to work through, but I'm spending the rest of tonight lost in my joy.

Jax still hasn't talked to me, and I know he's been around town because Becca's been keeping tabs on him. I call and text every day, but the only response is him saying he needs some space. It sucks, and I hate that I've hurt him.

I'm scared of what he'll do when he finds out about Chase and me. I don't want to lose him, but I'm no longer willing to give up my chance at happiness to appease somebody else. Not even

Jax. That being said, I don't want him to think I'll let him disappear from my life like he hasn't been the best thing in it. I grab my phone to send him a text. Again.

ME:

You don't have to respond. I know you probably won't anyway. That's okay. I just wanted to tell you again that I'm sorry for hurting you. And I hope you'll be at brunch on Saturday. I miss you, Teeth.

Sadness bubbles in my chest, breaking through my haze of happiness. I tap the phone against my mouth, praying for a response, but I don't really expect one, so when it vibrates against my lips, I startle. My phone drops onto the ground and I lean down quickly to grab it.

CHASE:

Made it home safe.

I smile.

ME:

Good. Is it weird if I already miss you?

CHASE:

No. Is it weird that I've spent the last eight years missing you?

My heart skips. I wish he had stayed at my place.

ME:

Are you free tomorrow night? My place is small, but it's all mine. And it's...cozy.

CHASE:

Damn, I wish I fucking could. I promised Anna I'd help her out tomorrow night with some planning for Sam's retirement party.

I try to tamp down the disappointment because I'm happy he's so close to his parents. I used to be pretty close to them, too. Anna was like a second mother to me, but after Lily ran away, things changed. When Mama died and Chase was gone for good, our families stopped talking altogether. Not that I noticed at the time, or would have cared either way. Still, there have been a few instances where I've seen Anna in passing, and the coldness in her eyes stings because there used to be only warmth.

My phone vibrates again, bringing me out of my thoughts.

CHASE:

How about Friday evening, you come over to my place and I'll cook you dinner? Work on that whole "wooing" thing.

ME:

Yeah, that's a good idea. You really need the practice. Will I see you tomorrow?

CHASE:

You couldn't keep me away if you tried.

I bite my lip, grinning. This feels good.

My eyes are burning from staring at the office computer, and a headache is on the verge of turning into a migraine. I am beyond ready for this day to be over. I've been doing menial tasks, like usual, but for some reason, it's harder than normal to be content with my job today. I'm stuck back here pushing papers when all I really want to do is teach dance. I heave a sigh and rub the palms of my hands into my eye sockets, trying to alleviate the pressure. My phone is on the desk next to me and when it rings, I don't answer, just watch it move across the desk.

I snap out of my daze long enough to realize it may have been my boss calling, so I grab it and light up the screen.

Jax.

It's three in the afternoon. Hardly a time where I'd be able to answer, which is probably why he called right now. An alert pops up letting me know he left a voicemail and my lips purse, my insides twisting at the thought of what it will say. I think I'll wait until I'm home to listen, just in case it's something awful, like him never wanting to see me again or that I'm the biggest mistake he's ever made in his life. I don't know if my heart can handle that kind of pain. Not when I've been so happy for the past twenty-four hours.

I think of Chase and the anxiety in my stomach unravels, the threads floating around until they twist up my insides for an entirely different reason.

My knees crack when I stand and stretch, my muscles burning. I've been sitting in the office for hours and I would kill for some caffeine. I make my way to the break room off the hallway and almost cry at the sight of freshly brewed coffee. I've just finished pouring myself a cup when hands touch my waist, making me jump. Hot liquid sloshes over the edge of my mug, spilling onto the Formica countertop.

My stomach jolts before settling with a simmer that blazes through my veins. I lean against the hard body that's pressed against me.

"Do you have any idea how fucking sexy you look right now?" Chase's voice rumbles in my ear, his nose trailing the length of my neck. Goose bumps blossom down my arms.

I close my eyes at the sensation and smile.

His fingers tighten and he pushes his hips into me. I can feel every single hard inch of him pressed against the back of my pencil skirt. *How have I gone without him for so long?* That simmer starts to boil.

Chase groans. "You like teasing me, don't you? Prancing around in that tight little skirt, knowing that every man here is wishing they could touch what's mine." He traces the curve of my hips, moving up until he's teasing the underside of my breasts. His hands rise and fall with each stuttered breath I take.

I glance at the open door. *Anyone could walk by and see this.* A shot of arousal rushes through me, my legs becoming unsteady from the rush. His thumbs brush over my nipples. The ghost of his touch tortures me. I wish he'd just rip off my blouse so I could feel him on my skin. He leans down, the tips of his hair tickling my shoulder as he bites my neck, gently. The thought that he might leave a mark makes a moan slip through my lips.

"Fuck, Goldi." He rests his forehead on the back of my head, his breathing deep and ragged. I push my ass against him, desperate to feel how much I affect him. He groans, pressing his thick length into me, thrusting slightly. I'm slick between my thighs. I press my legs together, worried my wetness will drip down them from how turned on I am.

Footsteps make us break apart, and I lean forward, grabbing a napkin to look like I'm cleaning up the forgotten spill. Chase moves to my side, cocking his hip against the countertop.

Benny and a couple of other guys walk into the room. Suddenly the air is stifling. I can feel the heat in my cheeks, my excitement at Chase's touch still surging through me, and I wonder if everyone else can feel the tension. I don't dare look up to see.

Chase, on the other hand, is unperturbed. I sneak a glance at him and he's smirking at me.

There's muffled conversation, but for the life of me, I can't tell what's being said over the pounding in my ears. I take deep breaths, my fingers tightening on the soggy napkin I'm still holding. Benny and the guys are sitting at the small round table in the middle of the room. Chase has his arms crossed, and he's still grinning at me with that knowing look in his eyes.

"What?" I try to scowl.

Chase's smile widens. "I didn't say anything."

"You didn't have to."

"Mmmm," he hums. He steps closer, grabbing a mug and the

coffeepot. His arm brushes against mine with the movement, and I suck in a breath. The fire in my body rages, still lit up from his earlier touch.

"You going to your dad's tonight?"

I frown. I don't want to think about Daddy or Eli right now. I'd much rather stay lost in my Chase bubble. "Nope. He's got Eli here. What's he need me for?"

Chase eyes me over the rim of his mug.

My throat tightens painfully. Eli hasn't even tried to talk to me. I know he's busy with Sarah and Daddy, but I thought he'd at least reach out. It's sad, realizing you don't know your own flesh and blood. His words from last night briefly run through my mind, but I brush them away. It's not *my* fault I don't know him. I won't let him place blame on me for his distance.

Chase levels me with a stare. "I'll be at Sam and Anna's for most of the night, but call me if you need anything. Or if you just want to talk. Say hi. Let me hear your voice."

I grin and his eyes spark.

He leans in close, placing his coffee mug on the counter. "I better get back to work."

I glance at his cup. He didn't even drink any of it. His hand brushes against my side, squeezing. He walks away, smacking one of the guys playfully on the back on his way out.

It's not until I get home from work that I find the courage to listen to Jax's voicemail.

"Hey, sweetheart. Sorry I'm just returning your calls. I've been…well, you know. Anyway—" He clears his throat. "I miss you, girl. I was hoping you were free tonight and maybe I could swing by to talk? I don't know. Let me know."

I fumble with my phone, trying to get my fingers to work

properly long enough to call him back, but he doesn't answer. *Of course.* We're forever playing phone tag. I send him a text instead.

ME:

Yes! I'll be home all night. You can stop by whenever. I miss you, too.

He doesn't write back, but there's a knock at the door a few hours later. I'm in pajamas—at the beginning stages of a movie marathon—a tub of ice cream in my hands. I jump, nerves making me jittery.

Jax has a soft smile on his face when I open the door, and the sight of him makes my panic dissipate. "Hiya, Teeth."

"Hey, sweetheart. Big night planned?" He quirks a brow at my attire and I look down. There may or may not be a chocolate ice cream stain on my holey Sugarlake High dance team shirt, and I know my hair is a knotted mess on my head.

"Ya get what ya get. Wanna come in?" I open the door wider and he walks through, going straight to the couch and making himself comfortable.

Good. This is a good sign.

I watch him closely as I sit, folding my legs underneath me. He stares, his leg crossed over his knee, his arm thrown on the back of the cushions. He seems relaxed. I chew on my lip, waiting for him to say something.

He sighs, running a hand through his hair. "You're making me tense, sweetheart. Cut it out. I'm not mad."

I look up from where I'm picking at my fingers. "You're not?"

"No. I mean…I was. I was *pissed* you've been spending time

with Chase, but I just needed a few days to lick my wounds. Once I calmed down, I realized how much of a dick I was."

"Jax, *I* was the one who said things to you I can't take back. You've been everything to me for so long, and I've taken you for granted. And I'm sorry—" My voice breaks. "I'm so sorry for how I've made you feel."

His eyes hold mine, emotion pouring out of them. "I forgive you. And I'm sorry for making you feel like you couldn't come to me. Like you couldn't tell me about Chase." He leans forward, grabbing my hands in his. "You're my best friend, Alina May. I love you, and even though I wish like hell you were mine, I'll live the rest of my life happy as long as you're in it."

Relief floods through me, dousing the burning ache in my gut. I squeeze his hands. "You deserve the everything kind of love, Teeth."

He chuckles, pulling back, but I grip his hands tighter.

"You'll find it someday. Mark my words, it's gonna knock you on your ass, and I'll be right there, front row. You just wait and see."

A tear trails down his face as he swallows, and my heart twists. I've never seen Jax cry before.

"Damn, you're a bitch. I can't stay mad at you to save my life." He laughs.

I want to grab his laughter and hold on for dear life because what I'm about to say might steal it away.

"There is somethin' you should know."

He groans, throwing his body against the couch and running his hands over his face. "Don't tell me, Lee."

"I have to."

"You're back with him, aren't you?"

"I am, and I love you, Jax, but I won't apologize for it."

His hands drop into his lap, a sigh leaving his lips. "You don't need to apologize to me, sweetheart. I just hope you know what the hell you're doing. He doesn't deserve you."

I nod, knowing this was the way he'd feel. "The boy he was didn't deserve me. But he's changed, Jax. Truly. You should talk to him and you'll see it, too."

"Yeah, well... I'll be at Sam's retirement party next weekend, so I'm sure I'll get my chance." He grimaces. Clearly, he isn't ready to forgive.

If I were a smart woman, I'd take this heavy moment between us and spill all my secrets. Tell him how Daddy's a sea of struggle and I'm drowning in his wake.

But I don't.

I've already seen the grief in his eyes tonight, I don't want to see pity there, too. So instead, I press play on my remote, and we spend the rest of the night getting lost in tales with happy endings.

Chapter 41
ALINA

I'M FIXING TO SNAP ON REGINA. IT'S NOT A GOOD look as her employee, but if she doesn't take a step away from Chase, I may just lose it. I've been standing in the corner of the dance studio, watching them have a "meeting" for the past twenty minutes. Regina told me I could leave for the day, but fat chance of that with the way she's been eyeing my man since she walked in.

I thought she was married, but she isn't wearing a wedding ring. *I bet she just took it off.*

Chase is taking me back to his place tonight for dinner, and instead of going home to freshen up like I originally planned, I'm here watching them like a jealous girlfriend.

I'm too far away to hear the conversation, but it doesn't matter. I know he's going over everything they've completed for the week. Regina wanted brand-new floor-to-ceiling windows installed in the main dance studio. She said it would help drum up business if people on the street could look right in and see the classes. He installed them today, and of course, she just *had* to come in and see them. It makes sense, seeing as how this is her place. But did she really need to undo those extra buttons on her blouse beforehand?

I watch her giggle and preen for what feels like hours, until she finally leaves. But not before giving Chase her personal cell number "just in case he thinks of anything else he might need." *Please.*

She breezes by, giving me a funny look and walking out the door. Chase stops in front of me, smiling like the cat that got the cream.

I cross my arms and scowl. "What are you lookin' so pleased about?"

He glances at the front door. Once he sees the coast is clear, his hands go straight to my hips. He squeezes, leaning in and stealing a kiss. "Can't I be pleased to see my woman?"

Butterflies go crazy in my stomach, but I maintain my glare. "I just don't think you should encourage her, is all."

"Who, Regina?" He laughs, backing up a step. "That woman's been out to get me since day one, Goldi. Hate to break it to you. There's no encouragement necessary."

Huh. I guess I was so busy trying to ignore Chase that I missed the signs. Probably for the best. If I had noticed her salivating over him, it would have made me green with jealousy, and honestly, I like her, despite the fact she's pissing me off.

"Are you ready to go?" I don't want to think about Regina anymore.

He leans against the wall. "What's the rush?"

I shrug, my hands out to my sides. "Aren't you hungry?"

"Starving." His eyes darken as he straightens.

He stalks toward me.

I take a step back.

He takes another step forward.

I stumble back another step.

I'm against the windows now, my hands pushing against his chest. "You're gonna smudge the new glass."

His head lowers and he nips my neck. "Don't care."

"Well, maybe I *do*," I say, leaning my head to the side so he has better access.

"Mmm…seems like it." He presses against me.

His palms move down my sides, his body following their trek. He drops to his knees, running the back of his hand up the inside of my leg. All the way up. My skirt bunches around my hips, and the cool air blows through the red lace of my panties.

Glad I wore my good underwear.

"What are you doin'?" I push on his shoulders half-heartedly.

"Eating." He leans in and kisses my clit through the lace.

My muscles seize and I bite my lip.

His hands glide along the outside of my underwear, slipping his finger underneath the material until he's sliding them down my legs. I'm vulnerable. Exposed. *At his mercy.* And then his tongue is on my clit and he's all warmth and wet, and I swear when he licks me from bottom to top and swirls around where I need him the most, I'm the closest I've ever been to heaven.

"I need… I need…"

His nose brushes against me, and he moves it back and forth. "I know what you need, baby. *Fuck*, you even smell perfect."

I can't find my words, so I grab the back of his head, my fingers tangling through his hair as I pull him into me. He smirks against my skin, the scruff on his jaw scratching the inside of my thighs. Finally, his tongue goes back to where I desperately need him.

"Oh, God." My eyes close from me being lost in the pleasure. He kisses down to my entrance, licking up my wetness and then dipping his tongue inside of me before going back to my clit and sucking.

One of his hands is on my stomach, pressing me firmly into the window.

His other hand traces down my side, moving between my legs.

"You taste so fucking good, baby. Even better than I remember." His fingers brush against me, lingering touches that don't satisfy the ache.

My fingers tighten in his hair. "Chase, please…"

"You sound good when you beg," he says. One finger dips inside, barely. Teasing. Driving me insane. "Please, what?"

"Make me come… I—I need to come." My body flushes red hot from my words. I've never talked dirty before.

Chase's eyes sizzle and his fingers dive into me, curling in and hitting *that* spot. He sucks my clit into his mouth. Not licks. *Sucks.*

My head slams against the window and I bite my lip to stop the scream. Pressure builds low in my belly until I can't focus on anything other than what he's doing to me.

Just a little more.

His fingers scissor inside me and my hips jolt forward. I'm so far gone I ride his face. I can't help it. He groans again, the vibration sending ripples of pleasure spiraling up my body.

The coil inside me tightens.

"You think people are watching you fall apart right now?" he murmurs against my skin. "Staring through the window and seeing what I do to you?"

I moan, the thought sending heat flaring down my spine and settling between my legs.

"You like that, don't you?" he asks.

His touch disappears. I'm about to protest, but before I can, he grabs my hips, hoisting me up. My legs drape over his shoulders and just like that, he's pinning me to the glass. His hands underneath me and his face between my thighs.

"Better give them a good show, then," he says before diving back in and feasting on me.

My head shakes back and forth, my body trembling. I'm so close. *So close.* He doesn't put his fingers back inside me, but he doesn't need to. One more pass of his tongue and I unravel.

The sensation shoots through me and my thighs tighten around his head. I feel him dive down, drinking up my juices. It's dirty and perfect and makes me feel so, *so* hot.

Chase lowers my legs and settles back on his heels, grinning wide and licking his lips as I slowly come back to earth. His face is glossy from my orgasm, and I have the strongest urge to kiss it off his face. So I do. I launch off the window and into his arms, making him fall back from the force. I can feel how hard he is, his thickness pressing against me. Between that and the taste of my pleasure on his tongue, I'm ready for round two.

He palms my ass and moans into my mouth, but eventually, I have to stop to catch my breath. Reason filters through me as I lie against his chest on the dance studio floor. I just let Chase eat me out against Regina's brand-new window, in broad daylight.

I don't regret it. *I'd let him do that to me anywhere.*

My legs are still shaky as I stand and then bend to pick my panties up off the floor. I slip them back on and rearrange my skirt, finger-brushing my hair as I smirk at Chase. "Well, that was unexpected."

"Best damn meal I've ever had." He winks. "You ready to go? It's my turn to feed *you*."

I'm sure he means dinner, but the double entendre in his words has me thinking wicked thoughts. I imagine him in my mouth and a tingle shoots through me.

I clear my throat. "Lead the way, Boy Scout."

I'm more than ready to go.

Chase's place is on the edge of town, a two-bed, two-bath, one-story house. I'm not sure what I expected. A bachelor pad, maybe? This definitely isn't that. It's manly, but also homey. Comfortable. Filled with solid oak furniture and dark brown leather.

I spin around and survey the open floor plan. The living room opens to the kitchen, a granite island separating the spaces.

"Surprised?" Chase is standing in front of the fridge, popping the top off a beer.

"Yeah. This isn't what I expected." I look around. This feels like a home. *How did he do this so fast?* "Did you hire a decorator?"

He chokes on his drink, coughing and sputtering. My eyes narrow.

"Uhh…kind of. Not really. My ex-girlfriend is an interior designer."

Hello, floor, meet my heart. *Ex-girlfriend.*

I shouldn't care. We've been apart for years. It's unrealistic to think he wouldn't have moved on in that time, but it still burns. As mad as I've been, as much as I thought I hated him, I was never able to give myself to another person that way. Hookups with no strings attached? Sure. But a relationship means there were *feelings*. Feelings that once only belonged to me. For the second time today, jealousy pricks at my insides.

"Oh." *Great job acting unaffected, Lee.* "So she was down here with you and decorated? That was…nice of her."

He shakes his head. "No, she just ordered the furniture. Helped out a bit. She didn't spend much time here." He gulps down another mouthful of beer.

"Was that the woman on the phone?" I blurt.

He cocks his head. "You'll need to be more specific."

"That night—the night you came and helped me with Daddy. There was a woman's voice in the background."

"There was," he agrees.

"Was that her?" I'm not thinking straight, and I know it. I have no right to ask him these things.

"Would it bother you if it was?"

"Yes. No…maybe? I don't know, Chase. It *shouldn't* bother me 'cause you weren't mine, but I won't lie and say it doesn't sting."

He walks around the counter and cups my face in his hands. His eyes are dark, his brows drawn. "I've always been yours."

I bite my cheek to stop myself from saying things I have no right saying.

"You don't think it drives me crazy to know you've been with Jax?" He growls Jax's name and my stomach jumps into my throat.

My head jerks back, surprised by his words. *He thinks I was with Jax?*

He crosses his arms. "Does he know about us yet, Goldi? Is he someone I need to worry about?"

"Where did you even get that idea? I was never with Jax."

His forehead creases. "What? That's not… I was sure."

I shake my head, stepping into him and running my hands over his arms. "He's my best friend, and yeah, he wants more."

Guilt swims around my veins. "But I've never felt that way about him. I've never felt that way about anyone. Only you."

"Are you saying you've never been with anyone else?"

My mind goes to Logan. "I'm not sayin' that...but you're the only relationship I've ever had." I shrug like that fact doesn't make me sound completely pathetic.

A grin creeps up his face. "Does it make me an asshole to say that I fucking love that?"

"Yes. But you've always been an asshole." I smile, leaning up to kiss him. "So, how long has this ex been an ex? If she—"

"I don't want to talk about her." He's quick to cut me off. "I want to focus on us." He walks me backward until I hit the arm of the sofa. His tongue traces my lips before he dips it into my mouth, kissing me deep. I whimper. *What was I talkin' about, anyway?*

He breaks the kiss, taking my hand, and leading me to the kitchen. "Contrary to what you may believe from what I've whipped up at your dad's house, I'm not a culinary genius by any stretch of the imagination. I hope you're good with pasta." He kisses his fingers like he's a chef.

"That depends. Will there be garlic bread?"

He grabs his chest. "I'm offended you even asked that."

Smiling, I watch him move around the kitchen while he makes dinner. Chase can act like he hasn't learned how to cook, but compared to the skills he had growing up, things have vastly improved. Honestly, he could have ordered pizza and I would have thought it was a gourmet meal as long as I was having it next to him. But it's truly delicious.

I lean back in my chair, patting my belly. "I ate way too much. I feel like I'm gonna explode."

"Don't tell me you didn't save room for dessert." He's clearing the plates, walking them to the sink.

"Depends." I rest my chin on my hand, watching him. "What's on the menu?"

A shrill noise interrupts the conversation, and the blood in my veins turns to ice. I know that ringtone.

"Daddy must be at The Watering Hole." I frown.

Chase stops doing the dishes and turns toward me. "How do you know?"

"Because that's the ringtone I set for when they call. It's the only one that wakes me up if it's the middle of the night." I grind my teeth, grabbing my phone out of my purse. "Hey, Johnny. Let me guess."

"Lee…the cops are here. I'm sorry, there was nothin' I could do. My owner's here tonight and wasn't havin' it."

I rub my forehead, the headache growing strong behind my eyes. "Don't worry about it. Should I head there or the station?"

Chase stands straighter at my words.

"The station. I'm sorry, Lee. My hands are tied."

"Stop apologizin', Johnny. The only one who should be sorry is Daddy. Thanks for the call."

I hang up, my tears of frustration boiling over. Chase rushes to me, kneeling between my legs. His hands squeeze my knees and I focus on his touch to keep me grounded.

"I'm so sorry. Our date is ruined and I was so lookin' forward—" My voice chokes, my hand coming up to cover my mouth.

"Hey, hey…it's okay, baby." He brushes my hair back. "Our date isn't ruined. We'll go take care of this, and then you're gonna come right back here. With me. Where you belong. Okay?"

I hiccup. "Okay."

He doesn't ask any more questions. Not until we're on the road and he needs to know where to go. The whole drive, he touches me, rubbing my knee, stroking the back of my hand. He's just there. Supporting. Letting me know I'm not alone. That he's in it with me now.

I don't remember when I fell in love with Chase Adams the first time around. It was mixed in somewhere with all the other feelings of growing up.

But this time? This time, I'll remember.

Chapter 42

CHASE

GOLDI'S FUCKING DAD, MAN. I SHOULDN'T BE surprised we had to pick him up from the county detention center, but I am. I assumed Eli would take his father's issues seriously. Goldi let me know that wasn't the case. Maybe this will be the wake-up call Eli needs because things are not okay here. He left Goldi with a hell of a burden on her shoulders, one she didn't ask for, and that she shouldn't have to carry alone.

Goldi's pissed. She didn't say the words, but I got the gist when she didn't even attempt a conversation with her dad. Not that he tried to talk to her. I've noticed he never does. My stomach burns when I think about it because I'm sad she has to experience how addiction steals people's love.

Craig struggles to walk himself to the front door. My arm goes around his waist, his around my shoulders. We've already learned the steps to this dance; it's one we practice often. All the while, Goldi's gearing up for battle. I see it in the rigidness of her features and the way she stomps through the door.

Eli and his fiancée are sitting on the living room couch, watching TV.

He shoots to his feet when he sees her. "What are you doing here?"

She walks right up to him and shoves his shoulders. He stumbles back, his legs hitting the furniture.

"What the hell, Lee?"

"When are you gonna get it, huh?" she bites out. "I thought you bein' back would make you see, get you to realize how bad things are, but here you are...sittin' pretty with your girl while Daddy's runnin' around town makin' a fool of himself."

"I'm not his babysitter. Pops is a grown man."

I scoff. I can't help it. This dude is being so fucking blind.

"Do you know where we just came from, Eli?" Goldi asks.

I'm still standing in the doorway, Mr. Carson in my arms. He shifts, his weight sinking into me. I move forward, setting him in his recliner, and as soon as I do, he hunches over, passed out. Sarah gasps when she notices the state of him, and Eli moves his gaze from Goldi over to me and his shit-faced father.

His mouth parts and he lifts a heavy brow. "What happened?"

Goldi huffs. "What do you think happened, Eli? The same thing that always happens. If Daddy doesn't have a babysitter, he gets behind the wheel, drunk as a skunk, and ends up at his favorite bar. Only his favorite bar has *banned* him 'cause he always causes a scene."

Eli cringes. "Lee, I didn't know..."

"I've told you a thousand times!" she cries, throwing her arms in the air. "Begged you a hundred more. You don't *listen*, Eli. You don't wanna hear it."

Eli looks over at his dad, the grief settling heavy in his eyes. "I didn't think it was this bad," he whispers. "Pops said he was meeting up with his buddies. He said you just like to hover, like to control things ever since Ma die—since Ma's been gone."

Goldi shakes her head, exhaustion blanketing her features. "The only buddies Daddy has are Jim, Jack, and Johnny, the liquor not the people. Oh, and the cops that picked him up and booked him tonight."

Eli's eyes grow big. "He was arrested?"

Tears well in Goldi's eyes, and it makes my stomach churn. I'd do anything to take this pain for her. I wish I could. I'm used to it—lived with it all my life, more wouldn't hurt me. But I know this is something that will dig deep in her soul and settle in, something she'll always carry.

I can't spare her from that. All I can do is help her navigate through the heartbreak.

"You gotta open your eyes. Daddy ain't the hero you've always seen him as. I just need a minute," she says, brushing past us into the kitchen.

The air is quiet but heavy. Eli collapses onto the couch. Sarah scoots closer, running her hand up and down his back as he leans forward with his head in his hands.

Eli looks up. "Thanks, man, for going with her."

I bite my tongue. There's a lot I want to say. Mainly, I want to ask where the hell he was and what the fuck he was thinking.

"Do you think she's overreacting a little?" He's looking at Sarah, so I assume his question is aimed toward her.

I blow out a breath, my small amount of restraint disappearing with his question. "You know, you may not want to hear it, but fuck it. Ignoring the problem won't make it go away, Eli. It won't make it stop. It'll just continue to spiral out of control, and then one day...one day, you'll wake up and wonder what the hell you were thinking. You'll wonder how you could have been so goddamn blind."

I pause to breathe through the sudden pain in my chest. "Trust me, when that day comes? The regret will rot you from the fucking inside. Because you'll know—you'll *know* that you didn't do everything in your power to save them when you had the chance. You didn't do *anything*." I shake my head. "I hope to God you wake up before then."

Eli blinks at me. I don't know if he heard a word I said, but I don't stick around to find out. I leave the room to find Goldi. She's coming out of the bathroom, her eyes puffy but her face clear.

She smiles when she sees me. "Ready to get outta here?"

I nod, gripping her hand. "You all right?"

She sighs, grasping my fingers tight. "Yeah, I'm all right. Just ready to leave."

I lead her out the front door and to my truck. I'm ready to get her home and take her mind off the heaviness. We were off to such a good start before her dad interrupted our night. I swear I can still taste her on my lips.

We're pulling up to a stoplight when I see Goldi unbuckle her seatbelt from the corner of my eye. She gives me a wicked smile as she leans over the console and trails kisses up my neck. A shiver races down my spine.

Her hand creeps over my chest, and I smirk. "What are you doing?"

"You promised me dessert." Her bottom lip gets fat as she looks up at me.

I'm already half-hard and her words stiffen my cock until it's trying to burst through my jeans. Maybe the right thing to do is to tell her she doesn't have to do this. Tell her to wait. She just went through an emotional moment with her family, and I don't want her to regret anything that happens, but on the other hand, if she wants an escape, there's nowhere I'd rather her find it than with me. So I lift my hips to give her better access.

She brushes her fingertips along the waistband of my jeans as the light turns green. Every touch sends a tingle through my body, making it difficult to concentrate on steering. The clank of my buckle and the sound of my zipper has me biting my cheek with anticipation. I can't see what she's doing since my eyes are on the road, but *fuck me*, can I feel it.

She reaches inside my pants, her palm rubbing against the bulge that's growing by the second. Goldi wastes no time, wrapping her fingers around my length. The coldness of her skin is a shock to my system, and my cock jumps in her hand.

We pull up to another stoplight, cars surrounding us even though it's well past nine at night. Fire sparks in my veins and the rest of my blood rushes to my groin. Goldi hums in approval and I glance down as her head lowers, licking my tip like it's a fucking ice cream cone.

I suck in a breath and fist her hair, pulling it away from her face so I can watch how gorgeous she looks as she swallows me. I glance back at the light. *Stay red. Stay red. Stay red.*

It turns green. I accelerate, trying to think about anything other than how fucking hot it is to have my dick in Goldi's mouth while I drive. She's so damn greedy for me, and I'm pretty sure being in public gets her off.

It turns me the fuck on.

She's teasing, licking up one side and down the other, swirling her tongue around the head. I'm about to go wild from how bad

I want to shove myself deep inside her. Her mouth. Her pussy. Fuck, I don't care as long as it happens.

I bite my lip as she sucks me down to the base, gagging slightly around me, and I grip her hair tighter. I throb against her tongue as she slips back up my length, and then drops back down again, deep-throating me. I grit my teeth so I don't come.

"Goddamn, baby." My hand tightens in her hair. She hums, fucking hums, around the base of my dick, and I thrust to see if I can get just a little bit deeper. She swallows and my foot jerks on the gas pedal.

She lifts her head, flattening her tongue as she slides back up, exposing me to the cool air. I take my eyes off the road to look at her. Spit connects her bottom lip to my shaft, saliva coating the length and making it glossy. *Damn.* She's filthy and I love it.

I grow harder, my balls tightening as I watch her dive back down and work up a rhythm. She starts slow, but by the time we're turning onto my street, she's got a fast pace, bobbing her head and working me so fucking good. I lift my hips over and over—completely blissed out.

I want to fuck her. So bad. I need her to stop. If she doesn't, I'm going to come down her throat, and I'd rather be balls deep in her pussy for that. But I can't form the words. The promise of pleasure steals my ability to do anything.

Her mouth pops off me and I moan in protest.

"Give it to me," she rasps, swallowing me again before sliding back up and off. "Come in my mouth."

And then she deep-throats me one more time. She isn't using her hands, but she doesn't need to because nobody has *ever* been able to take me as deep as she does.

Her words, coupled with the sight of her cheeks hollowing as she sucks, is all it takes.

My cock jerks and throbs, shooting into her mouth. The fear of veering us off the road makes my blood pump and heightens the sensation. I grip the steering wheel tight with one hand, my other still tangled in her hair. Her tongue massages the underside of my shaft, milking me for every drop.

She releases me, tucking me back into my jeans and leaving a kiss on top of the fabric, and then sits back, her eyes sparkling. Somehow, I've made it to my driveway.

"*Jesus*, Goldi." My chest is heaving, my brain trying to crawl out of the fog.

She wipes the corner of her lip, sucking her thumb into her mouth and winking. "Yum."

My cock twitches.

How the fuck did I think I could live without her?

She jumps out of the truck, sashaying that sweet ass all the way up to my front door. I hurry to meet her there, sweeping her into my arms. She squeals, locking her hands around my neck and laughing.

I smile down at her. "You are in so much trouble."

Chapter 43

CHASE

THE BLOOD STILL HASN'T REDISTRIBUTED TO ALL my limbs. The second I kick the door shut, Goldi is on me again, shoving her tongue in my mouth and rubbing herself on my dick. I stumble my way to the kitchen, setting her on the island that overlooks the living room. My hands grip her thighs and my body is between her legs, lost in her taste. I just came down her throat, and somehow I'm hard again.

I break my lips away. "I really do have dessert for us."

My eyes are drawn to her tits as they rise and fall with her heavy breaths. I want to tear her shirt off and see how long it takes to make her come from sucking her nipples. *Fuck. Keep it together.*

"Do you want dessert? Chocolate. It's chocolate. Cake," I stutter.

Her hand slides up my torso until she wraps it around my neck, tugging my face to hers. Our lips brush. "I kind of had somethin' else in mind."

She nips my bottom lip and pulls away, but I grip her face in my hands and bring her back. *She tastes so good.*

"Oh yeah? What's that?" I manage to ask in between kisses.

Her skirt is bunched around her hips, and she presses herself against me, looking at me from under her lashes. "This is somethin' that's a bit better if demonstrated."

My heart slams against my rib cage.

I lift her from the counter, wrapping her legs around my waist, my cock hard and thick against her. She starts sucking on my neck and *holy shit*, I need to get us to a bedroom—any bedroom, as fast as possible. I briefly think about throwing her against the wall and fucking her in the hallway, but I don't want that for our first time. My legs move fast, rushing us into my room. I drop her to the bed, my body covering hers. Immediately she starts grinding against me. She's aggressive as hell, and while it's the biggest turn-on of my life, I want to slow this down.

Savor her.

Take my time.

Commit every touch to memory.

I unwrap her arms from around me and stand, gazing down at her in awe. My stomach somersaults, my nerves lighting up. I've been waiting to have her like this for so long. *So fucking long.*

Her leg extends, trying to wrap around my waist and pull me back.

I grab her ankle in my hand and kiss her silky skin. "Slow down, baby. We have all night." I skim my hand up her calf. My lips follow, peppering kisses up her leg. On the inside of her knee. Her inner thigh. What she's giving me is a fucking gift—to have the chance to love her body as much as I love her soul.

She whimpers and fidgets and I lock my forearm against her stomach to keep her in place. My lips hit her skirt. I take the hem and drag it up with my teeth, putting her lace-covered pussy on display.

Delicious.

She shivers as I unbutton her blouse. Slowly. Methodically. After every button pops, I kiss the skin underneath because I want to worship every perfect inch of her.

Her shirt falls open, and I stop to drink her in. Her tits are fucking amazing, showcased in a red lace bra that matches her underwear, and I'm dying to know if her nipples are hard underneath. I kiss along the waistband of her skirt, grabbing it with my fingers and pulling it down. She lifts her hips to help. She tastes *so. Fucking. Good.*

I pull the cups of her bra, exposing her for my pleasure. My tongue peeks out, circling her areola, then sucking, until I feel it stiffen in my mouth. She moans and pushes into my cock. I have never wanted to be inside someone as bad as I want to be deep inside her.

Her hands reach down, unbuckling my belt. She fumbles, so I help, unzipping my pants, and shoving them off. My mouth never leaves her breast. I just lick my way over to work on her other nipple.

She wraps her fingers around my dick, over my boxers, and *God*, her hand feels better than any pussy I've ever had. She slides her palm up and down slowly, the fabric creating friction that has my cock weeping for more. There's a wet spot forming on the fabric and I know if she doesn't stop, this will be over before it really begins.

"Chase..." she begs.

I hum, my hand reaching down to press against her clit. She's drenching my fingers, even through her underwear.

Her breath blows against my ear, sending a shiver through my body. "Chase," she whispers. "I want you to *fuck* me."

My entire body spasms. Hearing Goldi say *fuck* is one of the most erotic moments of my life.

She grips my cock harder, massaging me so damn good. "I need to feel you...please."

I rest my forehead on her chest, trying to control the heat building in my groin. "*Jesus.* Okay, let me grab a condom."

Her hand pauses. "I don't—I don't want you to use one."

My heart stammers, my stomach flipping. I've never fucked without one before, and the thought of feeling her bare has my cock pulsing.

"Are you sure?"

"Yeah. I'm on birth control and I've never... I've never done it without one. I don't want there to be anything between us." Pink rises on her cheeks.

Her words undo me. I slide her panties down her legs, her pussy bare and on display. *Beautiful.* I eat her up with my gaze. She's naked from the waist down, her blouse splayed open and the cups of her bra bunched under her breasts. Her cheeks are rosy, her honey hair contrasting against the black of my bedspread, making her look like an angel. *My* angel.

Mine.

She leans on her elbows, watching me watch her. My hands glide up her arms, slipping underneath her blouse, sliding it down her shoulders. I trail kisses along her neck, nipping her earlobe as I undo her bra. It falls from her body and I'm drunk on the view. The outside is just as beautiful as her inside.

I push her up the bed, crawling over her. She pulls my boxers down and I rip my shirt over my head.

Now it's Goldi who stares. She licks her lips, a possessive gleam filtering through her eyes. *That's right, baby. I'm yours just as much as you're mine.* She grabs my cock and pulls me against her until the length of me is pressed along the heat of her pussy. I glance down at where we're touching and thrust forward, dragging every inch through her pussy lips until my tip grazes her clit. She gasps, and I bite my lip.

I repeat the motion, groaning as her wetness coats me, and then I move my hips back, pulling away from her warmth, and line myself up at her entrance. I pause, my breath stuttering in my lungs. I want to remember this moment forever.

"Chase, please," she begs again.

I hold her eyes with mine as I move forward, slipping inside her slowly. Inch by inch. She's hot and tight and wet as fuck, and *goddamn*, I can't believe this is happening. Her pussy clenches and my body reacts, sinking into her fully. I'm deep. So. Fucking. Deep. The threads of our connection light me up, zinging through every nerve ending, and I've never felt anything like this.

Goldi closes her eyes, turning her head to moan into the sheets.

My hand reaches up to grip her chin. "No, baby. Look at me."

I pull my hips back until just my tip is inside her.

She opens her eyes and I plunge deep and hard, making sure she feels every inch of me. I work up a rhythm. Long, deep strokes. Her pussy hugs my shaft on every thrust, and she moans, her muscles clenching again as the burn of arousal licks at my insides.

"Does that feel good?" I ask, grinding against her clit.

"Yes, oh my *God*. Chase…I didn't know it could feel like this."

I lean down to suck her neck, needing her taste in my mouth—wanting her to consume all of my senses. She pushes on my chest and she tries to turn us. I go willingly, turned the fuck on that she wants to take control.

Leaning back on my elbows, I watch as she positions herself over me, straddling my thighs. My eyes devour her, committing every second of this to memory so I can replay it whenever I want.

My breath is heavy from exertion and my gaze is glued to where she's sinking her pretty pussy down on me. Inch by agonizing inch, her tight cunt swallows my length. I fist my sheets to keep from thrusting up into her. I want to see what she does when she's in control. The view of her on top drives me insane, with her perfect tits and those parted lips that suck me so damn good.

She lowers all the way down until she's sitting in my lap. Her hips rotate. A tingle races through me.

She grinds down. My hands shoot to her hips.

"That's right, baby. Ride my cock. Take what you need."

Her hand traces along her stomach until she's cupping her tit as she rises up and then slams back down, over and over again. Her other hand tangles in her hair, gripping it tight as she rides me. *Holy fuck.* I wish I could take a picture because this is by far the sexiest sight of my life.

"Shit, Goldi. You need to stop."

She shakes her head, grinding on me faster. Every muscle in my body tightens, and I grab her hips, trying to slow her down. She doesn't, instead she fucking squeezes around me and I let out a moan, my eyes rolling in the back of my head. *Fuck.*

She smirks and does it again.

My grip becomes tighter as I flip her over, grabbing her wrists in my hand and pinning them above her head.

She inhales sharply, surprised by the sudden change in position.

"My turn." I grin down at her and thrust hard.

The slight sheen of sweat makes our bodies slick against each other as we move in tandem. Our lips are so close we're breathing the same air, and it heightens fucking everything.

She breathes out, I breathe in.

I wonder if she can taste how much I need her.

My hips drive into her steadily and hers rise underneath to meet me. My teeth graze her mouth, her chin, her neck, her breast. Anywhere I can reach. I'm fucking wild for her.

"Are you gonna give it to me, baby?" Our mouths brush. "I want to feel you come all over me."

She arches into me, closing her eyes as her body convulses, her inner walls gripping me tight as hell, contracting around me. The sensation envelops me, and I have to fight to keep my eyes open as the pleasure threatens to take me under. I want to see every second of her coming apart for me. Because of me. *With* me.

My balls draw up as my orgasm prickles. "Goddamn."

Goldi opens her eyes. "Come inside me."

My orgasm scorches through me, frying every nerve ending and making my vision go white. I push as deep as I can go, my cock jerking as I coat the inside of her.

Holy shit.

I collapse on top of her, my hair sticking to my forehead and my chest heaving. Goldi traces her fingers up and down my back. Aftershocks run through me, making my body jump from her touch.

It could be seconds or it could be minutes later, but I finally roll off her.

She laughs.

I turn my head. "Something funny?"

"I just…that was the best sex I've ever had. I wouldn't have wasted all those years if I had known I was missin' out on *that.*"

Leaning over, I brush my mouth against hers. "Well, guess we have a lot of time to make up for. But you know I still think we should talk about what happened earlier."

Her body stiffens but I don't let her pull away. "I know it's hard, but it's important. Trust when I tell you I learned that the hard way. So when you want to forget for a while, I'm here with you, baby. I'll be that for you. But you have to promise you'll let me be there for all the other things, too, yeah?"

She's silent for long moments, but then she blows out a shaky breath and kisses me again. "Yeah. Okay."

"Goldi?" I say.

"Hmm?" She rubs her nose against mine.

"You're the best *everything*. You know that, don't you? That I..." I shake my head, my hand gliding down her back and pulling her into me. "You're just everything."

A bright, beaming smile breaks across her face and her eyes sparkle as she reaches up, cupping my cheek.

"Yeah, Boy Scout. You're everything to me, too."

Chapter 44

ALINA

BEING WITH CHASE WAS MORE THAN I THOUGHT it ever could be. I always knew it would be explosive between us, but that was another level. I've never had someone take control of my body and just know what I need.

Dang, I want to do it again.

He's girthy. Bigger than Logan, for sure. He stretched me in ways I didn't know would feel good to be stretched. I'm sore and content lying in his bed, my fingers trailing over his chest, my head resting in the nook of his arm. He sweeps a kiss across my hair and I hide my smile in his side.

"Do you have plans this weekend?" he asks.

"Nope. Why?" It's semi-true. Technically, I have brunch plans with Becca and Jax, but I can cancel on them for one week.

"I want you to come with me to Nashville. There's somewhere I want to take you."

"You gonna show me where you've been all this time?" I look up at him.

He grins. "There's this thing I go to on Sundays. I'd like you to come with me."

"Oh yeah? What kind of 'thing'?"

"A meeting." His words carry a serious vibe that washes away my relaxation. "It's helped me a lot, and I thought maybe it could help you, too."

The cozy warmth in my chest starts to chill. I push against him, sliding away. "*Help* me? Why do you think I need help?"

He's quick to pull me back, his strong arms cocooning me as he drops kisses on my cheeks. The anger that was threatening under the surface melts away.

"I don't mean it like that," he says to reassure me. "It's a group for people who have been affected by addiction."

"I'm not an addict, Chase. I don't need a group to tell me that."

"I know, baby. It's a place for support."

I feel the scowl transform my face and Chase frowns as he stares at me. "I know it's the last thing you want to do. I mean, it was the last fucking thing I wanted to do, too. So I get it. Believe me. But this isn't a group that will judge you. You don't need to say anything. No one even has to know about your dad."

I run his words through my head. "I don't have to say anything?"

"No." He shakes his head. "I'd like you to come, though. It's an important part of me, and you're also an important part. The *most* important part. I really want to share this with you."

This is not what I had in mind when he asked if I was busy this weekend, but I can't deny the curiosity that's brimming, wondering what it was like for him in Nashville during our years apart.

"Okay. I'll go."

In the middle of the night, Chase slips inside me again. I

don't resist, even though I'm sore. And then again in the morning, when he takes me up against the shower wall, I revel in the sting.

After breakfast, he drops me home so I can pack an overnight bag for Nashville. I text Becca and Jax, canceling brunch. I feel guilty because I haven't told Becca about Chase yet, so I ask her to stop by.

The truth is, I'm nervous to tell her. Becca isn't known for her soft-spoken words or her understanding, especially since she was the one who was there from the beginning with Chase and me. From the first unrequited crush to the soul-crushing loss that swallowed me after he was gone. If anyone has a right to be upset about our relationship, it's her.

I'm throwing clothes in my bag when she shows up. She walks in like she owns the place, sashaying through the doorway.

"I know you think you can just ditch me and Jax for brunch, but I've come to force you to go."

I grin as I fold my shirt and place it in my bag. "I can't go, Becca. I'm goin' out of town for the night."

She plops down on my bed, frowning. "Oh. With who?"

I steal a glance at her, my nerves making eye contact impossible. Here we go. *Rip it off like a Band-Aid.* "Chase."

Becca blinks at me.

I continue flitting around my room, flinging clothes that I don't need for a one-day trip into my bag. Anything to keep busy so I don't feel the weight of her gaze.

After going through every possible wardrobe combination, I can't take the silence anymore. "Are you gonna say somethin'? You're makin' me nervous."

Becca tilts her head.

"Well." I raise my hands. "You've got *nothin'* to say about this?"

She sighs, breaking her stare and picking at her nails. "What would you like me to say, Lee? You've clearly made up your mind already. You're a big girl, I don't need to fight your battles for you."

My eyes sting from how wide I open them. I press the back of my hand against her forehead. "You feelin' okay? No snarky comeback? No witty retort?"

She bats me away. "Just so we're clear, you *want* me to be a bitch about this?"

I sit on the bed, frowning. "I don't...I don't know. I'm confused by your reaction. I was prepared to defend myself and here you are messin' up my plans."

She rolls her eyes. "I have other things to worry about, Lee. If you wanna go down a road that you already know I don't approve of, that's on you. I'll be here to wipe your tears when he inevitably fucks it all up. *Again.*"

I chew on my lip. "You really think he's gonna mess up again?"

She lifts her shoulders. "He's a man. That's what men do." She falls back on my bed, crossing her hands over her stomach. "Hey, how come you gave out my number, bitch?"

My eyebrows draw in. "What on Earth are you talkin' about?"

She levels me with a glare. "My number. You gave it to Eli's... thing." She waves her hand in the air. "Samantha or whatever her name is."

"Sarah," I correct.

"Whatever."

"Um. Okay, I'm sorry. I didn't think it was a big deal."

"Well, it is," she says, crossing her arms.

I narrow my eyes. "I gave it to her 'cause I'm tired of tryin' to figure out what the heck is goin' on with you and my brother.

It's *exhaustin'*, Becca. And while we're on the subject, just so you know…I'm not dumb."

Her face pales and she pulls her hair into a ponytail, moving it to her other shoulder before releasing it. She's always played with her hair when she's nervous. The fact she's doing it right now is a big tell.

"So what? I saw him around campus sometimes. He didn't like things I had to say and I didn't like the way he abandoned you. We didn't exactly get along."

"Okay. So what's the big deal with Sarah, then?"

"I don't like her." She shrugs.

"Mmhmmm. Well, I'm sorry. You've known Eli since you were in diapers. I really didn't think a thing of it."

She twirls the ends of her hair between her fingers, blowing out a breath. "That's all right. I'm just pissed off because my old man's thrilled to have somethin' for me to do. He keeps tellin' me 'idle hands are the Devil's playground.'"

"So he's makin' you help?"

She scoffs. "He's puttin' me in charge of the whole damn ceremony."

My jaw drops. "Do you even wanna do somethin' like that? Your daddy should realize you're twenty-six and capable of makin' your own decisions."

"Yeah, well…that's a fight for another day." She stares at her hands.

I watch her, wondering what it is that's making her so melancholy.

She looks at me, pasting a smile on her face. "You never told me where the asshole of the century is takin' you."

I want to keep pressing her on Eli. She's not thinking straight if she imagines I'm stupid enough to buy her story, but I let her steer the conversation in a different direction. Since she's in charge of his wedding ceremony, there will be plenty of opportunities for me to watch them together. Plus, I'm sure they'll both be at Sam's retirement party next weekend. Everyone in town is going. Even Daddy.

I'm not sure what to expect from this mini-trip with Chase. We're only here for one night, and I've already seen almost everything there is to see of Nashville, so I don't have any grandiose ideas. I'm anxious to experience a bit of what Chase's life was like without me. I want to see this side of him, even if that means sitting in a room full of people whose scars remind me I'm still bleeding.

We debate whether to order room service. I figure it would be a shame to not experience the Nashville nightlife, so we end up going to a casual spot downtown. A band is playing on the patio, so I'm thankful we're being led to a table inside where we can still talk. I slide into the booth, looking at our surroundings. It's busy, but then again, it's Saturday night so I shouldn't be surprised. The walls are bright pops of color. Neon greens and purples clashing against dark concrete floors. This place is clearly not known for its aesthetics.

"Is this your favorite restaurant?" I tease.

He smiles. "I don't really have a favorite, but their food's decent. Plus, I can't take you to a fancy place. Wouldn't want to ruin my reputation and make you think I was trying to woo you."

"No, no chance of that." I smile, glancing at the menu.

"See anything you like?" he asks.

"This is perfect. They have fried green tomatoes, which is all I need to be happy."

The waiter comes around bringing us drinks and taking our orders. We're left to relative silence, only the bass drum from the outside band thrumming in our ears. I see his mind working and I wonder what he's thinking. Does he regret bringing me here? Is he thinking about his ex? Did he bring *her* here?

Stop it.

"So, tell me about this thing you're takin' me to tomorrow."

He sips his beer, his eyes never leaving mine. "It's a group meeting. We get together in the basement of a church and share stories. My therapist actually encouraged me to go a few years ago, and it's helped me with…everything, really."

I still can't wrap my head around Chase seeing a therapist. I've tried to imagine it a million times, but I always come up short. "How often do you go?"

"Every weekend. I actually am the main organizer for it now." Something that looks an awful lot like pride fills his eyes. Shock weaves its way through my system as I listen to him. "I don't know how the fuck they decided I'd be the best for that. But here I am."

The waiter interrupts, dropping off our fried green tomatoes. They smell delicious, but I don't want to ruin the moment by indulging.

Instead, I urge him to continue. "How does it help?"

"Easy question." His fingers tighten around his beer. "I never processed all the emotion that came with being the son of an addict. Never let myself really feel it." His head is angled down, but his eyes glance up at me. "The shame that surrounds it. The feelings of complete fucking failure. The anger I have toward my mom…toward Lily."

My heart pangs with an ache so sharp it shoots to my toes. Even though he isn't talking about me, I'm rubbed raw from his words. Each syllable pulls at the emotions I keep hidden away.

"I've lived with that shit all my life, Goldi. I let it infect every fucking part of me, and it wasn't until I went to this group and heard other people's stories…saw the pain, and the anger, and the misplaced embarrassment on other people's faces." He shakes his head, taking another sip of his drink. "That shit makes you put things in perspective. For the first time, I realized I wasn't alone."

I don't really know what to say. Nausea is rolling around in my belly over the thought of going to this meeting with him—of being witness to the feelings I try to ignore, but I push down the anxiety. This is important to him, and I'm honored he wants to share this vulnerable part of his life.

"Do you—have you ever found Lily?" She was my best friend once upon a time, and I carry a lot of guilt for how I handled things with her.

I ignored my worries well before I spoke them, too naive to know what was really going on, and then too scared to speak up when I had the chance.

His mouth curves into a sad smile. "I don't know if Sam and Anna are still searching, but it wouldn't surprise me. I don't know where I'd even begin to look." He tugs on the ends of his messy hair. "She could be anywhere, you know? She could be happy as hell living a life without me in it. Or maybe she's dead in a ditch." I see the torment as it swirls around his face, darkening the hazel of his eyes.

My breath hitches at the thought. "Don't think that. Have you ever thought about lookin' again?"

"For Lily?"

"Yeah. I mean, I don't know how it works. But don't they have private investigators, or whatever they're called, that can do that? Hunt people down?"

His fingers scratch at the scruff on his jaw. "I've never thought about doing that. I'm not sure I'd even want to find her. Does that make me a shitty person?"

"No. It just makes you human, Chase."

"I just… I'm so angry at her for leaving. Part of me feels like she's had plenty of time to find her way back, and she hasn't, so I have to assume she wants to be left alone. And *that* makes me a piece of shit brother." He stabs his finger into his chest. "I should be turning the world upside down, right?"

"Maybe." I raise my shoulder as I bite into a tomato.

He frowns. "Yeah, maybe."

"Your sister was never known for her humility, Chase. You of all people should be able to relate to that. Maybe she wants to come home and feels like she can't. Or maybe you're right, and she wants nothin' to do with you."

He flinches, and I regret how blunt my words come across, but it's the truth, and he should hear it.

I reach across the table and grab his hand. "But…maybe Lily doesn't *know* what she needs. Or maybe it's not about her at all. If findin' her will give you peace, then it's worth doin'."

His eyes soften and he brings my palm up to his mouth and presses a kiss to it.

"At least talk to your folks. Maybe they know somethin'," I implore.

We don't speak of it anymore, changing the subject to something lighter. Something that doesn't take us to the darkest parts of who we are. I grab the surface level conversation and hang on tight because I have a feeling that tomorrow, we'll be back in the dark again.

Chapter 45

CHASE

IT WASN'T A SPUR-OF-THE-MOMENT DECISION TO bring Goldi with me to a Nar-Anon meeting. I almost didn't ask her, afraid that she'd take it the wrong way. I wasn't wrong, she *did* get defensive, but at least she's here. I'm grateful as hell for it. But I'm also antsy as fuck.

I rearrange the metal chairs in a circle, to a semicircle, then back again.

We arrived before anyone else, but now there's a couple of families filtering in. Goldi's been lost in one of the newcomer pamphlets, so I leave her to read in peace while I finish getting everything ready.

There's a group of about twenty tonight. Some adults, some entire families, a few lone teenagers. I envy the kids who are here of their own volition. *If only I had been here back then.*

It's been a while since I've told my story, but tonight I'm planning to share. I want to show Goldi the parts of me she's never seen—the pieces that were too broken to love her when I was a boy. Needless to say, I'm fucking nervous as shit. Telling a bunch of anonymous strangers was hard enough, but to lay it all on the line in front of Goldi? That's a whole different ball game.

I dive right in before I lose the nerve. I talk about Lily, even though most have heard the story. I talk about my mom and the wounds she caused that will never heal. I hear the murmurs of agreement when I speak of the weight of responsibility laid on my shoulders at such a young age. How it's still a struggle *every day* to remember that my mom's demons were her own. That the guilt I feel is misplaced. That it was never my job to make sure she was happy. I meet Goldi's eyes as I strip off my armor and show the naked man underneath. This is raw. This is real. This is me.

I talk about all of it, and then I listen. I listen to others share their grief. Some speak with hope, while others speak from loss.

It's easy to think about the ones with addiction. Easy to sympathize with their disease, mourn their deaths. It's simple to put out a social media post about what a tragedy it is and make comments on how we need to do something about the drug crisis, but nobody remembers to think of the people left behind. We're expected to dust off our knees from where we fell and move on with our lives like we aren't ripped to shreds. Like it isn't taking fucking everything to simply breathe through the pain.

We are the forgotten. Even though we're the ones left to struggle.

This moment right here, with strangers coming together and laying their souls bare—this is why I brought Goldi. So she could see that she isn't alone. She isn't invisible. She isn't to blame.

Goldi sits in her spot long after the last person leaves. I make my way over, the metal legs of the chair scraping as I sit across from her. Her face is dry, but her eyes tell the story of her tears. She opens her mouth, then closes it, her lips pressing together.

"I don't… I didn't…" She clears her throat. "I didn't think it was gonna be like that."

I nod because I fucking get it. I felt the same way at my first meeting.

"Those people," she says. "What they've been through…" Tears well up again, and her palms press to her eyes. She drops her hands, piercing me with her gaze. "*You* are strong. Stronger than I could ever be."

"You know that's not true. I see strength in everything you do."

"I don't feel it," she whispers.

Leaning forward, I tangle our fingers together and rest them on my knees. "I think that's pretty normal, baby. Do you want to talk about it?"

She shakes her head, looking at our hands. "Not really."

I don't push. I promised she wouldn't have to say anything, but I hope one day she will.

Mondays are always busy, and today is no exception. We're wrapping up the renovation at Tiny Dancers. As long as we stay on target, we'll be done next week, and while I'm happy things have gone smoothly, I can't help the disappointment that's filling me up. Being done means no more weekday Goldi. No more tight skirts and hidden corners where I can kiss her breathless like I've been doing every chance I get today.

I head back to the office. It's the end of the day, and I want to let her know I'm leaving and see if she wants to come over for dinner.

She's pacing the room, her cell up to her ear. She turns when I walk in and smiles. "Yeah, that sounds good, Jax."

Jax.

Bitterness sours my stomach. We'll inevitably continue to run into each other. He's best friends with the love of my life, but he was *my* best friend first. The loss of that friendship is something that still haunts me. I understand why he protected her the way he did, and as hard as it is for me to admit, I'm grateful she has him. Still, I can't help that part of me feels betrayed. It was just so easy for him to drop me, and even all these years later, it stings.

I walk toward Goldi, backing her into the wall. She pushes against my chest, pointing to the phone, her eyes widening.

"I don't care," I mouth.

My hands caress her curves as I kiss my way down her body and drop to my knees. *These fucking skirts of hers are going to be the death of me.* I lick my way up her thigh.

"Let me call you back, Jax." Her phone clatters. She grabs my hair and pulls. "Just what do you think you're doin'?"

"Checking up on your multitasking skills. They need some work." I tsk.

She breaks into a smile, smacking my shoulder and pushing me away.

I fall back, laughing.

"Regina's on her way, so I'll be stuck here awhile. You leavin' for the day?"

"That's a shame," I say, standing and dusting off my jeans. "I wanted to have the taste of you on my tongue for the drive home."

Her cheeks heat.

I love all the ways I can make her blush. I step into her and her arms wind around my neck.

"I could come over later if you want?" she asks.

"I'd love that." I kiss her deep, not wanting to leave because she feels so fucking good in my arms. "Guess that will have to hold me over."

There's a spring in my step when I leave, excited I'll have her in my arms again in just a few hours. I start up my truck, groaning when I realize my gas tank is sitting on empty. I hate getting gas out here because the price is higher than back home, but I don't think I have enough to make the drive.

There's a station before the entrance to the freeway, so that's where I stop.

I walk in, looking back to see which pump I'm on. There's nobody else here except the guy working the register. I grab some water and go up front to pay.

"Do I know you?"

I glance at the cashier as I place the water on the counter and dig in my wallet. *Is he talking to me?* "I don't think so, man."

"Huh. You sure? You look real familiar. I never forget a face." He taps his pointer finger to his head like he's a fucking savant.

I look at him closer, seeing if I can place him. He's skinny—almost too skinny, with pockmarks on his face and gaudy gold chains around his neck. *There's something about those chains.* His hair is short with frosted tips. My brows furrow, a buried memory pricking the back of my mind.

"Don't matter, I guess. This all for ya?" He reaches down and scratches his stomach.

Lightning strikes my entire body, bolting me in place. The memory of a skinny, pockmarked guy in a run-down house, with an unconscious Lily, slams behind my eyes.

Motherfucker.

I'm over the counter in less than a second, grabbing him by the chains I'm tempted to fucking murder him with.

"Yeah. You know me, you fucking bitch. Lily Adams. Ring any bells?" This time it's *my* pointer finger jabbing into his head.

His eyes widen and he squirms, trying to escape my grip.

I pull his chains tighter, twisting them.

"Oh, fuck. You're that brother, right? Listen…I got nothin' to do with her now, I swear!" He's panicking, his fingers clawing at my hands. "There are cameras, man. Just so you know. You hurt me, you won't be gettin' away with *shit*."

It's touching how he thinks I give a fuck.

"I will pull you over this counter and revel in the last fucking breath you take, smiling at the cameras once I'm done. So if you know where she is, if you know *anything*, you better tell me. Right. Fucking. Now."

He jerks away, but I yank him back. The chains cut into his skin, a trail of blood dripping down his neck. I've been waiting a long fucking time to get my hands on this prick. He's not going anywhere.

"Man, come on. I don't know! She ain't lived here for years. Last I knew, she was gone to Arizona."

"When was this?" I hiss.

"She called a buddy of mine a few months ago… Ow, quit!"

The door chimes and it distracts me long enough for him to wrench out of my grasp, the cheap chains breaking.

He runs over to the register and grabs the phone, pointing it at me. "Get outta here 'fore I call the cops. I told you what I know. I don't mess with that bitch no more, not in years."

I clench my fists. The urge to beat the fuck out of him is strong, but I hold myself together, repeating the serenity prayer in my head. The man who walked into the store is warily watching our interaction.

"You're fucking lucky," I point out.

Turning around, I speed-walk to my truck, knocking someone in the shoulder on my way out. I don't breathe until I'm in my seat, slamming my palms on the steering wheel.

"Fuck. Fuck. *Fuck!*"

My heart is racing and my mind is spinning.

Arizona. She's in Arizona.

Chapter 46

ALINA

I THINK I MIGHT BE IN SHOCK. BACK WHEN LILY overdosed and disappeared, a lot was left unsaid. Chase was closed off, and I was too afraid of pushing him to pry, so I didn't hear the details. I didn't realize he spent hours searching, and when he finally found her, she was on the brink of death. Chase has lived with this memory seared into his brain, torturing him. An entire experience that would shape the rest of his life, and I had no idea of its depth. *I never knew.* My heart cracks because I never thought to ask.

He tells me about the gas station. My eyes grow wide with every sentence he utters. I'm cozy in a pair of his basketball shorts and a tee, sitting on his couch, watching him pace a hole through his living room floor.

"I mean, I have to do something, right?" he asks.

"You don't *have* to do anything. Do you think you should?"

He rips at his thick, dark hair. I'm surprised he has any left on his head after the years of abuse the strands have endured.

"I should have killed that motherfucker. I'm gonna go back.

You think he's still there?" He stops in the middle of the room, spinning to face me. His fists open and close at his sides.

"I think you should take a deep breath." I inhale and blow it out to show him how it's done. He mimics me, and some of the rigidity leaves his posture. "Now, come over here. Sit down and we can talk this through." I pat the spot next to me.

He plops on the couch. I scoot him forward so he's on the edge, and I squeeze behind him, my fingers kneading the tension out of his shoulders. He groans, his head dropping to give me better access.

"Have you talked to your folks about any of this? I mean, do you ever bring up Lily?"

He blows out a breath. "No. We don't talk about her."

My hands pause their movements. His words surprise me. "Never?"

"Never."

"Well...then I think that's the first step. You need to talk to them. For all we know, they could've been in contact with her and not told you."

His shoulders tighten. "They wouldn't do that."

"Oh, no? Have you given them the impression you'd be open to hearin' about her?"

He quiets. The old Chase would clam up and change the subject anytime Lily's name was spoken, so I wouldn't be surprised if his folks were scared to bring her up in conversation. But I could be wrong because this new Chase is an enigma. He's more open than he was in the past; this weekend in Nashville proved that.

The Nar-Anon meeting was different than I expected. I've been spending the past twenty-four hours processing, and I'm still not sure how I feel. I've heard about Alcoholics Anonymous.

Heck, I've tried to get Daddy to go a thousand times, but I hadn't heard of a support group for friends and family.

Their stories were harrowing, digging deep inside, and pulling up ugly feelings I'd rather keep buried, exposing the rawness I only uncover in solitude.

I didn't think there would ever be a day where Chase spoke his story. I spent years hoping he'd share his burdens. Even though I get now why he kept them buried, the fact I wasn't what he needed to heal is a bitter pill to swallow.

There are some things the heart can't forget. Loving Chase is one. Being hurt by him is another. But losing my daddy to the devil makes me understand. Chase's mama ravaged his soul, leaving him to pick up the pieces, and abilities become stunted when something is battered and bruised. It doesn't excuse his behavior. It doesn't lessen the phantom pain of his betrayals. But it helps.

"I've been thinking about what you said," he blurts.

"I say a lot of things." I press my fingers into a knot on his neck.

"About a private investigator to find Lily. I wasn't planning on doing anything, but maybe this is the universe telling me I need to."

"Do you think that's what it is? A sign from God?"

"I don't fucking know." He tugs his hair again, leaning into me. "What do you think I should do?"

The lost look in his eyes makes me want to scour the world for him. I chew my lip, considering my words. "I reckon you should talk to your folks before you decide on anything."

He reaches back, palming my thigh. "Yeah, you're probably right. Will you come with me?"

My eyes bulge. "To talk to Sam and Anna?"

"Yeah. I don't want to do it alone." His voice cracks.

"Okay. I'll go." I slide my hands to his chest, wrapping my legs around his waist and squeezing tight.

I don't tell him how the thought of seeing them makes my stomach roll. How every time I've run into Anna, the air grows chilly. I don't open up about the resentment I feel knowing Sam dropped Daddy like he couldn't be bothered to help him through his pain.

I don't mention any of these things, but I sure do think them.

The smell of fresh coffee wakes me the next morning, and I inhale deep, groaning as I stretch my muscles. I take my time getting out of Chase's bed, rubbing the sleep from my eyes. Snatching my phone off the end table, I check the time. I'm relieved I didn't oversleep. I don't want to be late for work, in case Regina's there.

Grabbing my clothes from my overnight bag, I head to the en suite. I don't have any of my toiletries—other than a toothbrush—so I'll have to use whatever's available. The thought of smelling like Chase all day makes my insides flutter.

Showered and dressed for the day, I walk to the kitchen in search of some caffeine and some kisses from my man. Chase is leaning on the counter, scrolling his phone while he sips coffee. He looks up and smiles. My heart skips. *Those dang dimples.*

"You feeling good today, Goldi?" he asks.

"Hi." I grin, planting a soft kiss on his lips. "I feel great."

His big hand grabs me from behind and squeezes, pulling me further into him. "Fuck, I love having you here in the morning. Did you sleep okay?"

I nod, swiping his coffee and taking a drink. I hum as it hits my tongue. There's just something about that first sip in the morning that can't be beaten. Having Chase next to me while I savor the taste is the cherry on top. I could get used to this.

His eyes darken as he watches me. "You better stop that."

"Stop what?" I murmur, taking another gulp.

"Everything you're doing. You're making me want to bend you over this counter, and we don't have time for that."

My body heats as I imagine the feeling of him behind me, pushing my hips into the granite with his thrusts. I shift and bite my lip, arousal zinging between my legs.

He interrupts my daydream. "I'm gonna be at the main office all day. I'll talk to Sam about getting together for dinner tonight. Will that work for you?"

I rub my thumb over his lips. "Yep, works for me."

His teeth snap at my fingers and I squeal, jerking my hand away. He chortles, standing to grab his keys from the counter.

"I've gotta get going." His hands frame my face, his tongue parting my lips and dipping in my mouth for a quick taste. My eyes flutter closed, and the threads of our connection dance—content that we're finally together.

"Stay as long as you like, make yourself at home," he whispers against my mouth.

My fingers circle his wrists. "Maybe I'll just come straight here after work…if that's okay?"

"Baby, you could move in tomorrow and I'd be okay with it." He brushes my cheeks with his thumbs, leaving me with one last kiss.

That night, we pull into Sam and Anna's driveway, but I'm stuck looking at the house three doors down. I haven't talked to Eli or Daddy since our fight. Eli texted and tried to call, but I need to calm down before I answer, otherwise, who knows what will come out of my mouth. I may say things I'll regret, or I might ask what the heck he was thinking letting Daddy go to a bar. Or how come my best friend's acting a fool over him getting hitched.

"Hey, you okay?" A squeeze on my thigh makes me realize I've been staring in a daze.

I muster up a smile. "Yeah, I'm fine. Just worryin' is all."

"Do you want to stop by there after dinner?" He tilts his head toward where I've been looking.

Do I? Yes. No. Maybe. Nothing good can come of it, but I can't help that I miss Daddy even if I know he isn't missing me.

"Maybe. Let's just deal with one thing at a time."

As we walk the pathway to his front door, my nerves grow tenfold, jumping around at the thought of seeing Sam and Anna. Chase walks right in, pulling me with him. Being here after so long is a bit surreal. There are so many memories tied up in this place, and I spent years trying to forget them.

The smell of good home cooking makes me pine for my mama. I missed my weekly visit to her grave on Sunday and feel guilty for not making it a priority once I came home. *Tomorrow, I'm makin' time.*

"Anybody home?" Chase hollers.

Anna swings around the corner, her long blond hair twirling as she rushes into Chase's arms.

"Hi, honey." She palms his cheeks. The hole in my heart where Mama's love used to be aches.

"Hey, Anna." Chase beams. "Smells good in here, thanks for having us."

She smacks his shoulder, shushing him. "This is your home,

you're always welcome." She glances at me, her blue eyes cooling. "Alina. How are you?"

She's polite—her southern roots strong—but that's the extent of her hospitality.

Chase looks between us, reaching out and pulling me into his side. I don't miss the way Anna's eyes swing to where he holds me. Her lips purse.

I'm antsy, her judgment making my palms sweat. "Anna, thanks so much for havin' me. It smells delicious."

"Mmm. My pleasure." Her smile looks painful.

She turns back toward Chase, leaving me forgotten in the hallway, as she links their arms and walks to the kitchen. I follow behind, my stomach sinking at her disregard. *What did I do to make her hate me so much?*

"Is there anything I can help with?" I ask, looking around.

Anna doesn't spare me a glance. "I've got everything handled, thank you kindly. Make yourself at home."

Chase starts to walk toward me, but Anna grips his arm, stealing his attention back as she tells him about the new yoga group she's in. He gazes at me over her shoulder and I wave him off.

What the heck do I do now? I peer out of the sliding back door and see Sam lounging in a chair, beer bottle to his lips. I head toward him.

Stepping outside allows me to breathe easy for the first time since we've shown up. The twilight sky bathes the ground in orangey-pink hues, showcasing beauty that's lacking every other time of day. I plop in the lounge chair next to Sam.

"Beautiful evening, isn't it?" He smiles.

"One of the best Tennessee sunsets I've seen," I agree.

"That's high praise coming from a native."

"I call it like I see it, Mr. Adams."

He angles his head, his gray-speckled sandy-brown hair flopping as he looks at me from green eyes. "When have you ever called me anything other than Sam, Alina? Don't start being formal now, just because it's been a few years."

"Okay, Sam." My lips curl in a smile, relieved the animosity from inside hasn't followed me.

"So, how ya been? It's been a while."

"I'm great, thanks for askin'." It's an automatic response, and even though it isn't one-hundred-percent true, it's the only answer he'll get.

He bobs his head, staring at the horizon. "And your dad?"

I hesitate. My knee-jerk reaction is to say he's fine, great. Better than ever. But I can't find it in myself to lie for him. Not anymore.

"He's…strugglin'."

Sam frowns. I glance at my hands, the urge to vomit out the truth overwhelming me, but the back door opens before I have the chance.

"Dinner's ready, y'all!" Anna sings.

Sam looks like he wants me to keep talking, but I give him a small smile, shaking my head like it isn't a big deal.

Daddy's secret is safe for another day.

Chapter 47
CHASE

GOLDI STEPS ONTO THE BACK DECK AND SITS next to Sam and I want to follow her, but I'd like a minute alone with Anna. There are a couple of things I need to get across before dinner. I didn't miss the animosity she was spewing toward Goldi, and even though Sam warned me, seeing it with my own eyes is disappointing. It never occurred to me they would blame Goldi for things going sour, and while I can't go back in time and fix the wrongs of my past, I sure as hell can make sure they don't continue in the future.

I watch Anna chop tomatoes and drone on about yoga. I'm trying to stay focused on what she's saying, but I'm too irritated to pay attention. Before this moment, I've never felt anything but love and admiration—for that to be tainted so quickly is jarring.

"Anna," I interrupt her rambling.

She turns from her chopping board, stopping midsentence.

"What was that?" I keep my voice low, not wanting anything to carry out back. The last thing I want is for Goldi to hear this conversation.

"I don't know what you mean." Anna glances toward the deck, letting me know she does, in fact, know what I'm talking about. She resumes chopping her tomatoes.

"I mean with Goldi, but I think you knew that."

"I'm treatin' her the same way I always have."

She's avoiding eye contact even though I'm sure she can feel the weight of my gaze. That's okay, she doesn't need to say anything. She just needs to listen.

"Can I ask you something, Anna? Do you love Sam?"

"You know I do." Her eyes soften.

"Can you imagine what it would be like if you had to live your life without him? How it would feel knowing the love of your life was out there, wanting absolutely nothing to do with you because of things that you did?"

The knife in Anna's hand pauses.

"And then imagine that by some miracle, you get a second chance. That *finally*, you get to experience being loved by the other half of your soul."

"Chase, I don't know—"

I cut her off. "I know I've never opened up to you. That's on me, and I'm sorry for any pain that's caused you."

Her eyes gloss over and she curls her lips in, her hand rising to her chest.

"But listen to me when I tell you this, Anna, because I'm only gonna say it once. Goldi is *it* for me. She always was and she always will be. Anything that happened in the past, *everything* that happened in the past, is on me. *I* fucked up, and made her think I did things that broke her heart. I *did* break her heart. Alina did absolutely nothing wrong, other than try to save me from myself. And for some reason, she's still here with me, so she's not going anywhere. I lost her once, I won't lose her again. If you can't come to terms with that..." I blow out a breath. "If you force me into making a choice...I won't bring her somewhere she feels unwelcome."

Anna wipes under her eyes. "She was Lily's *best friend*, Chase. Do you really believe she had nothin' to do with what Lily got into?"

My chin rises along with my eyebrows. "Is that what you think?"

"I find it hard to believe anything else."

"Lily hid the truth from every single one of us, Anna. Hell—she *lived* with us and we didn't know. Or maybe we did and chose to be blind to what was right in front of our faces." I shake my head. "Either way, projecting that onto Alina isn't okay, especially since she's the one trying to convince me to *not* give up hope when it comes to Lily." I step closer, leaning my head down to catch her eyes with mine. "She isn't to blame. Not for Lily. Not for me. I know you love us, and I know we're your kids...but we're the ones in the wrong here. It's us who have to make up things to Alina, not the other way around."

Anna scowls. "She made you up and leave us. You couldn't even hear the word Sugarlake without your bleedin' heart spillin' through your eyes. You can say whatever you want, but...I struggled for *years* to have children, and then I finally got two. If it weren't for her, if she had never been in your lives"—she points the knife toward the back deck—"maybe I'd still have you both."

I keep my face stoic, but inside, my heart is being wrung out to dry from her words. This is a lot deeper than a simple misunderstanding. Anna and Sam had years of fertility issues. If she's blaming Goldi for the loss of her children, after years of struggling—that's going to be more than a ten-minute conversation before dinner.

"That's not fair," I argue.

She shrugs, her eyes sad even through her smile. "It may not be, but it's how I feel."

My jaw clenches. "Be upset at Lily. Be angry at me. Be pissed off at the hand life dealt you…but please don't think I'll sit back and let you take it out on her. I won't bring her here to be disrespected."

"I know." She nods. "You love her more than you love us."

My stomach sinks at her words. *I fucking hate this.* "I love you. You have been the best mom a guy could ask for."

She gasps. It's the first time I've said the words. The first time I've called her mom. I pull her in for a hug and she collapses against my chest. I hold her close, years of my mistakes and her longing culminating as tears stain my shirt. After a few moments, she sniffles and pulls back.

I hold her by her shoulders. "I'm in love with her. Try to understand, Anna, *please*. My world was black for so long, you know?"

"And she's the light?" Anna asks softly.

"She's every star in the sky."

Anna nods. "I'll try," she says finally before wiping her tears and heading to the back patio to let Sam and Goldi know it's time for dinner.

I set the table, my stomach rumbling from the smell of Anna's cooking. It's one of the things I've missed most over the years.

For the first half of dinner, we talk about Sam's retirement party. It's this Saturday, so Anna is trying to get all the last-minute details sorted. She's excited, almost bouncing out of her seat when she talks. Sam, on the other hand, isn't. I know for a fact he would rather not be retiring at all, but he's doing it to appease Anna. *Happy wife, happy life.*

I wonder if Mr. Carson plans on going. No one knows about his drinking, and I'm pretty positive he's past the point of being able to fake it.

There's a lull in the conversation, and I know this is my chance. Nausea rages through my gut, and my knee hits the bottom of the table from my jitters. It doesn't matter; my nerves won't stop me from this. Now that I know Lily's in Arizona, I won't be able to rest until I make sure she's okay.

"So." I clear my throat. "Something interesting happened. I want to talk to you guys about it, but I'm not really sure how to bring it up." I clench my fork, the metal stinging as it presses into my palm.

Anna places her napkin in her lap. "You know you can tell us anything, Chase."

"Right." I nod. "I ran into someone who knows Lily."

The table goes mute. Anna's smile drops and Sam's shoulders stiffen.

Goldi reaches over and links our fingers, giving me the strength to continue. "He told me she's in Arizona. Or at least, that she was a few months back."

Sam leans forward, his elbows on the table, his attention rapt. "How does he know that? She still talks to him?"

"I don't know, I wasn't exactly in the best frame of mind for asking questions." Even thinking about that motherfucker makes the rage bubble in my veins.

"Hmm." Sam's eyes are calculating. Anna is still frozen in her seat, her face drawn.

I look between them. "Do you guys still look for her? Has she ever reached out to you?"

Sam's eyes droop like he's disappointed I'd ask. "You really think we wouldn't tell you that, son?"

"I wasn't exactly open to hearing about her. Talking about her is hard for me." I squeeze Goldi's hand tight, using her to anchor me. "I've been thinking about hiring a private investigator. Actually, it was Alina's idea."

Sam leans back in his seat, sighing. "We hired one a few years back. He looked for over a year, but he never found anything."

Goldi pipes up. "Do you think it would help if he knew she might be in Arizona? You know, somethin' concrete to go on?"

Sam considers her words. "It's possible." He looks to Anna, who is stone-still, silent as a lamb. "I think his name was Don something. Based in Nashville. He's a bit seedy, but apparently, he's the best. I'll find his info and give it to you. Maybe you'll have more luck than we did."

I nod, my heart rising to my throat with the thought of finding Lily. It doesn't settle back in my chest—even after I go home, sleep, and get ready for work the next day.

After dinner, I thought I'd be able to talk everything through with Goldi, but then Becca called. I could hear her screeching from the driver's side of the truck, and when Goldi turned her worried look my way, I knew I was losing her to her best friend for the night.

I haven't seen her yet today. I'm supposed to be taking lunch, but I'm stuck staring at the contact info Sam just forwarded to my phone. Looks like I'm about to call this Don Calhoune guy. Sam warned me again that he's a bit sketchy, but I don't give a fuck if he's the slimiest crook in the world as long as he can find my sister.

With shaky fingers, I press call and bring the phone up to my ear.

It rings…once…twice…three times, before it stops.

"Mason."

I pull the phone away from my ear, squinting at the screen. *Mason?*

"Yeah, hi. I'm trying to reach a Don Calhoune? I was told this was his contact information."

"Uh-huh. And what do you want with Don?"

"I'd rather keep that between Don and myself."

"Well, considering that you called *my* number, asking *me* questions, that doesn't put you in a very good spot to make any demands, now does it?"

Is this guy fucking serious?

I sigh, exasperated already. "I'm calling for business. He did some work for my family in the past, and I'd like to hire him again."

"Mmhmm. You lookin' to find someone or to get lost?"

"I need to find someone. Listen, can you just put Don on the phone, or take a fucking message or something? I don't really have time for all this back and forth."

"I'm afraid Don's not in commission. I'm in charge now, so you can either talk with me or hang up. Doesn't make a hell of a lot of difference to me either way."

"Seems like a good business model," I mumble.

A throaty chuckle comes down the line. "Don't need a good business model when you're the best. I can find anyone for you, it's not a problem, but there's a price. And I prefer to meet in person before going over the details."

I lift my face to the sky, frustrated this isn't as cut-and-dry as I thought it would be. "Okay, that's fine. I can't get out of town until Sunday."

"Nope."

"What do you mean, 'nope'?"

"I mean, Sunday won't work. Saturday's the one."

"I'm busy Saturday," I say through clenched teeth.

"I'll come to you."

I consider his offer. I'll be busy all day with Sam's retirement party, but fuck it. I can disappear for a few minutes. I give him the info and he says he'll call if anything changes.

One step closer.

JOURNAL ENTRY #352

I SHOULD PROBABLY WRITE ABOUT EVERYTHING THAT'S GOING ON WITH LILY, THAT'S WHAT THESE JOURNAL ENTRIES ARE SUPPOSED TO BE FOR, RIGHT? EXORCISING MY DEMONS AND ALL THAT. BUT I'M FUCKING TIRED OF THINKING ABOUT IT. SO DOC, IF YOU'RE READING THIS, I GUESS YOU'LL HAVE TO HOPE I'M IN THE MOOD TO VERBALIZE MY SHIT WHEN I'M THERE.

BUT I'LL WRITE ABOUT GOLDI. I MISS HER. AND THAT MAKES ME FEEL A LITTLE PATHETIC BECAUSE I SAW HER EARLIER TODAY. I KEEP REMINDING MYSELF TO TAKE THINGS SLOW. I MEAN...NOT PHYSICALLY OBVIOUSLY. IF I THOUGHT SHE WOULD SAY YES, I'D MOVE HER INTO MY PLACE TOMORROW. I WANT TO BE NEAR HER. ALWAYS. IS IT TOO SOON TO HAVE HER HERE ALL THE TIME? IS IT NORMAL TO FEEL LIKE THIS? THE FIRST TIME AROUND THINGS WERE INTENSE, BUT I DON'T REMEMBER IT BEING THIS FUCKING OVERWHELMING. ALL I SEE IS HER. I TASTE THE MEMORY

OF HER ON MY TONGUE. I FUCKING SMELL VANILLA EVEN WHEN SHE ISN'T AROUND. I'M GOING FUCKING CRAZY.

BUT I DON'T CARE. I'LL LIVE THE REST OF MY LIFE CRAZY, AS LONG AS I GET TO BE CRAZY FOR HER.

Chapter 48
ALINA

"YOUR BROTHER IS AN ASSHOLE!" BECCA screeches, throwing the front door closed behind her.

I smirk, holding out the glass of wine I had poured and waiting. Chase and I were on our way to his place when she called in a tizzy. Her first official "meeting" with Eli and Sarah was today, and she threatened bodily harm if I dared to not be home when she showed up. So here I am, a bottle of wine and a listening ear.

"I take it things didn't go well?" I try to hide my grin.

She glares at me. "No. Things did not *go well*. Your brother is literally the worst person I've ever had the displeasure of knowin'."

My brow arches.

"I mean, how did you survive growin' up with someone who's so…so…"

"Particular?" I guess.

"Irrational!" she shouts. "Ugh!"

I grimace as I watch her gulp down her glass of wine. *Yuck.* Red wine is meant to be savored, not chugged like she's a frat boy with a beer. I try hard not to laugh, but it spills out anyway. It's nice to know that even if Eli and I aren't on good terms, he's still *him*. As picky as the day is long, and as controlling as the moon with the tides.

"You shouldn't let him get to you, Becca. He's doin' it on purpose. He loves gettin' a rise outta people."

"He'll get a rise out of my foot when I shove it up his ass," she mumbles, grabbing the wine bottle to refill her glass.

"Y'all have always been like oil and water. Remember how ticked he used to make you as a kid?" I smile at the memories. My heart squeezes, beating out a melancholy song that has me aching for my big brother.

"Well, I don't know how Sarah puts up with him. I could *never*. Really, there's no way I could ever marry that man, let alone live with him. It woulda been a terrible decision."

My stomach jumps in my throat, the wine that just passed my lips shooting back into my glass. "Come again?"

She yawns, running a hand over her face. "Huh?"

"You said it *would* have been a terrible decision. What exactly are you referrin' to in that statement? The marriage part, or the livin' together part?"

Her spine straightens. "I didn't say that. You misheard me."

"What'd you say, then?"

"Hmmm?" She's gulping down her wine. *Again.* "Hey, how was your trip with Chase?"

"Nope." I shake my head. "Nope. No way. You don't get to change the subject like that, Becca."

She groans, throwing her head back. "I don't wanna talk about Eli anymore."

"That's the whole reason you came over!" I throw my hands up.

"Well, I just needed to vent. I did and now I'm done." She shrugs, tossing her curly hair over her shoulder.

Playin' with her hair again. "You know, you and Eli are really startin' to tick me off. I don't appreciate bein' the go-between for you two when neither of you will tell me what's goin' on."

Becca doesn't say anything, just picks at her split ends.

I grab her hand. "You can tell me, you know? You're my best friend, Becca. Nothin' will ever change that. Just *please*, tell me what's goin' on."

"Nothin' is goin' on, Lee." Her voice is a whisper. She sounds exhausted by my line of questioning.

She should try bein' the one who has all the questions.

My intuition is an annoying gnat, flying around and nipping at my brain, but Becca's the most stubborn person I've ever met; continuing to try to get her to talk would be like beating a dead horse.

I narrow my eyes. "If you say so."

Becca ends up staying the night, passing out on my couch shortly after she decided to avoid all conversation regarding Eli. I know what I heard. But it's just too wild to believe. She's way too opinionated for someone like him, and he'd need to give up some of that precious control of his to have her. *Yeah right.* Plus, there's no way on God's green earth Becca would hook up with my brother and not tell me about it.

I'm still thinking about it the next day while I'm sitting in the office and typing up a blog post for the Tiny Dancers website. Chase waltzes in, interrupting my thoughts, and my entire body fills up with my smile.

I love him.

My heart grows wings, flapping around my chest at the thought.

"Hey, baby." He leans down, kissing me. "Fuck, I missed you. Please tell me I get to see you tonight."

"You get to see me tonight," I say against his lips.

"Do you want to go grab something to eat? I'm about to head out for some wings with the guys, thought I'd see if you wanted to come along."

I scrunch up my nose. I don't like wings. "Bleh. Pass. Thanks, though."

His face droops with disappointment, but I'd rather work through lunch and have time to stop for tulips on the way to Mama's grave.

"Okay. But I'll see you tonight? Want to go to the lake? Supposed to be a nice night."

I beam at the thought. "I'd love that."

He grins. "All right, I'll pick you up at your place."

"I won't be home until a little later. I'm gonna go visit Mama."

His eyes gain a sadness to their hazel hue. We haven't really delved into the "Mama" conversation yet, and that's okay. I don't particularly care for the weight that comes along with the topic.

"Okay, baby. Call me if you need me." He presses a kiss to my temple, then reaches down and slips his hand under my skirt, grabbing a fistful of skin.

"Hey! Watch your hand, mister." I laugh, smacking him away.

"Can't blame a guy for trying." He winks.

Just like that, he lifts the heaviness.

A few hours later, my feet slip over the freshly watered grass surrounding the path that leads to Mama.

My heart palpitates as I stand in front of her tombstone. I expected it to be in disarray—wilting flowers, some leaves that need to be cleaned, but it's pristine. Cleaner than I've ever seen it, actually, like someone took the time to meticulously scrub away all the dirt and grime. Fresh tulips sit in a vase with an envelope placed underneath. I step closer and peer down at the writing.

DEAR MA,

My heart squeezes tight, forcing tears to trickle from my eyes. Eli came to see her. I wondered if he would. All the anger I felt toward him washes away, and I cry for my big brother.

"Hey, Mama." I lay the flowers I brought along the bottom of her tombstone. "I see you had another visitor. I bet you've been missin' him somethin' fierce, huh?" I sit cross-legged, resting my elbows on my knees. "I've been askin' for you to bring Eli home for years, and you finally did it. So thanks, I suppose. Although, this isn't the way I expected it to happen.

"Did you know he was gettin' hitched?" I rest my chin in my hand. "I bet you were spyin' on every second of him fallin' in love, just couldn't help yourself."

Memories slide behind my eyes of Mama fussing over Eli and his "lonely heart."

"Did you send Chase back to me, too?" A leaf blows onto my knee, and I pick it up, fingering the delicate greenery. "You're just movin' down the list, huh?" I chew on my lip, frowning. "When ya gonna get to Daddy? Can you go be his guardian angel for a bit? I miss him almost as much as I miss you. For almost as long, too."

The breeze picks up, leaving a chill on my skin that's unusual for this time of year. I close my eyes and meditate on the feeling—try to reach out and grasp a connection to Mama's spirit. Eventually, a car door slams, bringing me out of my reverie.

With a kiss to her name, I leave.

There's a text waiting for me when I get to my car. I smile, seeing Jax's name on my phone. He's finally reaching out. I've wanted to smother him with my presence, but I know things are still raw. He says he needs space, so I've been trying to give that to him.

JAX:

Hey sweetheart. What ya up to? Can we get together tonight? I've got some news.

ME:

I'm busy tonight, but I'm all yours tomorrow evening! Wanna go out or stay in?

JAX:

Shit, can't do tomorrow.

ME:

You going to Sam's party on Saturday?

He's leaving town soon to go back to California, but I hope I get at least one more weekend with him before he does.

JAX:

Yep. I'll be there to steal the show.

I grin.

It's a beautiful night at the lake, but it always is when I'm there with Chase. Once again, we're lying on the blanket in the back of his black pickup truck, only this time, I'm not having to fight my feelings, so there's no need to hesitate before reaching over and grabbing his hand or rolling over and putting my head on his chest.

He tells me about the private investigator coming, and I vent my fears about Daddy. Mainly that he won't be able to string together a "congrats" for Sam at his retirement party. Once we've lightened the weight of what's bringing us down, we're able to relax, and just enjoy the peace that comes along with being together beneath the stars.

He trails kisses down the column of my neck, and my body trembles under his touch. My stomach tightens as his hand dips below my summer dress.

"Have I ever told you how much I fucking *love* the fact you always wear skirts and dresses?" He slips under the fabric and slides through my folds, spreading the wetness that's leaking out of me from his touch and his words.

"Wh-why's that?" I stutter.

"Easy access." His breaths puff against my neck as he talks, and it sends shivers up and down my spine.

"Chase," I breathe. "We're in public."

"And? There's no one here but us."

He bites my collarbone, a sting setting in from the marks his teeth leave behind. He pushes a thick finger inside me, and my eyes flutter closed as I gasp into his touch. He starts to slowly pump his finger in and out, frissons of lust sparking through my body.

"Besides," he continues. "I think you'd like it if people were all around us, knowing I'm about to make you come all over my hand." He grinds his palm against me as he speaks.

My mouth parts, my eyes rolling back. I love that he knows what turns me on without me having to voice it. *Is that why he keeps doing things where anyone can see?* Heat spirals through my veins at the thought. He slips another finger in and moves faster, making me writhe underneath him. Tingles bloom between my legs.

He leans in, swiping his tongue along the length of my bottom lip before he moves his way down my body. He pushes my dress up farther, his head disappearing underneath. I rise up on my elbows, scanning the shoreline to see if we're still alone. Before I can make sure, my vision goes hazy from the sensation of his mouth closing around me, right on that bundle of nerves begging to be touched. Licked. Caressed.

He twirls his tongue in tandem with his fingers, my heart beating to the pulse of my arousal. I drop back down, unable to hold myself up, tremors radiating through me. My legs wrap around him, his face fitting perfectly between them.

I lift my dress higher so I can watch him bobbing between my thighs. Reaching down, I grab fistfuls of his hair, pushing his face against me. He growls in response, his fingers twisting. Electricity lances through me.

I force my eyes open wider, wanting to watch every second as he makes me come apart. "Chase…I'm about to…"

His tongue moves faster. Circling. Flicking. Then he sucks *hard*, and I feel like I'm about to erupt. The pace of his fingers is audible from my arousal dripping on his hand.

I grip the strands of his hair tighter, twisting them as my back arches, pushing myself farther into his face. He groans like I'm the best meal he's ever had.

I'm so close and I just need a little…

More…

Distant voices fill the air, and the panic that seizes my heart is all I need to push me over the edge.

I feel the moan building and Chase's hand shoots up to muffle the noise. I bite down on his palm to keep from screaming. My inner walls clench around his fingers, sucking him in deeper as fireworks of pleasure explode and sizzle through my body.

He continues to lap at me as I catch my breath and float back to my body.

"Holy crap," I say on an exhale.

He pops up and smiles, his mouth glistening. "Guess there was someone here after all."

"You're the worst." I laugh, rearranging my clothes.

"You love me."

I suck in a breath, and the carefree grin drops off his face.

His words hang in the space between us.

I want to tell him that I do. *I do* love him. I don't think I ever stopped. But my tongue sticks to the roof of my mouth and I can't get it out.

"Hey, y'all got a light?" a voice interrupts our stare-down, and I breathe a sigh of relief.

"Nah, man, sorry," Chase responds before turning back to look at me. "You ready to get out of here?"

"Sure."

He grabs my hand, kissing the back of it, and the tension leaves my body with his gesture. "Okay, let's go."

We're quiet on the drive to my place. It's one of my favorite things about Chase. He doesn't fill the air with empty thoughts. I find more comfort in his silence than I do in anyone else's words.

We pull up to the front of my building and say our goodbyes, and just as I'm opening the truck door, I hear his phone ding. I look back to see him frowning at the screen. I lean in to give him a kiss, and his arm jerks, angling the phone away from me.

Alarm bells sound in my head.

I don't ask. Instead, I kiss him goodbye and run inside, thoughts of what he was hiding on his phone running through my head the rest of the night.

Chapter 49

CHASE

IT WAS A REFLEX OF A REACTION. ONE THAT I'M kicking myself over having. I saw the look on Goldi's face when my hand jerked, but damn, I did not want her to see what was on my screen. *Fucking Marissa.* I thought everything was under control—that when I told her to cut it the fuck out with the naked pictures, she had listened. It's only natural that when she decides to start up with her bullshit again, I'm with Goldi.

My insides feel jumbled. They aren't going to calm down until I explain things to Goldi, but I need to do it in person. I want to look in her eyes and know she understands that when I pulled my phone away it was to spare her the sight, not for any other reason. Unfortunately, my explanation will have to wait because I won't see her today. I'm stuck at the main office, and I'm tied up tonight and tomorrow setting up for Sam's retirement party.

Still, I need to make sure we're okay. I pull out my phone and text her.

ME:

Good morning, baby. I hope your night was filled with dreams of the lake. And us. Preferably the latter. Have a good day today. Anything planned tonight?

Goddamn, that was cheesy.

Sam walks in and I shoot him a grin. "Hey, old man, didn't expect to see you. I thought you'd be getting an early start on that retired life."

He plops down in front of my desk, making himself comfortable. "I can't seem to stay away. I just came to check in on you, have a chat."

I glance at my phone one last time, pushing it to the side and giving Sam my full attention. "How are you feeling about everything? You ready for your new slow and boring life?"

He runs his fingers through his graying hair, chuckling. "I don't know if I'll ever be ready. I never thought about what life would be like after, you know? I spent my whole life working toward a goal. Owning my own company. And then, building that company into something that would last."

"You've got it made now." I smile.

"Yeah." He sighs, lifting his arms to the side. "What do you do when your dreams have come true?"

"Fuck if I know. Make a new dream, I guess. You ready for your party?"

He shrugs and then brushes his hands down the front of his shirt. "I guess. It's more for Anna's benefit than mine."

"I think we all know that." I relax into my chair.

"The party's actually the reason I came to talk to you.

Everyone from our company will be there. I'm going to make the announcement officially that you're taking over as CEO."

My heart beats faster. *CEO.* I knew it was coming, but it's still a shock to the system. Back when I was a teen, I dreamed of this happening. When I became a man, I thought that dream was washed away in the stream of my mistakes.

I grit my teeth and nod, overwhelmed with gratitude for my second chance. Sam's eyes soften and I know he gets it. This is a big moment. I glance at my phone again, wondering if there's a text from the woman I want to share *all* my moments with.

My phone finally chimes three hours later.

GOLDI:

Sorry! I just saw this. Regina's in today and is being EXTRA special. I hope your day's good. Do you want to go to Sam's party together? Or should I plan to show up with Jax?

I want her to show up with me, not Jax. Not Becca. But I need to be there early, and I won't subject her to more one-on-one time with Anna.

ME:

I'll be stuck at the rec hall, you'll be bored hanging around all day. I'll just meet you there. You having a good day?

GOLDI:

Would be better if you were here.

The knot in my stomach unravels and contentment rolls through me. There won't be a good opportunity before the party to talk about what happened. Still, I need her to know it isn't something we should ignore. I'm not an expert on relationships by any means. *Fucking obviously.* But I do know there needs to be good communication at all times, from both sides. That was one of my biggest failures last time around.

ME:

Will you come back to my place after the party? I want to fall asleep with you in my arms. I also want to explain what happened last night. It was stupid and isn't anything you need to worry about. I'll show you whatever you want if you feel like you need to see it.

Typing bubbles pop up, disappear, then pop up again.

GOLDI:

Okay.

I've been carrying in trays of food for what feels like forever. Anna had a local eatery cater the party, but instead of having them deliver, she offered my services to lug it all in—which is fine, I really don't mind. But damn, it's hot as hell today, and she ordered what feels like the entire fucking store.

There are tables set up along the edge of the room, slowly filling up with all the food. I drop off the latest load and look around for Anna. I find her talking to some guy across the room. She throws her head back and laughs at something he says. She looks so happy, and it's enough to make my irritation at being an errand boy melt away. I walk over to them.

"Now's your time to think up the next stage of torture, Anna. A couple more trips and all the food'll be brought in," I tease as I approach her.

She laughs. "Oh, I have plenty of things to keep you busy. Don't you worry your pretty little head about that."

"I don't mind helpin' if you need an extra set of hands," the guy standing next to her chimes in.

I squint my eyes as I look at him. He looks familiar, but I can't place where I've seen him. I'm not surprised. In a small town like Sugarlake, you're bound to have seen everybody at some point. We probably went to school together—he looks about my age.

"Oh!" Anna exclaims. "Great! We can use all the hands we can get." She turns toward me. "Do you two know each other already?"

He lifts his chin at me. "Chase, right? We went to school together." My forehead scrunches as I try to remember him. My memory's a little hazy from trying to block out a lot of those years.

He offers his hand. "I'm Logan. I'm not surprised you don't remember, we didn't really run in the same circles."

The light bulb goes off as I shake his hand. *Logan.* He was a football player, I think. Hung out with that douchebag Reed—who I definitely *do* remember.

"Right. Yeah, man. My bad. You can help bring in the last of the food trays since you're offering."

"Lead the way." He grins.

After we're done, I grab us both some water. We sit on the floor against the wall, taking a break before Anna tasks us with the next thing.

"You're Sam and Anna's son, right?" Logan asks.

"Something like that." I look over at him. "How do you know Anna?"

"I'm a personal trainer here. She wanted some help promotin' her yoga group, asked me to spread the word." He unscrews his water bottle and takes a sip.

"She convince you to come to the party tonight yet?"

He snorts out a laugh. "You know it."

"I'm pretty sure she's invited the entire town. You'd be the odd man out if you didn't show up."

His eyes gleam. "The whole town, huh? Maybe my piece will be there."

I resist the urge to roll my eyes. *His piece?* "Oh yeah? You got a girl?"

He shrugs, tossing his water bottle up in the air. "She ain't my girl. I mean…she's cool, but she's just a nice way to pass the time. Haven't seen her in a few weeks, though."

I don't respond because I literally give zero fucks about this guy getting his dick wet.

"How about you? You got a girl?"

Now, *this* I do give a fuck about. "Yep."

He stares at me. When I don't elaborate, he shakes his head, chuckling. "You don't talk much, do you?"

I lean my head against the wall. "Not when there isn't much to say."

"Fair enough." He stands, dusting off his pants. "I'm gonna go find Anna and see what else she needs."

He leaves me behind with thoughts of Goldi and how happy I am that she's all fucking mine.

Chapter 50
ALINA

I'M AT BRUNCH WITH JAX.

Becca's down at the church, meeting with Eli and Sarah, so it's just the two of us today. It's the first time I've seen him since our talk, and I hadn't realized how much I missed him until this moment. We're spending the day together before heading over to Sam's party tonight. It's Jax's last night before he leaves for California, and he said he wanted to go with me, even if he had to give me up at the doors.

"I'm moving," Jax blurts.

My hands grip the edge of the table, my equilibrium suddenly thrown off from his words. "What do you mean, you're *movin'*?"

"To California. I spend most of my time there anyway, and… there's not much holding me here."

He's movin' because of me. My heart cries as it cracks in my chest.

"Oh," I whisper. His words are another jagged cut to my soul, like the marks are keeping tally of all the ways people leave. I don't know what to say. Even though I can't love him the way he wants, I still *love* him. The selfish part of me wishes that were enough.

He reaches out and grips my hand tight. "I'll still come back to visit. My mom would kill me if I didn't spend holidays with her, but this is something I need to do."

"Is it because of me?"

"A little," he admits.

My face crumples.

Jax rushes out his next words. "Please, sweetheart, don't cry. I just need to get some space. Find myself, get over you. I can't do that here… I need you to understand."

I sniffle, nodding. I get it, but it doesn't make it hurt any less. "Will w-we be okay?"

"Yeah, we'll be okay." With one more squeeze of my hand, he smiles. "No more of these tears, all right? I've got a hot date tonight, and I need her to be at her best."

I giggle, drying my eyes.

We spend the rest of the day together. Time with him moves faster now that I know he's about to be gone. He keeps the mood light, but still, anxiety eats at my insides as Jax pulls into the rec center's parking lot. I tried to get a hold of Daddy and Eli, but neither of them answered, and things are still on edge with Chase. He reassured me there was nothing to worry about, but the ghosts of our past still float inside my head.

"You ready for this?" Jax asks as he parks. "It's my last night here, sweetheart, let's make it count." His perfect teeth gleam in the artificial light of the streetlamps.

My heart twinges. *He's leaving and I don't know when he'll be coming back.*

I keep my eyes peeled for Chase as we walk in, but I don't find him. Maybe he's lost in the crowd. I think everyone in the history of Sugarlake is here.

"Shit, they really know how to throw a party, huh," Jax murmurs, his hand on my lower back as he leads me farther into the room.

There are long tables set up along the walls, appetizers covering every inch. A bar sits in the corner of the room, and that's where Jax steers me. He orders our drinks while I lean against the bar top, glancing around again for Chase. *Where is he?*

I don't see him, but my gaze snags on Anna talking to Logan. *Great.* I should have known he would be here. Logan notices me and a smile takes over his face as he says something to Anna and saunters over. We weren't in a relationship, but I still feel guilty about ghosting him the way I did. I haven't even thought about him because I've been so tied up in Chase.

Anna watches as he walks over to me, and my insides tighten at her stare. *Super, more ammunition for the Hate Alina Brigade.*

Jax tenses next to me, squeezing my waist. He leans in to whisper in my ear. "I'm gonna go find the men's room. I'll be back."

I nod, keeping my eyes on Logan. I'm sure Jax is really leaving to avoid him, but honestly, I'm relieved. I don't want to deal with the drama tonight.

"Alina. Hey, I was hopin' you'd be here." Logan pulls me in for a hug. I squirm, uncomfortable with his attention.

"Yeah? Here I am." I back up, drinking from my wine as I glance around for Chase.

His eyes dim. "Everything okay?"

I sigh, lowering my glass onto the bar top and wringing my hands together. "Logan, I—"

His laughter cuts me off. "Don't tell me. You're endin' things."

I grimace. "Was there ever really somethin' to end?"

"There could have been if you had wanted."

"You're an amazin' man, but I'm with—"

Logan puts his hand up. "I don't need the story, babe. We were just havin' fun, right? It was bound to end at some point." His eyes peruse my body. "But, damn, was it fun while it lasted."

"It *was* that."

His hands are in his pockets as he looks around the room. "Guess I need to rearrange my plans, then. Find someone else to take home tonight. I thought I had a sure thing once I saw you."

His words bring a grin to my face. "Sorry to be a night ruiner. I'm sure there's a line of ladies waitin' for their chance."

"Yeah, yeah. You don't have to butter me up after you break my heart," he jokes.

My eyes move past him as Anna walks up. "Alina, hi." She smiles.

Logan leans in to kiss my cheek. "It was good to see you, Lee. Don't be a stranger." He turns and tips his head to Anna. "Mrs. Adams."

"He's such a sweet boy," Anna says as she watches him leave.

"Mmm." I sip from my wine, unsure of what to say. I'm surprised she's even over here in the first place.

"Alina, I wanted to talk to you. This may not be the best time, but I'm not sure if I'll have the chance again. I don't see Chase willingly bringin' you around again after the way I acted."

The wine flows down the wrong pipe, and I bite back the cough. Is she apologizing? I wave her off. "Oh, no, Anna…"

"No, no. Let me say this." She puts her hand on my arm. "I've been placin' blame on your shoulders when you don't deserve it. Chase chastised me good and well for it the other night, and it's been on my mind ever since. I don't know what all Chase has told you, but Sam and I struggled with conceiving. I prayed for children every day. Having Chase and Lily come into our lives was God's answer." A small smile graces her face as she thinks of her children. "Then they met you, and you lit both of them up from the inside. Especially Chase. Truly, I've never seen anything like it. When I lost them, you were the easiest person to shift the blame to."

The sting of her thoughts bites at my sensitive heart.

"I'm not proud of the way I've acted toward you, but there's nothin' I can do to change it. I also won't lie to you. I've had years of buildin' up the blame in my head, and as much as I'd like to pretend I can turn it off with a flip of a switch, it's not that simple."

Now *that* I understand. "I appreciate your honesty."

"But I want you to know I'm gonna try like hell. I don't want to lose Chase again, now that I've got him back. And I can see how happy you make him. How happy you've *always* made him." She swipes a fallen strand of hair from her face. "Sam tells me I need to suck it up and just get outta the way, let love take its course."

Her words don't ring of a blossoming friendship, but they give me hope. "Thank you for tellin' me. And for bein' honest." I respect that she came to me. If anyone understands not being able to turn feelings off, it's me. I can give her time if that's what she needs.

Anna pats my arm. "Oh, look who just showed up." She points to the entrance. Daddy walks in followed by Eli and Sarah. My nerves sprout like weeds, wrapping around my chest and squeezing. *At least Daddy's still walking in a straight line.*

"I'll let you catch up with your family, Alina. Thank you for givin' me a moment of your time. You make sure that boy keeps comin' home, you hear me?" She gives me a look that only a mama can give, and I find myself smiling at her. I think we'll be okay.

I head toward Eli and Daddy, figuring I might as well get it out of the way. "Hi, y'all."

Eli grins as he sees me, and Sarah lifts her hand in a dainty wave. Daddy grunts and shoves past me, walking straight to the bar. *Okay, then. We're still in the ignore Alina phase, I see.*

"I gather he's in his usual form."

Eli watches Daddy's retreating back with a furrowed brow. "Yeah. I tried to convince him not to come. It caused a big thing at home." He runs his fingers through his blond hair, disheveling the strands. He looks tired, like being home has sucked the joy out of his soul.

"Hi, Sarah." I turn toward her. "How goes the weddin' stuff?"

"It's going okay." She smiles, but it seems forced.

The energy between the three of us is stilted and awkward. I'm dying to ask Eli about visiting Mama's grave, but this isn't the right place, and we have a host of other issues we need to work through. I stare at my big brother, drinking him in. The years have been kind to him, but I can see the stress he holds in both his posture and the few fine lines on his forehead. His eyes are stone, not giving anything away. Growing up, they were the window to his soul, and he always let people glance inside. I wonder what happened to make him feel like he needed to put up shutters.

Just as the thought crosses my mind, devastation swirls in

his irises, the grief stealing my breath away. It's just a second. A flash. But it's there. The space between my brow wrinkles as I watch him.

"Guess who the cat dragged in?" Jax's voice comes from behind me and I spin to face him. He's got his arm thrown over Becca's shoulders, a lazy grin on his face. Becca stares straight at Eli. I look back and forth between them. Eli's jaw is tight, and he reaches around Sarah's waist, pulling her to his side, leaning into her like she's a crutch.

Becca snaps her head to me and attempts a smile. "What's up, girl? You find the good booze yet? My chaperone over here"—she tilts her head toward Jax—"made me come find you first."

I gasp. "How dare he."

"I know, right?" Her hand lands on her hip. "I told him you of all people would understand. Especially in situations like these." Her eyes slide back over to Eli, locking on to where he and Sarah are connected.

"Becca! Hi. Long time no see," Sarah jokes, oblivious to the tension pulling the air.

"Hey, Sarah. You're lookin' just as pretty as you were this afternoon." Becca musters a grin. "A true beauty. Eli's a lucky man."

Eli clears his throat, his eyes narrowing in Becca's direction.

"The prodigal son returns home," Jax snarks before looking at Sarah. "Hi, I'm Jax. You must be the lucky lady?"

Sarah blinks at him, in a daze. I smother my grin behind my hand. Jax has that effect on people. I remember my first time meeting him and how he stunned me into silence, too.

He puts his hand out, his other arm still wrapped around Becca's shoulders. "Nice to meet you."

Sarah shakes her head slightly, before placing her hand in his.

"Pleasure's all mine, and yes. I am. The lucky lady, that is. Are you Becca's boyfriend?" She glances between them.

Eli stiffens, his eyes narrowing on Jax. A piece of the puzzle slots into place in my brain.

"Ha! He wishes," Becca huffs. "Excuse me, y'all, I need to step outside and get some air."

She breaks away from Jax's embrace and hurries toward the doors. Jax and I share a look. She's definitely not okay. *And I think I know why.*

"I'm gonna go outside with her." I turn back toward Eli. "Keep an eye on Daddy, would you?"

He nods, his jaw clenched, posture rigid—his gaze never leaving the space Becca left.

I find Becca on the edge of the sidewalk, staring at the parking lot. I don't say anything as I sit beside her. I just nudge her with my shoulder and give her silent support. A few minutes pass, watching the cars filter in and out of the lot before I decide to use a line from Chase's playbook.

"Do you wanna talk about it?"

"How many times do I gotta tell you, there's nothin' to talk about?"

"Oh, come off it, Becca. This ain't you. Anyone with two eyes can tell somethin' is wrong."

She stays silent.

I chew on my lip. "Is it Eli?"

She scoffs. "No."

I chew on my lip as I stare at her. "You know I don't believe you, right?"

She sighs, running a hand through her hair. "Your brother has nothin' to do with me, Lee. *That* I can promise you—Hey, isn't that your man?" She perks up, pointing her finger across the parking lot.

My eyes follow her movement and I make out Chase. *Has he been out here this whole time?* He's leaning against his black pickup truck, staring down at his phone. My heart speeds up at the sight of him.

"Yep, that's my man. I'm gonna go say hi." I'm standing to head over there when his head shoots up and swings from side to side. *Is he lookin' for me?*

A woman enters my line of sight, causing my steps to falter. She's gorgeous, her long jet-black hair swinging as she saunters up to Chase. She is the textbook definition of everything I'm not. My gut sinks and nausea builds, memories of our past playing out again in front of my eyes. I take a deep breath, trying to calm my racing heart. That was in the past, and he's grown. He's *different* now.

The woman steps closer to him. He grabs her shoulder and she smiles, letting me know there's a familiarity there.

"Who the hell is that?" Becca comes up next to me.

I shake my head, my eyes glued to the scene before me. I have no idea who that is. But Chase obviously does.

I'm frozen in place, the stitches holding my heart together coming loose with every beat. She rises on her toes. *No.* I can't look away, even as she slams her mouth on his, her fingers diving into his hair.

Bile rises in my throat and my stomach drops to the floor, making me dizzy. Becca's hand shoots out and grips my arm.

"Asshole!" Becca yells.

Her voice carries. Chase jerks back, whipping his head in our direction. His eyes lock on mine, widening in horror.

The woman pulls at his arm, but he shoves her away, racing toward me.

My feet back up, my head shaking. *I can't. I won't.*

I turn. And I run.

Chapter 51
CHASE

THE TEXT FROM AN UNKNOWN NUMBER TELLING me I look "tasty" has me snapping my head up and scanning the area.

I'm outside waiting for the private investigator to get here, and who shows up instead? My ex-girlfriend, who is proving with every fucking minute that it was a good decision to end things. Where was this other person hiding all the years we were together?

"Chase."

Mother*fucking* Marissa. I hear her voice before I see her, but soon enough she's standing right in front of me.

"Marissa, what the fuck are you doing here? How many times do I have to tell you this isn't going to happen?" I hiss at her, trying to keep my voice low.

She smirks, stepping into me. I grip her shoulders to push her back. Before I can get a word out, she plants her glossy, sticky lips on mine. They feel wrong and I rear back, but her fingers have locked in my hair and she presses harder against me. I try again, grabbing her wrists and wrenching my head just as I hear someone yell. I break free, looking at Marissa, disgusted, and turn toward the noise.

When I lock eyes with Goldi, my heart free-falls through my body and drops on the ground at my feet. *Fuck.* She looks gutted.

No.

Marissa tries to pull me back, but I don't spare her a second glance. All I care about is getting to Goldi. Determination invades my bloodstream, propelling me faster.

"Goldi, wait!" I yell. "Goldi!"

She starts running, stumbling through the doors to the rec hall, and I chase her. I don't want to make a scene, but I will if I have to. If I let her get away, I'm not sure I'll get her back. Fear prickles my neck at the thought, but I bat it away.

Goldi pushes her way through the crowd. The sea of people slows her down, allowing me to catch up just as she hits the doors on the other side of the room.

I grab her wrist. "Baby, damn. Hold up. That was *not* what it looked like. If you will just listen—"

She shakes her head and pushes through the doors. I follow her. I'll always follow her.

It's dark. Just a deserted hallway lined with empty rooms. Goldi runs to one of the doors and pulls, but I come up behind her and slam it closed again.

"Goldi, baby. *Please.* Just fucking talk to me. Say what you need to say and then give me the same courtesy. I'm telling you, that was not what it looked like." My tone is pleading, my desperation for her to understand obvious. I will do *anything* to be with her. I plan to spend the rest of my fucking life with her, but we both have to be in this, through the good and the bad. We won't make it if we aren't.

She spins around, tears making her cheeks glisten. "Talk then."

I open my mouth but hesitate, trying to figure out where to start.

"Go on then, Chase. Talk!" she yells, reaching out and shoving me.

My tongue wets my lips. "That was Marissa. My ex. I ended things for-fucking-ever ago, before I even knew there was a chance with you."

She huffs.

"It's true. I ended things because every time I looked at her, I wished she was you."

"Then what's she doin' here? And was that her the other night? On your ph-phone?" She sniffles.

"Yes."

She turns her head, twisting her body, but I step closer, pressing her into the door and blocking her path.

"Let me explain."

Her eyes search mine, and she must see the truth in them, or fuck, I don't know, maybe she's just tired of fighting me. Either way, she blows out a shaky breath and relents.

"Marissa didn't take the breakup well. She started sending me messages, and I swear to God, Goldi, I fucking shut them down every time. I blocked her number. I didn't know she would be here. Anna invited her when we were still together, but I never thought in a million years…" I hang my head, grabbing my hair.

"But you kissed her," Goldi bites out.

I lift her chin with my fingertips. "She kissed *me*."

Goldi shakes her head. "No—"

"Yes. Think about what you saw. Really think about it, baby.

Did you see me kiss her back? Did you see me encourage her in any way? I was out there waiting for that Mason guy. I didn't even know she was here. I promise you, Goldi."

Her eyes are locked on me as she chews that beautiful bottom lip. My thumb reaches out, tugging it from between her teeth. "You have to trust me. This won't work without it."

"So now you don't want us to work?" she accuses, again turning her head and trying to rip from my grasp.

I bring her face back. "I want us to work more than I've ever wanted anything in my life. More than Sam's company. More than my mom's love. More than finding Lily."

She gasps.

"I fucking love you, Goldi. Don't you know that? I love you. I'm *in* love with you. I have been since I was thirteen years old, and I want to spend every day for the rest of my life showing you just how much. I want to make up for all the days we've lost. But if you don't trust me…if we can't move past our history, we'll both end up miserable. I don't want that for you or for me."

I wait for her to say something. *Anything.*

She searches my eyes, sucking that lip between her teeth again and exhaling. "I love you, too."

Relief surges through every cell in my body. *Thank fucking God.*

I lean in and kiss her, not giving her a chance to take back her words.

"Say it again," I mumble into her mouth, my hands cupping her cheeks.

"I love you." She smiles against my lips.

A door bangs open, and I groan.

"Oh, shit. My bad. I didn't mean to… Lee? Is that you?"

We both turn toward the voice and my body stiffens as I see the guy from earlier today. What was his name?

"Logan, hi." Goldi pushes against my chest, forcing me back a step as she straightens her dress.

Logan. That's right. I look between them.

"So this is him, huh? Chase Adams? I never woulda guessed," he chuckles, shaking his head slightly.

Goldi's cheeks are flushed a beautiful shade of pink, and I don't know if it's from me or from *Logan*, who all of a sudden I can't fucking stand.

"Yep. He's the one." She beams at me, gripping my hand in hers.

My chest swells with her attention.

Logan rubs the back of his neck. "Ah, hell. I'm sorry, man. If I had known I was talkin' about your girl earlier today, I never would have brought it up."

Talking about my… My eyebrows lift as his words hit me. "*Goldi* was your 'piece'?"

He raises his hands in front of him, his face apologetic. "She ended things, though, so don't worry. She's all yours."

I laugh. Is this motherfucker serious? Of course she's mine. She's always been mine. I take a step forward, a smile on my face as I imagine all the ways I'll make him realize his mistake. Goldi's hand tugs me back.

"Chase, don't do this. You were just talkin' about trust. So *trust* me when I say I'm yours, just like I'm trustin' you."

I breathe sharply through my nose, leaning my forehead against hers. "Promise?"

"Cross my heart and hope to die."

I look back toward Logan. "Listen, man—"

Yelling cuts me off—muffled but close enough to the door that the voice carries.

Fuck.

Mr. Carson.

My head swings to Goldi. I don't let go of her hand as we rush through the doors back into the party. I stop short, watching the scene with wide eyes.

Mr. Carson has Sam's shirt crumpled in his fist and is being held back by Jax. His face is red and spittle flies out of his mouth as he slurs his attack.

"No! I don't give a good goddamn. I know...know what you said, Sam, you sonofabitch."

Goldi is a statue, her worst fear playing out in front of her. *Where the fuck is Eli?*

By the time I get across the hall to them, Mr. Carson has been wrangled somewhat under control. Jax's hair is a mess, half of it falling out of his bun, and his eyes are round with shock as he tries to contain the beast of Mr. Carson's despair. It's obvious he had no clue this was going on.

In any other circumstance, I'm sure Jax would love to argue my interference, but at this moment, he shows nothing but gratitude as I step between Mr. Carson and Sam to defuse the situation.

My gaze bounces to Sam. His face is red, and his lip is bleeding, but mainly he just looks sad.

I turn my attention to Goldi's dad. "Mr. Carson. Can you focus on what I'm saying to you?"

"Boy, you...you're always showin' up when you're not wanted. This here is men's business." He sways in Jax's arms. Jax's arms tense as he tightens his grip.

"I'm sure it is, sir. How about we take it outside and handle it there?"

The room is silent, hundreds of eyes watching as the Carson family secret spills into the open.

"I ain't got nothin' else to say." He points a finger at Sam. "You know... Gail was... I can't. How could you just bring her...up? My wife." He crumples, gripping his chest and sobbing.

I suck in a breath and twist around to peek at Sam. He watches his old friend with a frown, his forehead creased in concern.

"Mr. Carson," I try again. "Let's go out front, yeah?" I grasp his shoulder to steer him, but he jerks, the sudden movement pushing Jax back and allowing him to break free. He storms out of the hall, leaving a trail of gossip behind him.

"Shit," I mutter. I search for Goldi in the crowd. Her face is drained of color and she's clenching her fists. Over and over. Like the motion is the only thing that's keeping her together. I turn quickly to Sam. "You okay?"

He lifts his chin in a nod, and then I'm chasing after Mr. Carson. I'm not sure where he's headed, but I'm not going to let him get there on his own. I run into the fresh air, the calm of the night deceiving with its stillness. I search for Mr. Carson or his truck but can't find either.

Fuck.

Goldi bursts through the doors soon after me, panting from exertion.

"Is he gone?" She whips her head around.

"I think so. Want to go look for him?" I'm already grabbing the keys from my pocket, but she shakes her head, putting her hand on my arm to stop me.

"No. We'll never find him, and even if we did..." She shrugs.

"Daddy needs to learn to lie in the bed he makes. There's only so much I can do."

I pull her into me, hugging her tight and kissing the top of her head. I know how hard that is for her to admit, but I'm so fucking proud of her for realizing it doesn't fall on her shoulders. I peer over her head, keeping an eye out in case Marissa decides to make another appearance. I have no clue where she went.

Goldi says something, but the sound of an engine drowns her out. We turn toward the noise as a motorcycle rumbles into the lot, parking right outside the front doors. A man climbs off the bike, pushing his brown hair off his face and shrugging out of his black leather jacket. His arms are covered in ink. *He definitely isn't from Sugarlake.*

"Who is *that*?" Goldi asks.

I shake my head because I have no fucking clue. He lights up a cigarette, worn black combat boots crossing as he leans against his bike. He's got a cell in his hand, and after a second my phone vibrates in my pocket. I grab it, staring at the screen.

MASON:

Here.

My head snaps back to the biker. *That's* the private investigator?

"What is it?" Goldi asks, peeking at my phone.

"I think that's the guy, the PI. I'm gonna go talk to him. Want to come?"

She shakes her head. "I need to go hunt down Eli." She leans up and gives me a kiss. "Find me after?"

I nod, kissing her before she walks away.

We've caught Mason's attention and he swaggers over. The closer he gets, the more his details become clear. He's a fucking giant. I'm not a small guy by any means, but he towers over me.

"You Chase?"

"Yeah. Mason, I'm guessing?"

"The one and only." He smirks, taking a drag off his cigarette.

"Great. Thanks for making the trip."

He gets right to the point. "I don't have much time. There's a naked redhead in my bed back home just waiting for me to tear that ass up, so let's be quick. Who you looking for?"

"My sister. I don't really know much. Fucking nothing, actually, other than she might be in Arizona."

He flicks his cigarette and sucks in air through his teeth. "Oh. Nope. I don't go anywhere near the West Coast. Not even Arizona. I'll see what I can find by searching some records and making some calls, but you're shit out of luck for anything else."

"What the fuck do you mean, you don't 'go near the West Coast'? I was told by *you* that you could find anybody."

He stands straighter, his posture becoming defensive. His golden eyes flash. "I can. I'm just not *going* to."

My nostrils flare and I clench my fists, trying to stay calm. "Price isn't an issue. I'll pay you whatever you want. I just…I need to find her. I need to know she's okay." I point at him. "You're a fucking prick, but if you're the best, you're the guy I want."

Mason's chin lifts as he assesses what I've said. After a tense minute, a smile curls his face. "Yeah, all right. I'll do it. I'll give you my email and you can send me what I need. We do this on my timeline, you get me?"

"Yeah, I get you," I say through my teeth.

"Wonderful." The smile on his face grows. "Pleasure doing business. I'll be in touch."

"That's it? You needed to meet in person for that?" My brows touch my hairline. I have no clue why we couldn't do this over the phone.

He's already walking away, but he spins, walking backward. "You can't tell the soul of a man if you can't look in his eyes. I like to know who I'm doing business with."

What the fuck does that even mean?

I watch as he sits on his bike, his arms sliding into his leather jacket, that cigarette dangling from his lips. The engine of his motorcycle purrs, and he salutes me before peeling out of the lot.

Chapter 52

ALINA

I STARE AT MY REFLECTION IN THE RESTROOM mirror. My body is trembling from the extreme highs and lows I've experienced in the past hour.

Dang, get it together, Lee.

I believe Chase when he says it wasn't what it looked like. Maybe that makes me naive, I don't know. What I *do* know is that he's my forever. My soul recognized his from the moment we met, and he's right, if I don't trust him, what's the point? Now that the shock has worn off, I can look at the scene objectively. I see how my mind was lost in memories of the past, skewing my vision.

I think maybe I need to see a therapist to help work through our past issues and help me stay in the present. Maybe Chase would let me go *with* him to his.

Daddy is a whole different issue. Every bone in my body wants to jump in a car and chase him down, but I know it won't do me any good. I'm tired of being his punching bag, and after going to that meeting with Chase, I've realized as long as I'm there cushioning his fall, he won't ever feel the pain. He has to hit rock bottom, and he needs to do it alone. But that doesn't mean I'm not worried. *I need to talk to Eli. Where the heck is he?*

I splash water on my face to cool my cheeks and head back to the party. The last thing I want is to walk in there now that everyone's seen Daddy at his worst, but I have no other option. *I am not Daddy's choices.*

Pushing open the doors, I take a deep breath and work my way through the crowd. Music thumps from the speakers, and there's a group of people dancing in the middle of the room. My body instinctively wants to lose itself in the music, to forget about everything that's happened, but I keep my eyes on the prize.

I slink to a corner, hiding in the shadows while I scan the area for my brother. I find Sarah chatting with Sam and Anna, but Eli isn't with her. The thought briefly flitters through my mind to ask her where he is, but something holds me back. I'm not sure she'd be any more in the know than I am.

"Were you ever gonna tell me?"

My breath lodges in my throat as I spin around. "Jax."

His hands are in his pockets, a storm raging in the forest of his eyes. "Sweetheart, how long has he been this bad?"

"No. Don't you look at me like that, Jackson Rhoades." I point my finger in his face. "That right there is *exactly* the reason I never said anything. Ever since Mama died and Eli left, all I get is looks of pity from everyone in town. I can't stand the thought of you lookin' at me that way, too."

Jax rocks back on his heels. "But it's *me*."

A short laugh comes out with my breath. "That's even worse."

He flinches, and I struggle to find the words.

"Jax…I didn't tell you because you would have rode in on your white horse and saved the day. I didn't want that. You already hold me up whenever I'm fallin' down, and I knew, *I knew* that I couldn't be enough for you." I glance down, the sting burning me from my chest to my eyes. "I didn't want you to know I wasn't enough for Daddy, too."

"Alina. No. This is not your fault. *None* of this is your fault."

I sniffle. "I know that now, I do. He's really mean to me, Jax. Blames me for Mama…can't even look at me. I didn't want you to see it. I didn't want anyone to know it."

Jax's arms engulf me. "It kills me you've been going through this all alone, sweetheart. You say the word and I'll postpone my move. I'll stay here for as long as you need."

I shake my head against his chest. "No. You need to go. As much as I want you to stay, it would be the most selfish thing I could do, Jax."

He hugs me tighter, and I get lost in the comfort of my best friend's embrace.

"I'm sorry. I should have told you."

He lets out a deep exhale. "You're telling me now."

"I don't deserve you."

Jax pulls back, his hand cupping my cheek. "You deserve the world, Alina May. Promise me you'll go out and get it."

My belly burns and my heart rams against my rib cage. "Why does this feel like goodbye?"

"Maybe it is," he says with glassy eyes.

My head finds his chest again and my tears fall faster, soaking into his shirt.

"Maybe sometimes you have to say goodbye, even when it hurts. Maybe that's the only way to appreciate the hellos."

I squeeze my eyes tight as I cling to him. "I love you, Jackson Rhoades. I'll miss you every day."

He hums, and I commit the feel of him to memory. Even though I want to stay like this for as long as I can, I let go.

"Have you seen Eli?" I tuck my hair behind my ears.

Jax shakes his head. "I can help you look if you want."

"I'm gonna check the back hallway. Will you just keep an eye out? Tell him I'm lookin' if you see him."

I make my way to the hallway where Chase and I exchanged I-love-yous. My heart flutters at the memory. *He loves me.* If I'm honest, I think I already knew.

The hall is dark and quiet as I peer into the first couple of rooms. Nothing. I'm turning to leave when I hear a crash. The noise makes me jump, and I spin back around, cocking my head.

Thump.

I walk down the hallway, toward the last room on the left.

Thump.

I hear it again, and before I know what I'm doing, I'm turning the door handle, throwing it open and stepping inside. I gasp, my eyes bulging and my hands flying to cover my mouth. Eli snaps his head up. He sees me and curses. I should be running out of the room and pouring bleach in my eyes, but I can't move. I'm glued to the scene of my best friend laid out on a table with my brother hovering over her. They're both wearing clothes, but barely. The pieces of fabric are jostled, like they started to take them off, then realized they didn't have the time.

I cover my eyes. "I'm sorry, I'm sorry, holy crap. I'm sorry." The words spill out of me, even though sorry is the last thing I should be. "I'm not leavin' this room, so y'all do what you need to do and get decent quick. Let me know when it's safe to uncover my eyes. Oh my *God*."

A few minutes pass in relative silence, other than whispered words between them and the sound of zippers and snaps. It's enough time for my shock to morph into anger.

Eli clears his throat. "Lee, it's all good."

I drop my arms. "We must have different definitions of that phrase, Eli."

Becca walks toward me with her hands splayed in front of her. "Lee, this isn't what it looks like."

My face lifts toward the ceiling. "If I had a nickel for every time I've heard that phrase tonight." I laugh. "No. I think this is exactly what it looks like. And besides the fact Eli's engaged to be freakin' married, I probably wouldn't have cared." I pin her with my gaze. "But I *asked* you, Becca."

"I know, but—"

"Don't. Don't try and excuse this away. I don't wanna hear it. I can't even begin to process this right now. All I know is how much it hurts that you thought I wouldn't understand." My eyes well, and it ticks me off because I am so *sick* of crying.

I bite back the tears. "I need to speak to my brother, Becca. Alone."

She sniffs, nodding, not even glancing at Eli as she leaves. She pauses when she's next to me, her shoulder brushing mine. "I'm sorry." Her voice chokes on the words.

I stiffen my shoulders and keep my gaze on my big brother. I don't speak until I hear the click of the door. Eli sits on the table he was just mauling my best friend on.

"While you were busy gettin' your jollies with someone *other* than your fiancée, guess what you missed."

"She's not…" He shakes his head and then watches me with worried, cautious eyes. "What's that, Lee?"

"I'll tell you. Daddy gettin' in a fight with the man of the hour, Sam. Bein' a mess in front of the entire town and then stormin' off drunk as a skunk. *That's* what." I throw my arm in the direction of the parking lot. "Now he's out there, drivin', sloppy and upset."

"What?" Eli shoots up. "Where'd he go?"

"How should I know, Eli? Hopefully, home."

He starts to pace. "Well, let's go. We've gotta find him."

I shake my head, standing strong. "I'm not goin'. I just thought you should know."

Eli huffs, his eyes widening and his arms splaying to the sides. "What do you mean you're not going?"

"Look, if you wanna spend your time chasin' after Daddy and the devil on his shoulder, be my guest. He'll leave you in the dust, and all that'll be left is you chasin' your own tail."

His eyes soften. "I shouldn't have left you to deal with him alone. I should have come back. Should have done more." His voice raises with each declaration, and he resumes pacing.

My throat pinches with emotion because yeah, he should have. I put my hand up, stopping his rant. "Now's not the time, Eli. Literally any other day you've been here would have worked. But tonight? I don't wanna hear it."

His steps falter and his jaw tics.

I turn to go, wanting nothing more than to find Chase and tell him I'm leaving. Even though I shouldn't. I haven't even seen Sam yet to congratulate him, other than when he was licking the blood off his lip that Daddy caused him to spill.

"Lee," Eli says, his voice low and nervous. "You don't understand about Becca. It's not… We aren't… Just go easy on her, okay? You're the best thing in her life, and she'd be devastated to lose you."

I guffaw, my brows rising along with my chin. "You sure seem to know an awful lot about my best friend, Eli."

His cheeks puff out and he hangs his head. "No. I don't know her at all."

His voice cracks as he says it, sadness wrapping around his words and breaking them in half. But I don't have time to worry about the mess Becca and Eli are in. Not right now. Not after everything that's happened tonight. So I give a sharp nod and walk out the door.

When we make it back to the party, I spot Chase talking to Jax, which is surprising. My phone rings just as I'm walking over to them.

"Hello?"

"Hey, Lee. It's Buddy, down at the station. I uhh…your pa was just brought in. Thought I'd let you know. They're bookin' him now."

I lift my head to the sky. *What else could possibly happen tonight?* "What's he there for, Bud?"

"He crashed into another vehicle goin' down the wrong way on Main Street."

I suck in a breath, stumbling over my feet just as I reach Chase. I grab his arm to stay steady. Visions of getting a call about Mama flash behind my eyes. "Is everyone okay?"

"They're banged up, but nothin' life-threatenin'. There was a two-year-old and a pregnant woman in the car. He's lucky, it coulda been a lot worse. But off the record? Your pa's gonna need to get himself a lawyer. You can come pick him up in a few hours. Let him sober up a bit and get through his bond arraignment."

The urge to run to Daddy's side is strong, but I straighten my spine and remember what I just told Eli. "Nah, Bud. Thanks for the call. I think a night in jail will do him some good."

I hang up my phone and turn it off.

Chapter 53
ALINA

CHASE AND I ARE ON THE WAY BACK TO HIS PLACE. I begged him to stay behind, but he wasn't hearing it. I feel like a jerk for bailing on Sam's party before it was even halfway over, but I needed to get out of there.

His folks were extremely understanding. Sam hugged me as I apologized for Daddy, and he clapped Chase on the shoulder, saying, "Take care of your girl." It warms my heart to see a family that supports each other the way they do—the way mine hasn't in a long time.

I am mentally and physically drained by the time I plop down on Chase's couch. The fight with him seems like it happened light-years ago, instead of just three hours prior. *How can so much happen in so little time?*

Guilt spikes in my gut when I let myself think of Daddy sleepin' off his booze in a jail cell, but what else can I do? He wouldn't be grateful if I picked him up anyway.

Becca and Eli are something I can't even begin to scratch the surface of. The kicker is, I'm not even mad about the fact something is going on. I couldn't care less who they're with, as long as they're both happy. But Becca lied to me, even after I asked her, and that hurts worse than any secret ever could.

You've lied to her, too, the voice in my head reminds me.

Still, my heart hurts thinking about her planning Eli's wedding to someone else. I imagine what it would be like if that were Chase and my stomach revolts at the thought. I wish she had chosen to confide in me. I know how it feels to be collapsing under the weight of heavy secrets.

"You okay, baby? What a fucking night, right? Jesus." Chase rubs my shoulders.

I groan, the tension melting away under his skilled fingers. "Yeah, you ain't lyin'. But I don't really wanna talk about any of that."

"What do you want to do, then?"

"I want you to make me forget. Just for tonight. Can you do that?"

He stops rubbing my shoulders, coming around to sit next to me. "I can. You sure you don't want to talk about it?"

"I'm sure. Tonight should have been a celebration. Sam retiring. You becoming CEO."

"You telling me you loved me," he adds.

"And that." I smile, kissing his lips.

"We still can, you know."

"Can what?"

"Celebrate." His hand travels up my leg.

"I like that idea very much."

He leans in, parting my lips with his tongue, pushing me back on the couch. His body presses into mine, grinding, his hips hitting just the right spot even through our clothes.

I want him to push harder.

Press deeper.

He licks and sucks his way along my neck, pulling down my shirt and leaving a line of kisses on my collarbone. Every touch makes my body quiver. After everything that's happened tonight, all I want is this. I want to sink into his touch and forget the world around us.

I grip his hair, pulling his face up to mine. "Take me to bed, Chase. Show me how much you love me."

His eyes darken, lust rolling off him in waves and crashing into my skin, drowning me in his desire. He backs away, grabbing my hand and moving us down the hall.

Once we're in his room, he spins me around, his arms wrapping around my waist. We strip each other's clothes until we're bare. His hand touches the center of my chest, his palm resting against my speeding heart, and he pushes slightly, the back of my knees buckling against the bed frame until I fall onto the mattress. His body follows mine, every inch of his chiseled form pressed against me.

I feel needy.

Desperate.

His touch slides down my arm and he picks up my hand, bringing it to his mouth. He kisses each fingertip. Slowly, lovingly.

My fingers tangle with his as he raises my arms above my head. His length is pressed against my center and it pulses on top of me, making the ache between my legs unbearable. And then his mouth meets mine at the same time as he slides deep inside me in one solid thrust. His eyes burn so deep, I swear our souls can touch.

My hand tightens around his as he pulls back out, then goes

deep. Over and over. The friction between our bodies creates a buzz of energy that crackles and pops, weaving its way around us and infusing every pore.

I could stay like this forever.

My hips rise to meet his, grinding my clit against his pubic bone on each pass. I'm delirious with pleasure, every nerve ending firing off tingles that shoot through my veins. He lets go of one of my hands, slipping down my body until he fits it around the curve of my ass, bringing me into him farther, wrapping my leg around his waist.

He hits deeper this way. He plunges in, his hips speeding up.

If he keeps doin' that…

My orgasm races through my body like wildfire, touching every part of me. I clench around him, my body spasming.

"*Fuck*, baby."

He moves faster, slamming inside me with sharp thrusts, chasing his own high. My ears are ringing and my body feels fuzzy as I admire him. I run my fingers along the lines of his face, every dip and curve of his high cheekbones and his sharp jaw. Down the crease between his eyes. Over that scar in his eyebrow, the one I've wanted to trace since the moment we met.

His body shivers.

"Tell me you love me," he demands.

I lean up as far as I can, whispering it against his skin. "I love you."

His body jerks, his rhythm faltering.

"I love you. I love you. I love you."

"*Fuck.*" His thrusts turn erratic, his need trumping his skill, and I squeeze around him, trying to bring him over the edge.

His mouth parts, his eyes roll back, and he lets out the sexiest groan, his muscles flexing against me. He pulses deep inside me as he explodes and I moan at the feeling.

He collapses, and I can feel his heartbeat against my chest.

Soft kisses press into the crook of my neck. "You feeling good today, Goldi?"

Despite everything that's happened, there's only one emotion I feel right now.

"Yeah. I'm pretty damn happy."

I wake up to a text from Eli.

ELI:

> Picked up Pops this morning. Can you come by and talk? We all need to sit down and it should happen today.

I roll my eyes at his question but know he isn't wrong. As much as I want to stay in Chase's bed and forget the rest of the world forever, I need to face things head-on.

He gave me his house key and said he wants me waiting in his bed when he gets back tonight from Nashville. He offered to skip the trip, but I don't want to be the reason he misses his therapy session and group. Plus, I told him to handle whatever he needs to with his ex to make sure she gets the message. *Trust.*

He kisses me goodbye on his front doorstep and hugs me tight. "I'm so fucking proud of you. Go handle your shit, Goldi, and don't let them drag you back down. You aren't meant to wither away in the shadow of someone else's demons. You're meant to shine."

The darkness tries to seep into my conscience and steal my light on the drive to Daddy's, but I don't let it. I focus on the way Chase makes me feel instead. The way I'm beginning to feel about myself.

I park the car and let Chase's words wrap around me, so even if I stagger, his voice will cushion my fall.

With a deep breath, I walk in the front door.

The smell of coffee brewing makes me nostalgic. I follow the sound of clangs and muffled voices and find Eli and Daddy sitting in the kitchen. Eli is dressed for the day, looking sharp in a button-down and dark blue jeans. Daddy is still in his clothes from the night before, looking greasy and worn, his head in his hands as his elbows rest on the table.

Sarah is nowhere to be found.

"Hi, y'all," I greet them as I sit down.

Daddy's head pops up and his eyes meet mine. The baby blues are bloodshot, but they're clear and alert for the first time since Mama died. I suck in a breath, surprised he hasn't started numbing his pain.

"Alina," he rasps.

"Hi, Daddy. How ya feelin?" My lips curl into a sad smile, and I don't really know what to say. I'm not used to handling him sober; my ability to make conversation with him is rusty after all these years.

"Thanks for comin', honey." My stomach jumps at the term of endearment. My eyes bounce to Eli, his jaw muscle tensing as he watches us. Daddy's voice brings my attention back to him.

"I have some things I need to say, and you can take 'em or

leave 'em, I guess. I don't…I don't deserve your time." His hand comes up to wipe his mouth. "I'm messed up."

My eyes widen, my palms becoming clammy as I grip my thighs under the table. *What is going on?*

"Your mama…" His voice breaks. "Your mama was the best part of me. She pushed down the bad and brought out everything good. I never thought I'd have to learn to live without her. I guess we all know I never learned anyway. She's been gone for damn—damn near a decade and she'd be ashamed of what I've become." Tears line his lower lids and one spills over, dripping down his stubbled face.

"Daddy," I breathe. I'm stunned.

He puts up his hand. "No, no. Let me finish. I don't think I can say it more than once." He gulps his coffee then stares into the black liquid while he continues to talk. "I woke up this mornin' with a poundin' in my head, a sickness in my heart, and Bud the deputy tellin' me that I damn near killed a family."

I purse my lips, trying to keep it together while he talks.

"My first thought was to grab the nearest bottle and drown myself until I was sinkin' in the numbness. That's still what I want more than anything. But…" His eyes flick up to me. "My second thought was the guilt. I'm responsible for hurtin' those people last night. And then as I laid there in that cell, waitin' for someone to come and bail me out…all I could think about is how all these years, I've made you feel the exact same way."

I suck in a stuttered breath and the dam bursts, years of waiting to hear the words he's speaking form the tears that fall down my face. I bite my cheek to keep from interrupting.

"I don't…hell, I don't know what I'm doin', and it hurts to look at ya, Alina. You're so damn like her. I don't think I'll survive if I stare at you for too long."

"Pops," Eli starts.

I reach over, putting a hand on his arm, letting him know it's okay. Daddy's just being honest. He's not saying anything I didn't already know.

Daddy shakes his head, gripping his mug tighter. "Anyway, Bud says I'm gonna be lookin' at payin' that family's hospital bills, among other things, and that I'll need to lawyer up."

Eli pipes in again. "We've talked this morning and decided it would be in Pop's best interest to check into a ninety-day rehab program. I've been in contact with one over the past few days. They have a spot for him."

My stomach flips so hard it makes me lose my breath. Hope is a dangerous feeling. *Eli's been talkin' to rehabs?* A piece of my anger chips away.

"When?" I gasp.

Eli's face is serious. "Today. This afternoon. I had Pops pack a bag and we leave in..." He glances down at his wristwatch. "Thirty minutes."

I whoosh out a breath, overwhelmed. I never could have guessed this would be my morning. I gaze at Daddy, his head still hanging over his coffee cup, embarrassment and shame circling the air around him. Then I swing my gaze to Eli. Even though things are rocky between us, I can't help the gratitude that fills me. Because he's here now. He's helping. He's *present.* And at the end of the day, he's still my big brother.

"That's real good, Daddy." I try to grab his hand, but he jerks, moving it out of reach. My heart twists. These things take time, I guess.

Daddy doesn't say anything else. The words "I'm sorry" never cross his lips, and while I long to hear them, I'm not surprised.

We aren't okay. We're nowhere near healed. He has a lot to make up for, and I have a lot to forgive.

But for today, it's enough.

Thirty minutes later, I watch them leave, knowing Daddy's on his way into battle. I close my eyes and send up a prayer to God. And then I send one to Mama. I've been waiting on a miracle for years. Today feels like the perfect day to get one.

The breeze whips across my face, and I smile.

With a deep breath, I turn and walk away, heading back to Chase. To my love. To my future.

To the start of my happily ever after.

Epilogue

JOURNAL ENTRY #423

WELL, DOC. THIS IS IT. THE LAST JOURNAL ENTRY YOU'LL READ OF MINE. DOES IT STILL COUNT AS AN ENTRY IF I'M RIPPING OUT THE PAGE TO MAIL TO YOU? IT DOESN'T MATTER, I GUESS. IT'S BEEN A HELL OF A RIDE, EH? MAYBE YOU THINK THAT WAY ABOUT ALL YOUR CLIENTS. I'LL TELL YOU ONE THING, MY BANK ACCOUNT IS HAPPY AS HELL THAT I'M NO LONGER GONNA BE SEEING YOU. AND GOLDI'S HAPPY THAT I HAVE NO REASON TO GO BACK TO NASHVILLE. LESS CHANCE OF RUNNING INTO MARISSA THAT WAY. NOT THAT SHE'S BEEN A PROBLEM EVER SINCE I THREATENED HER WITH A RESTRAINING ORDER.

ANYWAY, THANKS FOR THE RECOMMENDATION OF SOMEONE CLOSER, SOMEONE WHO COULD SEE GOLDI AND ME. OTHER THAN STARTING A NEW NAR-ANON CLOSER TO MY HOUSE, THAT WAS THE LAST STEP TO LEAVE MY OLD LIFE BEHIND AND MAKE SUGARLAKE REALLY FEEL LIKE HOME AGAIN. HOME. CAN YOU BELIEVE IT? I CAN'T. A YEAR AGO, THIS ALL FELT LIKE A DREAM

THAT WAS OUT OF REACH, AND NOW WE'RE BREAKING GROUND ON A HOUSE THAT I'LL GET TO BUILD WITH MY OWN TWO HANDS. ONE THAT GOLDI DESIGNED FROM TOP TO BOTTOM. SHE'S STILL FUCKING PERFECT. FINALLY TEACHING DANCE AT THE STUDIO THAT HELPED BRING US TOGETHER. I HOPE THAT ONE DAY I'LL BE HELPING HER BUILD HER OWN STUDIO. SHE HASN'T TOLD ME THAT'S WHAT SHE WANTS, BUT I SEE IT IN HER EYES, AND FUCK, I WANT TO GIVE IT TO HER. I WILL GIVE IT TO HER.

I'M PROPOSING TONIGHT. I'M NERVOUS AS FUCK. SPENT A MILLION FUCKING YEARS TRYING TO PICK OUT A RING. ANOTHER HUNDRED TRYING TO PLAN THE PERFECT WAY TO ASK. I HAD A BIG CELEBRATION PLANNED, INVITED EVERYONE WE LOVE AND EVEN THE ONES WE DON'T. BUT I CANCELED IT. INSTEAD, I'M GONNA TAKE HER OUT TO THE LAKE. THE STARS THAT ALWAYS LIT THE PATH TO HER ARE GONNA BE THE ONES THAT ILLUMINATE HER FACE AS SHE TELLS ME SHE'LL SPEND THE REST OF HER LIFE WITH ME.

I CAN ONLY FUCKING HOPE.

GOD, GRANT ME THE SERENITY TO ACCEPT THE THINGS I CANNOT CHANGE, COURAGE TO CHANGE THE THINGS I CAN, AND WISDOM TO KNOW THE DIFFERENCE. DAMN, THOSE WORDS HAVE SAVED ME MORE THAN ONCE.

ALSO... SINCE I WON'T BE SEEING YOU AGAIN, I MIGHT AS WELL TELL YOU. THAT PRIVATE INVESTIGATOR I HIRED A YEAR AGO TO LOOK FOR LILY? HE CALLED TODAY.

HE FOUND HER.

CHARACTER PROFILES

Alina

Name: Alina May Carson

Age: 11 (beginning), 26 (end)

Place of birth: Sugarlake, TN

Current location: Sugarlake, TN

Education: High school diploma

Occupation: Dance instructor and server

Income: Less than $40K/year

Eye color: Sky blue

Hair style: Long, straight, honey-blond

Build: Tall, slender

Level of grooming: Always put together

Distinguishing mannerisms: Lack of filter, chews lip when nervous

Health: Healthy

Handwriting: Loopy with hearts that dot the *i*'s

How do they walk? Fast and light

Accent: Southern

Do they gesture? Talks with her hands when she's angry/excited

What's their laugh like? Light and airy

Describe their smile: The kind of innocent smile that lights up a room, quirks slightly higher on the right side

How emotive are they? As a child, she wears her heart on her sleeve and speaks her mind, so she's easy to read. As an adult she's guarded and difficult, has a wall up and doesn't let people in. Has a resting "innocent" face.

Family:

Father: Craig Carson

Age: 31 (beginning), 52 (end)

Occupation: Construction worker

Relationship: Was always solid during childhood, although Alina felt like he spent more time and attention on her brother, Eli, and Eli's basketball career, but he was a good father. As an adult, she has a strained relationship where she acts more like the parent although she enables his alcoholism for a majority of the book. He is toxic and abusive toward her because she reminds him of her mother.

Mother: Gail Carson

Age: 39 (beginning)

Occupation: Stay-at-home mom

Relationship: Mama's girl. Fantastic relationship and her role model/mentor. At times could be a little overbearing.

Brother: Elliot (Eli) Carson

Age: 14 (beginning), 29 (end)

Relationship: Close sibling relationship as kids, but Eli was all about basketball so he was never around much. As adults, their relationship is strained. Eli never comes home and sends monthly checks to "help" but never takes responsibility for anything, and avoids Sugarlake at all costs, including anything to do with their parents.

Closest Friends: Becca, Lily, and Jax

Who does Alina depend on?

Practical advice: Mama or Becca

Mentoring: Mama

Wingman: Becca

Emotional support: Jax

Moral support: Jax

The Core:

What do they do on rainy days? Dance or stay cozy inside with a good book and a hot drink

Book smart or street smart? Book smart

Outlook on life: Optimist in the beginning, realist in the end

Introvert or extrovert? Extrovert

Favorite place: At the lake in the bed of Chase's truck

Does she have secrets? Yes

What do they want most? Happiness

Biggest flaw: Naivete in the beginning, and using sex to replace facing emotions in the second half of the book

Biggest strength: Loyalty and the ability to see the good in everyone

Does she want to be remembered? Not by anyone other than family and friends

How do they approach:

- **Power:** Doesn't want it
- **Ambition:** Has it
- **Love:** In the beginning, she dives in headfirst; in the second half of the book, she shies away from it.
- **Change:** Adapts

What makes her angry? Liars

Moral compass: Strong. Only bends when Chase is involved or in dire situations for people she loves

Pet peeves: Chewing with mouth open, people who treat her like she's ignorant

What would her tombstone say? Alina May Carson: She lived, she laughed, she loved

Her story goal: Through the course of the book, we start with Alina as a naive, innocent child who has grown up in a stable and loving home and hasn't experienced any harsh realities of the world. In her mind, the world is black and white, and she sees the good in everyone and everything. As she grows older, she will go through major hardships that change her entire outlook on life and will cause her to build walls and shy away from facing emotions head-on. She is afraid of having her heart broken again, and she doesn't want to face her own feelings on how her father and brother treat her. She's ashamed of her family and hides secrets because she doesn't want anyone to look at her as weak. Her growth happens when Chase comes back to town and helps her see that she is more than what she's settling for.

She will start to trust again, will work on her issues regarding her dad's problem with addiction/alcoholism, and will stop enabling him, realizing that in order to have happiness and be at peace, you need to sometimes put yourself first and also forgive other people's faults.

Her character arc won't be one-hundred-percent complete at the end of this book because it will continue to grow throughout the series; however, she will have started to work on her avoidance of emotions, start therapy, and stop enabling her father.

Chase

Name: Chase Adams

Age: 13 (beginning), 28 (end)

Place of birth: Chicago, IL

Current location: Sugarlake and Nashville, TN

Education: Bachelors in business management from TSU

Occupation: Owns construction company

Income: Take-home salary $250K

Eye color: Hazel

Hair: Dark brown/black, short on sides, long and mussed up on top from him constantly tugging on it

Build: Tall, muscular from construction

Distinguishing features: Scar through left eyebrow and dimples in cheeks when smiling

Level of grooming: Clean

Distinguishing mannerisms: Broody and curses a lot

Health: Healthy

Handwriting: Chicken scratch

How do they walk? With purpose. Controlled. Like he's never in a hurry

Accent: Midwest

Do they gesture: Sometimes

What's their laugh like? Low, raspy

Describe their smile: When he occasionally smiles, it's crooked and he has dimples in his cheeks

How emotive are they? Holds things in, and doesn't show outward expression easily. Has a resting "asshole" face.

Chase's Family:

Father: Sam Adams (adoptive)

Age: 30 (beginning), 51 (end)

Occupation: Owns Sugarlake Construction

Relationship: Started out strained but turned into one of the most important and healthiest relationships of Chase's life. Father figure and dependable. Amazing role model, unconditional love.

Mother: Anna Adams (adoptive)

Age: 20 (beginning), 51 (end)

Relationship: Strained in the beginning, almost resentful, but turns into a good and healthy one. Not as close to Anna but still a strong relationship.

Sister: Lily Adams

Age: 11 (beginning)

Relationship: Very close and Chase is very protective of her. Co-dependent. Feels like he has to take care of her always since no one else has ever taken care of either of them. Feels responsible for her actions and choices.

Closest Friend: Jax
Who do they depend on?
- **Practical advice:** Sam
- **Mentoring:** Sam
- **Wingman:** Jax
- **Emotional support:** Alina
- **Moral support:** No one

The Core:

What do they do on rainy days? Build something or work
Street smart or book smart? Street smart
Outlook on life: Pessimist at first and then realist
Favorite place: Anywhere Alina is
Does he have secrets? In the beginning yes, but at the end no
What do they want most?: A family and to be enough
Biggest flaw: Letting his fears and insecurities lead his decision-making
Biggest strength: His ability to love
Does he want to be remembered? Only by people he loves
How do they approach:
- **Power:** Commands it
- **Ambition:** Lots of it
- **Love:** Doesn't trust that it lasts
- **Change:** Compartmentalizes it

What makes him angry? Thinking about his biological mother, being controlled

Moral compass: Flexible and believes right and wrong are subjective

Pet peeves: When people push him emotionally

What would his tombstone say? The serenity prayer

His story goal: Chase starts the book by being jaded by hardship and the fact he and his sister were abandoned by their mother. Before that, he was taking care of his mother and his sister through his mother's drug addiction. He has a lot of trauma for a boy so young and doesn't trust easily. He believes that everyone will always leave him eventually and that he isn't good enough for anything. His story goal is that through finding love in Alina and then losing both her and his sister, he will finally take a look at himself and his own issues. Through therapy and inner reflection, lots of self work, he will grow into a man who is able to communicate, support others, and love himself enough to realize what kind of love he can give. He isn't perfect by the end of the book, and will continue to have a character arc and growth throughout the series, but he is a changed man who no longer is afraid of everyone leaving and doesn't take the brunt of responsibility for other people's actions.

ACKNOWLEDGMENTS

There are a lot of people to thank for this story. But first, I'd like to thank myself.

That sounds ridiculous, but what a lot of people don't know is when I was a child, I had family go through addiction. I *was* that kid at the Nar-Anon groups, and then when I was seventeen, I was the person in rehab, and I've been clean ever since. Life gives us a lot of tough journeys, and I'm so grateful to myself for never giving up and for facing each challenge head-on. I'm so thankful for the past versions of me that allowed me to get to this point and bring my stories to *you*.

So I'd also like thank YOU, my readers. Some of you read this when it was first self-published. My very first book baby. And others are just now finding it after it was picked up by a publisher and re-released. No matter when you read it, thank you for reading. For supporting. For making my dreams come true. You are the best part of my life's journey.

To my best friend, Sav R. Miller: I don't even know how to thank you differently in each book I write, but there's really nothing I can say except thanks for being my soul sister and the best friend I could have ever asked for.

To my editor, Christa, my marketing manager, Katie, and the rest of Team Bloom: Thank you for believing in me, for always pushing me, and for being my McInCult council. I can never thank you enough for the opportunities you've given me.

To my agent, Kimberly, and the rest of Brower Literary Management: Thank you for always having my back and making sure that things are handled, especially when I'm too sick from chemotherapy to handle it myself. Having you in my corner and on my team is paramount to my success and I couldn't imagine anyone else I'd rather have by my side.

To my publicist, Jessica, and the team at Leo PR: Thank you for making sure people know about me and my books! I've always been a big believer that the team you surround yourself with is essential to how successful you are, and you are *integral* to me.

To my husband, Mike: Thank you for being my other half. For being the best husband and father. The one who holds me when I'm down, parents alone when I'm too ill, and supports me in every single way. I couldn't have asked for the universe to send me a better life partner, and I'm more thankful for you than you'll ever know.

And lastly, to my daughter, Melody: Everything I do is for you. You are my heart.

JOIN THE MCINCULT!

EmilyMcIntire.com

The McInCult on Facebook: facebook.com/groups/mcincult

Scan the QR Code to subscribe to Emily's newsletter and never miss an update.

ABOUT THE AUTHOR

Emily McIntire is a *USA Today*, *Publishers Weekly*, and Amazon bestselling author whose stories serve steam, slow burns, and seriously questionable morals. Her books have been translated into over a dozen languages, and span across several subgenres within romance. A stage IV breast cancer thriver, you can find Emily enjoying free time with her family, getting lost in a good book, or redecorating her house, depending on her mood.